North to Yesterday

WITH A FOREWORD BY A. B. Guthrie, Jr.

Number Four in the Texas Tradition Series
Tom Pilkington, Series Editor

Texas Christian University Press
Fort Worth

Robert Flynn

NORTH
to
YESTER-
DAY

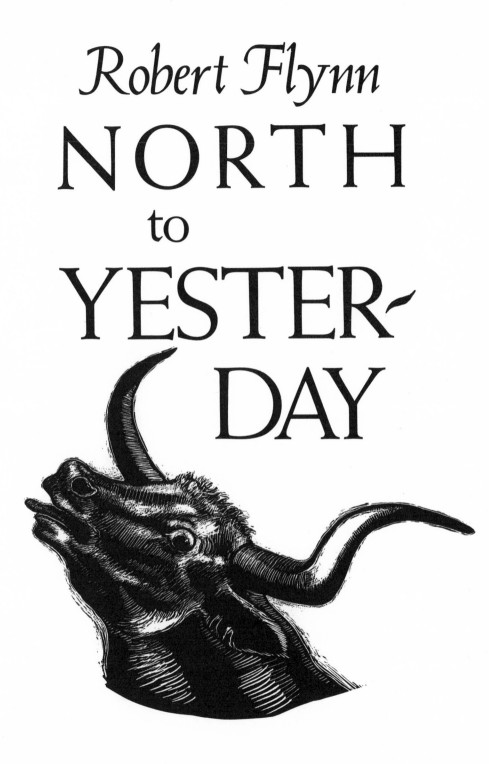

Copyright © 1967, 1985 by Robert Flynn

First published by Alfred A. Knopf, Inc. in 1967
Republished by TCU Press in 1985

Library of Congress Cataloging in Publication Data

Flynn, Robert, 1932–
North to yesterday.

(Texas tradition series; no. 4)
Reprint. Originally published: New York: Knopf, 1967.
I. Title. II. Series.
PS3556.L9N6 1985   813′.54   85-4688
ISBN 0-87565-014-7
ISBN 0-87565-015-5 (pbk.)

Foreword

IT IS RARE, after a lapse of years, to return to a book once enjoyed and find it more enjoyable than at first reading.

I have just had that experience with Robert Flynn's NORTH TO YESTERDAY, first published in 1967, and am tempted to indulge in superlatives.

The protagonist in the story is Lampassas, alias Marvin Darsey, a cowpuncher and handyman turned storekeeper, who has seen the great cattle drives start from Texas for the railroad towns of Kansas. He had dreamed for years of going along or, better yet, trailing his own herd. But one thing and another keep him from going or acquiring cattle.

Then at last he sells his store, though the money is not enough for 2,000 head of stock. A Texas rancher, on promise of a $500 payment on Lampassas's return, lets him choose longhorns from the Texas brush, longhorns the rancher was going to shoot anyhow.

So Lampassas leads out his crew and cattle, not knowing that the Kansas yards have not operated for fifteen years and longhorns have been out of favor for ten.

Among his crew are his son, Jamie, called the Kid, who yearns to be a railroad engineer; the Preacher, who is trying his hand at cooking and expects to establish a great church at Trails End, his biblical Nineveh; Pretty Shadow, so-named years before by a prostitute, who has his promise to return and take her as his own; a man named only June, who looks tough but isn't though he carries a revolver; and two or three others who decamp after a short time on the trail.

Adventures and misadventures follow. Those moss-horned cattle stampede at the chirp of a cricket. A town, overrun, threatens fines or jail for damages but forgets both on learning that the fines would have to be paid in cattle driven back to the scene of destruction. A stockmen's association, seeking to abort the longhorn drive, makes off with the horses, leaving the crew afoot and the grub wagon hitched to a couple of fractious steers.

Lampassas and company encounter a shiftless settler, a con man, a girl with an illegitimate baby and a sheepherder whose animals have fouled a spring. The girl joins the crew, adding the complications of baby care to the journey.

Each incident is detailed and rich in the telling and wonderfully inventive.

A man is lost at a river crossing. Pretty Shadow gets a horn in his side and dies, thinking to the last of his old girl. But Lampassas, the Kid, the Preacher, June and the girl persevere, on hobbling feet hazing along the thin, cantankerous cows, now reduced in number to about 500.

That's enough of an outline. Let the reader follow their arrival and experiences at the one-time railhead.

This book can be and no doubt has been called a picaresque novel, but it is much more than that. The picaresque demands an extension of credulity, a straining of belief, an indulgence in fancy. But Mr. Flynn knows his subject—the course of the trail, the necessary gear, the operation of the chuck wagon, the ways of cattle, the speech of the day—and he works this knowledge in so naturally that the reader accepts unlikely events with hardly a question. And the conversations are a delight, full of unexpected but logical turns. Neither is humor missing. Some of the scenes and parts of the dialogue are hilarious. Yet a note of pathos runs throughout the story. When Lampassas and the Preacher, a couple of doughty, old survivors, turn back for Texas, they are still dreaming.

Some years hence I shall return to this book in the full expectation that it will reward me again.

A. B. Guthrie, Jr.

To Gene McKinney

North to Yesterday

Chapter 1

LAMPASSAS reined up his rat-tailed, jug-headed, cow-hocked pinto horse on the little rise beside the lone, gnarled mesquite which had not yet admitted the end of winter. He brushed back the upturned brim of his full-crowned, still vaguely white hat, and grabbing the ends of the blue bandana tied about his neck, wiped the sweat from his forehead. Lampassas was a little man, wrinkled, dried up, and soured, and even on his horse he looked old and frail. But Lampassas did not feel old and frail. He felt like a young man full of destiny. He was swollen with dreams. Big with fulfillment. The horse lifted him above the earth; carried him swiftly and powerfully to his goal.

Lampassas stood up in the stirrups to stretch his legs and looked back. Behind him, across the valley, green with the first spring rains, the Preacher led out with the wagon. And behind the wagon were June and Pretty Shadow on the point. And behind them was a string of cows, their long horns tossing in the sunlight, as far as the eye could see. Behind the last cow and the men in the drag, beyond the cloud of dust that followed the herd, was a gray country store, smelling of hams, and pickles, new leather, and sour beer, dusty shelves packed with air-tights of peaches, apricots, and plums. Out back, through the bedroom and kitchen behind the store, and the weedy yard where larkspurs once had bloomed, beneath a live-oak tree, on land which now belonged to a stranger, was a single grave.

For Lampassas, this moment had been a long time coming. Hitching his leg up over the saddle, he sat back to savor it.

Lampassas had fought with the Confederacy in the West and had come back from the war without having really been away, having lost the war without ever losing a battle. He came back like the others; with nothing, to nothing, wanting nothing. Everything had been finished, or put aside and forgotten, so that now there was nothing to do. So that until something got started, he would drift, crossing and recrossing through country he was already familiar with, working a little, and waiting.

Lampassas got a job chasing wild cattle out of the brush where they were hiding, and rounding them up for a big drive up north where they were worth more than a dollar and six bits for the hide. When a sizable herd had been rounded up, the men were separated into two crews: one crew to drive the herd to Baxter Springs, and one crew to have another herd rounded up, cut, and branded by the time the first crew got back. Lampassas was left behind hunting cows. He didn't mind. He didn't have anywhere to go anyway. He was waiting.

When the drovers returned, they told tales not of Baxter Springs but of another town. Abilene. They told of getting up with the meadowlarks and going to bed with the whippoorwill; of going to sleep to the wail of the coyote and the song of the night herders. They talked of the loneliness, stampedes, river crossings, and dry drives of the trail; and of the fancy dealing, cheap whisky, and cheaper women at the end of the trail. Lampassas decided to go see for himself, but by the following spring he was too valuable a brush popper to go up the trail. For the next three years the outfit turned to rounding up the cattle and letting others drive them to the railhead. But Lampassas was determined to go up the trail himself. The next drive, the big one, the one he would remember all his life, to Wichita this time, he was to have been segundo, assistant to the trail boss. But that was the year he went to the Christmas Ball at the general store and met the storekeeper's plain-faced daughter, Marfa.

People had come to the Christmas Ball from fifty miles around, about four men to every girl, woman, and grandmother, but Lampassas didn't mind the competition. He hadn't come to dance anyway. He sat and watched the cowboys standing in line, maneuvering to get the young women when their turn came. He watched the girls whirling around the room, smiling. He tapped his foot to the music of the fiddle. He was already over thirty years old, and shy as a bridled mustang. But Marfa handled that.

"You haven't danced one dance, and neither have I, so let's dance this one together."

Lampassas danced the way he sheared sheep, not at all. But Marfa pulled him onto the dance floor. "I'm not afraid if you're not," she said, and they stomped their feet until the music stopped.

"Excuse me, ma'am, I've got to get out of here," Lampassas said when the music stopped. His face had darkened to the roots of his hair, and his stiff collar was choking him.

Marfa picked up her shawl and followed him outside. "I won't ask you to do that again," she said.

"I'm obliged."

"It was for them," she said. "Now if they ask me, I'll refuse."

They walked around to the back of the store and sat down on the steps of the porch. There was a room extending on either side of the back porch so that it was well protected from the wind. Lampassas pulled a bottle of whisky out of his coat and took a drink to warm himself and settle his nerves.

"Don't ever do that again in my presence," Marfa said.

"I won't."

"Whatever a man does when he is alone is his business, but whatever he does in a lady's presence is her business."

"I'll remember that," Lampassas said, thumping the cork

back in the bottle with the palm of his hand and putting the bottle in his coat pocket.

Marfa nodded her head with satisfaction. "Now that we've got that settled, let's talk about Christmas. I believe that Christmas is for children, and grown-ups shouldn't expect too much," she said. Lampassas didn't rightly see how he could disagree, seeing how she was a lady, and seeing how he wasn't going to hang up his socks in the bunk house this year anyhow.

Marfa wasn't a real plain-looking woman. Her skin was smooth, her forehead broad, her nose fine and not rough. Her eyes were gray but not plain. Her mouth was rather straight, but when she smiled she wasn't plain at all but warm and friendly. But some men didn't like the way she set her mouth when she said something. The way she talked made her plain. She was a real plain-talking woman.

"How many days do you have off?"

"I get four ever year, but generally I save one or two days for the Fourth of July."

"A man your age ought to have something better to do than get drunk on the Fourth of July."

Lampassas blushed and ducked his head. "I reckon I do," he said.

"You'll be spending your four days here?" she asked. He nodded. "Will I be seeing you?"

Inspired by the whisky and the conversation, Lampassas tried to take her in his arms, but she refused. "No," she said. "We just met."

"I think I could dance now," he said.

"Go ahead. I'm going to bed," she said, and standing up, she crossed the porch and entered the room on the west side. Lampassas followed her and took off his hat to say goodnight, but she closed the door in his face. Throwing the hat down on the porch, Lampassas kicked it out in the yard.

Lampassas finished the whisky, threw the bottle in the chaparral, picked up his hat, went around to the front of the store, and went inside, intending to push his way to the front of the waiting line, take the prettiest girl, swing her around the floor a couple of times, kiss her in front of everybody, and fight anyone who didn't like it.

Once inside the crowded, stuffy room, Lampassas decided he didn't feel like dancing or fighting either. The noise and the hot, stale air made him feel tired and dizzy. He made his way along the wall to the far corner where the counter, barrels, and boxes of goods had been shoved out of the way to make room for the dancers, sat down with his back to the counter, laid his head on a sack of flour, and went to sleep. He was awakened occasionally by the music and dancing, or by an argument which erupted between the men only to be quickly settled by the ladies. Once he was awakened by the whisky and went outside and into the brush a commendable distance from the store, gallantly by-passing the privy, which was reserved for the ladies and the store-keeper, who grudgingly allowed the use of his store for the ball but refused to suffer any consequent inconveniences. Lampassas returned to the store and stretched out comfortably on the top of the counter with a flour sack under his head.

As was his habit, Lampassas awoke at dawn, stood up, and stretched. The sore-fingered fiddlers finished the last dance. The sore-footed cowboys sat down to rest. The women went into the kitchen to fix breakfast. When the women returned with platters of fried steaks, flapjacks with molasses, biscuits, and pots of coffee, Marfa was with them. She filled Lampassas's plate, and after all the men were served, she fixed a plate for herself. Lampassas carefully placed his hands on her thin waist, boosted her up on the counter, and sat down beside her, where they ate in silence.

After breakfast the dancing resumed except for a few women who begged off to wash the dishes. Lampassas invited Marfa to dance, but she suggested they go walking instead. There wasn't any place to walk to. There were only three buildings in the settlement: the store, the blacksmith shop, and the blacksmith's house; and you could see from the porch everything you would

see in a lifetime of walking through the brush. But Lampassas
walked Marfa up and down the road, back and forth through
town, that day and every day until Lampassas had to go back to
the ranch. At night they sat on the front or back porch of the
store, whichever was out of the wind, and they talked while
Marfa's father thumped around inside and grunted about people
who came to the store and didn't buy anything.

They talked of religion. "I think the Presbyterians are too
hard, and the Methodists are too frivolous," she said. "Mostly
I'm Baptist." They talked of politics. "I'm not saying that
Abraham Lincoln wasn't a great man. All I'm saying is that Sam
Houston was a better one and should have been President," she
said. They talked of morality. "It seems to me that a man who
wanted the respect of his wife and children wouldn't drink
whisky." Or, "I know men have different notions, but a man
shouldn't trifle with a woman's affections. A woman has to wait
for a man to come to her, so he should make his intentions
clear."

The last night before riding back to the ranch, Lampassas
took Marfa's hand, kissed her on the cheek, and promised her
he'd try to see her before he left on the drive that spring.

"I've seen men go up the trail and come back so diseased
up they couldn't never marry a decent woman," Marfa said.

Lampassas promised her he wouldn't come back like that.

"I've seen men come back never satisfied to settle down and
build something, but always hankering to be off again for the
city, drinking and playing cards," she said.

Lampassas promised her he wouldn't come back like that
either.

"Seems to me if a man could do without whisky, and if he
was thinking to marry, there wouldn't be any need in him going
up the trail at all."

Lampassas backed out of going up the trail, and after the
spring roundup, he took a day off to marry Marfa. He found a
preacher who was taking a herd of cattle to Caldwell and brought
him to town to perform the ceremony. He forgot to ask if the

man was a Baptist. Lampassas moved his wife out to the line-rider's dugout. It was just a hole in the side of an embankment, but it had a wooden door, and a wagon sheet over the earthen roof that kept some of the dirt and water and most of the snakes and centipedes from coming through. Lampassas was proud of it, and Marfa didn't complain.

Lampassas wanted to make the drive the following year. "I don't think a man should go off and leave a woman to have a baby by herself," Marfa said. Lampassas didn't go. He worked the roundup. He represented the brand at more distant round-ups. He rode to Squaw Creek and back looking for signs of drift-ing cattle. "I don't think I'd better stay here any longer with you gone off two or three days at a time," Marfa said. Lampassas borrowed the wagon and moved her into the little room in the back of the store where she had grown up.

Lampassas was driving cattle from dried-up Squaw Creek to Huacho Tanks, where there was still water, when the baby was born. A boy. Five days old when Lampassas first saw him, small, sickly, gasping for breath. "He's been like that since he was born," Marfa said. "Can't get his breath. He won't live two days in that dugout." Lampassas drew his pay, put the rest of their belongings on his horse, and moved into the back of the store, where he, Marfa, and the baby, Jamie, lived in a bedroom on one side of the porch, and Marfa's father lived on the other, with the kitchen between them. Because he lived in the settle-ment, in the back of a store, people stopped calling him Lampas-sas and he became plain Marvin Darsey.

Marvin Darsey worked a few weeks during the roundups each year, and the rest of the time he sat around the store listen-ing to Marfa's father tell how Sam Houston had ruined the country, and how the Baptists were sending everybody to hell. He was a cranky old man and would hide things like lucifers or lamp wicks if he knew someone was going to ask for them, and say he didn't have any. Most folks just traded with him for spite, and because it was fifteen miles to the store over at Wall Town.

Lampassas never said anything to the old man. He listened, carried groceries, and drove the wagon for supplies.

After the old man died, Marvin stopped working the round-ups and tended the store, organizing the goods the way he would have organized a cow hunt. He cleaned up the store, finding a tin of rusty needles and a dried-up ham the old man had hidden and then forgotten. When he was through, the goods were arranged in methodical order: groceries to the left, saddles, clothing, and hardware to the right. Marvin dusted the store, checked to see what supplies he needed, and sat on the front porch waiting for customers. Other than the cleaning, nothing had changed. The store offered the same unimaginative variety of items, only now the customers could find things themselves.

Marfa and Jamie moved into her father's room. Marfa raised Jamie, taught him how to read and write, kept books for the store, and tried to raise flowers, watering them at sunup and sundown. Sometimes, early in the morning, Marvin would get up with her, help her water the flowers, and walk her back to his room. "I've got a hundred things to do today," she'd say. Sometimes, after Marvin had put out the lamp in the front of the store and finished his chaw on the front porch, he would crawl into Marfa's bed, being careful not to sit on Jamie. "You'll wake the boy," she would say. But Marvin had discovered that she was not a plain woman.

There wasn't much to running the store. Every month or so the ranches would send around a hand with a wagon and a list of supplies. Lampassas would fill it as best he could, making whatever substitutions he felt suitable. When they asked for cough syrup he substituted whisky; for tonic, sulphur and molasses; for perfume, vanilla flavoring; and when a new wife asked for a large china urn, he sent a crock chamber pot.

When one of the ranches sent for supplies, Marvin and the hand would load the wagon, and then Marvin would sit on the porch and chew while the hand ate an air-tight of peaches and talked about the grass, and the number of cows branded, and that hammer-head horse that had run him through the corral and busted him up to where he was driving a wagon.

When a cowboy came through, down on his luck, having lost all his money in the gaming halls or the little huts along the railroad tracks at the end of the trail, Marvin would give him cheese and crackers and an air-tight of tomatoes, and they would talk of life along the Musselshell, and the Yellowstone, and at Abilene, Ellsworth, and Trails End. Marvin would listen while the man dreamed of one more chance to make one more drive to get enough money ahead to start a brand of his own.

But the men in shiny black boots and brushed black suits, who came in to drink whisky and to buy flour by the hundred-pound sack, who paid cash for two months' supply of food for six hands, were the men who had taken their own cows up the trail and had brought the money back to buy up land and to stock their ranges. Marvin sat on the porch watching the huisache fade into darkness and listening to them talk, while his wife watered the flowers in the back yard and his son scratched the alphabet on a slate.

As he listened, Marvin began to see the trail. Along the Arroyo Hondo where the grass is good, until you are out of the brush, swing left of Jackson Springs, pass through Lost Valley, over Buffalo Branch, along Calf Creek through the Blanco Mountains, across the salt flats, Seven Lakes, Decision Valley, Nine Mile Creek, west of Mustang Springs, north of Tenderloin, the left fork of Hell Creek. Rest the herd in Dead Man's Valley. There's always running water in Osage Creek. The prairie dogs are bad around Seven Lakes. One herd lost three steers to a pack of lobos on the salt flats.

He saw the rivers across the trail: the Brazos, the Canadian, the Red, the Washita, the Cimarron, the Arkansas; rivers to be crossed—forded or swum as the case might be—and on the other side he saw the bright and gleaming city set on a hill, Trails End, the fortune and reward for the sweat and risk of the trail.

"The best time to start is early spring," they said. "A man with any luck will have good grass and water all the way."

"The grazing and the watering, that's the secret," they said. "Mostly it's the watering."

"Drive them hard the first few days and mill them at night until you get them away from their home range."

"Look out for the cows' feet and the horses' backs and the cook can look after the rest."

"You need at least six good horses per hand, and seven or eight is that much better. You need four tough horses for herding, a cutting horse and a roping horse if you can get them, a good horse for swimming, and a night horse you can depend on not to spook. One that can see in the dark."

"Stay away from the settlements. Dogs and washdays are hell on cattle."

"I've knowed women to hang up a pair of red bloomers and stompede the cattle and men both."

"Keep out of the timber."

"Beat the June rise on the Red."

"First time I made the trail, we didn't have nothing to sleep on but the ground and there was a whole lot of that, most of it covered with prickly pear and bullnettle. And we didn't have nothing for cover except a blanket we had tied to the saddle with our slickers. We rustled up some weeds and grass to scatter over the bullnettle and grass burrs and wrapped up in the blanket. After the first week we stopped rustling the grass."

"Don't drink no gyp water."

"That gyp water will sure draw a feller tight."

"The best place to cross the Brazos is just to the left of Shiloh. You come in just below the chalk bluffs. There's some salt cedar there, but not enough to bother. Even in high water a man on horseback can find the ford. You got to watch out for the wasp nests, though. I seen a steer hook into one of them and shake out yellow jackets like they was salt."

"That ain't as bad as jackrabbits along the Red. I recollect the time it took us three days to get the leaders into the water, and the minute they hit the north bank a big jackrabbit jumped up right under their noses. Well, they turned back into the rest of the herd that had just hit big swimming, and before we could break the mill we lost over three hundred head."

It always came back to that—treachery and death on the Red. They would sit chewing or smoking, thinking of floods, dropoffs, suction holes, quicksand, remembering old fears and terrors, and their favorite friends, their best horses that bore them up, that carried them through. Their eyes misted over remembering.

"You know, I lost my youngest boy in the Red," an old man said, pulling at his long yellow beard.

"That was Ike, wasn't it?"

"Ike. We was crossing about mid-afternoon. Just as still. Warm. Not a cloud in the sky. The water was low. The boys didn't even pull off their clothes. No trouble at all. The herd didn't even slow down. Walked through the water like they didn't know it was there. Then all of a sudden Ike's horse went under. No warning. No sign of trouble. Just stepped in a dropoff. Some of the boys jumped in, but Ike never even come up. Took us two days to find the body. We buried him right near where we found him. Couldn't find a preacher. One of the hands knew some Bible. He said that. Kind of a prayer, seems like. And then we sang Ike's favorite night-herding song. The one about the boy who gets in trouble up the trail. 'I've paid my debt now, They let me out today, So sell my saddle, jailer, I'm going home to stay.'"

The old man's eyes glistened, and his pink lips trembled as he pulled at the yellow beard. The other men looked away, past the yellow-blooming huisache, past the land—yellow, white, and scarlet with mild mustard, prickly poppy, and Indian paintbrush—past the hackberry, post oak, and cottonwood motts and shinneries to the big river which lay across the trail.

Marvin listened long after the men had left him sitting on the porch alone, hearing sounds he thought he had forgotten: the contented grunting of well-fed and watered cows bedding down at night, the snuffing of an angry steer, the bawling of a lost calf, the deep-throated grunts of a bronc trying to throw its rider, the satisfying creak and jingle and clop of riding alone. Marvin would go into the store, put out the lamp, and find his way to bed in the dark, not needing a light. Lying in bed sleepless and alone, he would go over the trail, calling off the towns, the rivers, the landmarks, recalling where the grass was good, the water clear, the bedgrounds safe.

One morning Marfa didn't get up to water the flowers. Marvin went in to see about her. "I'm all right," she said. "It's just a fever. I'll be all right tomorrow." She was one of thirteen people who were carried away in the epidemic. Marvin rode over to Wall Town to get the Baptist preacher, and they buried her beneath a live-oak tree back of the store.

Marvin took the frightened boy to his room and gave him an air-tight of peaches for supper. The boy sat in the rawhide chair in his best clothes, eating the peaches from the can. Marvin sat on the bed watching him. He could think of nothing to say. Outside it was growing dark. The black satin bow he had hung at the front of the store could be heard fluttering in the wind, rustling against the door. Marvin listened for a while, and then he went out on the porch to lean against the side of the house and thoughtfully chew his tobacco. When he went back inside, the boy was gone. Marvin found him asleep in his mother's bed. Marvin thought about sleeping with the boy, but he did not want to disturb him, and he did not want to lie in Marfa's bed. Quietly, while the boy slept, he took Marfa's things out of the room and put them in the store to give to friends. Then he went to his own room and lay down fully dressed. He thought of Marfa. He thought of the boy, the store, the trail. And when morning came, Marvin had decided to wait until Jamie could go with him. When Jamie was ready, the trail would be also. They would go up the trail together.

Marvin tried to take over his son's education, but Jamie was a puzzle to him. Marvin couldn't teach him reading and writing, and the boy was already keeping books for the store, so Marvin decided to teach him what he knew. How to judge a horse by his teeth, back, and legs. How to keep a tally book on brands and ear marks. How to ride a high roller or a sunfisher. How to treat a setfast. How to throw a Blocker loop, heel catch, horn catch, over the hump to catch both front feet on the off side and throw a big steer without stepping out of the saddle. He set up a saddle on a sawhorse and gave Jamie a lariat to play with, but Jamie didn't play with it.

Some surveyors came through laying out a track to El Paso. They were around for a while, coming by the store every two or three days to sit on the porch and drink beer. Marvin and Jamie sat on the porch and listened to them talk of paddies who could lay ten miles of track a day and brawl all night about who drove the last spike. Of highballs, air brakes, boudoir cars, double-headers, moguls, and spark-arrester caps. Of shacks, brass pound-ers, tallow pots, and hog heads. Of gandy dancers. Of flange bolts. Of stringers, spanners, side plates and spike mauls. Marvin wished they would leave so he could go to bed and map out the trail again, but Jamie listened to the new and singing words and dreamed of the railroad as Kansas boys dreamed of river boats. Jamie was polite, asked questions about the railroad, brought them beer when they asked for it; and when they left, they gave him a railroad book and an engineer's cap. Jamie read the book, but he put the cap under his pillow because Marvin didn't like for him to wear it.

Marvin didn't approve of Jamie's interest in the railroad, which he considered to be the ruin of the country. When cow men came to the store, Lampassas would get Jamie and sit him close by so he could hear them talk of the long trail and the adventures and hardships along the way. But he could tell the boy was not listening. Jamie's eyes were fixed on a faraway dream, his ears heard a distant rumbling and roaring in the earth, his mind was set on change. The only time the boy showed interest was when the men talked about loading cattle, and then he would ask questions about the trains: what kind they were, what they looked like. The cow men looked at him in surprise. None of them could remember much about the trains, even those who had ridden with the cattle to Chicago or Kansas City. They

could remember every horse in their string when they went up
the trail—Churn Head, Aunt Betty, Maida the Castrator—but
the train was a machine, a tool, like a plow or a branding iron.
It merited no remembrance.

Marvin was disappointed in his son. The boy was a green-
horn. A tenderfoot. Marvin watched the boy grow thin and pale,
with a round middle and soft hands, a storekeeper like himself.
Marvin wanted the boy to get out in the open air, to get his
hands dirty, to do a man's work, but Jamie didn't want to, and
Marvin needed him to tote up the grocery bills. But Marvin
didn't want to die a storekeeper, and he didn't want to raise a
storekeeper for a son. More and more clearly Marvin saw the
way. A single successful trip up the trail would not only make a
man of his son, it would set them up with a brand of their own.
He and Jamie could put up a house, run a few cows, and live
like men, free to sit and rock on their own porch, looking over
their own cows, spitting on their own land, and not own one
thing that was for sale.

When Jamie began walking with Tertia Birnbaum and
rolled and tossed about at night so that neither he nor his father
could sleep, Marvin knew the time had come. Tertia was a sweet
young thing, seventeen, plump, and ripe for marriage, daughter
of Seth Birnbaum, who had just opened a feed store, the fifth
store in town. Marvin watched as Tertia teased and tormented
the young men, now favoring this one, now that one. He saw her
set her cap for a storekeeper and town life, with a shingled roof,
chocolate and butter whenever she wanted it, and sewing circle
every Thursday afternoon. He watched as she showed disdain
for Jamie, then indifference. She began coming to the store
every day to show her indifference. Marvin knew that unless
he did something, inside of a year Jamie would be married and
a storekeeper for life.

The railroad was rapidly building along the route laid out
by the surveyors, and one of their buyers stopped by to arrange
a base of supplies. "You and me ought to be able to work out a
little deal which is mutually advantageous," the buyer said,

putting his arm around Lampassas's shoulder and giving him a wink. "Economics being what they are."

Marvin didn't know what economics were, but he sold out to the surprised buyer, keeping only enough things to equip himself and his son for the trail. The buyer quit his job and waited for economics and the railroad to catch up with him.

Marvin threw away the storekeeper's clothes and the white apron Marfa had made him wear and outfitted Jamie and himself in sturdy denim trousers, flannel shirts, wool vests, slickers, good hats and boots, and took the two best saddles in the store.

Free of the store after almost twenty years, Lampassas and his son rode off to buy a herd and find some hands to drive it. Lampassas rode back to the Treefork ranch where he had worked as a young man. He was surprised to see the fences, the windmills that stood in the pasture like trees, the new white house that replaced the old adobe. "I hope they still got cows," he said to Jamie.

"This is a horse ranch now," Fulton said. "Race horses."

"I heard you'd changed things around since old man Naylor died, but I never thought you'd rid the place of all them cows."

"Well, I ain't exactly rid it," Fulton said, giving a thoughtful pull to the crotch of his trousers. "There's still lots of them old longhorns back in the brush. My boys don't seem to be able to get them out of there."

"I'll take them," Lampassas said.

Fulton, who had been trying to shoot the cows to get rid of them, was pleased to discover that no matter how worthless something was, there was always someone who would pay cash for it. Working Lampassas until he found the size of his pocketbook, Fulton agreed to sell every cow Lampassas could find and hold long enough to brand, plus a broken-down wagon and fifty horses he had culled out of his own caviard, for whatever Lampassas had. Then he had to loan Lampassas five hundred dollars to outfit the wagon so Lampassas could move the herd off his ranch. Lampassas promised to pay the five hundred at the end of the drive, which Fulton didn't believe was very far away.

However, being a sporting man, Fulton was willing to bet five hundred dollars the old man could move the cows far enough to become somebody else's problem.

Lampassas considered it a sign of good luck that he found a herd so easily, and an even better sign when the first hand approached him looking for a job the next day. He and Jamie were riding out to look for the longhorns when a man driving a hayrake pulled up his mules and waved them to stop.

"There's talk you're going up the long trail," the man said. "If so, I'd like to go with you."

"Have you ever worked with cows?"

"Most of my life. I'm a little down on my luck right now," the man said, indicating the team of mules and the hayrake. "But I'd sure like to get back in the saddle, and I'd particularly like to get back to Trails End."

"What do they call you?"

"When I was riding the long trail, they called me Pretty Shadow."

"That's an honest name," Lampassas said. "Take that hayrake back to the barn and draw your time."

"Like I say, I'm a little down on my luck," Pretty Shadow said. "I don't have a horse or saddle no more."

"You sold your saddle?"

"No sir, I never sold it. They didn't want me riding none of their fine horses, so I just hung it up in the barn until I could buy me a horse. The other day I noticed it was gone. Mr. Fulton said it didn't look like it was any good and he had one of the boys throw it out. I should a quit right there, but I sure did hate to have to walk away from a job afoot."

"I'll advance you the money to outfit yourself with a suit of clothes and a good saddle against the end of the trail," Lampassas said.

Lampassas took Pretty Shadow back to the store and let him select the clothes he wanted. Pretty Shadow looked around the store, pulled out the items he wanted, and dropped them in a pile on the floor. "How much?" Lampassas asked, waving a hand in the proprietor's face to indicate his opinion of both the store's goods and storekeepers in general.

The man, who had been jotting down the prices as Pretty Shadow dumped the goods on the floor, quickly added up the figures and handed the book to Lampassas, who looked at it in disbelief. "That ain't right," Lampassas said.

"What's the tally?" Pretty Shadow asked, taking the book and whistling under his breath.

"It's the railroad," the man said. "Everything has gone up."

"How much did you put down for them boots?"

"Thirty dollars."

"I sold them boots for fifteen dollars," Lampassas said.

"It's the railroad," the man said. "Prices has gone up."

"Do them railroad hands buy many of these boots?" asked Pretty Shadow.

"Why no. None atall."

"Then what do you reckon made the price double like that?"

"Economics," the man said, shrugging his shoulders.

The horse pawed impatiently beneath him. Lampassas shifted in the saddle and took one last backward look at the life behind him, seeing instead the Preacher lustily singing revival hymns as he drove the wagon, Pretty Shadow and June on the point, and behind them, the herd. Turning, Lampassas looked ahead, beyond the rolling hills where blackjack oaks were beginning to green, past the morning clouds of the horizon, through the bluebonnet, Indian Blanket prairie, the gray-green chaparral, across the rippling red of the river, where Trails End, the Golden City of the West, was shining in the sunlight.

Lampassas knew the way, not as a traveler knows the way by map and waybill, not as an explorer knows the way by compass and guide, but in a more certain and rudimentary way, as a bird knows the way across the sky to its winter home, as a fish finds a path through the sea to the river's mouth, or as the elephant goes home to die.

With his hat, Lampassas motioned the point to follow him,

then spurred his horse down off the rise, riding majestically through the wet grass, down the trail that opened before him. Behind him the herd was beginning that sudden and complete dissolution known as the stompede.

The Preacher, being the camp cook, was not required to chase after the stampeding cattle, and since the wagon had remained in the same place so the men could find it, he had spent the day greasing the running gear, mending the harness, killing a beef that had been crippled in the stampede, and fixing something special for the boys to eat.

The Preacher was an old man, as old as Lampassas, with short, thin legs, thick chest, and large head. His hair and beard were uncombed and his face was lined and drawn with the long days and hard work of the trail. But he was a patient man, having waited on the Lord a long time; he expected to live by the sweat of his brow, and he asked only that tomorrow's campfire be closer to Trails End than today's. When the team was hitched and the wagon was on the move, he sang; when the brake was set, the tongue pointed north, and the lid of the chuck box dropped, he worked; when the herd was bedded and the fire banked, he prayed; and when he got to Trails End, he would preach. It was the Lord's way.

Picking up the gouch hook, the Preacher jerked the lid off the stew and stirred it around with a ladle, dipping out a bite to cool before touching it to his tongue. It was done. Carefully scooping out the ashes that had sifted into the pot, he replaced the lid and straightened up. The Preacher was pleased with the stew. Lampassas and the hands, having been without food all day while trying to round up the scattered cattle, would be expecting something special, and this was a favorite of theirs. Only they called it son-of-a-bitch stew. The Preacher believed such language to be inelegant and the proof of an irreligious mind. He called it Chauncey Gray stew, that being the name of the bishop who had closed his meeting in the Big Thicket.

"Chauncey T. Gray," the Preacher exclaimed, jerking his

finger back from the hot dutch oven where he had been melting bacon grease and sticking it in his mouth. Seeing the grease had melted, he wadded up a gunny sack, removed the dutch oven from the fire, and placed it on the propped-up tailgate of the chuck box. He got out the sourdough keg, looked into it, scooped out a handful of working batter, and carefully replaced it with flour and water and a pinch of salt. He began making dough, working in flour and water and pinching out the gnats that got rolled up in the batter. With a doughy hand, the Preacher took off his hat and waved the gnats back a few paces. Pinching off some of the dough, he rolled it into a biscuit between his hands, daubed it in the melted grease, and placed it in the bottom of the dutch oven. He wiped back the gnats from his eyes, scratched at his beard with the back of his hand, and pinching off another biscuit, began rolling it between his hands.

The Preacher didn't particularly like cooking, and he particularly didn't like the taunts of the men about his cooking. He had done a lot of cooking for himself while following the will of God, but he had never cooked for others. And he had never dissipated himself with fancy foods like Chauncey Gray stew and boggy top. He kept up his strength and the vigor of his preaching on plain cornbread, pinto beans, and lots of good, strong coffee. The Preacher placed the dutch oven in the fire, raking coals around the side and over the top to bake the biscuits evenly, and then he waked the Kid, nudging him with the toe of his boot.

Jamie was dreaming of a giant locomotive which was pounding across the trembling earth on rails of steel, throwing clouds of black smoke into the air, its bell clanging. With his gloved hand securely on the throttle, his cap pulled down firmly, his neckerchief fluttering in the breeze, he watched out the window, his narrowed eyes fixed on the widening tracks. Up ahead he saw the signal light slanting down the rails. "Green on the semaphore," he shouted to the fireman, who echoed back the call as he swung a shovelful of coal into the firebox. "Green on the semaphore."

Jamie grunted from the nudge in the ribs and tried to hold

on to the dream. The Preacher nudged him again. "Get a move on, Kid. I let you sleep longer than I should have."

Jamie sat up and vigorously scratched his head. "How long did I sleep?"

"Fifteen minutes, maybe."

With a groan the Kid fell back on his blankets and had to be nudged some more. "Get up, now. I hear your pa coming in."

The Kid put his hat on his head and got to his feet. "I was having a dream," he said, yawning.

"There'll be time for dreaming when you get back home," the Preacher said, getting out the plates, cups, and eating tools. "Now, hurry up. I don't want them horses getting too close to the wagon and getting sand in my cooking."

The Kid got out the washpan, the towel, and the comb, and then went out to meet Slim and Quill, who were taking the first watch. The two men rode down wind of the wagon and quickly stripped the saddles and bridles from their horses. The Kid turned the tired horses into the remuda, and while Slim and Quill ate he caught up two fresh mounts for them, having them saddled and ready by the time the men had finished eating.

Slim and Quill rode back to begin the night herding, and the rest of the hands came in to eat and rest before taking their turn with the herd. They unsaddled and let their sweaty horses roll before running them in with the rest of the remuda, then spread their ropes and helped the Kid catch the night horses. Due to the poor condition of the horses, Lampassas directed that they be staked close to the wagon, but left unsaddled. "These poor horses is just about played out," he said.

"If Fulton had any good horses, I reckon he's still got them," said Pretty Shadow, who was a good judge of horseflesh.

Lampassas led the way to the wagon. Dropping his saddle and leggings by the fire, he asked about Slim and Quill. The Preacher, who had seen several men ride off from the wagon and never come back, replied that they had eaten well but had seemed down in the mouth to him. Too tired to face up to any more desertions, Lampassas washed his face and hands at the wagon, ran the comb through his tough gray hair, and handing it to the next man in line, picked up a tin plate and helped himself to the chuck. Hitching up the dusty, baggy trousers which had once been uncomfortably tight, he sat down cross-legged beside his saddle to eat.

Gattis, a red-faced, red-headed Georgia farm boy, dropped his saddle, his batwing chaps, his ornate Chihuahua spurs, pushed back the huge, white sombrero, which was decorated with a band made from the hide of a diamondback rattler, and which added a foot to his stature, and sat down to pull off the high-heeled, pointed-toe boots. Gattis's feet were not made for boots. They were big Georgia feet, the soles flat, the toes splayed, the nails thick and yellow; feet made for walking the warm, moist Georgia furrows behind the heaving haunches of a mule.

Tugging off the boots with a sigh, Gattis stripped off the damp, soiled socks and wiggled his toes, free for the first time all day, in the cool air. Hanging his socks over his boot tops to dry, he carefully placed his bare feet on the hard, flinty ground and stood up. "Fire and fall back," he said to Pretty Shadow, who after Lampassas was the first hand to the washpan, and who took more time combing his hair than any two men in camp.

Pretty Shadow paid no attention. Neatly dividing his long hair down the middle, he raked it down the side and, with a flip of his wrist, tossed it back. Pretty Shadow, who had spent more than half of his thirty-five years around cow camps and cow towns, was no longer the tall, straight, carefree boy who first went up the trail. The years had softened his shadow, hardened his face. He had a bum knee from a fall with his horse, a stiff, knocked-down shoulder from a tangle with a bogged cow, and a dent in his nose caused by a reluctant steer. Bad food, bad water, and bad women had left other marks less visible but just as crippling.

Picking up his hat from the wagon stanchion where he had deposited it, Pretty Shadow carefully fingered the crease down the top, clamped it on his head with a solid tug, and took his place before the pot of stew with the unhurried authority of one who knows his way around cow herds, cow camps, and cow towns.

June, who followed Pretty Shadow and Gattis to the wash-pan, showed little interest in appearances. Dropping his hat in the wagon, he dipped water at his face with one hand and reached for the towel with the other. After drying his face, June took the comb, brushed the straight black hair out of his eyes, and set his hat back on his head. Dropping one hand to the butt of his six-shooter, June turned to survey the night through his small, close-set eyes, his crooked mouth hanging open. June was not so tall as Pretty Shadow, but he had broad shoulders and strong arms which made him look big, and the small eyes, heavy six-shooter, and scar on his cheek made him look mean and dangerous.

The herd was quiet, the fire burned brightly. The night herders sang the story of Sam Pitch, a handsome cowboy who got the traveling itch. He left his girl along the trail, and died, the son of a bitch. Satisfied that no Indians or cattle rustlers were about, June tugged the six-shooter around to the front where it wouldn't get in the way of his eating and tried to beat Gattis to the stew.

For a while the men ate silently and steadily. Then, having taken the edge off their hunger, they helped themselves to more sourdoughs and stew, or another cup of coffee. June magnanimously declared that son-of-a-bitch stew was his favorite dish.

Pretty Shadow, an authority on camp cooking, noted that the Preacher was the only man he knew who could get four hundred pounds of biscuits out of a fifty-pound sack of flour.

The Preacher suggested that those who did not like his cooking, not eat it.

Pretty Shadow confessed he liked his biscuits boggy. "That's the way I like my coffee, too," he said. "Barefooted."

The Preacher was about to reply when Lampassas dropped his plate in the wreck pan and got his bedroll out of the wagon. The other men followed suit, unrolling their soogans before the fire. Placing a pan of water on the chuck-box lid, the Preacher began washing dishes.

"Three times them cows have stompeded this week," Lampassas said, too tired for his evening chaw. "I don't believe we've got fifteen hundred head left out of the two thousand we started with."

"Thirteen hundred would come closer to it," said Pretty Shadow.

"I believe they're getting used to trailing," June said. "They didn't run near so far this time."

There was a long discussion as to who had chased the cows the longest and the farthest, which ended with the conclusion that Bill was not back yet. "We better go look for him," Lampassas said with a groan. "He might be out there somewhere crippled up or afoot."

"I don't reckon you need worry about him," said the Kid, who had just returned to the wagon from the remuda. "He rode off."

"What do you mean rode off?" Lampassas asked.

"He just rode off," the Kid said. "Quit."

"You mean with the herd scattered and us already short-handed, Bill rode off on my horse, on a saddle I paid for, and you didn't do nothing about it?"

"He looked like he had made up his mind to go," the Kid said. "I couldn't stop him."

Lampassas looked at his son. "He wants to quit too," he thought. "I'm making this drive for him and he ain't man enough to stick it."

Pulling the blanket over his shoulder, Lampassas turned his back to the fire and looked out across the dark land where the herd was bedded. His herd. His and Jamie's. But Lampassas was not thinking of the herd; he was thinking of the trail. Along the Arroyo Hondo where the spring grass had been good, left of Jackson Springs, through Lost Valley where they had rested the herd, across Buffalo Branch which was running water, along Calf Creek, through Blanco Mountains, and then—He closed his eyes trying to get the picture again. Through the Blanco Mountains, across the salt flats—

"Maybe I done wrong," he thought. "Maybe I waited too long. Ten years too late. I lost my wife. I lost the store. All I got left is a weakling son and a dwindling herd and both of them wants to run." Lampassas looked over the herd, trying to see the trail beyond the salt flats, Seven Lakes, and then—and then Mustang Springs.

"Kid, grab a cup towel and start wiping these dishes," the Preacher said.

The Kid took a cloth that showed signs of having once been white and began wiping the tin plates and stacking them on the propped-up lid of the chuck box. "Preacher, were those fellers that quit bad men?" he asked.

"Cowards. Ever living one of them."

"Just because they changed their minds?"

"Boy, you don't take on a herd of cows and then change your mind. When you take on a herd, you take it all the way. You might lose part of it, or you might pick up a few strays, but you don't never let it go. He that putteth his hand to the plow and turneth back is not worth snuff."

The Preacher finished scouring the dutch oven, rinsed it in the cool, greasy water, and handed it to the Kid to dry while he took the shovel and banked the fire.

"Do you think it makes sense to risk being trompled just to stop a bunch of cows that will stompede again the next time you belch?"

The Preacher stopped his work and leaned on the handle of the shovel. "It ain't a matter of what makes sense," he said. "Cooking don't make a whole lot of sense to me. It don't never get done, and it ain't something I especially like to do. But cooking is getting me where I want to go so I can do what I want to do. So I do the cooking, and it don't matter whether it makes sense or not."

"What if you don't want the job? What if you didn't ask for it?"

"I don't reckon any man ever asked for the job he got. Moses didn't."

"I am minded," said Pretty Shadow, "of a feller I once saw that had aholt of a bull by the horns. 'How'd you get aholt of that bull thataways?' I asked him. He said, 'It don't matter how I got aholt of him. It's how do I get shut of him that counts.'"

The Preacher finished banking the fire and replaced the shovel in the jockey box while the Kid threw the dish water under the wagon to lay the dust. The Preacher hung the lantern from the tailgate of the wagon to light the way to camp for the night herders. The night was black, without moonlight. The stars were brilliant. Jamie and the Preacher got their soogans from the wagon and spread them on the ground, arranging their few personal belongings which they kept rolled up in the blankets. The Kid laid on the ground beside him the new clothes which he planned to wear when they got to Trails End, and kicked the engineer's cap to the foot of his soogans before anyone saw it. The Preacher placed his Bible under his head.

"Pretty Shadow, does chasing these cows make sense to you?" the Kid asked.

"Like the Preacher says, I got a job and when it's done I'll be in Trails End, and I got a gal there waiting for me. Been waiting for fifteen years. Hell, if I was to wait much longer, I reckon it wouldn't be no use to go atall."

"The Lord told me to go to Nineveh and build a church there," the Preacher said. "That's why I'm going. I don't reckon He cares if I take a few cows with me."

"If this herd is going to Nineveh, I sure as hell ain't going with it," said Pretty Shadow. "I ain't got no gal in Nineveh."

"It's Trails End that I am talking about," the Preacher said.

"Then why the hell do you keep calling it Nineveh?"

June groaned and rolled over. "Leave him alone, Pretty Shadow, or you'll have him preaching again, and I'm trying to get some sleep. I got the next watch."

"Well, a feller that's always talking about what's right and what ain't right ought to be accurate or folks'll lose confidence in him," Pretty Shadow said.

"It's the Lord called it Nineveh, not me."

"There are some folks that wants to blame everything on the Lord," said Pretty Shadow. "Them that are foolish say it is God's wisdom, and them that are cursed say it is God's blessing, and them that are hot say it's God damn hot."

The Preacher, who had strong feelings about the name of the Lord, took offense. Pretty Shadow pulled his hat over his eyes and pretended to be asleep. June became curious about Nineveh. "If the Lord told you to go to Nineveh, why ain't you going there?"

"Because there ain't no Nineveh no more," the Preacher explained with Christian patience. "That is just a name. The Lord spoke to me and said, 'Go to Nineveh, that great, wicked city, and build my church there,' and I said, 'Where, O Lord?' and He said, 'Across the River Red. Across the Arkansas and the Cimarron.' And I knew then he meant Trails End."

"Why didn't the Lord just tell you to go to Trails End?"

"Because that ain't the way the Lord speaks. The Lord don't speak like a common man, like you and me. He speaks poetic. He uses words that means something else. When He says there are seven lean cows, He means there are seven years of drought. And when He says Nineveh, He means Trails End."

"Why don't the Lord say what He means?"

"Because He knows it ain't good for a man to be too smart. A feller is a better Christian if he's a little confused. When he has to trust to the Lord to find the way, and not just go riding off on his own," the Preacher said. "I prayed as to where was Nineveh, and I sought God's wisdom, and when Lampassas offered me a chance to go to Trails End, I knowed then that it was Nineveh, and the Lord had opened the way for me to go there and build His church."

"They have a church in Trails End," Pretty Shadow said, forgetting he was supposed to be asleep. "I seen it oncet. It was on fire."

"Yes, they may have a church. A white-washed church for folks who wash, and wear silk hats, and make themselves fancier than God intended with stockings and belly cinches; folks who never broke a law or kept a Commandment. A little narrow church for folks that always takes the same trail to water. A little round church for folks that are always milling about, smothering and trompling one another, and never take to the trail. Little churches that makes little shoe-and-stocking folks feel comfortable. But a man can't pray big in little churches that are all filled up with pews and choirs and little people. There ain't no room in them for a man who reads brands the way he sees them. There ain't no room for folks that stompede now and then, for folks that has a mean string of horses to ride. But when I come to build my church—" He looked about him, his eyes full of the dream. Everyone was asleep. "June? Kid? Pretty Shadow?" he called.

Pretty Shadow grunted and turned in his sleep, holding tightly to his dream of Diamond Annie. Clad only in her embroidered flannel drawers, with a lacy silver garter on her leg, she was reclining against the red satin bolster of the brass bed. Pretty Shadow himself was sitting on the bed trying to remove his tight boots while Annie ran a brush through her sparkling black hair. Her rosy lips curled back in a smile and she whispered his name. "Pretty Shadow."

"Pretty Shadow," the Preacher called, a little louder this time. "Stompede," he whispered. Pretty Shadow threw off his soogans, grabbed his hat, and jumped to his feet. The night was still, the herd was bedded down, and he could hear Slim singing softly to the cattle of Sweet Bessie who married a man of poor behavior. Full twenty times he told a lie. Full twenty times he made her cry, till Sweet Bessie lost her flavor.

Pretty Shadow looked about at his companions, all of whom seemed to be asleep except the Preacher, who was droning on about his church. Pretty Shadow stretched, yawned, and lay back down to roll himself a smoke. "Dammit, Preacher, I was dreaming about Diamond Annie," he said.

"Is that one of them cheap women you're always talking about?"

"I don't know whether they was cheap or not," said Pretty Shadow, thoughtfully blowing smoke at the stars. "But they was sure inexpensive."

"Is that why they call you Pretty Shadow?" the Kid asked. "Because of the women?"

"Why, boy, I thought you was dead to the world."

"I woke up. I guess it was hearing you talk about women," the Kid said, rolling over on his back and looking up at the stars, full of wonder and love. "Tell me about them, Pretty Shadow. Tell me about the girls I'll see at Trails End."

"It ain't respectful to talk about such things in front of a boy that way," the Preacher said.

"Why, when I was half his age I had already pointed my first herd, emptied my first bottle, and broke half a dozen women. I reckon I was what they call a child prodigal."

"Is that why they call you Pretty Shadow?"

"They call him Pretty Shadow because he rides along admiring his shadow running along the ground beside him," the Preacher said.

"I'll tell you about that, Kid," Pretty Shadow said, throwing his cigarette into the fire. "One night I was on the dodge, and since I couldn't find no other place to go, I ducked into the first window I seen. Worse luck, it was a girl's bedroom, and when she started to scream, there wasn't nothing to do but kiss her to keep her quiet. Well, her pa opened the door and stepped in, and I stopped kissing that girl right there and went out the window a whole lot faster than I came in it. 'Who was that in here with you?' I heard him say, like he was intending on going for a shotgun and a preacher. 'I don't know,' she said. 'But he sure had a pretty shadow.' Well, the name just kinda stuck. I have been called Pretty Shadow by girls from Cheyenne to Shawnee."

"God a'mighty, can't you fellers let a man sleep," June said, raising up on one elbow. "We chased them damn critters all day and no sooner than get to sleep before Pretty Shadow starts chasing women."

"He was going to tell me about the bad girls I'll meet at Trails End," the Kid said.

"To Pretty Shadow all whisky is good and all girls is bad," June said, rolling over in disgust. "He don't have no prejudices."

"You've been everywhere and done everything, ain't you?" the Kid asked.

"I've been about everywheres there is to go except hell, and I hear that's east of the Mississippi."

The Preacher, knowing that men were men and rough in tongue and deed even when pure in heart, could take a measure of irreverence when he was not provoked. However, he chose to take offense at Pretty Shadow's irreverent use of the hell he believed in. The Preacher ranked that name right alongside the name of the Lord, neither to be taken lightly nor in vain. "I warned you, Pretty Shadow," he said.

"Hell ain't cussing," Pretty Shadow said. "Hell's a place."

"And wide is the trail to it, and many there be who find it," the Preacher said, taking this opportunity to make his point clear.

"Have you ever been there?"

"I can say of a certainty that I am free of the power of hell forever," said the Preacher.

"Well, if it's a place, and you ain't never been there, how do you know it ain't east of the Mississippi?"

"I don't know where it is any more than you do," said the Preacher. "But I ain't never going to find out, neither." Considering Pretty Shadow sufficiently warned, the Preacher, who never punched anyone into the Kingdom of Heaven, turned his back on him and closed his eyes in the sweet repose of the blessed.

But the Kid could not sleep. "Pretty Shadow, tell me about Trails End," he said.

"Oh, there's lots to see, Kid, lots to do. Course I ain't been there in fifteen years, but I don't see how it could have improved any."

"What's the first thing you do?"

"The first thing you get to town, you go to the barber shop and take a bath with lots of soap and hot water. Then you get a haircut and a slick shave with lots of sweet-smelling oils and bay rum. Down the street you'll see this fine store, the New York and Trails End Clothiers, where they got about ever kind of duds a man would wear, and some that a man wouldn't. You get you a new suit of clothes, a good hat, some fancy boots, and you're all set to take a stroll about town.

"Best I remember there's about two dozen saloons, all of which serve the same whisky. What they charge you for is the accessories. Duggan's is the cheapest; they don't have nothing but a bar and some buckets for wetting down the dirt floor. Over at the Bullshead, they got some good lamps, a real floor, and some tables if you want to try your luck at the cards. If you win anything you might want to work your way up to the Red Dog Saloon where they got a carpet on the floor, brass spittoons, and girls. If you see a girl you like, you might dance her around, buy her a drink, and take her upstairs where they got brass beds and painted lamps. Real high class. After that you might want to howl some. Go back to Duggan's, raise a little sand, get drunk, and then if you got any money left you can go down to Texas Street to spend the night.

"There's all kinds on Texas Street. Some of them have windows, and lamps, and floors, and others ain't nothing but a roof and a bed. I've knowed fellers to start at the top and work their way down, and I've knowed fellers that let their payroll be their guide. It don't matter. They got girls to fit ever pocket-book."

The Kid lay blinking up at the stars, trying to imagine dancing a girl about the dance floor, and then steering her masterfully up the stairs and into bed. His imagination failed him. The only women he had ever known were his mother, who would stop on the first step and drag a man outside by the ear, and

Tertia, who could be coaxed up the stairs, one step at a time, to the top, where she would promptly toss her hair and flounce right back down. That there was a third type of woman had never occurred to him. "What kind of girls are they, Pretty Shadow?"

"Bad girls. Ever last one of them."

"I mean, how do you know which one to pick?"

"Well, there's a lot to choose from, but you can't go far wrong if you stick close to nature. Black-haired girls is more natural. Blondes and redheads is a curiosity, worth looking into, but not dependable. And I like them a little plump. There's something mean about a gal that don't eat.

"Admire the curiosities if you want to: Winnie the Widder-Maker, Jacqueline No Bottom, Big Tit Bess. But when you're down to your last night on Texas Street, stick to Betty Big Heart, Dumb Denise, and Pam from Three Rivers, girls that will help you down to the train station, put you aboard the right one, and set you in the aisle so you can't roll out."

"You've seen the trains, ain't you?"

"I've seen lots of trains, boy, lots of them. Kid, there's more pretty women riding the trains than there is riding up the long trail. Why, if I weren't on my way to Trails End to get married, I'd sure be tempted to give up this wayward life for riding on a train."

"What kinds have you seen?"

"Well, there was this one I seen in Utah. An accommodating widder woman with two—"

"No, I mean the trains."

"Oh, the trains. Well, to tell the truth, usually I wasn't seeing too clearly when I got on the train, and lots of times I got off before it stopped."

"Did you ever see the Prairie Zephyr?"

"Well, I seen her dance once in—"

"That's the king of the line," the Kid said. "Oh, you must a seen it. A 4-8-0, the biggest thing on rails, and it has a tender capacity of thirty tons of coal, and twenty thousand gallons of water. It's got roller bearings on the drivers and pony wheels,

and can take the Rockies in one huff. Why, I bet the engineer
on that train don't even eat with common folks."

"Where did you learn all them things?"

"From a book that some surveyors give me."

"Now, I ain't got nothing against books you understand.
Personally, I've always admired them. But books don't never
tell you what you want to know. You can't learn nothing about
trains from a book. You take me, I reckon I have read everthing
written about women from Ruth to Calamity Jane, and I ain't
never found out nothing helpful. They don't never tell you what
all them little hooks and buttons is for, and which ones count
and which ones don't. I remember one time I spent half a hour
undoing hooks and buttons and wasn't no nearer then than
when I commenced.

"And another thing you won't find nowhere in a book is
how a man is supposed to excuse himself when he is sitting in a
parlor with a lady and needs to be excused. And where to go
when he can't get out of sight of the house in a hard day's ride.
And it don't tell how to ask, neither.

"There are lots of complexities to being a human being that
a feller wouldn't know just being a man. Like which words are
proper and which ain't, where to put your hands when you're
boosting a fat gal into a wagon, and how to inquire after a lady's
condition.

"Now me, was I writing a book, I'd fill it up with things
a feller would like to know. The first chapter would cover what's
a bustle and what ain't. I have seen seasoned cowboys take up
with hunchbacks thinking it was a new style of dress. Then I
would cover parlor conversation and what to talk about after
there's nothing to look forward to, how a feller can undress
hisself and his girl at the same time, and where to look when a
girl loses her sachet. I'd like to inform a feller how to tell what
he's getting, but you can't never tell how they'll dress out till you
get the wrapper off. You can't uncover everthing even in a
book."

"What would you write about trains?"

"I'd cover the subject thoroughly from how to get on without assistance to how to get off without the law."

"Have you ever been in the cab?"

"Hell, I've been all over the trains, boy, but mostly under them, trying to prod the cows to their feet. Once I was riding on the U.P. all liquored up when we hit a 'snakehead.' A rail came loose, popped up through the car, and killed six people not counting myself. I come to three days later, and the doctor said if I'd a been sober enough to know how bad I was hurt, I'd a died too. Hell yes, I've been in the cab. Once on a Rio Grande freight I crawled over the tender and into the cab to get warm. The engine driver and the fire stoker was going to throw me off, but I offered them a drink, and they was kinda cold too. It was good whisky, and before we had finished it, we had run through two red eyes, a flag man, half a dozen torpedoes, and the back end of a stalled train.

"There ain't much to them railroad men," Pretty Shadow said with a yawn. "Always getting drunk and carousing around, hanging them red lanterns on women's doors and giving them a bad name. Always a long way from home and likely to get maimed tomorrow."

"I aim to work on the railroad," the Kid said. Pretty Shadow only grunted. The Kid raised up on his elbow and looked at his father, small beneath his blanket. Since leaving the store, he seemed to have shrunk, hardened, like a bois d'arc apple. "I'll go with him," he said. "But just because of the train."

The banked fire glowed a dull red, the coffee pot hissed. The lantern reflected faintly on the wagon sheet draped over the bed, looking ghostly in the darkness. Fresh beef quarters hung from the wagon to cool. The harness was draped over the propped-up wagon tongue, pots and dutch ovens lay about the fire. Bridles, saddles, ropes, lay scattered about the bedrolls, and beside Gattis stood a single boot, its mate having fallen on its side.

"I aim to get up there in the cab where a man's out of the

dust," the Kid said. "I aim to drive one of them fine locomotives clear across the country."

Lampassas ground his teeth, chasing the scattering herd over the hills, popping after them through the brush, following behind them as they scattered and thinned one by one, and never able to stop. The Preacher snored gently. Gattis heard the river running through his sleep, and Pretty Shadow dreamed of Diamond Annie. June breathed heavily in his nightmare as he fired the six-shooter at an old man. The hammer fell softly, the bullet emerged slowly from the barrel, striking the old man without effect but surprising him. The old man looked at him in sad astonishment. June groaned. Only the Kid was awake to hear the melancholy ballad of the boy from Pecos who died in jail at the end of the trail. The doctor took his saddle, and the outfit paid his bail. His mother got his boots through the U.S. mail.

The Kid lay back and snuggled down into his soogans, finding the engineer's cap and holding it in one hand. He closed his eyes to see the steel rails that bound together the many faces of the continent. The Prairie Zephyr stood on the rails, immobile, contained, but trembling with power, straining to be free. The Kid pulled his cap down with authority. Catching the chain, he pulled the watch from the pocket of his overalls so that it lay open in his palm. For a moment he studied it, then replaced it, pulled on the heavy gauntlets, looked over the train order sheets and a clearance, and handed them to the fireman. The car inspectors finished their examination of the journal boxes. The head brakeman signaled from the end of the train. The Kid swung up to the cab. His eyes swept over the silver-faced gauges and checked the water glass. He tried the gauge cocks. Down the tracks a green light glimmered.

"Green on the semaphore," the fireman shouted.

"Green on the semaphore," he echoed.

Behind him, the conductor waved the highball. The brakes went off, the bell clanged, there were two shrill blasts of the whistle, a hiss of steam, a throaty cough in the stack, a bump, and the sound of the giant knuckles coupling. The Kid dropped the reverse lever into the full-forward position, and eased back the throttle. There was an explosion in the stack, steam poured into the cylinder driving the piston out, pushing the crosshead between the steel guides; the main rod slid back, the side rods cranked forward, the drivers crunched into the sanded rail. There was another explosion in the stack, driving the piston forward, the side rods cranked back, the cars lurched forward. The stack huffed, the main rod slid back and then forward, the drivers ground into the rails, the engine began its powerful stroke. The exhaust thundered, the cars rolled slowly behind as one. The churning engine increased its stroke, the stack panted and puffed, the cars rolled freely, losing their inertia. The Kid leaned out the window, watching the dull glow of the headlight on the rails.

The switches and frogs rattled under the weight of the drivers, the cab swayed gently as the train gained its head and leaned easily into the breeze. The Kid latched back the reverse lever, hooking it up. The fireman, down on the deck, swung back and forth between the coal gates and the fire doors, pouring the coal into the firebox with his number two scoop.

The Kid crouched over his arm rest, one hand on the throttle, looking over the gauges on the boiler head, glancing down the track as the wind whipped his neckerchief and the smoke billowed above him. Without slackening speed, the engine swung into a curve, stringing out the bumping cars behind it, hurtling free and unstoppable across the earth, and inside the cab the Kid rode high, free of the earth, ringing the bell not in announcement or protest but in joy as he passed through the night and across the prairie.

A signal appeared ahead of him down the track. "Green on the semaphore," he shouted. "Highball," answered the fireman, as the giant train roared on, past the lights of the town, the violence of its passing tossing the hair and swirling the dresses of the white-toothed girls who stood waving beside the tracks as the Kid hurtled past, leaving them to wave and to watch as the red light of the caboose dimmed down the track and the sound of the bell faded into silence.

The Kid felt the drag of a grade. Quickly, he dropped the reverse lever forward for more power as the side rods whipped the churning drivers into great crunching strides up the mountain that rose before him. The sweating fireman shoveled coal into the firebox, the engine huffed, spewing red and gold sparks and plumes of black smoke into the air. With his hand on the throt- tle, the Kid coaxed the groaning engine up the steep grade, swinging around the sharp curves, doubling past its own caboose. The engine slowed, laboring mightily, grinding sparks from the rails. The panting locomotive reached the summit; the headlight swung in a downward arc, and the stack rumbled with a racking cough before regaining its breath. Slowly, the locomotive crawled along the ridge and headed into the downgrade, dragging its enor- mous load behind it. One by one the cars rolled over the ridge, faster and faster, so that the cars began leaping over the summit, throwing their weight behind the engine. The caboose rose over the summit, its red light seeming to hang motionless for a mo- ment, and then the entire train dropped, clacking and rattling, the cars swaying from side to side, slamming into the curves, the wheels shrieking, the couplings popping, the springs groaning in protest. The night whipped past the dim glow of the headlight on the rails as the rails turned and twisted out of the light and away into the darkness; and down the track, a signal.

"Red eye!" the Kid screamed.

"Red eye!" the fireman shouted.

The Kid turned the brass brake handle but nothing hap- pened. There was no pressure on the wheels, no grab on the tracks, no slackening of speed as the train went rushing on, past the signal, past a white-faced brakeman swinging his forlorn red lantern, the torpedoes exploding under drivers as the train thun- dered onto the creaking wooden bridge, the lurching cars push- ing the locomotive out toward the dark chasm where the bridge spans were down.

The Kid opened the throttle, pulled the whistle; the fireman fired the box, and with a shrill blast of the whistle and clanging of the bell, the drive wheels churning, the locomotive shot over the chasm and into the dark gulf, dragging the racketing cars behind. The Kid lost his breath at the sickening drop of the locomotive, but still he stood in the cab, and with one hand on the whistle cord and one hand on the throttle, he coaxed the cowcatcher up until the pilot came level, up until the headlight, which had lighted the dark gray water, rose up to light the stars, lifting the silent cars above the water, lifting them over the mountains.

The Kid strained to keep the train up, his teeth clenched. Only by the utmost effort and concentration was he able to keep the train in the air, and whenever he relaxed, it fell again. His fingers ached, his head throbbed with the effort. The heavy locomotive dipped and rose, dipped and rose sickeningly as it drifted out into the night, as the clang of the bell and the red gleam of the taillight dimmed and died in the night.

Chapter 2

A *HERD* of longhorn cattle being driven up the trail fifteen years after the trail had been closed and ten years after most folks had decided the longhorn cow had gone the way of the bone man, attracted a lot of attention, all of it unfavorable.

The Brazos County Cattleman and Stockraiser's Association heard the news with dismay. Ten years before anyone else the members of the association had realized the day of the longhorn and the trail drive was over and had started raising cattle that couldn't walk to water but could be eaten without danger to teeth or stomach. They had taught their cowboys how to string wire and repair windmills and had fenced off their ranges to protect their tender stock from the fever-ridden trail herds, the exuberance of longhorn cows, and the malice of drunken cowboys who stubbornly mistook the muley bulls for large sheep.

Time had proven them right and they had ceased being self-conscious about carrying water to the cows and walking the bulls to settle them. And now their investment was threatened by a herd of barbaric cows and a man who didn't understand that the trail had been plowed under, fenced off, and overgrown with towns and farms. A meeting was called in a back pasture, the problem was reviewed and resolutions were considered.

"Worse-looking bunch of cows I ever seen," said one man. "Some of them are fifteen and sixteen years old and so tough you couldn't carve them with a Winchester. Fulton even sold them an old blue bull. They had to castrate him to drive him, but it didn't tame him none. Take my word, there ain't a fence or a bull in the country that's safe from them cows."

"We got to do something," said another. "I just bought a five-hundred-dollar English bull and he could plumb wear himself down to a steer on one of them old longhorn cows and not get nothing better than a two-bit dogie. Not to speak of the mortification of being chased around the pasture by one of them old cows."

A resolution to oppose the herd with saddle guns died for lack of a second. "If I was to show a Winchester to my hands, they'd think it was a new-fangled post-hole digger," said one man.

A resolution to stampede the herd was laughed off, as the cattle had been stampeding two or three times a week steady without any help at all.

A resolution to steal the horses, setting the drovers afoot, a position which was not advantageous to driving cattle, was debated, denounced, deplored, and adopted. "And we see to it that nobody sells them any horses," the president said.

One man lamented the downward path he had trod, from cow man to cattle raiser to stock breeder to horse thief. Another philosophized upon the paradox that the better things got, the worse a man had to be to keep them.

"When do we put the poor son of a bitch out of his misery?"

"The first time they get all them horses and cows together again," the president said.

Gattis McCullough was the first to observe the arrival of the Association. Unaccustomed to dust, dry air, and sleeping on the ground, Gattis had been plagued with a dryness of the nose and throat. He wanted to get up and get a drink of water; but his watch was coming soon, and he would have to get up then anyway, so if he could wait until then he could save himself one getting up. If he did get up, he would have to consider whether or not he could go back to sleep without relieving his bladder. If he relieved his bladder, he would have to leave the camp far enough so as not to incite the anger of the cook, yet stay near enough to the fire not to intrude upon a skunk or a rattlesnake. If he walked far enough from the campfire to suit the cook, he would have to put his feet in the stiff, sweat-dampened boots or chance stepping in a cactus.

Gattis decided to wait. Rolling over, he was beginning to hear the river again, the river back home that had always lulled him to sleep. He was listening to it sucking softly at the bank when he realized something was wrong. He sat up. Seconds later Lampassas sat up also. Around the campfire, other men lifted their heads, listening for something they had not yet identified, but which had changed the quality of the night.

"Slim has stopped singing," the Preacher whispered.

The men began to move, quietly laying back the covers, putting on their hats and pulling on their boots. June's hand went unerringly to the six-shooter in its holster beside his head. Gattis held one boot poised, ready to stuff his foot into it only if absolutely necessary.

"Something's bothering the horses," Pretty Shadow said.

The remuda, which had been grazing off to the left of the wagon, was now standing motionless. The absence of movement indicated to Pretty Shadow's experienced ears that the horses had scented something and were standing absolutely still, nostrils twitching, ears set forward. The hoofbeats were sudden in the stillness as the horses wheeled about and began trotting off in a single direction, not scattering.

"Somebody's driving off the horses. Rustlers, rustlers," Lampassas yelled, seeing a man riding after the night horses. "Shoot him, June, shoot him."

"Where?"

"There. There," Lampassas yelled, waiting for June to shoot the man off his horse. Behind him he heard the empty click of the hammer. "Catch the night horses," he yelled. "They're driving them off."

Lampassas ran after the night horses, trying to step on the

trailing stake ropes in the darkness. The night horses, gentlest in the remuda, were trotting, heads held high for fear of stepping on the ropes. Lampassas headed them and turned them back toward the wagon, hoping the other hands could catch them as they ran past.

"Here they come. Get a rope on them," he yelled as Pretty Shadow threw a loop over the head of one of the horses and went running along behind it trying to pull the horse down. The other hands jumped about, trying to dodge the horses and catch the stake ropes in the darkness. As Lampassas chased the horses across the campground, June was trying to fire the pistol, Gattis was hanging to a horse by the neck, and the Preacher headed off three of the horses and turned them back.

Lampassas caught a stake rope, and the horse, feeling the pressure on the other end of the rope, reared, dragging Lampassas with it. Holding tightly to the rope, Lampassas talked to the horse, trying to calm it. Gradually he worked his way along the rope, a hand at a time, trying to get close enough to catch the horse's ear. Someone began shooting close at hand, frightening the horse. The horse backed away, trying to rear. Lampassas held on, throwing his weight against the horse, and then the rope went slack as the horse dropped to its knees and rolled over on its side, shot through the head.

Lampassas stood holding the rope, looking down at the dead horse. At first he thought what he heard was the echo from the gunshots, and then he realized it was the sound of the cattle running. The shots had stampeded the herd. Too exhausted to run for cover, Lampassas sat down beside the dead horse, hoping to hide behind it if the cattle came his way, but they veered away to the north.

Lampassas sat beside the horse until all was quiet, and then he took the stake rope off the horse and walked back to the wagon. Someone had put out the lantern. He lighted it so that the others could find their way back and set it on the chuck-box lid. June was sitting under the wagon, covering him with the six-shooter.

"Put that thing away," Lampassas said, and June put the pistol in the holster and crawled out from under the wagon, dusting his trousers. "June, what was you shooting at?"

"Sounded like someone was trying to steal a horse."

"How do you know it wasn't one of us trying to catch a horse?"

"Never thought of that," June said. "Hope I never shot anybody."

"You shot my horse," Lampassas said with remarkable restraint. "I caught a horse and was fixing to jump on his back when you shot him."

"Ain't it lucky it wasn't you?" June said.

Lampassas sought the words to adequately express his emotions at having his remuda stolen, his herd stampeded, and the one horse he had managed to save shot out from under him. But Lampassas was not an eloquent man, and after several false and blasphemous starts, he sat down beside the wagon.

"Maybe someone else caught a horse," he said hopefully, as the men began straggling in one at a time and sat down beside the fire to examine their wounds. But it soon became evident that the men had been unsuccessful, that all the horses had been driven off—including those which pulled the wagon—that the herd had stampeded, and that Slim and Quill had either joined the rustlers or had ridden for home at the first sign of trouble. Fortunately, none of the men had been seriously hurt except Gattis, whose foot had been stepped on.

"I reckon we better get that boot off while we still can," said the Preacher, but despite Gattis's protests and June and Pretty Shadow's efforts, the boot did not yield.

"We'll just have to cut that boot off there so I can put a dung poultice on the foot," the Preacher said.

"You ain't cutting my new boot," said Gattis.

"Well, I'll see if I can find something for it in the wagon," the Preacher said. Rummaging through the shelves of the chuck box for the medical supplies, he found a large bottle of castor oil, quinine, some axle grease for burns and skin rashes, some horse physic, a bottle of horse liniment, and a box of dusty, faded pills, which the Preacher used indiscriminately as he had forgotten whether they were for the men or the horses. Looking under the box, he found a can of coal oil.

"Some folks swears by the horse liniment, but I prefer this," he said, pouring Gattis's boot full of coal oil. "That ought to ease the swelling some and lubricate your foot."

While the Preacher soaked a rag in the coal oil and liberally doctored the cuts and bruises, Lampassas tried to decide what to do next. Concluding that the rustlers were after the horses and that the cattle had been accidentally stampeded by June's shooting, he decided to stay with the herd.

"We don't even know if there is a herd," the Kid said.

"We're going to find out as soon as it's daylight. We'll try to round them up and drive them to Mustang Springs where we can notify the law and maybe get our horses back. If not, we'll have to see about getting some more."

"Ain't we going after them rustlers?" June asked. "It don't seem right to let them get away."

"It ain't right," Lampassas said. "But we can't turn the cows loose to go chasing them."

"I've knowed folks that can't leave nothing till they've set it to rights," the Preacher said. "They attend a few necktie parties, but they don't never get no cows to market."

"How are we going to drive them cows afoot?" asked Pretty Shadow, rubbing his bent nose. "Likely them old cows ain't never seen a man afoot before."

"I don't know how," Lampassas said. "I don't even know whether or not it can be done. But I know where the trail is, and by God, I'm following it with as much of a herd as I can get behind. I know you boys didn't sign on to go driving cows afoot, but you signed on, and there just ain't nothing else to do till we get some horses. No real cow hand ever deserted a herd, but if there's anybody here that thinks he can't make it to Mustang Springs afoot, he had damn sure better pick up his gear and get away from my wagon."

"Mustang Springs ain't so far to walk if there's horses there," June said, looking mean enough to walk it barefooted.

"I don't know whether there's horses there or not," Lampassas said. "But why else would they call it that? Gattis, if your foot's broke maybe you better ride in the wagon."

"How do you intend to move the wagon?" asked the Preacher.

"The first steers we come to, we'll harness to the wagon."

"We don't have no yokes."

"I reckon it'll be a little rough till we get them broke in," Lampassas admitted.

"Oh, I reckon I can get them started," the Preacher said. "It's convincing them to stop I ain't got worried out."

"I think I'll be able to walk by morning," said Gattis, who viewed walking as safer and at least as comfortable as riding in a wagon the steers were tied to.

"I hope one of them ain't that old blue steer," said the Kid. "He might be difficult to harness."

"Maybe so," said Pretty Shadow. "But I'd just as soon he was harnessed to something that don't move no faster than I do."

"You ain't scared of him, are you?" June sneered.

"Hell no, I ain't scared of him. It's just that I ain't used to looking up at a steer."

But June shook his head contemptuously. "There won't no cow charge you if you stand your ground and look him straight in the eye. Why, I've knowed fellers was throwed in the middle of a stompede and they just stood their ground and looked them critters right in the eye, with cows veering to either side of them, and come out not harmed in no way."

"They must a had considerable eyestrain," said the Preacher.

"I don't know what them cows will do when they see us afoot," Lampassas said. "But there's nothing we can do till it's light enough to track, so we might as well get some rest."

The men took off their hats and crawled into their soogans, too tired to remove their boots. They gazed at the stars or watched the dark and unknown horizon for signs of daylight, conscious of the earth beneath them slipping away toward morning.

"I feel like there's something I ought to be doing," June said, rolling over on his side.

"It's just so quiet," said the Kid. "If you could hear the horses grazing, or the cows, or someone singing."

Lampassas sat up and signaled the others to be quiet. "Listen," he whispered. "You fellers hear that? There's something out there."

"I think I shot one of them rustlers," June said, suddenly remembering. "Seems like it was over there."

"Well, go see," said the Preacher. "Don't leave the poor devil out there to die. Besides, he might do to hang."

"You mean go looking for him in the dark?"

"Well, why not?"

"Well, for one thing, if I shot him he might be mad at me."

"More likely his horse fell on him," Lampassas said. "You'd need a extra batch of luck to hit the wagon with a handful of gravel."

June laid his hand on the six-shooter and looked out into the darkness, squinting his eyes so the scar on his cheek was visible. "I don't hear him no more," he said. "I reckon he died."

"Go see for sure," Lampassas said.

"Here," said the Preacher, handing him the lantern. "Take this with you so you can see him."

"You want him to see me coming?" June asked. "I reckon I can face up to a man in a fair fight, but I don't take too strongly to the notion of walking out to meet him carrying a lantern."

"Go on out there, or give that six-shooter to somebody else and let them do it," Lampassas said.

Holding the lantern at arm's length, June slowly started out into the darkness, squinting his eyes against the light, his right hand resting on the butt of the six-shooter. The lantern gave off a yellowish glow, making the brush look gray and forlorn, casting long, deceptive shadows across the ground and creating a little circle of light which illuminated June and little else. Being extended from the length of his arm, the lantern swung with every step he took, so that the shadows rolled and slithered about the ground.

After a while they noticed the light was getting brighter again and the arc of the lantern's swing was getting larger, and then they could hear June's boot heels hitting the ground, heavy, like a man who was walking fast and looking back over his shoulder. The light flickered and flared as the lantern swung back and forth, and June came trotting in, slowing as he neared the fire. He sat the lantern on the end gate and stepped away from it, catching his foot in the fork of one of the saddles and falling down. He rolled over a couple of times away from the light, sat up, and brushed off his clothes. "Wasn't nothing," he said.

"The hell it wasn't," Lampassas said. "I heard it."

"I mean it wasn't nothing but a cow," June said. "It had done died. Somebody must a shot it."

"There wasn't nobody shooting but you," Lampassas said. "And can't nobody blame you because if you hit it, the poor critter must a run right into the bullet."

"I think there was two of them," June said.

Lampassas opened his mouth to say something and then lay back down. "I take back what I said, June. Two cows and a horse with a six-shooter on a dark night is pretty fair shooting for anybody."

Slowly, June unbuckled the belt and let the pistol fall beside his bed. "I shouldn't a let them get away with the horses," he said. "I feel bad about that. I believe if I hadn't a been scared of shooting one of you fellers, I could a withstood them."

Pointedly, the others ignored him, stretching out again, looking up at the distant, coldly glittering stars. Despite their weariness, they were tense and restless. Without the herd they felt free, but also lost.

The Preacher thanked his Lord that he had been delivered from the dangers of the night, that his feet had been fixed on righteousness, that his hands had not shed blood. But it did seem to him that losing the horses was an unnecessary trial to a man who was following the Lord's will and a herd of cows to Trails

End. And now that he had tried it, it seemed an uncommonly slow way to travel and nearly as dangerous as riding the train. But he was not doubting God's wisdom, nor questioning His way.

"Lord, I give my word to follow You to the end of my days, and I aim to do it. If this be the way Thou choosest to get me to Trails End, then will I take it. But, O Lord, we are afoot in the middle of nowhere, no way to get horses, and Thy servant is impatient to commence building Thy church. Deliver me out of this wilderness, O Lord. And punish them malefactors that rustled our horses. Amen."

Pretty Shadow fingered his bent nose, wondering if Diamond Annie would notice. Of course she would have changed too, he would have to expect that. Gattis groaned and shifted his throbbing foot to ease it. He thought of the river back home. If he could just put his foot in that and let the cool dark water heal it. June lay on his back, smelling the flat, acrid staleness of the six-shooter beside his head, remembering the shock and power of the gun as it exploded, whipping in his hand as though it had a life of its own. It was an awesome, fearful thing. Rolling over on his side, June gently placed his hand upon the gun.

The Kid had just gotten his train on the track, puffing along, building up a head of steam when the Preacher woke him. "Kid, take the lantern and see if you can find some brush or chips and build up the fire. Get the round browns, not the flat whites. It'll be daylight soon. I reckon we should have breakfast ready."

The Kid threw back his soogans and got up, cursing the Preacher, the cows, and the sun that came up in the middle of the night. The Preacher rolled over to doze until the fire was ready for biscuits, leaving only Lampassas to watch the wavering lantern disturbing the peace, and darkness, and loneliness of the empty land.

Now that the worst had come, now that the blackest part of the night was known, Lampassas felt a sense of relief. The herd was gone, and every horse. But he had not quit. He still had hands to drive the cows if he could find them, and he still knew the way. Maybe his luck would change. With any luck the herd might be running toward Mustang Springs. With any luck the herd might still be together, peacefully watering at the springs. Dawn would come soon. Today he would be in Mustang Springs. Today would be better.

Chapter 3

ED MEHARG, forty-year-old Mustang Springs farmer, had invested the ten dollars he got from selling his dry milk cow in enough warm beer and red-eye whisky and enough Bonnie Bess to blunt his despair at the red, flinty earth that cracked open to absorb a man's sweat and life, and at the dirt-floored, two-room paling house and withering fields he called home and hope. Groping for his shoes in the darkness, he put them on, and standing up, pulled on his shirt over his head and stepped into his overalls, hooking one gallus. Mercifully blinded to the raw, gritty town with its leaning, unpainted shanties, he stepped from the darkened house of the pock-faced, pimple-bottomed Bonnie Bess, and catching the door by the leather strap, drew it across the dirt floor until it leaned in place.

Remembering that he had promised his wife enough money from the sale of the cow to buy some thread and maybe a piece of calico, he searched through his pockets, hoping he had saved the money so he could buy one last drink before leaving Mustang Springs. He found no money, but he did find a bottle in a back pocket. Holding the bottle up, Ed tried to skylight the level of the whisky. Unable to judge the number of drinks left, he turned the bottle up and finished it in one, then threw the empty bottle, smashing it against the house.

"Door's open," Bonnie said drowsily.

Hunching his shoulders and shoving his hands in his pockets, Ed turned his back to the town and started down the long road home, kicking his foot when his shoe became spongy and heavy with manure, and cursing when his foot slipped in the mule-puddled street.

Now he had neither cow nor money nor the heat of passion to keep him warm. By the time he got home it would be daylight. He would eat breakfast in silence across the table from his hard-eyed wife and his four sore-eyed, ringwormy kids. Then he would begin another day under the sun, working with the dry, dead soil, coaxing the feathery seedlings out of the ground into the sunlight where they sickened and died. He thought of crawling into bed with his stringy-haired wife, but the thought gave him no comfort. "Just the same, I should a done like I thought and saved a few cents for my wife," he said. "She could a fixed herself something pretty to wear to church."

Church! Today was Sunday. He wouldn't have to get up and work in the field. He wouldn't have to get up at all. "At least I'll be too sick for church," he said to himself.

Even with his dulled senses, Ed Meharg was aware that something was wrong. Twice he stopped along the road to listen, but he could not make it out. It was a sound more felt than heard, a shifting and soughing and tossing about. It was a fearful, eerie sound, like voices heard when one is alone, and it made him uneasy. The night was at its darkest before sunrise, even the white thread of the road being indiscernible. But Ed knew that he was not alone in the night. There was something else. It was not that he was being followed, but that he was surrounded, encompassed by something of the night.

Being of a religious rather than a superstitious mind, it occurred to Ed that he should go to church whether he felt like it or not. Even if his head did throb. Even if the preacher shouted, the pump organ squealed, and the women's choir shrieked and howled, he should sit quietly in church, his trembling fingers pressed to his temples, allowing his soul to find peace

and rest. He had promised to save some of the ten dollars for
his wife. Now he wished he had saved it for the Lord.

Ed stopped again as something moved near him. It was like
something heavy being tossed through the air without falling. Ed
had heard of devils casting lots for a man's soul. Now he was
afraid he had heard them.

"I done wrong, Lord," he said, praying aloud to frighten the
devils, who trembled at the mere mention of God's name. "I
should a saved You some of that money, but I am still a child of
Yours, and I aim to walk right on down this here road and not
be harmed by any fool thing," he said, taking a tentative step.
Something flicked lightly across his face.

But one thing the demons feared, and that was the singing of
praises to God by a good man. "Praise to thee, O Lord, for my
lovely wife and my healthy children," Ed began. Before him,
directly in his path, one of the demons raised its huge and gro-
tesque head. Ed recoiled in horror, stepping back and treading
on a devil's tail. The devil jumped into the air and exploded into
action, its four feet going in different directions, its eyes and
horns pointing the way.

"O Lord," Ed screamed as a thousand devils lunged at him.
Ed turned and ran toward Mustang Springs, running for the sanc-
tuary of the church, the thousand devils behind him, clicking
their pitchforks together, their cries of anguish inhuman, belched
forth like thunder, shaking the very ground he ran on.

Ed Meharg ran as he prayed. First he vowed to the Lord
that he would never take another drink. Then he vowed to himself he would never again mix beer and whisky. Then he vowed
to save his breath until he got into the church. But by the time
he got to town, he was completely surrounded by the fiends, who
raced with him down Main Street, uprooting hitching posts,
shoving shanties off their foundations, knocking down porches,
and tossing the paling fences into the air. "Door's open," he heard
Bonnie Bess call as the front wall of her house collapsed, as he
led devastation through the streets.

Ed Meharg passed the church surrounded by the devils,

pricked by their pitchforks, lashed by their tails. He felt them crowd against him, massive and unyielding, harder than ever his wife had crowded against him, hotter than Bonnie Bess after a succession of crowdings. Smoke rose from the ground, choking him and stinging his eyes as he ran through the town and down the road. "I will run like this forever," Ed cried. "Cursed to run for the rest of my life, pursued by devils."

Unaccountably, the herd swerved to the left, knocked down a fence, a picket corral, and a pigpen. Ed, seeing his chance, dived into a haystack, only to have the demons dive in with him, the straw exploding in the fury of their pitchforks. He emerged running as the herd circled back toward the town. Soon Ed could see a few cautious slivers of light where single, curious eyes peered through the cracked doors of the houses, as a legion of demons attacked the town from the east with the first faint promise of dawn appearing over their shoulders.

Deacon Jack Lewis lovingly lifted the silver chalice he had given to the church in memory of his mother and turned it slowly in his yellow, wrinkled hands, so that the reflected light from the single candle on the altar glinted faintly on the three stained-glass windows along the east wall. Already the lighter pieces of glass were revealing traces of the morning, and with the help of his memory, Deacon Lewis could make out the figures of Jesus being tempted by the devil in the wilderness, which he had given in memory of his first wife, the frail, hysteric Eula Mae; Jesus preaching by the Sea of Galilee while the happy fish leapt for joy, given in memory of his present wife, the buxom, bucolic Rita Murl; and Jesus riding down a palm-strewn street in Jerusalem, given in memory of his favorite wife, the dark-skinned Rose.

Flecks of saliva formed in the corner of Deacon Lewis's mouth and ran down his cheek as he sat holding the chalice and thinking of his wives. Because his mother, a fat, tearful woman, had taken to bed when he was twenty, never to rise again until the Resurrection, Deacon Lewis had been unable to marry until after her death, when he was already in his forties. Two weeks after his mother's death, he married Eula Mae, eighteen-year-old belle of the town, who died of love and consumption at twenty-one. A short time later he married the flashing-eyed, dark-skinned Rose, whom he was rumored to have met in a border-town bordello. After a brief spell of connubial bliss, Rose had run off with a cigar drummer. Deacon Lewis had then married his third wife, a stout farm girl, strong enough to help him upstairs at night, ample enough to keep him warm, soft enough to tickle his senses, and simple enough not to run away from a bad bargain.

In his later years, burdened down with physical infirmity, cares, and tragedies, Deacon Lewis had become a religious man. At first, perhaps, it was because he encouraged Rose to go to church, needing all the help he could get. Later on, perhaps, it was because Rita Murl went to church, and the simple girl dressed him and took him with her out of habit. Perhaps it was also because spiritual pleasures were the only ones left him.

But Deacon Lewis had grown tired of teasing glimpses of spiritual enjoyment, half-hearted spiritual pleasures. Deacon Lewis wanted ultimate gratification. He desired consummation. The real thing. A vision.

On the morning of Communion Sunday, Deacon Lewis came to the church before anyone else except Rita Murl, who had to help him to the church and then went back to bed, to polish the silver chalice, prepare the wine, and wait for a vision. Yet the pearl of great price had been denied him.

Sometimes Deacon Lewis wondered if it weren't an oversight on the Lord's part that he had never been given a vision, and sometimes he feared that he had been given a vision and had not recognized it. Such thoughts greatly disturbed him, and he would lie awake all night, his head on Rita Murl's young breast, trying to see a vision. Sometimes he almost captured it, as for a moment he had a glimpse of the sun breaking above snowy-white clouds, of ruby-peaked, alabaster mountains, and then, tantalizingly, it would be gone.

On this most important of mornings, he had come to church

before dawn after spending the night on Rita Murl's bosom in prayer. He had prepared the wine and polished the chalice. Then, catching hold of the altar, he fell on his knees, one knee at a time, beside the single candle, and prayed. Sincere as was his spirit, his flesh was weak and weary with sleep. His prayers became rambling and pointless, full of unfinished sentences and lengthy pauses. His head nodded, his shoulders sagged. Slowly, he lost the sodden weight of the tired old flesh and was running tirelessly across the flower-flecked prairie with Rose at his side.

Somewhere he heard the mighty wind, the rush of great waters. He took Rose in his arms and pressed her down, and the earth trembled and shook beneath them. A sharp pain shot through his knees, and with a groan, he fell on his face before the altar. Painfully, he tried to straighten his cramped and throbbing legs. Rubbing his numb legs, he searched the shadowy church. Nothing had changed. But what of the noise, the rush of great waters, the passing of angels' wings, the trembling of the earth? Had it been only a dream? Or had the vision come while the flesh slept?

"Could ye not wait one hour?" he heard the Master say. And then he heard it again. The rushing void. The sound of many waters. The thunder of angels' wings, until the earth began to tremble and the candle on the altar beside him wavered and flickered, then fell, giving one last, brilliant flash before it sputtered into darkness. In that flash Deacon Lewis had the consummation of his desire. In that flash Deacon Lewis saw horns appear over the head of the devil, a cow eating fish by the Sea of Galilee, and Jesus riding a steer down a palm-strewn street of Jerusalem.

Miss Fairy Nell Prosper, schoolmistress, awoke from her prim, gentle sleep, and as was her habit, dressed in the early morning darkness because she did not wish anyone to know that she was dressing, and that for a transitional moment between proper night clothes and proper day clothes, she was improper. She was troubled by a foreign sound, totally out of place in her neat, well-organized home. For a moment she huddled in the darkness, clutching the lacy throat of her gown while she tried to identify it. Unable to do so, she called it "noise" and blamed it on the evil boys of the town who loved noise and destruction just as she loved peace and order. After the noise had passed, she peeked out the window to see if any of the young gentlemen were still about. The eastern horizon was beginning to redden. That was the first clue she had that the dreadful noise had put her off schedule and that she must hurry to perform her duties before it was daylight. Miss Prosper had so arranged her affairs that she took care of her body predawn and postdusk so that no one might see her in the compromising position of walking to the privy. This was easy in the foreshortened days of winter, but required severe discipline in the summer.

Hurriedly, Miss Prosper dressed and put on a bonnet, although it was still dark, and slipping the straw flower basket over her arm, she backed out the back door, and with clasped hands, smiled at the lovely flowers still hidden in the dark shadows of the house. With great care she picked half a dozen irises to demon-strate that was all she was going to do, selecting the last one near the outhouse door. Picking the last one, she placed it neatly in the basket, and while pretending to smile upon it, backed into the privy, slamming the door behind her.

This was the moment of terror. Miss Prosper had never seen the inside of the privy in the daylight, but she had seen the granddaddy longlegs that congregated in huffy tangles on the outside of it. She had seen the hairy caterpillars and toads in the garden. She knew that Mustang Springs was inhabited by spiders, centipedes, vinegaroons, rattlesnakes, and fuzzy tarantulas that could jump six feet in the air. And she had no way of knowing which of these had crept into her outhouse during the night to drop on her bonnet, catch at her long skirts, or jump on her bare limbs. Shuddering, she lifted her skirts, half expecting to feel the cold, clammy skin of a toad against her exposed ankle, the sharp sting of a rattlesnake's fangs in the soft flesh back of her knees, or the furry body of a tarantula on her bare, naked thighs. Brushing the spider webs from her face with a trembling hand, she stepped up on the stool and brooded over the dark and threatening unknown.

She was surprised to hear thunder, or perhaps those young men were trying to frighten her by thumping on a rawhide stretched over a rain barrel. The privy began to shake and tremble and there was a genuine bump. Someone was trying to turn the outhouse over with her inside it. She was terror-stricken at the thought of being tumbled about in an outhouse full of tarantulas and toads.

"Get away, you nasty, nasty boys," she called.

There was another bump, and then the outhouse began to slowly turn on its axis and to tip dangerously. The door was banged open, knocked off its hinges, and in the light of the early dawn, Miss Prosper saw the entire garden filled with twisting, writhing snakes. With a cry of terror, Miss Prosper leapt from the outhouse, her skirts billowing as it crashed on its side.

The curious early risers on the west side of town were standing in the middle of the street, rubbing the sleep from their eyes and surveying the broken-down porches and tipped-over houses in disbelief, when Deacon Lewis led a congregation of cows out of the church. While running for cover, the citizens were further amazed to see Miss Fairy Nell Prosper, who was riding a lobo steer, carrying a basket of flowers over one arm, and was the nearest thing to Lady Godiva the town had ever seen.

By the middle of the morning, the ladies were standing in the street waving scented handkerchiefs and gossiping while the men put houses back on their foundations, propped up the sagging porches, and cleared the litter from the street. The mayor was making a survey of the damages. The tall, bald, bare-headed sheriff sat on an overturned rain barrel in the middle of the street and worked on a fresh chaw of tobacco. In the church, Deacon Lewis was gathering up the shattered, stained memories of his three wives.

When Lampassas led his limping, sore-footed hands past the wreckage of the pesthouse and down the main street, folks jumped, and some of them had started for cover before they noticed the cowboys didn't have any cows, or any horses either.

On a day of surprises, the cowboys were no disappointment. Natural they might look on a horse, but afoot, on a Sunday morning, in a wrecked town, they were picturesque. They had left their chaps and spurs in the wagon, but they limped on the high-heeled boots, and beneath their wide-brim hats their faces were chapped and rough with beard. Lampassas mumbled to himself self-consciously as he followed the outrageously visible cattle trail down Main Street. Behind him the Kid supported the limping Gattis, who, minus the spurs and batwing chaps, managed to appear highly ornate in his white sombrero, checkerboard trousers, and cowhide vest. Pretty Shadow was in the swing, admiring and tipping his hat at the ladies, and June brought up the drag, his hand on the butt of his six-shooter, his eyes squinted and mean, looking for trouble. The townspeople stepped back to let them pass, and then fell in behind, forming a procession that paraded up to the man sitting on the rain barrel.

"You folks seen any cows passing this way?" Lampassas asked, stepping over a diamond-shaped privy seat.

"Yeah, we seen some cows," the sheriff admitted.

"Did they have an undercrop with a 4F trail brand?"

"I didn't get a good look at the ear mark or the brand," the sheriff said. "All I spied was that they had two horns apiece and they couldn't seem to get both of them through the street without knocking into something."

"I reckon them was my cows, all right," Lampassas said.

"You must a been chasing them cows pretty hard to a wore your horses down to where your feet touch the ground."

"I mean to tell you about that. Our horses was rustled last night. Ever last one of them except the one that was accidentally shot. I reckon you better get up a posse."

"Tell you what I'll do," the sheriff said. "I'll spread the

word, and if anybody spots them horses, I'll have them picked up and sold to pay for the damages done to this town. But until we get the horses, I reckon we'll have to hold you responsible."

The mayor bellied his way through the crowd, shaking hands, patting backs, carrying a yellow ledger in one hand. "Sheriff, is that man in custody?" he asked when he had attained the center of the crowd.

"He is."

"Charge him with aggravated and atrocious assault and the willful destruction of public and private property."

"We've got reports on you boys and the damage them wild cows has been causing along the way, and I reckon we got a good sampling of it right here," the Sheriff said. "Mr. Mayor, have you got an accounting there?"

"Yes sir, I sure do," the mayor said, smacking his fat lips and waving the ledger for the crowd's approval. "First, the personal damages. Ed Meharg has a broke leg. Buster Breedlove had a horn stuck through his—the seat of his britches and the fatty portion of his back, and Miss Fairy Prosper lost something she held dearer than life. That unfortunate woman, so dear to us all, was gathering flowers in her garden when she was caught in the very center of the stompede and borne away. And she is at this very moment hiding in a ditch at the end of town waiting for the Ladies' Aid Society to fetch her some decent clothes. And sends word that school will meet tomorrow."

The mayor returned his attention to the ledger, ignoring the boys who ran for the ditch at the far end of the town to inquire about tomorrow's assignments. "Now as for the property damages: the citizens of Mustang Springs lost seventeen outhouses, three clotheslines without clothing, one clothesline with, six houses knocked off their foundations, approximately half a mile of fence, six porches, and a vacant shanty. In addition to which, there ain't a sign left hanging in the whole damn town. No Doctor, no Welcome, no Nickel Beer, no Church, no Ladies, no Gents. A stranger could pass through this town and not have no idea what we're like.

"The church lost three stained-glass windows, two doors, a silver chalice, and extensive damage to the carpet. In addition to which, the city lost three hitching posts, three horse troughs, the city limits signs, the jail two-holer, and the finest pesthouse west of Fort Worth."

"Was there anybody in the two-holer?" asked the sheriff.

"No, but there was three unfortunates in the pesthouse. A case of the mumps, a case of the smallpox, and one undetermined."

"Was the unfortunates hurt in any way, Mr. Mayor?"

"The smallpox and the undetermined was spreading the contagion as fast as they could run, the last I seen of them, but that poor devil with the mumps was down to a crawl."

The sheriff apologized but declared he was holding Lampassas in jail unless Lampassas had the money to pay the damages.

Lampassas said he didn't have the money. June said Lampassas wasn't going to jail.

The sheriff apologized but explained that he was holding Lampassas for the destruction of property and June for carrying a six-shooter on or about his person.

June allowed he wouldn't give up the six-shooter.

Lampassas allowed he wouldn't go to jail.

The sheriff allowed that June wasn't to go around carrying a six-shooter on or about his person and that Lampassas wasn't going off and leaving the town all busted up, since it was his cows that did the busting.

Lampassas explained that the cows had run free all their lives, and that if they broke down a fence, it was the fence that was at fault. If they ran down a horse, it was because the horse wasn't fast enough. If they fell and broke a leg, it was their own leg. If a man had to be responsible for them, he would never have owned one, much less tried to drive it across the country. "No sir, there ain't nobody liable for a longhorn cow. A feller just tries to stay out of their way."

The sheriff explained that there were property rights, that

property couldn't get out of the way, and that Lampassas was liable for any standing property that was no longer standing, or any property that was moving or had moved. And that Lampassas was not at liberty to leave until he had paid his liabilities to the last outhouse and farthing.

June and Lampassas allowed they weren't staying, and the sheriff allowed there was going to be an altercation.

The trouble might have become serious had not the participants been distracted by a spectacle at the far end of town. Four wide-eyed, trembling steers, linked to each other and the wagon by a tangle of harness, were trying to stampede, but because of the harness, succeeded only in propelling themselves and the wagon in a conspicuous and erratic manner down the street. The driver stood on the wagon, holding the hopelessly snarled lines and yelling at the steers. "Woe unto you, Sodom. Whoa. God strike you dead, Judas." Seeing the group of men standing in the street, the driver took courage. "Head them off, somebody. Get a rope around them and slow them down."

Pretty Shadow quickly made a loop and tossed it over the horns of the lead steer on the off side. With the Kid's help, he dallied the rope around a splintered post that was all that remained of the hitching rail. The steers plunged on past until the rope jerked them down in a tangle of horns and harness. While Pretty Shadow snubbed the lead steer up close to the post, the Preacher jumped down from the wagon, and, with the help of the Kid, rolled the wagon back, stretching the harness taut, and kicked the steers back into line. "Jump in, boys, and we'll get after the herd," the Preacher said.

The sheriff explained that the Preacher would have a slow start if he waited on Lampassas and June; that he was holding Lampassas for owning a bunch of cows (the sheriff felt herd was inaccurate) that had busted up the town and June for carrying a six-shooter on or about his person.

"Have you ever trailed cattle?" the Preacher asked.

"I went up the trail to Abilene oncet."

"Did you carry a six-shooter?"

"Things was different then. We had to protect the herd from rustlers."

"Ain't our horses been rustled?"

"Yeah."

"Then don't you think the law might excuse his carrying a six-shooter under the circumstances?"

"I'm going to overlook it this time," the sheriff said. "But he's going to have to put that six-shooter away and get himself out of town pronto. And I don't never want to see his backside around here again."

"Is that agreeable to you, June?" the Preacher asked.

"I don't know," June said. "Ain't nobody taking my six-shooter."

"Put that thing in your pocket and get up in that wagon or I'm going to wrap it around your head," the Preacher said.

With one last scornful look at the town, June jumped majestically into the wagon.

"But I got to hold this feller for the damage his herd done," the sheriff said.

The Preacher sat down on a barrel, took off his hat, and scratched at his head. "Well, we ain't got no money. I don't know nothing else to do but for Lampassas to go to jail. Me and the boys will go round up the herd and head them back this way. That's the only corrateral we got."

Unexpectedly, the townspeople expressed sympathy for Lampassas's cause, and the mayor regretted the extra work of returning the cows, suggesting instead that the herd be driven as rapidly as possible towards their destination.

"They're his cows," the Preacher said, pointing his hat at Lampassas. "If we was to drive them off, that'd be stealing. But we'll bring them back here to pay the damages."

The mayor was adamantly opposed to the return of the herd.

The sheriff explained that it was pointless to hold Lampassas unless he were able to pay the damages.

The Preacher volunteered to bring back the herd.

In an informal meeting, the town council decided that
Lampassas could pay the damages on the way back from Trails
End, provided he was unaccompanied by cows.

The sheriff assured the crowd that the excitement was over
and they were free to return to whatever homes were still standing. In somewhat more direct terms he told Lampassas and his
hands they were free to go.

"I was hoping to buy some supplies here," the Preacher
said. "We're running a mite low on flour and coffee."

"This here is Sunday," the sheriff said.

"We can't go no farther without supplies," the Preacher
said. "I reckon we'd best wait here until the store opens."

"It's open, it's open, no need to wait," said the storekeeper,
gesturing at the general store, which was minus the front door
and two windows. A bolt of gingham had been snagged on a
passing horn and lay twisted and soiled along the street. "I
don't want to disconvenience you boys none. I know you're
anxious to be on your way," he said, as with a strength surprising in one so frail, he began carrying sacks of flour, beans, and
coffee out to the wagon.

"That's too much flour," the Preacher said.

"Ain't no need in you boys having to come back for more."

"I don't believe we got the money to pay for that much,"
the Preacher said, looking at Lampassas.

"Not unless you want some cows," said Lampassas.

"No, no," said the storekeeper. "No cows, please. Just pay
me on your way back. And here's a bucket of blackstrap molasses
in case you boys get hungry for something sweet."

"Well, I reckon you can go now," said the sheriff, when the
wagon was loaded. "There ain't nothing for you here."

"I ain't going nowhere till I get some horses," Lampassas
said.

"Ain't no need to get sore, mister," the sheriff said. "We're
doing the best we can. Anybody know where we can get some
horses? Folks around here is farmers. They don't keep nothing
except a mule or two."

"Then why is it called Mustang Springs?" asked the Preacher.

"The springs down there used to be a water hole for mustangs. But since the farmers come, there ain't been any mustangs. There ain't been any springs, neither. It's all filled with silt now."

"How far do you reckon we'd have to go to get some horses?" Lampassas asked.

"Can't never tell. Maybe on the other side of the river. Folks don't keep horses like they used to."

"How in the hell are we supposed to get the herd across the river without horses?" asked Lampassas.

"How in the hell are we supposed to get the herd to the river without horses?" asked Pretty Shadow.

"How in the hell are we supposed to get horses if we don't have any money?" asked the Kid.

"We'll worry about them things when we come to them," Lampassas said.

"I can't go no farther," said the Kid.

"I can't hardly even stand on this foot the horse stepped on," Gattis said, letting go of the Kid and easing himself into a sitting position, his swollen foot stretched out in front of him.

Lampassas and the Preacher sat down too, and June climbed out of the wagon to join them.

"I wouldn't quit now," said the sheriff.

"I could give you five more pounds of coffee," said the storekeeper. "And some tripe."

"It ain't a fur piece to the river," said the sheriff.

"And the river's low. A feller could just walk them cows across it," said the blacksmith, wiping his hairy hands across the front of his suit, conscious of his nakedness without the leather apron.

"There's sure to be horses on the other side," said the storekeeper.

Lampassas rubbed his bearded, sweat-stained face and looked

at the men who were sitting on the shambles of a store front, their heads between their shoulders, staring at the ground.

"Hell, I got to get to Trails End some way," Pretty Shadow said. "Might as well walk."

"I believe if I had yokes on them steers instead of bridles, I could handle the wagon," the Preacher said.

"I ain't got one," said the storekeeper, wringing his hands and looking at the crowd.

"Seems like I used to have one," said the blacksmith, breaking into a run. Two or three other men also ran to look for a yoke.

"Will two be enough?" asked the blacksmith, carrying a yoke on each shoulder as he came out of his shop.

Harnessing the steers properly was slow because of the number of hands and the enthusiasm involved, until, out of patience, the blacksmith shoved the others aside and finished the job himself.

"I reckon we're ready," Lampassas said, slowly getting to his feet. The crowd was flushed with relief. Pretty Shadow, the Kid, June, and the Preacher pulled themselves erect. The crowd beamed.

"I ain't going," Gattis said.

The crowd blanched.

"I can't stand on my foot."

The crowd hastened to set Gattis on his feet.

"I can't walk," Gattis said.

"You can ride in the wagon with me," the Preacher said.

"Foot's too sore to take all that jarring around."

"What he needs is some pain killer," June said.

"Do you think you could make it if you had some pain killer?" the Preacher asked.

Heroically, Gattis nodded his head.

"The saloon is closed on Sunday," Pretty Shadow said, spitting in the street in disgust.

"Folks thought it was quieter that way," said the sheriff.

"There's not a doubt in my mind but what it's quieter,"

said June. "But it sure does show little heed for the troubles of your fellow man."

"Wait right here," the sheriff said. "I got a little something in my office."

Tenderly, the citizens of Mustang Springs lifted Gattis up to the wagon seat, and the sheriff placed a bottle in his lap. The Preacher climbed up beside him, Lampassas, June, Pretty Shadow, and the Kid caught hold of the wagon stanchions, the blacksmith cut the lead steer loose, and with a shout from the crowd, off they went down the street. Old men waved good-bye and young girls threw them kisses.

"Do you think they'll come back?" asked the storekeeper.

"If they do, let's just move off and give them the town," the blacksmith said.

"We won't see them no more," the sheriff said, spitting on a pile of fresh manure. "We won't see nothing else like them, neither. But I reckon we got enough to remember."

The Preacher sat on the wagon, which was being propelled toward the river in a series of stampedes alternated with balks, first in one direction and then in another. Disconsolately, the Preacher held on with one hand and with the other attempted to direct the steers by hitting them with a knotted rope. It was a hard lesson in humility the Lord was teaching him. The Lord had not spared the rod, and inwardly the Preacher smarted.

The Preacher knew that a man driving oxen was supposed to walk beside them with a goad, but he would be dogged if he would do it. It was humiliating enough to have to ride in the wagon they pulled. And they were slower than hot sheep. He could scarcely keep up with the hands, who were having all kinds of trouble driving the herd afoot and spent much of their time dodging the overcurious and often belligerent cows. At this rate they would never get the herd to the river, and if they did, what then?

To the Preacher it seemed impossible that the cows could be driven across the river afoot. But he was a man of faith. The

Lord had gotten them this far. He had rescued them from Mustang Springs. He could get them across the river. As a pledge of his humility and faith, the Preacher got down from the wagon and trudged along beside the panting, wild-eyed steers.

Jake Johnson was following the Lord's will, as he had been ever since he had discovered the Lord had a will, ever since that time after the war when he had walked all day through desolation, so that every step he took, every puff of devastated dust about his bare feet was a curse on the Yankees who had destroyed and then returned to ravage. He was walking with no gun and no horse, and only a pair of torn gray trousers and a faded shirt he had stolen from a clothesline to cover his short, thin legs and thick chest. He was returning from the war minus everything he had taken to it—home, hope, and youth—except for the family Bible his mother had placed in his hands as he left, so that no matter where he was, no matter how far from home, the family names would be with him to remind him of honor and that God whom he not only did not know but did not care to know. He returned with a single souvenir of the war, a pen case containing a pen holder, three steel-point pens, and a vial of liquid ink. He carried the Bible because for three years it was all he had to read, and because it was old and familiar and the last thing he had. Twice he had risked his life to save it from thieves who believed that anything a man would carry on foot a thousand miles must be worth stealing.

It was a large leather-backed Bible, the pages grimy and torn with much reading. On the frayed and wrinkled flyleaf someone had written "Oct. 8, 1842," making immemorial the time of a personal and secret victory or defeat or, perhaps, appointment. In one corner an unknown hand had initialed "C.K.N.," not a family name. On the brittle, yellow pages favorite passages and the scripture that had been read at his father's funeral had been marked and re-marked. Separating the Old and New covenants, written by different hands, were the old and honorable family names and the family history told in terms of births, and deaths, and baptisms. Annie Lee Johnson,

April 1, 1834, died at birth. Aunt Hattie and three children, killed by Comanches, July 23, 1859. Grandpa Favor, killed by Mexican soldiers at Salado Creek. Lucy, age nine, died of appendicitis. And the newest name, that of his mother, written on a hill before Gettysburg, with a pen case he had borrowed from an officer and never returned because there was no one to return it to.

Jake had been sitting at the edge of the road reading the Bible the day he began to suspect the Lord had a will, reading not the imperishable words of prophets or apostles, but the perishable names of his dead and forgotten kin. Seeing a shadow fall across the page, he looked up. A strong young Negro, probably a field hand, obviously the leader of the band of Negroes in the road behind him, still a slave despite Lincoln, Gettysburg, and Juneteenth, stood between Jake and the sun, holding his hat in his hand, his head slightly bowed, his eyes lowered. "Suh, could you tell us which way is the Promised Land?"

All day Jake had passed bands of Negroes, in rags like himself, walking aimlessly up and down the roads, waiting in despair at crossroads, not knowing which way to go, the bread and roof of their slavery gone and freedom not yet come. At least he had that. Even though he had no place to go, he knew how to get there. "This is it," Jake said. "Go back where you came from."

"We can't," Ezra said, "It's all gone. The house is gone, the crops is gone, the folks is gone."

"White folks knows," a young woman said bitterly, catching Ezra's sleeve. "Lincoln give it to us."

Jake looked into the thirty despairing faces. One of them, a scabby-headed, sore-faced little girl, began to cry. Jake had never been a slave-owner; he had not been suckled by a Negro mammy, nor taught to hunt by an Uncle Tom. Slavery was as foreign to him as bakery bread. He had no opinion at all on the war except that what a man had was worth fighting for, whether it be a farm or a colored slave, or just the right to have a farm or a colored slave. The plight of the Negro had never concerned him, as he considered them to be another form of life. For the Negroes on the road he felt the same pity he would have felt for a lost and starving horse.

"That's what Lincoln give you," he said, pointing at the little sore-faced girl, whose tow-sack dress scarcely covered the swollen joints of her knees. "There's your Promised Land."

"Then I reckon we got to get her there," Ezra said.

"White folks knows," Maybelle said, clutching Ezra's sleeve.

"I reckon that way's north," Ezra said, taking the left fork and starting down the road with Maybelle. One or two at a time the others looked down the road, straining to see the end of it, and then getting up to follow. "How far is it?" the old man asked. "Ain't far. Some yet," the old woman said, helping him to his feet. When Ezra reached the top of the ridge and looked back, he saw that Jake was at the end of the broken, straggling line, carrying the little girl.

When night fell they built a fire because they had no roof and sang songs because they had no supper.

> *Jericho is up ahead. Lead us out of the Wilderness,*
> *The road is long, but Pharaoh's dead,*
> *Lead us out of the Wilderness,*
> *O Great Jehovah, who Moses led,*
> *Lead us out of the Wilderness.*

The children were fretful and could not sleep, so Jake took the Bible and by the flickering firelight read to them the old familiar stories of love and hate, of Samson and shepherds, Saviours and Saul, until they stretched out on the damp ground and dreamed of freedom, whimpering in their sleep.

They drank hot water for breakfast, and Ezra led the way north. They ate whatever they could find or whatever Jake could steal. By mid-afternoon they reached a fork in the road, neither branch of which led north. Ezra sat down in the middle of the road to puzzle it out. "Whichaway do you reckon it is now?" he asked.

"That way," Jake said.

"Do you reckon that road goes north?"

"West."

"Ain't it north?"

"West," Jake said. "New country."

They followed him west. When he stopped, they stopped. When he provided, they ate. Whatever fork of the road he chose, they took as their own. He did not know where he was going, but he believed it was toward a new and better land. Perhaps a land of freedom.

"Maybelle say she going to have a baby," Ezra said. "She say she ain't going no further till she married."

"Do you know who the father is, Ezra?"

"Yes suh, I'm the father. Me and Maybelle, we been together a long time. Only we ain't never had no chance to get married. But Maybelle say she ain't going another step until we do."

"Where does Maybelle think we're going to find a preacher?"

"Maybelle, she say you do it."

"Ezra, I ain't a preacher."

"You got the Book."

Jake looked back where Maybelle was sitting cross-legged in the road. "Well, if it'll make her happy, I don't reckon it'll hurt anything," he said, setting Jo down and taking the Bible. Jake read the story of Jonah and pronounced them man and wife, and for a while they were happy.

"When we going to eat, white man?" they said. "Ain't we there yet? When we going to get some meat? Whyn't we take that road back there? It wasn't uphill. Ain't we there yet?"

Ezra stood beside him, hat in hand, head bowed slightly, after the others had gone to sleep. "What is it, Ezra?"

"Maybelle say she can't tell no difference."

"What?"

"Maybelle say she can't tell no difference since we been married. She say she don't think you're no regular preacher."

Jake learned to pray. He had said words before, earnest,

sincere words. "Help. Someone please help." But they weren't prayed to anybody. They were prayed to everybody, mostly himself. But now he prayed to God. "God, I will do anything You ask of me if You will just get shut of these people. I'll go anywhere, Lord, I'll do anything if You will just let somebody else take care of them. Make the Yankees take care of them, Lord."

"Old man says he can't go no further. Says he wants to be baptized. Says he's knowed the Lord for a long time, but he never took no time to be baptized. Says he wonders if you'd do it."

"I can't baptize him, Ezra."

"I reckon you the only one there is," Ezra said.

Jake baptized the old man in the river, and while sitting beside the fire drying his clothes, he opened the Bible to the family record and under marriages he wrote "Ezra and Maybelle."

"What's your other name, Will?"

"I never knowed I had no other name," the old man said.

Under baptisms he wrote "Will," and the next day, after reading the Bible over him, he recorded Will's death also.

They followed Jake for over a hundred miles before the trail ended at a sawmill at the edge of the woods. A longhaired, mustached man sat on the porch of the store, watching through a large right eye that pushed up his eyebrow and wrinkled half his forehead, as Jake passed down the road carrying Jo. The man watched the straggling, broken procession go by until Ezra and Maybelle came along at the end of it. "Hey, boy, where you folks going?"

"To the Promised Land."

"Well, I reckon you found it. I reckon you're tired, too. Here, sit down here on the porch in the shade. Hey, folks, come on back here now, you about to pass it up."

At the bend of the road, Jake looked back and saw that everyone had turned back and was crowding around the porch. He thought of putting Jo down to wait for them and going his own way. Instead, he turned and went back.

"I got houses for all of you, and ever man that wants it can have a garden of his own. I got work for everybody that ain't afraid of a axe or a saw. Twenty-five cents a day. And I got a store right here where you can come in and get whatever you want, chicken, bacon, molasses, whatever you want. You just come in and say, 'Mr. Laurie, I want a turkey, or a pair of shoes for Liza's birthday, or a hoe to work my garden,' and I'll just write it down in the book. You don't even have to pay for it. I'll just take it out of what I owe you." His right eye opened wide so that the forehead wrinkled above it. "That's right. Go ahead and look," he said.

The children jammed against the openings, trying to fill their senses with the wonders of sugar-cured hams, sides of bacon hanging from the walls, sacks of coffee, sugar, and flour. "Help yourself, folks, and I'll just write it down and take it out of what you earn tomorrow."

By the time Jake got to the store, the Negroes were already coming out laden with hams and chickens and sacks of flour. "Stop, stop," he said, trying to hold them back.

"We ain't stealing," Ezra said. "We got jobs."

"This ain't it, Ezra. This ain't the Promised Land."

"I know it ain't, Mistah Jake. But my people are hungry. They're tired. Don't look like it would hurt none to stop off here for a little while."

Jake went into the store, which was stripped of groceries and looked barren and dirty. Mr. Laurie sat behind the counter trying to catch up with his accounts. "Looks like I'm sold out," he said.

"I want you to let them go."

"Sure," he said. "Any time they got a mind to. Soon as you or them pays me the hundred and twenty-three dollars."

"One hundred and twenty-three dollars?"

"That's right," said Mr. Laurie, his right eye swelling to run over the figures. "One hundred twenty-three dollars and twenty-eight cents. I'm going to have to get another load of groceries tomorrow."

"I'm staying," Jake said.

"Suit yourself."

Jake was put in a shack with the other three white hands, and the Negroes were divided into the remaining shacks, seven or eight to each. When the bell rang at five, and the men picked up their axes and went to work, Jake went with them. He worked beside them all day, pleading with them not to buy from the store.

"We got to eat, Mistuh Jake."

"Where are those gardens he promised you?"

"This is them, Mistuh Jake. As soon as we gets the trees cut down, we can clear out the brush, plow it, and plant us a garden."

"But that'll be next year."

"We got to eat."

When Jake got back to his cabin, he found a tub of water, a suit of new clothes, and a razor waiting for him. "Mr. Laurie wants you to have supper with him," one of the men said.

Jake bathed and shaved, but put on his old clothes after shaking them out. "You can take these back," he said. "I ain't buying nothing in that store."

Mr. Laurie met him at the door and ushered him into the sitting room. "Sit down and let's have a cup of coffee and a cigar," he said. "Tommy, bring the coffee."

A golden-haired, golden-skinned, blue-eyed girl offered him coffee. "My daughter, Tommy Lou," Laurie said as the girl returned to the kitchen. Laurie drew on his cigar thoughtfully. "I figured you and me better have a little talk. Them niggers owes me money, but I reckon they're still your niggers."

"They ain't mine."

"I reckon you're down on your luck right now, but you got some place to go or you wouldn't be taking them niggers with you. And you need them for something or you wouldn't be waiting."

"I don't need them."

"I'm going to level with you. Them trees ain't going to

last forever. By the time the last one's cut, them niggers will have that ground cleared of brush and turned under. I'm going to plant it in cotton. But farming won't keep all of them niggers busy, so I got to cast around for another scheme. Now it appears to me you got a scheme under your hat, and that it would profit both of us to go in cahoots."

"I ain't got a scheme."

"Close-mouthed, ain't you?"

They went to supper, and Jake ate slowly, aware of his rough manners, his dirty clothing, and the soft warm girl beside him, who spoke so quietly he involuntarily leaned toward her. After they had eaten, Tommy Lou began cleaning away the dishes.

"You let them dishes go, honey. I'll get one of them nigger gals to clean them up. You and Jake go sit out on the porch where it's cool."

"Don't you just hate it here?" she said as they sat gently swaying in the porch swing. "We used to live in a nicer place than this, but it's all burnt up now. But I just hate this place. First chance I get, I'm going to leave. I bet you got some place to go to."

"No."

"Sure you do. You got some place to go to."

"No, I was just going."

"I wish you would stay a while."

"I guess I'll stay a little while."

"I'm glad," she said, smiling at him.

She closed her eyes, and he swung her slowly, gently, looking down into her moon-softened face. Carefully, he touched her smooth cheek with his trembling fingertips, and she opened her eyes and smiled at him.

"Forgive me for asking," she said, "but what are you doing with them niggers?"

"Nothing. It's like we was going the same way, and we just started walking together. Mostly, I guess I stayed because of Jo. There was this little girl, and she couldn't hardly walk her knees were swollen so bad, so I started carrying her. Then at night I'd read the Bible to her, and sleep next to her to keep her warm. We had to sleep on the ground."

Tommy Lou closed her eyes and Jake swung her gently so as not to disturb her. He kissed her lightly, and she trembled in his arms.

When the bell rang the next morning and Jake stepped outside, the Negroes were wearing new cotton shirts, overalls, and heavy shoes. "Dammit, Ezra, don't you realize you'll never be able to pay for these things? You'll never be able to leave? He's making a slave of you."

"No suh, we're free. We can go to the store any time we like and buy anything we want."

Jake devised a desperate plan. By eating with the others and buying nothing at the store, he could use his money to help pay Ezra's debts, then the two of them could pay Maybelle's debts, then the three of them could pay off the debts of someone else. At the end of the month, he asked for his wages.

"You ain't bought nothing, have you? Let's see, six days a week for four weeks, that's six dollars."

"How much does Ezra owe you?"

"Let's see now, I keep Ezra and Maybelle's account together. You know, they've sort of taken up with each other the way niggers will. Subtracting a month's wages for the two of them and that leaves one hundred and eighteen dollars."

"It'll take him two years to pay that off if he doesn't buy another thing."

"You know how niggers are, big eaters, can't save nothing. I told Maybelle how she could earn a little extra, but somebody's already got to that gal," he said, winking his enormous eye at Jake.

"I'm taking them," Jake said.

"Any time you got the money."

"I'm taking them right now. It'll take a gun to stop me."

"What do I need a gun for?" Laurie asked. "I got the law. How far do you think you'd get before the law was after you?

Likely they wouldn't do much to you, but they'd have them nigggers working on the roads for nothing. Hell, I'm giving them two bits a day."

"This man is cheating you," Jake yelled at the Negroes who were sitting before the cabins waiting for supper. Curious faces appeared at the doors. "This is just another kind of slavery. We're leaving right now. And don't take nothing with you." The Negroes did not move. "Right now. I'm taking you out of here."

"Where you aim to take us?" they asked. "We got homes here. We got jobs. Whatever we want we can get at the store."

"Tell them, Ezra," Jake said. "Tell them they got to go."

"You ain't old massah," Ezra said.

Angrily, Jake faced them, wanting to strike them, wishing for a whip or a gun to make them do his bidding. "Can't you see I'm doing it for you? For your own good?"

"You ain't old massah," Ezra said.

Abruptly, Jake turned and went into his cabin. He came out a moment later carrying the sack with the Bible in it. No one seemed to have moved. Laurie stood on the porch of the store watching.

"Mistuh Jake, we don't want you to leave," Ezra said.

"I got to," Jake said. "I'm a slaver, too. You go with me, Ezra. You and Maybelle. You know this is wrong."

"Where can we go with you?" Ezra asked.

Because he could not answer, Jake laid his hand on Ezra's head and said a prayer over him. Then he laid his hand on the heads of the others, praying for them also. He picked up Jo and kissed her, then went to the house and knocked on the door until Tommy Lou answered it.

"I'm leaving, Tommy Lou. I don't know where I'm going, but I want you to go with me."

"I can't."

"I'll take care of you, Tommy Lou. I want to marry you."

"I can't marry nobody that's slept with niggers."

"She was just a little girl," he said, reaching out to her. "Just a little nine-year-old girl."

But she was crying, and she turned away and closed the door without looking at him. Jake stepped off the porch and walked into the sun, into the successive stages of light and shadow, moonlight and darkness, until his shadow was running along the ground before him. He sat down under a shade tree, opened the sack, and took out the Bible. He opened the Bible, and there were their names: Lucy, Annie Lee Johnson, Aunt Hattie, Grandpa Favor, along with Will, and Jo, Maybelle and Ezra. He took out the pen case, fitted a steel pen into the holder, dipped it into the vial of ink, and under Marriages, he scratched a large X, deliberately canceling the line of blood and family honor. Then he closed the Bible and put it into the sack. "I don't know where to go, Lord, unless You tell me," he said.

Jake Johnson went to and fro about the earth planting cotton, laying crossties, and following the Lord's will. All day he worked as a man among men, and every night he read the Bible and talked to the men about God. Not everyone wanted to listen to Jake and some of them were frank in saying so. However, Jake was obstinate about it, and after they had whipped him two or three times, it didn't hardly seem worth the effort. After they had listened a while they realized he was talking about them and all their stumbling, clumsy efforts to be men. They didn't care much for storekeeper's churches with their fancy dress, and fancy singing, and everyone pretending they weren't the same people who had overcharged and shortchanged on Saturday. But they trusted Jake, and in time they even came to like him.

The men would come and sit on stacks of lumber outside the sawmill, or bales of cotton along the river, or on the ground behind the gin, and listen to Jake talk, sometimes not even listening, but just sitting, whittling and chewing, enjoying the company. Soon the women would start coming to see what the men were doing. They'd come in their Sunday-go-to-meeting clothes, making all the men feel shy and embarrassed, because a woman dressed up in church in no way, shape, or tone of voice resembled a woman undressed at home. The women would all say what a fine thing it was that the men were going to church, and that they'd come too if the men would just shave and dress up a little. Some of the men would stop coming, and others would dress up and come with their wives, looking scrubbed and constipated.

"Wouldn't it be a fine thing to have a ladies' choir?" the women would say. "Wouldn't it be a fine thing to have a pipe organ, and a regular church building, and some stained-glass windows, and pews in which to sit? Would the Reverend Mr. Johnson please not speak so crudely in the presence of ladies? Wouldn't 'Fallen Woman of Babylon' serve the same purpose? Shouldn't there be a Bible school for the children? Wouldn't a church picnic be nice? Would the Reverend Mr. Johnson come to a tea party Friday afternoon? Would the Reverend Mr. Johnson get a haircut, a shave, a frock coat, and a wife before Sunday?"

Before the Reverend Mr. Johnson's amazed eyes, a church would spring up, full of pipe organs, ladies' choirs, comfortable pews, stained-glass windows, palm-leaf fans with the Last Supper on one side and the funeral parlor on the other, church picnics, and women. Sometimes Mr. Flack, the piano teacher, would be the only man present. The Reverend Mr. Johnson would begin looking for a call from the Lord. Then, a few days later, between the soprano solo and the first meeting of the Christian Women United To Promote Church Attendance, Lye Soap, and the Church Fair, the Reverend Mr. Johnson would saddle his horse and follow the will of God.

Following the will of God, the Preacher rode into the Big Thicket to warn of the destruction and wrath to come. He tied his horse in the clearing, close enough that it wouldn't be stolen, and sat down to read his Bible and pray until the people came. An outsider in the thicket was his own herald, like a rock thrown into a still pond. Soon the denizens were coming to see what all the noise was. For three weeks they came, hidden behind the dogwood and loblolly, and watched as the Preacher read his Bible aloud and wept at what was coming.

"O Lord, if it be Thy will, let it not come. If it be Thy will that it come, then spare us this day. O Lord, hold back destruction from us. Let it not come today."

When they could resist no longer, they charged into the clearing and demanded to know what was coming, and Jake began preaching of the judgment to come. Some of the men slipped back into the thicket, and some were baptized in Lost Cow Creek, but every night men came to listen.

In a few days the women started coming to see what the men were doing. Then Chauncey Gray came to say that he was a bishop, that Jake was an impostor, and that they were dupes for listening. Jake answered the charges with a well-aimed blow to the eye of the fat, red-faced bishop, and the bishop retracted.

The next day the bishop appeared with a black eye and the sheriff. The bishop reiterated his charge, and the sheriff read a paper to the Preacher. The Preacher took the paper, tore it up, and stuffed it into the sheriff's vest pocket. The sheriff objected. The bishop reiterated his charge. The Preacher repeated his response to the bishop's good eye. The sheriff remonstrated. The Preacher replied to the sheriff's eye. The sheriff and the bishop took exception to the Preacher's attitude, put the Preacher on his horse, escorted him to the county line, and gave him explicit directions as to where to go.

The Preacher replied by giving them fair warning of what was to come, and was vindicated ten years later when Wilbur Crutchfield announced that his hogs had come back from the wallow covered with oil. The wrath and the Yankees descended. The hills were leveled, the land was stripped bare, the hunters, fishers, and moonshiners were dispossessed, and oil towns and oil wells sprang up like stills. The sheriff ran for governor, and Chauncey Gray built a new church where folks could worship in the beauty of holiness without having to look upon the wretchedness of their neighbors who had struck a dry hole.

After being run out of the thicket, it came to the Preacher

that the East was getting too fancy for his taste. "Where to this time, Lord?" he asked, drifting west.

While he was praying about where to go and looking for signs to follow, the Preacher met up with a man named Marvin Darsey who was getting together a herd of longhorns to take up the trail. It came to the Preacher that this was the call he had been waiting for and the Lord had provided the way.

"I ain't never done any cooking except for myself, but I've worked with cows, and I've worked with men, and I want awful bad to get to Trails End and build the Lord's church there."

Lampassas assured him he could do the job, and showed the Preacher an old, wide-tired wagon with a chuck box built on to the tailgate. The wagon was loaded with the heavy supplies: sides of bacon, a keg of molasses, sacks of flour, salt, beans, and coffee. In the chest that hung on one side of the wagon to balance the water barrel were stored the hobbles, horse-shoeing equipment, and the axe and shovel. "She's all yours," Lampassas said, as the Preacher doubtfully surveyed the old, overloaded wagon and the gaunt horses that were hitched to it.

"Do you think she'll make it to the river?" the Preacher asked.

Chapter 4

THE river rises on the Llano Estacado, the Staked Plains of Coronado, who sought Seven Cities of Gold and found instead the plains, the canyon, the river, treachery, despair, and death. Water falling on the plains begins its downward course to the sea, seeking an outlet off the level mesa, plunging into the canyon, the Palo Duro, cutting deep through clay and sandstone, cutting through the ages, leaving perpendicular blue, red, yellow walls, eroded bluffs, high, lonesome sentinels and towers that brood over their own desolation. Rushing downward through narrow defiles, the river spreads free, mile-wide-and-foot-deep thin over a broad, sandy bed through a semi-arid plain. Free now of its headlong plunge, the river sinks into the sand, separating into several channels, slow, sullen, through chalk bluffs, sand hills, among the cattails, salt cedars, past tangles of mustang grapes, thickets of wild plums, past forgotten Indian campfires and cowboys' graves, over deep holes where catfish big as hogs lie deep in shadows and bump lazily against the red prison walls, treacherous with shifting sands where cattle and horses mire and die.

But when it rained on the high plains, the river had another face. Heavy, thick, ponderous with its own power. Tearing out new channels, washing away old bluffs, rising up out of its bed to sweep away cottonwood and hackberry, mesquite and willow, here and there carrying away a field of cotton or a stand of corn, or a farmhouse built solidly upon a crumbling bluff. High, turgid, out of its banks, the river lay athwart the trail. Death and destruction were on its face.

Lampassas knew nothing of rivers. The Brazos, the Nueces, the Frio he had seen. The Mississippi he had heard of. The Hudson, the Niagara were up north. The Amazon, the Ganges were unknown to him. The Nile had something to do with the Bible. The Styx, the Acheron, the Lethe he had never heard of, and he would have scoffed if he had. The Jordan he would cross when he died, hopefully not alone. But this river he knew, although he had never seen it before, the river of cattle crossings and trail drivers—the Red.

The late afternoon sun broke through the clouds so that the slow drops that fell into the heavy river were long and sun-streaked, the short wet grass glistened. Lampassas dipped his head to shake the water from the brim of his hat and looked up, appraising the heavy bank of clouds in the northwest that foreboded more rain. It had showered all day, but not enough to make a difference in the river. The rise of the river had to be due to heavy rains on the plains, and if it was raining there now, the river would be even higher tomorrow. Lampassas turned to look at the sun breaking briefly through the clouds before dropping beyond the edge of the world. If it didn't rain any more tonight, and if the weather were pretty tomorrow—

Lampassas looked back at the wagon, which stood between the river and the sun, rigid, immobile, thirty feet above the flood, upon the red clay bluff that was slowly crumbling in the rush of red water. From the bank of the river where Lampassas stood, the wagon seemed to float lightly upon the crimson sky below the purple clouds, buoyed up by four shimmering, spidery wheels. The wagon sheet, set on a pole to protect the firewood from the rain, soared upward into the low-hanging sun like a sail. Before the wagon, the Preacher hovered over the smoldering fire, protecting it from the rain with his spread slicker.

The intermittent rain had almost stopped. "But it's too

late now," Lampassas thought, remembering that cattle will not cross a river when the sun is low and in their eyes, blinding them as it sparkles on the water.

Lampassas looked across the river to the open country on the other side, trying to see the trail. Lampassas had waited a long time to look across this river, and now he could not see a trail on the other side. "There is something about a river that it will always run across a trail," Lampassas thought.

Lampassas turned his back on the river, looking across the valley where the herd made its way between the sand hills. The hands walked beside the cattle, watching for his signal. They walked slowly over the bright red-and-white mounds, their shoulders slumped, their feet heavy, yet holding something back for the crossing. Already they were chousing up the drag, prodding them into a faster walk, holding the formation tight for the crossing. For three days they had driven the herd over the same path to the river, and each time he had waved them off to wait another day. The cattle were getting restless; the men were on edge. Lampassas knew he had to cross them soon or he would lose them. He looked back across the river, high and running fast.

"We'll wait one more day," he said, signaling for the point to turn the herd upstream to water rather than holding them in tight trail order to cross the river.

"We'll have to cross them tomorrow, irregardless," he said. "We can't wait no longer."

Behind him the herd swung upstream as the hands strung out the cattle along the muddy river to water. The cows approached the water cautiously, suspiciously, snorting as their hooves slipped on the slick wet grass and bogged in the soft bank, tossing their horns to keep the other cows from crowding them into the water.

"We'll never get them into that water," Lampassas thought, "We couldn't get them into that river if we had horses. Water the herd at Mustang Springs. Stay on the left bank of Sandy Fork. Pass through the sand hills and come out in a little valley

with low banks on either side of the river. That's the ford. Over
to the west is a big red bluff. Near thirty foot high. Hug the
bluff when you take to the water. The river will swing you right
a little and you'll hit solid footing about two thirds of the way
across. On the other side of the Red—on the other side—"

Lampassas called Pretty Shadow over to him. "This look
familiar?"

"To tell you the truth, I don't remember much," Pretty
Shadow said. "You know how it is the first time you cross. You're
too excited to see anything except the other side. Then too, I
was in the drag most of the time. About all I saw was dust
and tails."

"We're crossing tomorrow," Lampassas said.

"They look mighty skittish to me," said Pretty Shadow. "I
ain't sure they'll set foot in that water."

"Tomorrow," Lampassas said.

The Preacher, his shoulders hunched forward, his legs
and slicker spread, stood, protecting his fire from the slow, slanting
rain that still fell, hissing when one of the big drops hit the
fire. "You get the logs?" he asked the Kid, who was returning
to the wagon with the axe in his hand.

"Yeah, they're down on the river. Cottonwoods. They'll
float the wagon if anything will," the Kid said, replacing the
axe in the tool box on the side of the wagon.

"What we'll do is run the wagon axle-deep into the water,
float the logs up under it, and lash them to the axles. We'll
run a rope over to the other side, and when she rises off the
wheels, the river will swing her right on across."

"You think she'll float?" the Kid asked, looking at the old,
clumsy wagon, encumbered with tools, cooking gear, bedrolls,
and the useless saddles.

"She'll float if you got some good logs. Not too wet."

"I think it's stopped raining," the Kid said.

"Well, you can put that slicker up and start grinding the

coffee," the Preacher said, rolling out dough. "That's a pretty sight, them cows watering."

"It'd be a prettier one to see them take to the water."

"You'll see that too. One of these times you'll see them cows come down to the river and take to the water without even slowing down, like it was the most natural thing in the world," the Preacher said. Putting the biscuits to one side to rise, he wiped his hands on his dirty apron, pulled the slicker-wrapped side of beef out of the wagon, and began slicing off steaks. "That is the law of progress. If you keep doing the same thing over and over long enough, somebody will come along and change it, just to be different."

Cutting off the last steak, the Preacher checked the Kid's coffee-making to see that he was generous with the coffee and stingy with the water, and began beating the tough, stringy meat with a butcher knife to make it digestible. "Don't never make the mistake of thinking of that herd as one thing. There's a thousand cows down there and ever one of them has his own reason for not wanting to cross the river. Old Blue is the leader. He's a smart steer and he don't like the looks of things, so he ain't going to set foot in that water. But there's half a dozen other leaders down there just waiting for Old Blue to falter so they can take the lead. If one of them takes to the water, Old Blue will have to go in too or drop behind. There are some steers that are always up front, not good for nothing but following. They'll follow anything. I have to beat back half a dozen of them ever morning that want to follow the wagon," the Preacher said.

Laying the steaks in the big dutch oven, he set it on the coals, standing up and turning his head to avoid the smoke from the wet wood and cow chips. He looked around for the Kid, to see only his boots protruding from under the wagon. "Are you listening, boy?"

"What?"

"I said get out from under that wagon. What are you doing under there anyway?"

"I was just studying to see how they put it together."

"I've never seen a man yet around a machine that he didn't have to get down on his hands and knees to it. Get out the lantern and fill it up; it'll be dark soon. And since you like that wagon so much, you can grease the axles when we get it across the river. People that can stand here in the middle of God's creation and not find nothing better to look at than the underside of a wagon!" the Preacher said in disgust.

"First watch is coming in," the Kid said.

"Bury the sourdoughs in the coals."

"They look kinda flat and pink."

"They don't rise much in damp weather, and the water's half mud. I can't help what they look like," the Preacher said.

The herd had been driven back from the river and up the valley to drier ground, and the hands were bedding it down. Pretty Shadow, who had the first watch, left the herd as soon as it was thrown on to the bedground and made his way to the wagon, circling around the cattle. Most of the cattle were already down, but here and there lone cows stood chewing their cuds. The hands circled the herd slowly, keeping it properly spaced, singing to the cows as they bedded down. As Pretty Shadow passed behind one of the cows still standing, the cow suddenly snorted and whirled around to face him.

Old Blue, actually a steer, was theoretically a bull, having the short horns and short temper characteristic of that gender. Although Old Blue's operation had changed his character, it had done little for his personality. Naturally surly, he kept to himself when the herd was grazing. On the trail, he remained on the point, and at night when the herd was bedded down, he selected a spot off to himself, within the circumference of the bedground, yet apart from the other cows. Pretty Shadow, his thoughts on the river, had intruded into Old Blue's mood. Snorting, Old Blue whirled about. Dropping his head, he pawed the ground.

Pretty Shadow recognized his mistake. He stopped and stood absolutely still so as not to challenge the big steer, and when Old Blue lowered his head and began pawing the ground, Pretty Shadow attempted to withdraw. But Old Blue was not content to let him walk away, and followed, trotting forward a few steps with his head held high, then stopping to paw the ground again.

The other hands watched the herd closely, fearing any sudden movement on the part of either Pretty Shadow or the steer might stampede the herd. June, who was closest to Pretty Shadow, nervously fingered his six-shooter, afraid to shoot for fear of frightening the bedded herd.

Pretty Shadow backed away cautiously, slowly. Turning to look over his shoulder, he tripped and fell down. Old Blue, startled by this sudden movement, raised his head and trotted forward to investigate. Pretty Shadow, seeing the steer's approach, jumped to his feet and ran for the wagon. Dropping his head, the steer charged.

Seeing Pretty Shadow could not outrun Old Blue, the Preacher grabbed his slicker and ran out to wave the steer to a stop as Pretty Shadow and the Kid jumped into the wagon, knocking down the wagon sheet. "Get back," the Preacher said, waving the slicker. "Don't you get around my fire."

Old Blue stopped. Snorting, he pawed the ground and waved his horns. The Preacher stood his ground, talking quietly and gravely to the steer. Old Blue raised his head and looked about him. The Preacher backed slowly away. Old Blue, losing interest, turned and trotted back to the herd.

The Preacher returned to the wagon and hung the slicker on a wagon stanchion. "Well, get out and eat," he said to Pretty Shadow, who had thrown back the fallen wagon sheet to watch Old Blue.

"Whew," Pretty Shadow said, climbing down from the wagon. "I sure as hell thought I was a goner. That damn old steer has been chasing me all day. I'm going to ask Lampassas to put me back in the drag."

"Cows is naturally curious," the Preacher said. "The thing you got to do is either stand your ground or lay down where they can't see you. Because if you run, they're just naturally going to light out after you."

"You think June is right about a cow not charging a man that looks him in the eye?" Pretty Shadow asked, groaning as he pulled his boots from his swollen and blistered feet. The raw flesh had bled, and his worn, holey socks were caked and stiff. Carefully, he pulled the socks from his feet, beat them across his knees, and hung them on the wagon wheel to air. "He didn't charge you, did he? You just stood there and looked him in the eye, and Old Blue turned and walked off."

"I got some rawhide in the wagon," said the Preacher, looking at Pretty Shadow's worn, run-over boots. "I'll see if I can patch them tomorrow."

"I don't reckon you'll have time tomorrow, since we're going to cross the herd. That's what Lampassas says."

"He's said that ever day for the past three days," the Kid said.

"And that's why I think it'll be tomorrow," Pretty Shadow said. "He's put himself in the position where he can't say it no more without doing it. Hey, I thought you was supposed to have my chuck ready when I got here."

"I didn't know you was coming in so fast," the Preacher said. Taking a plate, he put in four biscuits, covered them with beans so that Pretty Shadow wouldn't notice the color, and placed the steak over the top. "You better eat quick. The men will be ready to come in."

Pretty Shadow washed his face and hands, combed his hair, and sat down with his plate. "Kid, would you get me a cup of coffee? I'd like to save what's left of my feet for night herding. And you might bring me a couple more of them muddodgers, too. The Preacher didn't give me anything to push with."

"The only water we got is muddy," the Preacher said. "If you don't like them biscuits, don't eat them."

"I like them muddy," Pretty Shadow said. "Puts grit in your

craw. This is the way I like my steak, too. Cut right off the horn."

"I've got more important things on my mind than to quarrel with you about the food," the Preacher said.

"Preacher, why is it, no matter what we're talking about, you always bring the subject back to women?"

"I'm talking about that river there," the Preacher said. "I ain't the hand to question the Lord's judgment, but wouldn't it a done just as well somewheres else?"

"Do you think we can make it without horses?" the Kid asked.

"Can't never tell till we try," Pretty Shadow said.

"A man's got a lot of rivers to cross, boy," the Preacher said. "There's the rivers of childhood—"

"But what's it like?" the Kid asked impatiently.

"Well, it's kinda like going down for baptism," the Preacher said. "Behind you you're leaving—"

"It's kinda like the first gal you ever have," Pretty Shadow said, deliberately rolling himself a cigarette. "At first you can't think of nothing else, and then when the time comes, you can't imagine yourself doing it. Then before you know you're doing it, it's done, and you're on the other side trying to remember what it was like. You feel proud that it's done, but you don't hardly even remember doing it."

"That's the way it is the first time?" the Kid asked with obvious disappointment. "I mean, something important like that and you don't even remember?"

"For some men, that's the way it is ever time," Pretty Shadow said, running the rolled cigarette across his tongue to stick it together and lighting it from the fire.

"You ought to be ashamed talking to the boy like that," the Preacher said.

"I was just telling him about rivers."

"Well, you ought to know. You're the only feller I ever knowed that floated downstream all his life without making a ripple."

"Now, that ain't so," Pretty Shadow said. "Why, I reckon I've wrestled with temptation as much as any man."

"Then you must be as sorry a wrestler as you are a man," the Preacher said, setting the other steaks at the edge of the fire to keep warm.

"Preacher, you've done gone too far and become offensive," Pretty Shadow said. "As a matter of fact, it was resisting temptation that caused my downfall."

The Preacher snorted and made, vaguely toward heaven, a gesture indicating his ready-formed opinion of the story. But Pretty Shadow did not begin. For a moment the Preacher waited, and then, disgusted with himself, he turned to look at Pretty Shadow, who was nonchalantly flicking the ashes from his cigarette toward the fire.

"I reckon when a feller is all swole up to tell a lie, he ought to tell it, or he'll bust," the Preacher said.

"Which lie is that?"

"That lie about—that lie about how resisting temptation caused your downfall," the Preacher said.

Pretty Shadow unhurriedly finished his cigarette, tossed it into the fire, and crossing his bare feet and lacing his fingers behind his head, he leaned back and began. " 'Twas just the other day I was minded of the first horse I ever owned. I was about the Kid's age, a little younger. Old Snuff, I called him. And it was a devil of a cold morning, when a man's joints was stiff from sleeping on the ground. That horse would wake up ever morning thinking he was a mustang. While the other men were riding out to work, I'd still be running through the prickly pear with Snuff at the other end of the rope, trying to slow him down enough to slap a saddle on his back. And for the first five minutes after I saddled him, he was a bronc. After that he was as fine a cow pony as a man could wish.

"But Old Snuff sorely tried my soul, shaking me around and rattling hell out of me when I was stiff and half asleep. And now and then Old Snuff would land me in a bed of cactus or a pile of rocks. It got so I woke up ever morning cussing, and by the time

I had taken the edge off Old Snuff, my tongue was warmed up on evil words till they would come to mind without being called. I reckon I became the worst cusser in the outfit," Pretty Shadow said, chuckling at the recollection.

"I got to the point where I couldn't go to sleep at night thinking what Snuff was going to do to me the next morning, so I started taking a drink at night just to help me go to sleep. Just a little one. But before you know it, it was taking bigger and bigger drinks to put me to sleep, and there I'd be having to ride that devil of a horse with a hangover.

"Some mornings my head would hurt so bad I couldn't face that horse, and I started paying some of the boys to top Old Snuff for me. Just take the edge off him. But what they charged for five minutes of rough riding was a crime, and the only way I could raise the money was by card playing. And there I was, sixteen or seventeen years old, and the worst cussing, drinking, gambling son of a bitch in the outfit. Well, one happy day I met one of the Lord's helpers, and he told me if I was ever going to break them evil habits, I was going to have to put temptation behind me."

"He told you right, too," the Preacher said, edified by the story. But Pretty Shadow had not finished.

"So I traded Old Snuff for a horse called Pic. Pic was the prettiest horse I ever seen. He was a paint with a white tail and mane that was as fine as a girl's hair. Well, there are two kinds of horses, work horses and show horses, and Pic was a show horse. He wouldn't work and he wouldn't run. That horse couldn't catch nothing but girls. I could ride into town and I would just be surrounded by pretty girls, oohing and aahing, and wanting to pat him, and run their fingers through his mane, and rub his ears, and stroke his nose. And pretty soon they'd start talking to me, and winking their eyes, and wagging their tails, and the first thing you know, I'd be walking off down to the river with two or three of them. I'll tell you the truth, Kid, if it hadn't been for resisting temptation and trading off Old Snuff, I never would a noticed girls, and I never would a got the clap and been in the shape I'm in today. And I made a resolution right there that I'd never resist temptation again."

Feeling a sudden stomach cramp, the Kid stood up and walked around to the other side of the wagon. The Preacher studied Pretty Shadow's face in silence and then calmly set about pointing out the flaws inherent in Pretty Shadow's reasoning. "But that wasn't—you didn't—that was—"

"Well, I reckon I'd better get back to the herd," Pretty Shadow said, pulling on his socks and boots. Taking a final drink from the coffee cup, he spat it on the ground and started down the face of the bluff.

"It don't do no good to swap horses if you're going to make a jackass out of yourself," the Preacher said. Pretty Shadow walked on toward the herd, seeming not to hear.

The Preacher drew in a heady lungful of air, ready to yell in a voice that Pretty Shadow would have to hear, but common sense got the better of him, and remembering the bedded herd, he kicked at the fire, sending up a cloud of sparks and ashes.

Deciding it would be best not to be there should the Preacher turn around and look, the Kid walked away from the wagon, along the top of the bluff, to a spot where it overhung the river. He looked down at the dark water, scarcely able to locate the slightly darker edge of the bank. Something yellow and bloated, the color of old ivory, came floating down the river. At first the Kid thought it was a large dead fish, but when he saw it turn slowly around in an eddy, he realized there wasn't any fish that big in this river and that it was either a cow or a man. He watched it as it bobbed and rocked down the river until it too faded into the single blackness of distance.

He had not wanted to come on this drive. He did not want to cross the river. On this side was everything he had ever known: home, boyhood, Tertia. Ahead of him was Trails End, the railroad, freedom. The Kid knew that once on the other side, he would not be this way again.

He had listened to his father talk and dream, believing it was just talk and dreams. But when his father had sold the store

to buy cattle that no one had seen for five or six years, that had
to be found, and then chased through the brush like jackrabbits
and rounded up before he could even see what he had bought,
then the Kid knew he was mad. And not only mad but addicted
to madness, surrounding himself with other madmen who tore
recklessly through the brush for days, chasing cows that no one
else ever saw, and then mysteriously disappeared at night like the
cattle, without even being paid for their trouble. He had talked
to his father, reasoned with him, quarreled with him, and at
last, desperate as the rest, had decided to go with his father on
this mad adventure, help his father get the herd to Trails End,
and then, his father's dream fulfilled, he would be free to leave
him, to get a job on the railroad, to find his own life. But they
would never get to Trails End. They would never get across the
river. They would all die here. For nothing. For talk and dreams.

The Kid did not want to die. He was too young to die before he had ever lived. Why, he had never really done anything
yet. The only girl he'd ever known was Tertia, and he'd never
done anything but kiss her on the cheek one time. Well, it was
sort of on the mouth. But that was all, all he'd ever done, and
now he was supposed to cross the river. And he'd never even lived
yet. He'd never had a woman, or a drink, or a ride on the train.
Maybe when he got to Trails End—but he'd never get to Trails
End.

Above the sound of the river he heard another sound. High
and lonely. Sounding lost and sad. At first he thought it was the
wail of a coyote or the song of the night herders, distorted by
distance and the noise of the river. But when he heard it again,
he knew it was not the call of an animal and it was not the high-
pitched cry of a water fowl. It was at the same time human and
unearthly. Involuntarily, he shivered.

"River got you worried, Kid?" the Preacher asked, walking
up behind him. "Maybe we'll cross tomorrow and the hardest
part will be over."

"Do you think anybody ever crossed a herd before without
horses?"

"I reckon not. I reckon we're going to be the original," said the Preacher. "Across the river there might be horses for us. I been praying."

"We're not going to get any more horses, and we're not going to get to Trails End. We ain't even going to get across the river. Don't you think we ought to quit? Don't you think it's smarter to quit when you make a mistake than to go on making more mistakes?"

"I reckon it takes a smart man to know when to quit," the Preacher said. "Back in the war, we marched off with a lot of fine reasons for killing and getting killed. Well, after a while we all seen there wasn't no reason to fight any more, that it wasn't going to change anything, that we weren't even fighting for what we went to war for. Well, most of us quit. Them that quit too early was cowards, and them that quit too late was criminals, and some of them ain't quit yet. Fools, I guess."

"Then how do we know we ain't fools too?"

"Maybe we don't," the Preacher said. "But them that was cowards knew it."

Disgusted with the whole discussion, the Kid stood staring across the river, hoping the Preacher would go back to the wagon and leave him alone. Then he heard it again, lonely and sad, yet lovelier than any song he had ever heard. "Did you hear that?" he asked.

"Hear what?"

"I thought I heard singing. Coming from the river."

"Singing?"

"It was kinda high and lonely. But pretty. Not very loud, though."

"I didn't hear anything. Probably just the wind."

"Preacher, have you ever heard that a river sometimes sings to a person that's going to drown?"

"Yeah, I've heard that. I thought it was the ocean."

"It was kinda like a woman's voice. Calling to you—not calling you to come, exactly, but making you want to come just the same. Making you want to quit everthing else and just come."

"I heard that once," the Preacher said.

"Was it a river?"

"No. No, it was right after the war. I was going home."

"What do you think it is?" the Kid asked.

"I think it's just the first time. When you're young and you try something new, life seems to be singing to you. When you're my age, you don't hear the songs much any more."

"From here it don't look like much."

"No, it don't look like much, and most of the time it ain't one tenth of what it is now."

"How deep do you figure it?"

"Oh, it's not deep. If we're on the ford and don't hit no holes, the cows might not have to swim atall. But the current's running pretty strong. It's going to be hard to keep your feet."

"I can't swim, Preacher."

"I can't neither."

"What do you aim to do?"

"I aim to keep my feet down and my head up, and pray I don't step in no hole."

"I don't want to cross the river, Preacher."

"Boy, behind you is home and all the comforts you ever knew. Ahead of you is life and adventure, and you won't never get the both of them inside the same pasture again."

Together they stood before the river, the Kid looking into the dark and unknown future beyond, the Preacher, his eyes dimmed by time, looking over the Kid's shoulder and seeing nothing but rivers to cross and golden cities to discover. Behind them they heard the men coming to the campfire, their voices distant, tired, yet cheerful that the day was done. "Where the hell's the Preacher?" they heard Gattis say. "I'm so hungry I could eat that damn blue steer."

"You may be doing it, too," said June. "If he takes a look at me, I'm going to shoot him right between the horns."

"I thought you said he wouldn't charge if you stood your ground and looked him right in the eye," Gattis said.

"That's what I said, and I'll stick by it," June said. "But I'll sure as hell shoot him if he gets familiar."

"Squat, sit, or hunker, boys, the chuck's ready," the Preacher called. "Come on, Kid, let's go eat." By the time they reached the wagon, the others had washed, spread their bedrolls, and begun eating.

"We're crossing tomorrow, irregardless," Lampassas said, looking at the Preacher. The Preacher nodded.

"I'd like to meet up with that sheriff that said the river was so low you could walk across it," June said.

"If I wasn't so tired, I'd take Old Blue back there and run him through town for another bottle of whisky," Gattis said.

"Well, I'll be pleased to move on to some more scenery," June said. "I been here long enough to take up farming."

"How's your foot, Gattis?" the Preacher asked.

"Better. I believe by tomorrow I'll be able to get my boot off."

"How do you keep up?" the Kid asked.

"Well, we ain't been going very fast, and if I walk mostly on my heel—" Gattis stopped and held up one hand, signaling for quiet. "Did you hear that?"

"Hear what?"

"Sounded like singing."

"Singing?" Lampassas asked in disgust.

"Now, that's what I call a happy man," June said. "Give him a blanket under the stars, a little beefsteak, and a plate of beans, and he hears singing."

"Well, I did."

"That ain't nothing but the wind along the river," Lampassas said. "It'll lay in a little while."

"What I heard was singing," Gattis said.

"Kinda like a girl singing?" the Kid asked.

"Yeah."

"Forget the music and keep your ears on the herd. If they start moving around, we'll have to get down there and give Pretty Shadow a hand."

"I believe we finally got those cows trail broke," June said. "They only stompeded once this week. The other two times they just scattered."

The Kid finished his supper, dropped his plate in the wreck pan, and walked up to the front of the wagon where the tongue pointed north across the river.

"The Kid can't get his mind off the river," the Preacher said. "This waiting around has got him jumpy."

"Ain't we all," said Gattis, pulling out a twist of tobacco and biting off a chew. "I reckon I'm the onliest one can swim."

"Yeah, with that sore foot, you'll do better in the water than you do on the ground," June said.

"I been thinking about that," Lampassas said. "There ain't no way of knowing how deep the water is. I thought you could take the point because you can swim. We'll get the herd headed into the water pretty good, and you can go out with them to keep them from turning back. The water's too swift for them to turn upstream. Go out as far as you can. If they hit the main channel and have to swim, then find a place to stand, and keep them headed across. You can grab hold of a horn if you can't keep your feet under you. The rest of us will keep them moving into the water, and we'll follow you out as far as there's good footing. If there's swimming, we'll cross with the drags. We can grab hold of a horn or a tail to steady us.

"That leaves the wagon on this side. Preacher, you drop off after the drags has taken to the water. Pretty Shadow is going to take the rope over. As soon as we get it around something pretty strong, we'll wave a shirt and you can ride the wagon across. I aim to drive the herd back from the river until they get good and thirsty. Then we'll run them into the water until they hit the opposite bank or hit bottom. Sink or swim."

"What do we do if there's a mill?"

"I don't know what we'll do if there's a mill," Lampassas said. "I don't know what we'll do if we hit a drop-off. I don't even know how we're going to get them cows in the water. I've been holding this herd for three days hoping the river would go down, hoping something would happen to get us across it, trying to think of some way where we don't have to cross it. If I wait any longer, I won't have the nerve to try. That's why we're crossing first thing in the morning."

"Are you sure this is the ford?" Gattis asked.

"Hell yes, I'm sure," Lampassas said. "Didn't you see them graves back there?"

"But that was years ago. Mightn't the river changed since then?"

"I've thought about that," Lampassas said. "Chances are it has changed, but what can we do about that? This used to be the ford; we don't know of no other one; we can't find one without a horse, and we ain't got a horse. I figure it's better to trust an old crossing than none."

Talk of the coming day and its dangers had a sobering effect upon the men, and they lay back silently on their bedrolls, heads pillowed on the familiar saddle leather, smoking or chewing, watching the fire or the night with tired but sleepless eyes.

"Back home I used to go to sleep ever night listening to the river," Gattis said, raising up on one elbow to spit. "There's just something about the sound of running water that's restful. But I never heard a river as loud as this one. It don't lull you to sleep."

"Maybe that's because you ain't never heard one sing before," June said.

"I never said it was the river singing. I said it sounded like—"

"Pa, Pa." The Kid's voice rose above the sound of the river, faint and quavering.

"Jamie fell in the river," Lampassas said, jumping up, cramming his hat on his head and stomping into his boots. "Hold on, Jamie. Don't yell or you'll stompede the herd," he muttered, as he struggled into his boots and ran to the edge of the bluff over the river with the rest of the men behind him.

"Where are you, Jamie? Can you hear me?" he called hoarsely, trying to prevent his voice from carrying to the herd.

"I'm down here, Pa."

"Hold on. I'll be right down to get you out."

"I'm all right, Pa."

"Then what the hell are you yelling for?" Lampassas asked, relieved that the boy was safe and angry that he had been needlessly frightened.

"There's a girl down here."

"Is she drowned?"

"No. She's got a baby with her."

"Well," Lampassas said, leaning over the bluff, trying to make something out of the darkness below. "Don't bother her none."

"She's kinda wet."

"What's she doing down there?"

"She was singing," the Kid replied.

"What the hell do you make of that?" Lampassas asked, turning to the men, who had crowded around him and were looking over his shoulder, although he didn't know where the Kid and the girl were any more than they did.

"Well, tell him to bring her up to the fire and we'll see what this is all about," the Preacher suggested.

"Bring her up to the fire," Lampassas called.

"We're coming," the Kid said.

"Better bring the baby, too."

The men huddled on the edge of the bluff, trying to make out the figures, and following by ear the progress of the Kid and the girl through the underbrush until June, crowding in to see, almost pushed Gattis and the Preacher over the edge. Angrily, they pushed him away.

"Maybe it's Pretty Shadow's girl come to meet him," June said.

"With a baby?" the Preacher asked in disgust. "He hasn't seen her in fifteen years."

As they watched, the girl reached the top of the bluff and walked toward the wagon. The Kid followed behind her, gallantly trying to guide her to the wagon without touching her.

The men followed warily behind Lampassas, stopping back from the wagon where they could see without being seen. When the girl, aided by the Kid's gestures, stood between the fire and the lantern, they saw that she was young, wet, and set on traveling. Her limp hat, which had once been stiff and flat, folded about her head, and the once colorful but now damp and bedraggled flowers hung down over her forehead along with a lot of her hair. She was wearing a dark jacket and skirt, full sleeved, tight waisted, and full skirted, with a lacy, high-collared, grimy blouse. The skirt was muddy from the knees down, and when she turned, they saw there was a large swatch of mud across the seat. Under one arm she carried a small baby, dressed in a blue cap and gown and partially wrapped in a wet flannel blanket, and at least as grimy as she was. In the other hand she held a carpetbag. In climbing, she had caught the hem of her dress on a corner of the carpetbag, and the upturned skirt revealed muddy underskirts, muddy, high-cut shoes, and equally muddy, baggy white cotton stockings.

"What do you think?" Lampassas asked.

"There are three things a cow hand feels obliged to help against his better judgment," the Preacher said. "A horse in a fence, a cow in a bog, and a woman in trouble. Let's go see what we can do."

The girl watched the men as they sauntered in out of the protection of the darkness. She did not move but tightened her grip on the carpetbag and the sleeping child.

Lampassas took off his hat and addressed her. "Evening, ma'am, I hope my boy didn't bother you none. I raised him myself, and he don't know how to act—"

The girl watched Lampassas angrily, defiantly, and when he looked up and met her eyes, he forgot what he was going to say, his voice trailing off. Nervously, he looked about soliciting help from the other men.

Gattis, who had been taught how to treat a lady by his mother, swept off his hat, stepped forward, and made a little bow. "I'll take your bag, ma'am."

The girl only glared at him and jerked the bag behind her.

Gattis looked at the other men uncertainly, but Lampassas gave him an encouraging nod. "Ma'am, was that you singing?"

"What if it was?"

"Nothing. I just—I just thought it was pretty," he said, stepping back into the comforting company of the other men.

"Why, that's a little baby," June said, staring at the small, dirty bundle in her arm.

"What did you expect, a calf?" she asked, curling her short upper lip and flashing her black eyes at him.

"He was crying. That's why she was singing. To stop him from crying," the Kid said, looking unaccountably guilty.

"Well, sit down, everbody," Lampassas said, so gruffly that the men all jumped and then quickly sat down. The girl only looked at him. "Sit down, sit down, gal," he said, more kindly. "You must be tired."

Gattis and the Kid jumped up to offer her their bedrolls to sit on. The girl set down the muddy carpetbag and sat down on it cross-legged, laying the baby in her lap and primly smoothing the dress over her knees.

"Now, let's see," Lampassas began. "What's your name?"

"Covina."

"What's the last of it?"

"There ain't no last."

"He means what's your husband's name," the Preacher explained.

"I ain't got a husband."

"Bless your heart, just a child and a widder already," the Preacher said. "Did you lose him in the river?"

"I ain't got a husband," the girl said defiantly, looking the Preacher in the eye.

Several of the hands had coughing fits, and Lampassas's attention was caught by a falling star, which he could miraculously see through the dark and overcast sky. The Preacher studied the girl, who wiped the damp hair and flowers back from her forehead with the palm of her hand and sat holding the baby in her lap, looking defiantly at nothing in particular.

"Have you had supper?" the Preacher asked, when the men had finally swallowed down their throat irritations and the falling star had passed clear on the other side of the universe. The girl did not answer. "Kid, get the lady something to eat. And a cup of coffee. She looks a mite lank to me."

The group about the campfire exploded into activity as everyone but Lampassas and the Preacher jumped about with a great show of efficient energy. The steak had all been eaten, but there were some biscuits left. The Kid put them in the plate. Gattis dumped a ladle of beans over them, and while he and the Kid wrestled over the plate, June handed the girl a cup of coffee, which she gulped, although it was fresh from the fire. The Kid, managing to get the plate from Gattis, handed it to the girl, who seemed not to notice the bean juice that ran over the rim of the plate and dripped on her dress. Taking the knife June handed her, she began to eat, holding the plate clear of the sleeping baby.

"Gattis, see if we don't have a fork," the Preacher said, deploring the manners of his fellows. He turned to the girl, who was still watching them while she ate. "If you like, I'll hold the baby while you're eating."

The girl stopped with the knife halfway to her mouth and watched them through the hair that had again fallen over her forehead. Gently, the Preacher picked up the baby, careful not to touch the girl's lap, while she watched him, holding the knife poised like a weapon. When the Preacher got the sleeping baby balanced on his lap without touching her, the girl poked the knifeful of food into her mouth, accepted the fork from Gattis, and continued eating.

The men gathered around the Preacher to smile and make faces at the baby, who slept with most of his left hand inside his mouth.

"Leave him alone," the girl said. "Can't you see he's asleep? It took me long enough to get him quiet, and I don't want to have to do it again."

The men tiptoed back to their places, getting themselves

fresh coffee or rolling cigarettes, observing a respectful silence while the girl ate. When she had finished, she set down her plate, drank the rest of her coffee, and leaned back, stretching. "God, that was awful."

The men nonchalantly blew their noses, scratched their heads, examined their worn boots, and hummed to themselves, pretending not to notice.

"Now that we got you fed, I reckon we'd better decide what to do with you," the Preacher said.

"It ain't that we're not concerned," Lampassas said. "It's just that we're mighty busy men, and you sure caught us in a bind. We're planning on crossing that damn—excuse me—river tomorrow with a herd of cows, and we don't have no horses, and we don't know how in the hell—pardon me—we're going to do it. But I reckon we're bound to help you all we can. How long you reckon you been lost?"

"I ain't lost," Covina said. "I'm on my way to Trails End."

"How'd you get here?" the Preacher asked.

"I rode with a feller part of the way, and the rest of the way I walked."

"How do you aim to get to Trails End?"

"The same way."

"Well, it's purely going to short-hand us, but I don't reckon there's anything to do but let the Preacher take you back home in the wagon," Lampassas said.

"I ain't going back home," the girl said. "I don't reckon you'd loan me a horse?"

"I told you we don't have no horses," Lampassas said. "What about your folks? Where are they?"

"I ain't got no folks," the girl said. "My pa run me off and said he didn't never want to see my face again. My ma didn't say nothing different. I ain't going back there."

"What are you going to do?" the Kid asked.

"I'm going to Trails End and go to work so's I can take care of the baby."

"But how is a girl going to support a baby by her—" The Kid's voice failed him. His eyes and mouth popped open.

"I reckon I know what I have to do," she said.

The Kid turned from the girl to look at the other men for confirmation, but they all happened to be carefully looking the other way. The only sounds that could be heard above the rustle of the fire and the rush of the river were June humming to himself and faint snatches of Pretty Shadow's song about the girl back home, who was plain as a door, fragrant as a stable, she promised her love to everyone, and was as true as she was able.

June's humming was becoming noticeable, and Pretty Shadow's song approached a poetic description of how the girl back home was disappointing in both fidelity and ability. The men fidgeted at the dearth of conversation.

"We're going to Trails End. Why can't we take her with us?" the Kid asked, and this time he had no need to search for their eyes; they were all turned on him. But it was his father's eyes that the Kid's eyes met.

"It ain't done," Lampassas said, quietly but finally.

"A lady can't travel about the country in the company of men, or would one want to," the Preacher explained to the Kid.

"I don't mind," Covina said.

"Nor could a girl endure the trials and rigors of the long drive, walking for days and weeks—"

"I can stand it."

"Nor would a female wish to spend months getting to her appointed destination," the Preacher said.

"I'm in no hurry," Covina said.

"It ain't done," Lampassas shouted, banging his fist on the ground and ending the conversation by waking the baby, who gasped once and let out a blood-curdling squall.

"Oh, hell, now you've done it," Covina said, lifting the screaming child out of the Preacher's arms. "You've waked the baby, and now I'll never get him back to sleep."

"I'm sorry," Lampassas mumbled.

"Maybe he's just wet," the Preacher said, pulling his damp trousers away from his leg.

"He's not wet, he's hungry," the girl said, angrily shaking the baby about to pacify it. The baby responded by turning red in the face, waving his clenched fists, and screaming at the top of his lungs. This brought results. The excited hands took one backward look at the nervous, high-strung herd and crowded around the baby, making faces, trying to distract the child.

The girl stopped shaking the child and laid him in her lap, resigned to his crying. "That's why I was singing to him down at the river," she said, shouting over the baby's cries. "To get him to sleep without his supper."

"Then why don't you feed him?" June asked. "Ain't what we got good enough for him?"

"He's a baby," the girl screamed. "What he wants is milk."

"Oh," the Preacher said with sudden insight. "Well, what's the matter with you boys? Get away from here. Get on the other side of the wagon."

The hands took one look at the thin, flat-chested girl and scattered into the darkness like sheep.

"We'll be right over here if you need anything," the Preacher said, following Lampassas behind the wagon.

Instead of replying, the girl began crying too. The Preacher listened for a moment as the girl's sobs mingled with the wails of the child, and making sure that none of the other men were doing the same, he peeked around the wagon. The girl, still holding the baby in her lap, was sitting cross-legged on the carpetbag, crying. The Preacher took another look to be sure. The girl was decent.

The Preacher stepped around the wagon and walked back to where the girl sat by the fire. "We're rough, ma'am," he said, "but we don't aim to be, and if we said anything to offend you—"

"I can't nurse him," Covina said, freeing a hand from beneath the wet child to wipe at her nose.

"What have you been feeding him?" the Preacher asked.

"I stopped at a farmhouse yesterday and they gave me some

milk, but I used the last of it this morning, and it gave him the colic. He hasn't had anything to eat since."

The Preacher stepped back to the wagon. "Kid, do we have any more of that milk?"

"We used the last can yesterday," the Kid said, sneaking a look past the Preacher. The men peered from behind the wagon, and seeing all was clear, began drifting back to the fire.

"What's the matter?"

"Well," the Preacher said. "This girl here—the little mother— Well, she don't— See, she's just a young girl, and she—"

"I don't have no milk," the girl said, looking at them so spitefully that they all quickly sat down.

"It's two or three days' walk back to Mustang Springs, at best," the Preacher said to the girl. "How far is it to the farm-house?"

"It's a day away. Don't you have any cows?" she asked.

"That's what we got," Lampassas said. "A herd of cows."

"I mean cows. Milk cows. Aren't any of your cows fresh?" the girl asked, again trying the shaking tactics on the wailing child, and stirring him up to a higher pitch.

Lampassas hung his head. "I'm right sorry, ma'am, but you see, we can't slow down the herd for calves to keep up, so when a cow throws a calf, June here goes out and shoots it, and after a while the cow goes dry."

The girl, aligning herself on the side of motherhood, glared hatefully at baby-killer June, who stood before the fire, his hat in his hand. "You kill little baby calves?" she asked, hugging the screaming child to her breast. June looked away.

"Well, nobody likes it," Lampassas said. "But it's got to be done. And June here volunteered to do it."

"I didn't exactly volunteer," June said. "See, I'm the one that carries the six-shooter, so—"

"You volunteered to take baby calves away from their mothers and shoot them? Just so you could carry a six-shooter?"

"No, ma'am. You see— Lampassas, I been meaning to tell

you," June said. "You know, after losing the horses, we been traveling kinda slow, and well, them little fellers looked so helpless, and they was keeping up—"

"You mean you didn't shoot them?"

"Well, they was keeping up and all. And they never stompeded."

"You mean them newborn calves was keeping up with the herd?"

"Well, sure, except right at first when I had to carry them some."

"I don't know what kept them old cows from hooking you, messing around with their calves thataway."

"Well, they didn't like it, but I just stood my ground and looked them in the eye," June said.

"I knew I should a checked, since I can't depend on you for nothing," Lampassas said. "That's probably what stompedes the herd. Them cows and calves stumbling onto the bedground and stepping on some steer that's already asleep."

"No it ain't, Lampassas, they're real quiet."

"Well, how many fresh cows do we have?"

"Three."

"We got three fresh cows if you can use them," Lampassas said to Covina. The girl said nothing, only looked at him. The baby screamed. "We ain't got nobody to milk them," he said. The girl looked at him, scarcely holding the struggling baby, who jerked his clenched fists and kicked his feet in anger and frustration as he cried.

"Boys, I purely hate to ask it of you," Lampassas said, looking at the men around him. "I've asked you to take the herd through places where the trail was closed, to trail cows afoot, to drive them across a flooded river, and now I'm going to ask you—" He paused, looked at the men and then looked quickly away. "I'm having to ask you— Hell, I've done a lot of low things in my life. I've run a store. I've sold corsets. I've patted butter. But by God I've never milked no cow, and I ain't asking nobody else to do it." And looking away, Lampassas attempted to turn a deaf ear to the cries of the hungry child.

The child, however, was not to be ignored. Turning red in the face from anger and lack of breath, the child launched scream after scream at the mother, who seemed to be used to it, and the men, who did not. Covina no longer made any effort to stop the child's cries. The men fidgeted and swore under their breath.

"Well, you can see this girl is in no condition to do it herself," the Preacher said. "So I reckon we'll have to do it. It's hard to ask it of somebody who ain't never turned a hand to it before, but maybe there's one of you fellers that's already—already done it."

"I've cleaned stables, I've dug for water, I've picked cotton," June said, bent on humiliating himself. "But I ain't never pulled a cow's teat, and I ain't never going to."

Gattis ducked his head, and even in the flickering, uncertain light of the fire they could see the color rising to his face. But Gattis could not destroy himself in the eyes of these men. "I— I saw Ma milk a cow once," he said. "But hell, that's the reason I left home."

In sympathetic embarrassment, they all looked away. All except Covina, who had none of their finer feelings. "Hell, is that all you're going to do? Sit and talk about it? Show me the damn cow and I'll milk her myself," she shouted, as tears welled up in her eyes.

"Do you think you could do it?" the Preacher asked Gattis, while Lampassas looked away in shame.

"I ain't refused Lampassas yet," Gattis said. "But I ain't going to volunteer."

The Preacher looked at Lampassas, but Lampassas refused to meet his eyes. "If that baby keeps on crying, he's going to stompede the herd. It wouldn't just be milking a cow," he explained to Lampassas. "It'd be averting a stompede."

"I reckon I could give it a try to avert a stompede," Gattis said.

Lampassas looked up, full of resolution and command. "Gattis, you go down there and see if there's anything you can do about averting a stompede."

Gattis fitted his hat on for business, picked up a lariat, and started in the direction of the herd.

"You'll need somebody to help you throw her," Lampassas said. "Kid, you get down there and give him a hand. June, you'll have to go along and help them find the trouble. You're the only one that knows what they look like."

"And hurry. This little feller ain't had any chuck since this morning," the Preacher said, anxious to have peace again.

Without a word to grace his departure, June got up, gave a menacing hitch to his gunbelt, and limped after the others.

"Be careful you don't frighten the herd," Lampassas said. "Cut her out and drive her away from the bedground first."

While Lampassas and the Preacher tried to make themselves comfortable and to shut out the noise of the baby, Covina mechanically shook and rattled the red-faced child, who waved his fists and screamed to the sky of injustice.

"When Jamie was little, his mother used to give him sugar and water for something," Lampassas said. "I forget what it was."

"Do you reckon he'd take a little sugar and water?" the Preacher asked in desperation.

"We could try," the girl said, wiping her eyes with the hem of her dress and wiping the hair and flowers back from her forehead. "Maybe it would stop him for a while."

"Let's do that," Lampassas said.

The Preacher scooped a cupful of water off the top of the barrel, strained it through the dirty cup towel, and mixed in some sugar. "I'll put just a drop of coffee in it to kill the taste of the mud," he said.

The girl took the cup without a word and offered it to the child by dipping her finger in it, and after tasting it herself, poking the dripping finger into the child's open and loud mouth. The liquid strangled the baby, and enraged, he screamed louder than ever. Covina alternately sang to the baby and shook him until he calmed down enough to suck the sweetened finger.

"That's pretty good, ain't it, little feller?" the Preacher said, wiping a drop of the water out of the baby's eyes with a corner of the cup towel. "What's his name?"

"We already been through that once," Covina said.

"I mean, what do you call him?"

"I been calling him Little John. His pa's name was John."

"That don't seem right," said the Preacher. "It don't seem right to name him after somebody that don't want him."

"Well, there wasn't nobody that wanted him. I wanted to name him after my pa, but he said he didn't want no bastard named after him. I've been thinking about calling him Trouble," she said, looking at the Preacher for approval.

"No, that ain't right. He ought to have a real name."

"Since I been calling him John, I ought to keep it similar I guess. So I don't forget it. I could call him Jack, or Jake, or George, or—"

"Jake's my name. Well, the boys all call me Preacher, but my real name is Jake."

"Would you mind if he was named after you?"

"I wouldn't mind."

The girl looked down at the baby in her arms and held him close. "I wouldn't feel right about calling him Jake if you didn't like him. I mean, I wouldn't feel right about using your name if you didn't care about him, if you wouldn't look after him."

"Why, sure I'd look after him," the Preacher said. "Any man that wouldn't protect a baby—"

The girl reached out and touched his hand. "Then that's what I'm going to call him. Little Jake." Roughly, she hugged the baby to her breast. "Smile for us, Little Jake," she said, pinching the baby's cheeks together so that his mouth flew open and he puckered up to cry. "I know you'll come to good for being named after a preacher, and you won't never have to worry, because Uncle Jake is going to look after you," she said, smiling at the Preacher. "I like him better already."

"Now that we've decided on a name for the baby, maybe we can get around to deciding what to do with him," Lampassas said.

"He's not yours to do with," Covina said.

"Well, maybe we ain't got the right, but it does seem like we got the honor."

"I ain't going back home."

"You ain't going with us," Lampassas said.

"We can't just turn her loose out here with the baby," the Preacher said.

"We ain't turning her loose," Lampassas said. "We ain't turning her no way atall. We are going to leave her just like we found her. She ain't no worse off now than then."

"But we did find her," the Preacher said. "And we can't go off and leave her like we found her."

"Well, hell, if we're going to have to help everbody we run into, we'd a done better to of stayed home."

"We can't refuse her milk for the baby."

"She should a thought about that before she left home and fenced herself into this corner," Lampassas said, turning on the girl. "You ain't very smart thinking you can get to Trails End afoot."

"Maybe so, but you ain't so smart yourself. You're taking a closed trail, and I'm taking the only one that's open to me."

"What would you a done if we hadn't come along?" Lampassas asked. "I reckon I'm obliged to help fools and misfortunates, but I don't see how I'm called to help a she-wolf raise her young."

"I ain't asking no favors," Covina said. "I was just offering to help."

Lampassas started to say something, but everything that came to mind was unsuitable in the present company, so he expressed his feeling by loudly snorting.

"Until you get some horses, you're going to be short-handed," Covina said.

"That's true," the Preacher said. "We are short-handed."

"And getting across that river is going to take all the help you can get."

"We can use the help," the Preacher said.

"I reckon I owe it to the boys to get all the help I can," Lampassas said.

"Damn right," said Covina.

"But I'm only taking you on until we get across the river and get some horses. And I ain't giving you nothing but a fire to sleep by and whatever there is to eat."

"That's fair enough," Covina said, holding out her hand. Annoyed, Lampassas got to his knees and reached over the fire to shake hands on the bargain.

"You can do the cooking and drive the wagon, and I'll help chouse the cows," the Preacher said.

"I don't know nothing about cooking," Covina said, "but I can drive cows as well as anybody."

"We can't have a woman working alongside the men," Lampassas said.

"Why not?" the girl asked, dipping her finger in the water and poking it in the baby's mouth.

"Because I ain't going to have you— Because them men are— Because it ain't done, that's why," Lampassas said. "Wandering about the country begging milk for a sooner baby. Asking to do a man's work. You wouldn't be saddled with that little stray right now if you hadn't tried to run with the stallions."

"You needn't feel sorry for me," she said.

"Who the hell is sorry for you? I'm just sorry for that poor child that doesn't even have a name."

"The hell he doesn't," Covina said. "I just give him a name, and it's the second one he's had, which is more than you can say."

"I been married myself," Lampassas said. "And I know that sometimes things can just come over a body. Even a woman. And I can understand how you got this way. But I ain't going to have no goddam cussing woman at my campfire."

"Look who the hell is cussing," Covina said.

"I'm a man," explained Lampassas. "And a man that works with cows all day has a right to cuss now and then."

"I'm a woman, and I'm just as good as any goddam man, and I've got the same goddam rights."

"No goddam woman has the right to cuss," Lampassas said.

"I can do anything any goddam man can do," Covina said.

"You think you're pretty mean, don't you?" Lampassas said. "Well, I've seen wilder heifers than you milked in a gourd."

"Not by you," Covina said.

The baby whimpered and set his face to cry again. Covina dipped her finger in the sweetened water and gave it to him.

"You-all start that shouting again and you'll have him crying for sure," the Preacher said.

"Well, do I go or not?" Covina asked. "I can drive cows as good as any man you got, and any time I can't keep up, I'll drop out."

"If it was just me, I'd rather drown than have your help," Lampassas said. "But I don't rightly see how I can leave you out here alone."

"You and the baby can stay with the wagon," the Preacher said.

"I aim to earn my own way and for the baby. But I'm not cooking, and I ain't washing dishes, so why waste a hand? You don't have to worry about me. I can handle cows and I can handle men."

"I ain't never seen you handle cows," Lampassas said. "But if you don't have no more to recommend you than the way you handle men, then I reckon we'll find you underneath the next stompede."

"Well, ain't you got a nasty mind."

"Covina, there's something better for you than herding cows and running with men," the Preacher said.

"Hell, you sound just like a preacher now. Can't you get it through your head that I don't intend to be a nice girl that carries slops, and washes dishes, and looks like hell? I don't aim to clean up after a bunch of men. I aim to live just like you do. Any damn way I please."

"It's kinda hard living any way you please when you're wagging a baby around on your hip," Lampassas said.

"Just a minute," the Preacher said. "Who's going to take care of the baby while you're gallivanting around with the steers?"

"God, you can't trust any man," Covina said, appealing to heaven. "You said you'd take care of him."

"I never said that I'd take care of him," the Preacher said. "All I said was that I cared—"

"If you hadn't a told me that I wouldn't have called him by your name."

"How am I going to take care of him?" the Preacher asked. "At this moment I am taking care of four oxen, the wagon, the education of the Kid, chuck, and the spiritual welfare of six men, and I don't aim to start wet-nursing somebody else's child."

"Okay," Covina said. "I'm not asking you to. I know men don't feel any responsibility to children. I'll just carry Little Jake on my back."

"You can't carry him on your back and drive cows," Lampassas said.

"The hell I can't. I been carrying him one way or another for over a year now and I ain't dropped him but once, and that was when he was born."

"I reckon he can ride in the wagon," the Preacher said. "If he can drink out of a cup, I don't reckon he needs a mother anyhow."

"You can work near the wagon," Lampassas said. "That way whenever you get a chance, you can tend to Jake."

"Which Jake do I have to tend to?"

"There are three things I don't take off nobody," the Preacher said. "A drink, a loan, or a sass word."

"Oh, take it easy. I was just hurrahing you. I don't guess I can expect any freedom around here."

"If you wore your cinch a little tighter, you wouldn't be saddled with that little maverick right now," the Preacher said, nodding his head and looking at Lampassas. Lampassas nodded in return, and both men folded their arms and lay back on their saddles in supreme self-satisfaction, much to the annoyance of the girl.

"Bullshit," she said.

Sighing, both men sat up and exchanged looks. "The boys will be coming back pretty soon," Lampassas said.

"Yeah. And before they get back, I reckon there's something we ought to explain to Covina."

"You mean about Pretty Shadow?"

The Preacher nodded. "I think we ought to tell you, ma'am, there's one of the boys you haven't met yet. They call him Pretty Shadow, and he's about the worst human being for women I ever seen. And if you don't watch him, he'll—he'll try to charm you."

"Tell her about June."

"Well, June carries a six-shooter, and he sometimes looks mean on account of that scar, but he wouldn't shoot anybody, so you needn't worry about that. But he's—he's healthy. So you do need to worry about that."

"And Gattis."

The Preacher nodded again. "What I'm about to tell you about Gattis I want you to hold in strict confidence, because I'm sure Gattis don't want it known. Gattis has a good heart, but he got mixed up with a girl in Georgia once and had to run away from home."

"I see," said Corvina. "What about the young one?"

"That's my son," Lampassas said. "I promise he won't bother you none."

"You mean he's too young to be a son of a bitch?"

"What I mean to say," Lampassas said, "is that we got some rough edges to us, but we ain't mean minded. There ain't nothing we respect more than a—a good woman. But now, when these boys meet up with a—a woman that—that ain't exactly—nice—"

"I think what Lampassas is trying to say," the Preacher

said, much to Lampassas's relief, "is that these men have been working with cows and all. They've been away from civilization, and they've kinda forgot that things ain't always the way they look. And when they see a cow with her back up, well, they naturally—"

"You mean whatever happens, I brought it on myself."

"What I mean to say is that these men take things the way they see them, and when they hear a girl cussing like a cow hand and wagging around a fatherless child, they're liable to have hard thoughts about her."

"Bullshit," Covina said. "That's the only kinda thoughts men ever have."

The Preacher was setting his face to answer when the baby grew tired of the sugared water and, rejecting Covina's wet fingers, began squalling again. For a moment, both men stared at the baby, and then Lampassas discovered it was time for his watch. Promising to hurry the other men back to camp, he left. The Preacher busied himself building up the fire and getting a bedroll ready for Covina, while Little Jake calmed down to a steady and long-lasting howl.

"You must be wore out. I'll hold the baby for a spell if you want to get some sleep," the Preacher said.

"I reckon I'll wait till I find out about the milk," she said.

The Preacher stretched out in his blankets, hoping to sleep, but the stars still blinked before his eyes and the baby's cries still rang in his ears when the men returned to the wagon. Gently, he shook Covina, who had fallen asleep sitting up.

"We got the milk," June said to the Preacher, pointing to the Kid, who was slowly emerging from the darkness, one foot at a time, carefully holding the bucket in both hands. "I hope to hell you didn't spill any of that precious stuff coming in," he said to the Kid. "We had a hard enough time getting it."

"I just hope the baby will take it," Covina said.

"Well, if he don't like that, we'll go out and get some bear milk," June said.

Covina took the bucket of milk and began pouring it into a

cup to feed the baby. Anxious eyes followed every movement. "Careful you don't spill none of that," Gattis said.

Covina held the cup for the baby to drink. The thirsty baby fought for the cup, spilling some of the milk, while the men watched in outraged silence. "There's hardly enough here for one feeding," Covina said.

The men looked at her in disbelief. "You mean that kid drinks more milk than a calf?" June asked.

"Little Jake takes four feedings a day, and today he missed three of them," Covina said.

"That was all the critter had," June said. Angrily, he turned on Gattis. "You said that was all the milk she had."

"Hell, when I got through milking her, her hide was already beginning to shrivel," Gattis said. "You picked it out. You must a picked out a steer."

"This'll do for now," Covina said, putting down the cup and putting the baby on her shoulder to burp it. The hungry child was gulping down the milk so fast that he required frequent and savage burping. "He'll be up before daylight wanting more and there's not enough here for two feedings."

The men fell into their blankets without a word and pretended to be asleep. "Boys, we ain't going to have no time in the morning for milking cows," the Preacher said. "So I reckon it had best be done tonight. June, do you think you can find another fresh cow in the dark?"

"By God, if I drag it out of the herd and throw it, he's going to get milk out of it, I don't care if it's Old Blue."

"Ain't you boys gone to bed yet?" asked Pretty Shadow, who went to the wagon to get his soogans. "I've done finished my watch and am ready for sleep," he said, stopping short as he caught sight of Covina. "Bless my heart if that ain't a girl."

"This here is Covina, Pretty Shadow. She's going to stay with us for a while," the Preacher said.

"Well, I'm right happy to hear that," Pretty Shadow said, throwing his soogans between the girl and the Preacher.

"Other side of the fire," the Preacher said.

"I was just going to have a look at that pretty baby," said the offended Pretty Shadow, bending over and patting the milky, preoccupied baby on the head. "And a pretty sight it is. Now, that's what I call a pretty baby. Just look at them eyes. Just like his ma."

"He's got eyes like his pa," Covina said. "That son of a bitch."

Pretty Shadow squatted down beside the girl and carefully scanned the faces of the men gathered around the fire. "Is the father present in our little group?" he asked politely.

"That bastard is in California by now," Covina said.

"Covina's going to Trails End," the Preacher said. "Since we can't leave her and the baby out here alone, she's going to stick with us for a while."

"We'll take care of you," Pretty Shadow said, placing his hand on the girl's shoulder. "You just leave everything to old Pretty Shadow."

"In that case, the first thing you can do is to take this bucket and go fetch some milk for the baby," June said.

"Milk?"

"That's right," Covina said, shrugging her shoulder so that his hand fell off. "What do you think a baby eats, tamales?"

"I got no time to play milkmaid. I got to cross a river with a herd of cows tomorrow."

"Then I reckon we'd best get at it," June said. Gattis picked up the bucket and started limping toward the herd, the Kid following him.

"I've got a suggestion if you was to ask me," Pretty Shadow said.

June stopped and turned around. "What?"

"I'd take some salt. That'll make it a lot easier to lead the cow away from the herd."

"Let's try it, June," Gattis said.

June went to the wagon, got a handful of salt, and picked up his rope.

"Don't forget your milking stool," Pretty Shadow called

after them. He picked up his soogans and rolled them out across the fire from Covina. Lying down, he stretched and yawned luxuriously. "No need to wake me up when you get back."

Turning their backs to the fire, the three men walked quickly away in order to give proper expression to their feelings without offending the ears of the girl.

By the time the men reached the herd, having properly classified Pretty Shadow as to moral stature, legal pedigree, mental capacity, and national origin, they had regained some of their good humor, and June quickly spotted one of the cows he remembered as being fresh. Luckily, the cow was on the edge of the herd, and they slipped a rope around its neck and were dragging it away from the herd when the Kid discovered it was a steer. There was a short conference during which Gattis and June exchanged whispered confidences, accompanied by much waving of arms, shaking of fists, shoving and pushing, climaxed by a brief exchange of punches, and ended by the Kid, who stepped between the two men and dispassionately spoke of the virtue of reasoning.

"You're going to stompede the herd," he said.

With Gattis limping and June holding his nose, the men tiptoed back to the sleeping herd, and June's next selection proved to be more accurate. The men gently prodded the sleeping cow awake and erect by thumping the bucket against her scarred, rib-studded side. Slipping the rope around her neck, and with the aid of the salt June had brought, they coaxed the straight-horned, long-faced, rail-backed cow from the bedground. Once outside the protective circle, the cow became less attentive to the salt and began to look back toward her former position of refuge with rolling eyes and protruded tongue. June tightened up on the rope so as to keep the cow choked down, and with his other hand, held on to a horn, while Gattis pulled on the opposite horn and kept a tight grip on the cow's muzzle to prevent her from expressing her dismay. The Kid twisted the cow's tail and leaned his shoulder into her high, bony hip to propel her forward, and the innocent calf trotted along behind on wobbly legs, stopping now and then to nuzzle the Kid's hand or to bump into Gattis's sore foot.

"Can't somebody hold that damn calf? He keeps stepping on my foot," Gattis said.

"Shut up and pull," June said.

"Don't tell me to shut up. I'll turn the damn cow loose."

Again June and Gattis began their pushing and shoving, this time across the cow's horns, until the Kid let up a little on his tail-twisting and reasoned them back to peace. Angrily, they renewed their hold upon the cow and resumed their progress away from the herd.

When the cow had been pushed and prodded, tugged and goaded a sufficient distance from the sleeping herd, Gattis and June twisted the cow's head until her nose pointed at the sky, and the Kid grabbed her tail and swung her posterior to one side with sufficient force to throw her down, had not her head been twisted in the opposite direction.

"The other way, dammit," June said.

The Kid swung the tail to the other side, and the cow gratefully fell down. The Kid grabbed one kicking hind leg and pulled it to his chest, holding the other leg forward with his feet. June tried to lock the cow's front legs between his own while he kept the horns pointed earthward and the nose pointed skyward and lay on her neck. Gattis took the bucket and, after cautioning the Kid not to let go under any circumstances, placed himself between the cow's legs and proceeded to milk with one hand, with the other holding back the curious calf that nuzzled his neck and stared at its mother's predicament. Despite Gattis's strenuous efforts, the nature of the longhorn and the nervous condition of the cow combined to frustrate his designs so that the outcome of all their efforts was scarcely more rewarding than the previous attempt had been.

"Well, that's it," Gattis said to June. "Unless you can squeeze a little more out of her at that end."

"Is the bucket full?"

"Hell, you couldn't fill the bucket with the whole damn herd."

"We got to do better than we did last time or we'll be back down here before daybreak," June said.

"Maybe this is the same one we milked before," the Kid said.

"No it ain't," Gattis said. "That first one just had five teats." Cautiously, he backed out, holding the bucket away from the calf. "You can let her up now."

"Okay, Kid, you let go of her legs real easy like, but hold on to her tail," June said. "If she goes running and bawling back to the herd, the whole shebang will jump into the river."

The Kid did as he was told, and June let go of the cow's horns and held to the rope, but the cow did not get up. After being dragged, tortured, choked, thrown, and milked, she appeared to have given up. "Get her up," Gattis said. "We got to get back to the wagon."

The Kid twisted and pulled on her tail, and June tugged on the rope until they got her on her feet. "Hang on, now," June warned, "or she'll run right through the herd."

But the abused cow made not a move. June tightened up on the rope, and grabbing a horn, he pulled the cow toward the bedground while the Kid twisted her tail and shoved her from the rear, and Gattis followed, holding the bucket of milk away from the calf that followed at his side.

The hands got the cow back to the bedground, threw her down to sleep, chased back the calf that was following the bucket of milk, and returned triumphantly to the wagon with the precious milk, where they found everyone asleep and the fire dying out. Disappointed, they stood looking at the sleeping figures.

"Well, she was dead on her feet," June said. "But she'll be mighty happy when she sees this milk."

The Kid knelt beside the sleeping girl, and not daring to touch her, softly spoke her name until she awakened.

"What the hell do you want?" she asked, shaking her head and blinking her eyes open.

"We got some more milk," June said, showing her the bucket.

"What's that in it?" she asked, blinking.

"Where?" Gattis asked.

"Looks like cow shit," she said. "Didn't you think to hold the cow's tail?"

"That was your job," Gattis said to the Kid.

"I was holding her legs," the Kid said.

"Well, it was your end," June said.

Gattis plunged his hand into the milk, picked out something, and threw it over his shoulder into the night. "Just a straw," he said.

Covina lay back down and closed her eyes.

"Aren't you going to feed the baby?" June asked.

"You want me to wake him up to feed him?" she asked. "You can go to hell." Rolling over, she pulled the blanket over her head and went to sleep.

June raised the bucket and would have thrown it into the fire had not Gattis restrained him. "We better go to bed," the Kid said, taking the bucket and placing it on the lid of the chuck box. He laid a cup towel across the top to keep the bugs from falling in the milk.

June found it necessary to cross over Pretty Shadow's bedroll, stepping on Pretty Shadow, before he could take off his gunbelt and lie down to rest. Exhausted, he was sinking into sleep when he was startled by a strange new sound. June laid his hand on the butt of his six-shooter and raised his head to listen. When he heard it again, he rolled up on his elbow and pulled back the hammer on the single action pistol. Little Jake was noisily sucking his thumb. June shoved the six-shooter back into the holster and turned over. "Maybe he'll drown tomorrow," he said.

Lampassas's voice rose in the distance, across the sleeping herd, above the rumble of the river:

He was only a lonesome cowboy
Who made his bed where he lay,
He had no home and no mother,
And was known as the Wild-eyed Stray.

Gattis lay on his bedroll, trying to put the river out of his mind and to go to sleep. But no matter how he lay, his feet hurt. Gattis was used to walking, following a plow as long as there was light to see. But following barefooted the straight lines of a plow in no way resembled chasing in high-heeled boots the crooked path of a cow through prickly pear and over sharp rocks and flinty soil. Gattis believed if he could just keep his swollen feet out of the tight, iron-hard boots for a while, they would be all right. Promising himself that when he crossed the river, it would be barefooted, he kicked the heavy boots out from under the cover to cool his feet.

For as long as Gattis could remember, his feet had followed the plow, walking straight lines, placing one foot before the other, back bent, shoulders hunched into the plow, to the end of the row, where he pulled the mule around by the single rein looped over his shoulders, reset the point in the earth, clucked up the mule, and started another straight, parallel line. Gattis added row upon row, from the river to the woods, until the failing sun let the work be done. Then Gattis would unhitch, leaving the plow standing in the field ready for another day's work, hang the singletree over the collar, roll up the plow rein, and hanging it over his shoulder, he would swing up on the mule's back and ride to the house, for the first time all day above the dirt, the plodding, the hot, stale breath of the mule, free of the earthward pull of the plow.

Unharnessing the mule, Gattis would let himself out of the lot, avoiding a collision with the big, square-headed dog. Fighting off the dog, Gattis would go to the house and sit down with his mother and father around the table, where the smoking lamp was already drawing millers that flitted about the light and fell into the steaming peas and left gray dust on the soft butter. Gattis and his parents ate rapidly, without speaking, without pleasure.

"How much did you get done?" his father would ask after he had finished eating and had moved back from the insect-ridden lamp to smoke his pipe. No matter what Gattis answered, it was never enough.

While his mother cleared the table, his father would outline everything that needed to be done the next day, and then Gattis would climb the ladder to the attic and the bed of corn shucks, so he could be up early the next morning, to eat by lamplight, hitch the mule by feel, and ride back to the field into the first rays of dawn. But he did not always go to sleep. Sometimes he would lie awake and listen to the river, running below the house, bending back, forming on its west side one high bank beyond which Gattis had never been. String Town was to the east.

As a concession toward Christian morality, southern convention, and Georgian laziness, no work was done on the McCullough place from dusk Saturday until dawn Monday. Instead, the entire family availed themselves of the pleasures of driving to the store at String Town, where they could buy tobacco, and coffee, and sometimes a bolt of material or a pair of shoes.

After shopping, Gattis's mother went down the road to sit on Ma Hamrick's porch and watch the wagons come to town; his father went down to the mule barn to swap yarns; and Gattis hung around the front of the store watching for Mattie, who didn't wear a bonnet, or shoes, and whose hair was not tied back but hung stringy and tangled about her shoulders, and whose thin dress revealed nothing beneath it but Mattie, but revealed a lot of that. Gattis watched her as she climbed out of the wagon, walked up the steps, and sat on the edge of the porch swinging her bare feet and eating berries, but Gattis did not know how to make her acquaintance.

Gattis had never had any money because his folks grew what they needed, and what they didn't grow they charged at

the store. He had never needed money because his mother
bought his shoes and his father bought his tobacco. But now
Gattis decided he needed some money.

One night when he reached the house before his father,
Gattis told his mother he needed some money. The woman was
not only surprised, she was frightened. Frightened because
money meant buying from some place besides the store, and she
knew of only two commodities which were not charged at the
store. Whisky and women. His father came tromping across the
porch, and Gattis sat down to eat, and nothing more was said.

That night after he had climbed up to the attic and was
listening to the river, he heard a strange sound. It was his
mother and father talking. The sound kept him awake for a
long time. The next morning as he and his father started out to
the barn, his father stopped him and handed him a dirty,
wadded bill. "Don't you never say nothing like that to your
ma again, or I'll thrash you, big as you are," his father said.
"You feel an itch, you come to me."

Gattis worked toward the coming Saturday, never slackening his pace, but his parents were aware of his restlessness. They
watched his face become drawn, his eyes hollow. When the day
came, Gattis waited in the wagon until his folks had gone off
to their amusements, and then he went into the store and
looked at the harness until he was alone.

"Give me some candy," he said, holding out the crumpled
bill.

Mr. Culbertson took one look at the bill and knew that he
didn't have that much candy. "You getting this for a girl?
Look over here, don't you think one of these pretty handkerchiefs would be nice to put with it? Ain't no girl can eat that
much candy."

It was a white, useless handkerchief, and since he was
ready to chuck the whole thing and run outside, Gattis agreed.
Mr. Culbertson wrapped the handkerchief and the candy in an
old newspaper, and Gattis took it outside to wait in the wagon.
He waited until Mattie and her folks started home, then he

jumped down, ran up beside the wagon where Mattie was sitting in the back, and handed her the package.

Gattis's mother and father said nothing to him, but they noticed that he was even more agitated than before, even more restless. His father watched him as he plodded behind the plow, leaving a serpentine trail behind him, and now and then forgetting where the end of the row was. But they said nothing. Saturday night Gattis found another bill beside his plate. Silently, he slipped it into the breast pocket of his overalls. After supper he hitched the team to the wagon, rode to town with his parents, and sat at the corner of the porch, away from the other men. When Mattie arrived, she was wearing a lacy white handkerchief pinned over what Gattis believed to be her heart. She turned to look at him over her shoulder and then went around the corner of the store.

Gattis looked to see if any of the men had noticed, but they seemed to be paying no attention, so he slid off the porch and followed. As he walked around the corner of the store, Mattie giggled and ran. Gattis caught her, grabbed her around the waist, and they fell to the ground rolling together in a tangle.

"Mattie? Mattie?" her mother called.

Gattis tried to hold her, but she pushed him away. "Marry me," he said, trying to hold her.

"I already got a feller," she said, getting to her feet, leaving Gattis lying on the ground, the taste of dust in his mouth, pounding the earth with his fist in bitter disappointment. After a while he dusted off his overalls and went back to sit in the wagon, holding the crumpled bill in his fist, watching for another girl to buy candy for.

Gattis went back to plowing behind the mule, but he slept even less and scarcely ate at all. The plow moved slowly across the field, the land no longer dividing itself in parallel lines. His father complained about how little he did. His mother would scarcely look him in the face. And at night he could hear them talking long after they had gone to bed.

"He's got to get married," his mother said. "What he's doing is a shame to us."

"I need him to work."

"We could fix them up a room in the smokehouse. It's clean and dry, and it smells good. She could help me around the house, keep a garden, pick cotton, and he could still do the plowing. That way it wouldn't be like we was losing him."

"All right. But it's got to be a country girl."

"It's got to be a girl who can help around the house without getting under foot. A girl who can bear children and see after him when we're gone," his mother said. "Seeing the way he's been acting lately, I reckon it had best be an older woman. One that don't scare."

Gattis went to sleep hearing their whispered names like the sweet sounds of the river. Carla, Minnie Claire, and Ruth. Bertha, Beulah, Anna Mae, Laura Lee, Hazel Pearl.

The next morning when Gattis came down, his mother and father were sitting at the table. "Gattis, we think it's time you were getting married," his father said.

"We think it's high time," his mother said righteously. "So we asked a girl over to Sunday dinner. She's related to my cousin Minnie by marriage, and I know she's a nice girl. And knows how to work. She's a Methodist," his mother said. "But she ain't stuck up about it."

"We don't never work on Sunday noways lessen we have to, so your ma and me thought that after dinner you and Evalena might like to walk down to the river."

"And I don't want you carrying on none, neither," his mother said. "Just talk to her and get acquainted."

"If she's agreeable, we'll get the parson to marry you before he leaves String Town to go to that other church, and you-all can have me and Ma's bed till we can fix you a place in the smoke-house."

"And there'll be no cutting up until you get off to your-selves," his mother said. "I'm done with that."

"Well, I reckon you'd better get to the plowing."

Gattis picked up his hat and walked out of the house. He jumped off the porch, ran across the yard, almost tripping over the excited dog, vaulted the fence, leapt upon the back of the surprised mule, and had started to the field when he realized he had left the harness and had to go back and get it. That week Gattis laid the land open, cutting the rows as straight as his feet could walk it. And every night after supper his mother gave him lessons on how a gentleman should treat a lady, as best she could remember.

Sunday morning, Gattis and his folks got up early to be the first ones at church. After church they walked outside to meet Evalena. Everyone who had been in the service, plus two or three families who had come only for this occasion, formed a circle. Inside the circle were Cousin Minnie and Evalena. Girls tittered and grown men stopped chewing to solemnly watch. Gattis looked up quickly and nodded. In that glance he discovered that Evalena was almost as tall as he and was already beginning to look like his mother, long necked, flat chested, and thin flanked.

Gattis offered Evalena his arm and helped her into the wagon the way his mother had taught him, where she sat between his parents. Gattis sat in the back, pretending to watch the turning wheels that raised a thin cloud of red dust. But he noticed something else about Evalena. She did not bounce. Even on the sharpest bumps, her flesh was as rigid and solid as stone. His father bounced, the round haunches puffing like a bellows. His mother sagged, the tired flesh sagging up and then sagging down again. Mattie had not only bounced, she had bobbed, jiggled, and sprung. But Evalena did not bounce.

While his father beat back the dog, which with unlimited curiosity and gall was always poking his nose into other people's private business, Gattis assisted Evalena out of the wagon and into a chair on the porch, where he planned to entertain her by requiring the dog to play dead. However, Evalena jumped up from the chair, and with Gattis following, inspected the house.

"Needs paint on the outside, paper on the inside, and new

shingles," she said. "The privy is too close and the barn is too far." Then she went into the kitchen, hung her bonnet on a nail, gave a twist to the tight bun on the back of her head, and set the table, putting the plates and glasses down in a manner which was hard to argue with.

"Hard worker," Gattis's father whispered, poking him with a thumb.

"She don't bounce," Gattis said.

His mother detoured by him on the way to the table. "Knows what a stove's for," she said, giving him a meaningful glance.

"Hard worker," his father said. "Anxious to please."

They ate in silence, everyone careful not to be caught dropping food or picking his teeth with his fork. When the last of the food had disappeared, Gattis's mother suggested he show Evalena around the place.

"First the dishes," she said, slipping the apron over her neck and going to work. She washed each dish with an expertness and placed it on the folded cup towel with a finality that dared inspection.

"She don't break dishes," Gattis's mother said, nodding at him and winking. "You won't never have to use tin."

When she finished the last pan, Evalena wiped the table and stove and then took the dishpan outside, throwing the water under the porch and hanging the pan on the nail. "All right, let's go if you're a mind to," she said to Gattis, starting down the steps and across the yard.

The primrose path of love crosses avenues of a coarser nature, and this way of love across a Georgia farm was no exception. For one thing, the red rooster was running about the yard making a spectacle of himself. For another, the path which Evalena had chosen to follow to the river went past the mule, which Gattis was dutifully pointing out as a specimen of rural fauna when the mule spread its legs and began making a specimen of its own.

Gattis jerked Evalena back to save her skirts, but it was

too late. The damage had been done. Evalena looked down at her spattered skirt, and then raising it a little, she stepped up and gave the mule a kick which made the animal self-conscious for a month.

"Well, there it is," Gattis said, when they had overcome all obstacles and had at last reached the river.

"You ought to clean up that fence. Cut back the weeds and put in some new rails. Cut down the woods to make room for more cotton. Put a garden here in the pasture. What's down that way?" she asked, nodding her head toward the high bank where the river curved away out of sight.

"I don't know," Gattis said, determined to find out the first chance he got.

"Let's sit down here," she said, pushing him down on the trunk of a fallen tree. "I'm strong, a good cook, keep a clean house, and expect to provide my husband with eight or ten kids to work beside him in the field. Now tell me about yourself."

It was a slow, sunny fall day, still plenty of daylight left. Gattis stalled. "I'm not much of a farmer," he said.

"I'd expect to prod a man a little."

"A man gets mighty dirty and smelly from following a mule, and I never did go much for washing."

"A nose don't never lie about a working man or a dead skunk."

"I'm hard to get up in the morning."

"Them that goes to work late don't go to bed early."

Gattis sighed and hung his head shamefacedly. "Maybe you ain't heard," he said. "When it comes to women, I'm a brute."

"After the work's done," she said.

"You don't understand. I do things to women."

"I done noticed," she said.

Gattis spent the rest of the afternoon hiding in the haystack, and as soon as it was dark, he put the bridle on the mule and rode off to see what was around the bend. Thoughts of Evalena kept him on the mule's back through the following days.

Gattis rode down the dusty roads between the cotton fields, and the field hands would stop picking cotton long enough to raise up and stretch, watching as he rode past, aware that he was not one of them. Weary, unwashed, unfed, on a saddleless mule, he was above them, forever free of the downward pull of the cotton sack. It was then that Gattis realized what he wanted to be. A man on horseback. A cowboy.

A handful of Broken Circle cowboys, who were sitting around a windmill, were startled by an apparition, a gaunt, red-faced man on a gaunt, long-eared mule. He sat bareback on the mule, holding the plow reins in both hands with the excess wrapped over his shoulder. The hands watched him in astonishment.

"I'm looking for a job," he said.

"Fix a windmill?" the foreman asked.

"I never seen one to the other day."

"Build a fence?"

"Not bob-wire."

"Treat a sick cow?"

"No."

"Can't use you."

It was the same story wherever he went, except that sometimes they laughed and hooted him off their place, and one time they threw rocks at him and the mule, driving them away.

Gattis came across a cow camp in the brasada. At first he thought about going around it; but he was hungry, and the mule was footsore. Brazenly, he rode up to the wagon.

"Light and help yourself to the chuck," the cook said. "But get that jackass down wind so he don't kick no sand in my cooking."

Surprised at his good fortune, Gattis filled his plate and sat to one side. When a man came over to give instructions to the cook, Gattis knew he was the boss. He was a small dried-up man, older than the foremen he had seen, as old as his father. "I don't reckon you could use a hand?" Gattis said, out of habit. "I can't repair windmills, I can't fix no bob-wire fences, and I don't know nothing about doctoring sick calves. But I can sit on a horse as long as anybody."

"You anxious to get back home?"

"I ain't never been no place I'd like to get back to," Gattis said.

"As soon as we get through trail-branding these critters, we're driving them to Trails End. That's a far piece, and it'll take a while to get there. Some of the boys got impatient and quit, but if you're willing to stick, I'll put you on."

"I got as much patience as any cow."

"I reckon you can learn as we go," Lampassas said. "I'll furnish what you need, to be taken out of your wages at the end of the trail."

"That's fair," Gattis said. "What about my mule?"

"I reckon there's folks that would buy one," Lampassas said.

With regret, Gattis swapped his mule for a saddle. "It's a good saddle, and it'll outlast the mule," Lampassas said. "As long as you sit it like a man, you can call yourself a cow hand, and as long as you call yourself that, don't never sell your saddle."

Gattis picked out the rest of the equipment: a pair of bat-wing chaps, a striped shirt, checkerboard trousers, red bandana, cowhide vest with the hair side out, a white sombrero, and a pair of nickel-plated Chihuahua spurs.

Lampassas looked over the pile of outlandish goods he was paying for in dismay. "I'm picking out the boots," he said. He got the highest-heeled, sharpest-toed boots he could find. "So you don't look like you're walking behind a plow any more."

They had trouble getting Gattis's feet into the stiff, high-topped boots, but when they got them on his feet, he didn't put one foot in front of the other any more.

> They buried him there by the river,
> There at the close of the day,
> They raised no stone to remember
> Where lay the Wild-eyed Stray.

Gattis turned around on his bedroll and propped his feet up on the saddle. That relieved them some. He was a cow hand now, but he was afoot again. And following a cow was harder than following a plow because a cow didn't walk straight lines, and a cow didn't leave a warm, moist furrow to walk in. And he had never had to follow a plow across a river. "But I'll do it," Gattis swore. "I'll stick. Spite of hell or sheep."

Chapter 5

"ARISE and shine, wake up and aspire; God's in his heaven, the beans is on the fire," the Preacher called cheerfully in the early morning darkness, banging a spoon against the lid of a dutch oven out of sheer exuberance.

The hands awoke to darkness, drizzling rain, wet bedding, and the sounds of the tumbling river. Putting on their wet hats, they greeted the day with groans and curses, which died in their throats as soon as they remembered the girl. Rolling up their soogans in an attempt to keep them from getting wetter, they pulled on their wet boots, shivered into their cold slickers, and with the brims of their hats turned down and the collars of their slickers turned up, they lined up before the wagon to wash. Covina picked up her flowered hat, put it on her head, and got up, carefully replacing the bedding over Little Jake to keep his wetness all his own. The Preacher picked up the lantern and waved in the Kid, who had stood the last watch.

June was drying his sore and enlarged nose when Covina joined the men at the washpan. Courteously, they all stepped back to allow her passage to the dirty water and grimy comb. Covina dipped both hands into the water, vigorously rubbed her face, and blowing the excess moisture from her lips, she reached blindly for the towel. "Give me the towel, dammit," she said, and June placed the wet, soiled towel in her hands. She wiped her face dry, cleaned out her ears, and hung the towel back on the wagon.

Setting her hat on the wheel, she took the comb from Gattis, giving him a look which placed the blame for several weeks' accumulation of grime solely on his own head. After wiping the comb on her dress, she combed the hair back from her face, biting her lower lip as the comb jerked through the tangles. By the light of the lantern, the hands could see that her hair was straight, brown, and short, and that her front teeth were slightly discolored, probably because her short, crooked upper lip never quite met the full lower one, which protruded slightly. Dropping the comb on its leather thong, Covina replaced her drooping hat on her head and led the way to the food.

Huddled against the rain, the hands ate quickly in hollow-eyed silence, staring at the fire, watching the shadows flickering over the wagon, thinking of the task ahead. Covina sat in her bedding, holding the covered baby in her lap, eating with one hand and feeding Little Jake from a cup with the other. The baby, unaccustomedly warm, was fully content, gurgling and blowing bubbles and spilling milk as June watched with mean eyes.

"Eat your fill," the Preacher said. "We got a long way to go before supper and there won't be any more eating till then."

As quickly as they finished, the men dropped their dishes in the roundup pan for the Preacher to work on and began tying their soogans to place them in the wagon.

"If there's anything you don't think you'll need, it'd be a good idea to leave it here," Lampassas said. "No need to weigh yourself down. We can leave our boots on the bank."

The hands pulled off their slickers and emptied their pockets, some of them stripping off vests and belts, rolling them up in their bedding and placing them in the wagon. Covina wrapped the contented baby in her soogans and laid him under the wagon out of the rain.

"Ain't you going to lighten up any?" Pretty Shadow asked

June, who was standing beside the wagon in full battle attire. "You'll drown."

"Well, if I do I want to have my clothes on."

"At least leave that six-shooter and the gunbelt in the wagon. That must weigh fifteen pounds."

"Might need it," June said.

"It'll weigh you down," Pretty Shadow said, but June's modesty was invincible.

"If there's any wading to be done, I'd better get out of this," Covina said, catching her skirt in both hands and swishing it about.

The activity around the wagon came to an abrupt end as the men, too decent and chivalrous to turn around and look at the girl, and too honest to abandon hope, watched out of the corners of their eyes just in case.

"Just what do you intend on wearing?" the Preacher asked.

"I thought one of you gents might lend me something."

"No self-respecting female would be caught dead in men's clothing," the Preacher said.

"Well, I ain't no self-respecting female, and if I was that's exactly how I'd be caught in the river in these self-respecting clothes. Dead."

"There is a right way and a wrong way to dress, and them clothes you have on is the right and fitting way for a young lady."

"They might be fitting for a woman who lives in a parlor and has servants to carry the slops, but they are an inconvenience at wading through rivers and cow manure."

"Right is right, and wrong is wrong, and right never wronged nobody," the Preacher said in his best and most persuasive preaching voice.

"Bullshit," said Covina. "Trying to dress according to them St. Louis fashions has sent more women to hell than men and whisky put together."

The Preacher, not wishing to provoke another obscene outburst, sulked in pious silence.

"Well, didn't none of you bring any extra clothes?" the girl asked.

"We all planned to get a new suit of clothes when we got to Trails End," Lampassas said.

"Well, I don't see how I can cross the river in this thing," Covina said, swinging the skirt around and trying to tuck it up between her legs.

"I got some things that would be about your size," the Kid said.

"Why, how did you know my size?" Covina asked.

While the others chuckled, the Kid, blushing, went to the wagon, unrolled his soogans, and removed the bundle of clothing he had been saving to wear into Trails End. He handed them to Covina without looking at her and went back to drying dishes.

"You boys throw the wagon sheet over the side there, and she can dress behind the wagon," Lampassas said. While June and Pretty Shadow arranged the tarpaulin under the critical eye of Lampassas, Covina examined the clothes the Kid had given her. "You don't happen to have another pair of boots, do you?" she asked. The Kid shook his head. "Well, I guess these high-tops will have to do. Here, I don't have no use for these," she said, handing the Kid a pair of men's drawers. "Besides they got a hole in them."

Again the men chuckled, and the Kid, blushing so hard he could scarcely see, wadded up the drawers and stuffed them into his bedroll.

"Don't none of you boys peek, now," Covina said, going behind the wagon.

To the Preacher's disgust, all the hands turned to, getting the wagon packed and ready for the crossing. They put the yokes in the wagon, buried the fire, pulled up the fire rods, put the pothooks and the shovel in the jockey box, and watched the wagon seat, across which Covina tossed her discarded clothing.

"If she was to flap her skirts just once, the whole bunch of you would stompede into the river," the Preacher grumbled as the men stood in the half-light and drizzling rain, listening to the girl's quick sighs as the cold drops hit her naked skin, and watching the accumulation of clothing on the wagon seat. First the bonnet, then the jacket, skirt, blouse, drawstring petticoat, hip bustle, bust pads, corset, and two dirty cotton stockings.

"As soon as the sun comes out, it'll be too hot to wear stockings under trousers," she said, looking over the wagon and catching all of them gaping at the mysterious pile of clothing, the uses of which only Pretty Shadow pretended to know. Caught looking, the men turned away and became very busy at their self-appointed tasks.

"How do I look?" she asked, stepping from behind the wagon and standing before them in her high-button shoes, a blue suit and vest with the cuffs and sleeves rolled back, a white shirt, and a four-in-hand tie. "Anybody got a hat?" she asked. "I got to have something on my head."

The Kid got the striped and billed engineer's slouch hat and gave it to her. Covina brushed back her hair with her hand and pulled the cap on her head. "Let's go get them cows, boys," she said.

"Might just as well," said Gattis.

"Why didn't you tell us you had a brother?" Pretty Shadow asked the Kid before turning and walking off with Gattis toward the herd. Lampassas and June studied the girl for a moment and then followed them.

Covina wadded the pile of clothes into the carpetbag. The Kid rolled up his soogans once more, threw the wagon sheet back over the wagon, and began tying it down. The Preacher put away the last of the pots and pans and closed the lid of the chuck box. "Here's the last of the milk," he said, pouring it into the whisky bottle Gattis had brought from Mustang Springs and thumping the cork into it.

Covina took the bottle and stuck it inside her vest. She rummaged through the carpetbag, pulled out a scarf and some extra diapers. She stuck the diapers inside her vest and tied the scarf about her neck. When she turned around, the Preacher and the Kid had almost disappeared into the early morning gloom.

Wrapping the baby in the Kid's coat and tying the sleeves tightly, she picked up Little Jake and started off into the rain.

Scattering out in the first gray light of day, the hands started the herd back from the river, not stringing them out in trail order, but letting them graze. By mid-morning the drizzle had stopped, and from time to time the sun broke through the overcast, glinting off the wet grass. At noon, after giving the hands a few minutes to rest, Lampassas turned the herd back toward the river and strung them out in trail order, Gattis and himself on the point, June and Pretty Shadow in the swing, and Covina, the Preacher and the Kid prodding the drag.

Nearing the river, the leaders picked up the pace. The point gave them their heads and stayed with them; and in the drag, the hands shouted and whooped, urging on the slow, sore-footed cows. The leaders took to the river and for a moment Lampassas thought they were crossing, but when the water reached their muzzles, they stopped to drink. Cursing and yelling, Gattis and Lampassas floundered in the swift water, holding to the cows to keep their feet under them and prodding the cows deeper into the water. The frightened cows bawled and hooked, threatening to fight.

Pretty Shadow and June tried to keep the herd in tight formation so that the oncoming cows would force the leaders far enough into the water that they would head for the opposite bank. The leaders turned back, fighting the cows being pushed into them. There was a brief mill which Gattis and Lampassas broke up before any of the cows were trampled into the water, and the herd scattered out along the bank despite the best efforts of the hands. The cattle ventured close enough to the river to drink and then stood stupidly immobile, ankle-deep in the water.

"Don't let them bull up on us," Lampassas yelled. "Get them to moving."

For perhaps another hour, the frustrated men wrestled with the cows in the treacherous water, trying to force the leaders into the river. From time to time one of the men would lose his footing and, splashing and kicking, be swept down the river past the frightened cows until he could catch a leg or tail and get his feet under him again. Back from the river, the Preacher, the Kid, and Covina, with the baby in the coat tied to her back with diapers, Indian fashion, kept the cattle from turning away from the river and scattering out in the valley.

When about mid-afternoon a light rain began falling again, more cattle grazed in the valley than stood before the river. Lampassas was trying to chase a small, smoky red steer into the water when the steer wheeled about, dropped its head, and knocked Lampassas backward into the river. Lampassas got up, shook off the water that ran down his arms, and called off his hands. Stumbling up the bank, he fell exhausted under a mesquite tree that gave no protection from the rain that continued to fall although the sun had broken through again. The others fell down beside him, panting for breath.

"We'll give them a little while to calm down, and then we'll round them up and try it again," Lampassas said to the others, who were too tired to protest. "We still got time to get them across today."

Covina made use of the first break of the afternoon to pull the diapers out of her vest and change the soiled baby, who, because he was becoming weaned, or because the constant motion of being carried on his mother's back had amused him, had cried only intermittently throughout the day. Covina walked down to the river, washed out the diapers in the muddy water, and hung them over a mesquite limb to dry. Then she fed the baby from the bottle, giving him the last of the thin milk that due to the warmth of the day had already become clotted and sour.

"Milk's gone," she said, setting the empty bottle on the ground before them.

"There's not going to be any more milk until we get on the other side of the river, so I reckon we'd best get started," Lampassas said.

With a sigh of relief at having to face the river rather than one of the sore-teated cows, the men got up and started after the herd. "Get them diapers," Lampassas called back to Covina. "If the cows see them flapping in a tree, they're liable to turn around and head for home."

Covina gathered the wet diapers from the tree, stuck them inside her vest, and rinsed out the whisky bottle before swinging the baby on her back and following the men.

The hands fanned out in a wide circle to rebunch the cattle that had scattered out to graze, shaping them in trail order and heading them for the river. Now, however, the cattle were not thirsty, and they trailed along at a leisurely pace, patiently allowing themselves to be prodded and yelled at by the sweating, swearing men who ran excitedly alongside them. The herd marched to the river, stopped before their hooves touched the water, and turned back, to mill and bawl in confusion.

"They've sulled on us," Lampassas yelled. "Get in there and bust them up."

Through the long afternoon the stalemate lasted, the drovers keeping the herd at bay, the cattle, heads down in exhaustion, legs trembling from excitement, refusing to take to the water. While Lampassas, Covina, the Kid, and the Preacher kept the herd from scattering, June, Pretty Shadow, and Gattis worked along the river, dodging hooves and horns and trying to force the cattle into the water.

Lampassas watched the sun move steadily west, watched his last hope fade and die, his dream become a past and bitter thing. Sick with frustration and fatigue, he waved the drovers in. "Let them go," he called in anger and despair and turned and walked back from the river, sitting down on the wet ground. The sky was dark and heavy, threatening more rain, and despite the season, Lampassas felt a chill.

He did not look up as the men fell down beside him, or as Covina unslung the baby from her back and sat down beside it. The baby, wet, hungry, and displeased at being no longer carried and jostled about, began to whimper and then to cry, but Lampassas was beyond caring. Out of the corner of his eye, he saw Covina take out the empty bottle and place it on the ground before the men. Turning his head, he looked at her, and she shrugged and put the bottle back inside her vest. Sighing, she pulled out the diapers, picked out the driest one, and tied it around the baby, who was becoming as red as the river. Lampassas watched as she picked up the baby and walked down to the river through the excited cows that scattered before her and rinsed the diapers in the river, hanging them on the limb of a dead mesquite.

"We'll let them scatter out and calm down a bit, and then we'll try to bed them down. We got them so jumpy they won't even lay down," Lampassas said.

"I'll get up in a minute and fix some chuck," said the Preacher, who made no effort to move.

"The river's bound to go down some tonight," Lampassas said. "Maybe by tomorrow or the day after we can walk right on across."

"Moses couldn't walk them cows across that river," the Preacher said.

Pretty Shadow was of the opinion that the flood would leave deposits of quicksand that would be even more dangerous than the flood. June gave it as his opinion that either up or down the river could not be crossed without horses. The Kid held the prospect of buying horses as unlikely since they had no money and still owed five hundred dollars on the cows.

"I reckon you can rest easy about that five hundred dollars," Lampassas said to the Kid. "I ain't forgot about it yet."

Pretty Shadow explained that he had as good a reason for wanting to get to Trails End as anybody, but that he hadn't planned on waiting beside the river until someone came along and gave them some horses. The Preacher suggested that when a man went as far as he could go, for him that was the end of the trail.

Covina came back and sat down beside the men. She studied the sky a moment and expressed belief that it was getting dark early. Pretty Shadow predicted more rain before morning.

"We still got time for one more try," said Covina.

The men forcibly restrained themselves from giving expression to their opinions.

"Well, ain't that what we're here for?"

"We can't cross that river without horses," June said.

"Hell, how do we know until we've tried?"

June was of the opinion that they had already tried. The others concurred. "I've done everything I know to do and we're still on this side of the river," Lampassas said.

Pretty Shadow was of the opinion that Covina was not interested in getting the herd across the river but was only seeking a way to get herself and the baby on the other side.

Covina explained that her reason for wanting to get across the river was not the point, and that anybody that would quit a herd was a sorry bastard.

Gattis believed that while it was undoubtedly a social error to quit a herd, it was at least unethical to ask a man to risk his life in the river.

Lampassas expressed dismay at having to choose between being a bastard and being a son of a bitch.

"Was it me," June said, "I'd rather be a bastard."

Covina inquired as to what, since he wasn't going to cross the river, Lampassas intended on doing with the herd.

Lampassas admitted he didn't know how to quit a herd. The Kid reminded him that there didn't seem to be a market at hand for longhorns, and Gattis was satisfied they couldn't be sold for milk cows. June suggested they drive them back to Mustang Springs for another grub stake, and the Preacher believed they ought to take them back to Mr. Fulton since in a way they were still part his. Gattis objected to all that walking, and Pretty Shadow complained that it was as far back to Fulton's as it was to Trails End.

The Kid wondered why they couldn't abandon the herd like sailors abandoned a ship, but the Preacher reminded him that when sailors abandoned a ship, it was going down and not left floating around to bump into things.

"When you take something up, you got to lay it down," Lampassas said.

While Lampassas searched for a way to get rid of the herd, the dark, heavy clouds brought an early twilight, the herd scattered along the river to graze and sniff the air, and Old Blue investigated a strange object flapping in a tree.

Idly, Lampassas watched as Old Blue pawed the ground and shook his horns at the waving diaper. Old Blue sniffed at the diaper and the diaper flapped in his face. Old Blue jumped back, snorted, and lunged forward, impaling the diaper on one horn. The diaper fell over his eyes.

Lampassas and the hands laughed as the big steer snorted, and pawed, and tossed his horns, trying to shake the limp rag from his eyes. Dropping his head and grunting, he lunged forward, crashing into the mesquite tree. The mesquite quivered. A dead limb gave a sharp, dry crack and fell across the steer's haunches.

The hands started to laugh again as the steer jumped into the air with a loud snort, but the laugh died in their throats when the herd jumped with Old Blue and came down running. For a moment the hands watched the cows in disbelief. "Stompede!" Lampassas yelled, and forgetting their exhaustion, the others leapt to their feet and ran after the cows. "Stompede! Head the leaders!"

Lampassas ran, dodging the scattered cows that ran after the leaders. He was almost in the water before he realized the cows were stampeding into the river. The thought that the cows had resisted all his efforts to put them in the river and then had jumped in themselves because of a diaper struck him as being funny. "They're taking to the river," he said, looking back over his shoulder. Seeing nothing but a solid mass of hooves and horns bearing down on him, he turned and dived into the river to avoid being trampled.

Lampassas came spluttering out of the water, trying to keep his feet under him in the strong current and to dodge the cows that were plunging into the river. "Gattis," he yelled, trying to be heard over the noise of the river and the stampeding cattle. "Gattis, take the point and we'll try to take them across."

Colliding with a cow, Lampassas went sprawling into the water, caught hold of a steer's leg, was swept away again by the swift current, washed under some cows, and came up holding to a horn. Getting his feet set, Lampassas released the horn and tried to get back to the bank, reasoning that it was as good being trampled on land as in the bottom of the river.

Reaching shallow water where it was easier to keep his footing, Lampassas began yelling again. Now that his own danger was past, he feared for the cattle. Without the men to direct them, the panicky cattle would turn back, milling in the water, crushing and drowning one another. Or they might drift downstream, past the ford, under the high banks where, unable to climb out of the water, they would drown. Or they might disperse in the water and end up some on one side of the river, some on the other, hopelessly scattered.

The surge of joy that he had felt when the cattle first took to the water was gone now, and he felt helpless and afraid. "Gattis, take the point," he yelled, weaving his way through the cattle as he tried to get to the downstream edge of the stampede to keep the cattle from scattering. "Gattis. Pretty Shadow. June. Somebody, take the point."

In his desperation, Lampassas blundered into the cows which had been slowed by the water, and hitting and shoving at them, he tried to force his way through them, looking for his men. It was not yet sundown, but the heavy clouds shut out the sunlight so that it seemed almost twilight. Distant objects had lost their focus. Even with his experience, Lampassas had difficulty making sense out of the chaos and darkness, but he believed he was seeing some order, some sign of direction. It wasn't a tight formation, but the cattle were becoming less scattered and were heading straight into the water instead of drifting down the bank. Soon Lampassas could see some of the hands, formed in a line along the bank and out into the water, pointing the cattle across the river. Beyond the last man, the current swept the cattle into a large arc, almost doubling them back to the south bank. And then Lampassas knew that Gattis was on the point, that far out in the river, the thing that kept the herd moving into the current rather than turning back to the near shore, was Gattis on the point. Lampassas stopped for a moment to catch his breath, and then pulling off his boots and throwing his hat back over his shoulder, he ran into the river to help.

Wading into the water to assist Pretty Shadow, Lampassas took heart at what he saw. The cattle were moving into the water, the hands were pointing them across, and standing far out in the river, Gattis was turning the leaders toward the north bank. They were going to make it. Even without horses they were going to cross the river.

Lampassas felt his fear dissolving so that he could breathe again. Gaining confidence, he worked his way deeper into the treacherous water, his feet feeling for the uncertain bottom.

The leaders were two thirds of the way across the river when they hit swimming water and turned back into the face of the oncoming herd. With the crush of bone and the snapping of horns, the cows met head-on in a giant mill that crushed and drowned the weaker animals, and only Gattis could reach them. At the top of his voice, Lampassas began yelling at Gattis, at first calling for him to do something, to turn the leaders, to break the mill, and then urging him to swim clear before he too was caught in the mill and crushed between the frightened cattle.

Helplessly, unable to make himself heard above the roar of the river, Lampassas watched as Gattis, in trying to turn the leaders, was swept into their floundering midst. Desperately kicking at the pressing cows, Gattis tried to climb upon their backs, but was caught between them, and hung, helplessly pinned.

For a moment Lampassas thought June was going to rescue Gattis as June crawled over the backs of the cattle, firing the six-shooter into the center of the pack and beating at the cows

with the barrel of the six-shooter. The mill broke apart and both
June and Gattis disappeared into the water between the pawing
and thrashing hooves.

With a groan at what he had just seen, Lampassas looked
back and saw that only Pretty Shadow and Covina were still
with him. Pretty Shadow, holding to a tail to steady himself
in the water, was still turning the cattle across the river, un-
aware that no one was on the point. Covina, who appeared to
have lost the baby and the engineer's cap in the excitement, was
waist-deep in the water, grappling for the Preacher, who had
stepped in a hole and disappeared. The Kid stood on the bank,
afraid to step into the water, hoping he would be left behind.

With a cry for help, Lampassas turned his back on his son
to follow his herd. He had not taken twenty steps before he lost
his footing and was swept away by the current. Unable to get
his feet down, he was rolled over and over and washed against a
cow. Grabbing in desperation, he caught the cow around the
neck, blindly hanging on until he felt his feet dragging over the
bottom of the river.

Getting his feet under him, Lampassas stood up, not caring
which side of the river he was on. It was the north bank. He
climbed out of the slippery river, fell against a tree and looked
back across the river for sight of the others. Battered, exhausted
cows with broken horns and peeled hides struggled up the bank.
Pretty Shadow sat in shallow water, unable to move another
step. The Kid crawled out of the river on all fours and fell down
beside Lampassas. Disinterestedly, they watched as far downstream Covina walked out of the darkness of the river, dragging
the Preacher behind her. Falling as she climbed the bank, she
slid partially back into the river. Rolling the Preacher on his
back so that his face was out of the water, she lay unmoving as
the water lapped at her breast and tugged at her clothing.

When they had caught their breath, Covina and the
Preacher walked out of the water and started along the bank
toward the others. The Preacher stopped short as he saw something bobbing at the edge of the water. Knowing already what

it was, Lampassas and the Kid got up, and joined by Pretty Shadow, who waded out of the river, they stood looking at Gattis's body, half buried in the mud at the edge of the river.

"God, we must a run the whole damn herd over him," Covina said, turning away.

Gently, the men carried Gattis out of the water, and laying him down, they fell down to rest. "By God, we crossed her," Lampassas said, when he was able to speak.

"We got to go back," Covina said. "The baby's on the other side."

The fire burned timidly beside the river, gnawing at the wet brush and giving off faint flickers of light that cast eerie shadows at the figures about the fire. The men blinked and rolled their eyes at the smoke, pretending not to notice that Covina was squatting in the darkness across the fire wearing only the Kid's long-tailed shirt, which was clinging wetly to her body. Spread on a green bough and held over the fire to dry were the trousers and vest. The Preacher sat on the ground fully dressed, holding over the fire Gattis's hat, which he had found in the river. Pretty Shadow and the Kid, stripped to the waist, were drying their shirts. Lampassas hunkered near the fire in his drawers as he dried his shirt and trousers.

"The Lord wouldn't ask a feller to risk pneumonia for the sake of appearances," Lampassas said to the Preacher, who shivered before the fire in his wet clothing.

"I got to go back and get the baby," the Preacher said, guilty because Covina had laid the baby down in order to pull him out of the hole he had stumbled into; and then she had been unable to go back for the baby because in his panic he had clung to her, dragging her across the river with him. "It was on account of me that she left it."

"It's too late to cross tonight," Lampassas said. "As soon as it's light, we'll tie the rope around a log, and someone can float it across to the other side. Is that all right, Covina?"

"I keep thinking I hear him crying," Covina said.

"That's just the river," Pretty Shadow said. "I figure June's on the other side with him. He'll look after him."

"If he was on the other side, we'd a seen a fire by now," Covina said. Standing up and turning her back to the fire, she stepped into the damp but warm trousers, that smelled of wood smoke. Unbottoning the wet shirt, she dropped it over the Kid's shoulder and slipped on the vest, buttoning it all the way up. "June is somewhere in the river," she said.

"I wonder if we'll ever find him?" the Kid asked.

"I count it lucky that we found Gattis," said Lampassas.

"What if Gattis wasn't drowned?" the Kid asked. "What if he had swum across the river and was trying to crawl out when we ran all them cows over him, stomping him into the mud. Maybe he was calling to us. Calling to us to help him."

"I don't figure it that way," Pretty Shadow said. "And I ain't never going to figure it that way."

Covina untied the scarf from around Gattis's neck. "I'm going to wash his face," she said. "We can't bury him like this." She wet the scarf in the river and then knelt down and began washing Gattis's face. The men watched.

"Well, at least we can get his boots off now," the Preacher said, turning away.

"What for?" asked Pretty Shadow.

"For the girl," the Preacher said. "Can't you see she lost one of her shoes crossing the river? And the other one looks ready to fall apart."

"It ain't right to bury a feller without anything on his feet," Pretty Shadow said.

"Better the dead should be barefoot than the living," said the Preacher. "You can have his hat, too," he said, handing Covina the hat he had been drying over the fire. "That snake-skin hatband come off in the river."

"I lost the cap," she said, looking at the Kid, intending to apologize, but the Kid had turned away so as not to look at Gattis. For a while no one spoke, as Covina washed Gattis's face.

"I sure wish I had the makings with me," Pretty Shadow said, tasting his mouth.

"I wish I'd thought to stick some sourdoughs in my shirt," the Kid said.

"The wagon and everything else we got in the world besides cows is on the other side of the river," Lampassas said. "We don't even have a shovel."

"We can't bury him until we get to the wagon anyhow," Pretty Shadow said.

"Why not?"

"We don't have nothing to wrap him in."

"Well, what difference does that make?" Lampassas asked in exasperation. "He's dead."

"It makes a hell of a lot of difference."

"I don't see what difference wrapping a feller in a saddle blanket can make after he's dead."

"Well, for one damn thing, it keeps the damn dirt off of him."

"I don't know what possible difference that could make," Lampassas said. "He was trompled into the bottom of the damn river. He died face down in the damn mud. He is going to be buried in the damn dirt. What difference is a damn dirty blanket that will rot the first time it rains going to make?"

"Well, if you don't know that, then you ain't got enough human feelings to make a man," Pretty Shadow said in disgust. "You can't just put a man in the ground and throw dirt on him like a misborn calf."

"Shut up," Covina said.

"I don't know why you boys want to upset everybody arguing about it," the Preacher said. "We ain't got a shovel to bury him with, and besides, my Bible is in the wagon."

"Don't you know the words?" asked Pretty Shadow, who was feeling argumentative.

"Of course I know the words."

"Then what difference does it make which side of the river your Bible is on?"

"Because you've got to have a Bible at a burying. That's what folks do."

"Tradition," sneered Pretty Shadow.

"It ain't tradition, it's what's right."

"Superstition," snorted Pretty Shadow.

"Well, if that ain't the stupidest thing I ever heard out of a grown man. You think wrapping a blanket around him to keep the sand out of his eyes is civilized and reading a Bible over him is superstition. Why, you wouldn't know the difference between a piebald steer and a spotted skunk."

"Shut up," Covina yelled, standing up and clapping her fists to her ears. "Shut up, shut up, shut up."

Before Covina had finished her admonition, the men were on their feet, pulling on their clothing and listening for sounds of stampede. The echoes of the girl's screams died across the river. All was quiet.

"Whew," said the Preacher.

"Girl, don't never do that again," Lampassas said. "I reckon you got reason to be edgy, but this ain't no time nor no place for yelling."

"I thought the herd was going to hell for sure," Pretty Shadow said. "They must be logy from the water."

"What if they'd stompeded back across the river?" asked the Kid.

Ruefully shaking their heads at the narrowness of their escape from disaster, they sat back down in silence.

"Listen," the Kid said.

"What is it?" asked the Preacher.

"Did you hear singing again?" asked Pretty Shadow.

"No, it was—it sounded like a baby crying," the Kid said, not daring to look at Covina.

"You couldn't a heard the baby," Lampassas said. "Now, you put that out of your mind. I don't want you upsetting everbody."

"But I heard—"

"Just stop listening," Lampassas said.

"How many head do you reckon we still got?" the Preacher asked, trying to fill up the silence.

"Well, we lost close to a hundred head in the river. There must be about the same number still on the other side that we never got across. I figure we got right at eight hundred head on this side of the river."

"If we keep losing cows the way we been doing, by the time we get to Trails End we won't have enough to make a herd," Pretty Shadow said.

"We'd sure be short-handed if we had any more," the Kid said.

"We wouldn't a had none left if it hadn't been for June and Gattis breaking up that mill," the Preacher said.

"It was a brave thing they done," Lampassas said.

"Stupid," the girl said. "It was stupid. Dying in the mud so them damn worthless cows would have something to stand on."

"It ain't a question of how much a cow is worth," Lampassas said. "It's a question of how much it's worth to a man to get his job done. Gattis and June did more than I would a asked of them, but I reckon it was worth it to them, or they wouldn't a done it."

"Bad luck," said Pretty Shadow.

"The will of God," said the Preacher.

"Bullshit," said Covina.

By common consent, the men ignored Covina. "What are we going to do about June?" asked Pretty Shadow.

"We can't leave him to the coyotes and buzzards," said the Preacher.

"As soon as it's light enough, we'll scout down the river to see if we can find him," Lampassas said. "If we don't find him on this side, whoever crosses over can look for him on the other side."

"He may be tromped down in the mud where we'll never find him," the Kid said.

"It just don't seem right that a man should do what June

did, climbing over them cows that way, and then just be forgotten," Pretty Shadow said. "I figure June bought a piece of this land whether we find him or not. And I think we ought to make him a grave, same as Gattis, and put rocks on it, so if we ever come by here again, we'll remember him."

"We could put a cross on it," said the Kid. "So that if anybody else ever sees it, they'll know somebody is buried here."

"And we'll have a drink on him in Trails End," Lampassas said.

"And we'll tell folks what June and Gattis done," the Preacher said. "Thataway they'll be remembered."

"Bullshit," said Covina. "What do you know about remembering? What do men ever remember except trails, and brands, and horses? Men just ride around burying friends and planting kids and forgetting where. It's the womenfolks that stay put to bear the kids and bury the dead. If June and Gattis don't have no womenfolks to remember who they were and what they were like, it won't make no difference whether they're under a pile of rocks or in the bottom of the river."

The men sat in angry silence, angry because she was wrong and there was no way they could make her admit it, since the only effective argument was violence.

The Kid sat upright. "Listen."

"Oh, hell," said Pretty Shadow.

"There's something out there," the Kid said.

"I heard it too," said the Preacher.

The men watched the darkness along the river bank, listening as something moved in the brush. "Maybe it's a cow," the Kid said.

"That ain't no cow. That's—that's June," the Preacher said as he saw June, still weighed down with clothes and six-shooter, blundering through the brush.

"How in the hell do you expect a man to see a little biddy fire like that?" June asked in exasperation as he pushed his way through the brush. "I've been looking everwhere. Falling in the river. Bumping into trees."

"June," the Kid said.

"Don't be yelling, now," June said, warding them off with one hand. "You'll wake the baby and I just this minute got him to sleep."

"The baby?" Covina asked.

"I guess it was the walking that put him to sleep."

"Is he all right?"

"Well, he was kinda fly-specked when I found him, but he dropped right off to sleep when he seen it wasn't no use to cry."

Covina grabbed the baby out of June's arms, pressing him to her breast and unwrapping him to be sure he was all there.

"I wish you wouldn't do that, ma'am, I just got him to sleep," June said.

"We thought you was dead," the Kid said.

June looked down at Gattis's body beside the fire. "I knowed he wouldn't make it when I seen the way them cows had him packed in. He must a been dead by the time I got to him," June said, and then looked about him apologetically. But the men were looking at Gattis, and Covina was examining and pinching the baby. "Stand back and let a man to the fire," he said.

"I told you to take your boots and that gunbelt off or it'd weigh you down," Pretty Shadow said.

"Hell, that's what saved my life," June said. "I got knocked under in that mill, and I knowed there wasn't no use coming back up and getting stepped on, so I just started walking; and I kept on walking till I walked right on out of the river. Only thing, I got turned around and come out on the other side."

"Then how did you get on this side?" asked the Preacher. "You mean you walked back across the river?"

"Well, when I finally walked out of the river, it was dark, and I was wore out, so I laid down a spell to catch my breath, and when I recollected my senses, I realized I was way the hell downstream and the river was running the wrong way. So, I stood up to get my bearings, and by damn, as dark as it was, I missed it at first, but there was a bridge there. Then it come to me that I was on the wrong side of the river. So I walked back to the wagon to see if anybody was left, but there wasn't nobody there but the baby, and I'd a missed him if he hadn't been crying. I picked him up and went back to the bridge. It was almost under water but still standing, so I just walked across it, and I been wandering around ever since looking for your fire."

"Is the bridge still there?" asked the Preacher. "You didn't dream it up or nothing, did you?"

"I told you I walked across it."

"He got the baby," Pretty Shadow said, and the Preacher believed in the face of this incontrovertible evidence.

"There was a bridge there all the time," the Kid said, "and we swum the river. We risked our lives and there was a bridge there the whole time."

"You can't never tell. It was pretty near under water. Likely it wouldn't a held no cattle," June said, unwilling to admit his heroism was unnecessary.

"Cows don't take to bridges nohow," said Pretty Shadow. "Likely we never would a got them on it."

"But it was there," the Kid said, and that fact had a sobering effect upon the men. "Gattis might still be alive if we'd a tried the bridge. And there wouldn't a been no need in June risking his life."

"What's done is done," said Lampassas. "There ain't no point in arguing about how it should a been done now."

"Anyhow, it's there if we need it," said Pretty Shadow.

"Is it big enough for the wagon?" asked the Preacher.

"It's big enough, but I ain't sure what it'll hold."

"As soon as it's light, we'll cross over the bridge, round up the rest of the cows, and get the wagon," Lampassas said.

"How many cows do you reckon we lost crossing?" June asked.

"Near a hundred head," Lampassas said. "There's eight or ten cows down there with broken legs, or busted up to where they can't make it. As soon as it's light, I reckon you'd better go down there and put them out of their misery."

"Why do I always have to do the killing?"

"Because you're the one that carries the six-shooter."

For a moment June balked, unable to decide between throwing the gun away and shooting Lampassas with it. Then he slumped before the fire, mumbling to himself. "I chased them damn cows into the river like I was told. I ran across their damn backs like they was crossties to break up the mill. I walked across the damn river on the damn bottom. I got the damn baby. I found the God damn bridge. And now I got to go down there and kill them God damn crippled cows."

The baby began to cry.

"I hope you're satisfied," said Covina, who was washing the baby's face with her shirttail, which she had wet in her mouth.

"I asked you not to bother him," June said. "I just got him to sleep."

"You woke him up with all that cussing," the Preacher said.

Covina deftly ran a finger under the baby's diaper. "He's hungry," she said.

"I reckon we'll all be hungry before we get back to the wagon," said June, unable to remember when he had last eaten.

"Little Jake can't wait until morning," Covina said, looking at Lampassas. "You told me he'd be fed once we got across the river."

With dead, hopeless eyes, Lampassas looked at the girl, remembering no such thing. But Lampassas was not the man to name the mother of a hungry bastard a liar. "I reckon you boys ought to go see if any of them fresh cows made it across the river. They may be hard to find. The cows is pretty scattered out, and likely the calves drowned."

"The bucket's in the wagon," June said. "On the other side of the river."

Covina produced the empty bottle, setting it on the ground before him.

"You can milk a longhorn into a whisky bottle," June said.

Covina looked at Lampassas.

"Pretty Shadow, with Gattis gone, I reckon you'll have to give them a hand," Lampassas said.

Pretty Shadow looked at Lampassas.

"I ain't asking it for me," Lampassas said. "But it does seem like you could do it for a dead man."

"God damn," Pretty Shadow said, spitting into the fire. "How in the hell are we supposed to find them cows in the dark?"

"I reckon you'll just have to look until you find them," Lampassas said.

Pretty Shadow looked at Lampassas.

"It's a lucky thing you brung the rope," the Preacher said.

Pretty Shadow looked at the Preacher. The Preacher lapsed into silence. Pretty Shadow got to his feet and picked up the coiled lariat. He looked at the Kid. The Kid got up also. Together they stood at their ease, looking at nothing, Pretty Shadow idly twirling the rope.

"Don't wait for me, because I ain't coming," June said. Shivering, he bent close to the fire and chafed his arms. The fire hissed and smoked. The baby cried. The river ran. Pretty Shadow and the Kid waited, Pretty Shadow idly twirling the rope. "I hope ever damn one of them cows drowned. I hope their udders dried up and their teats fell off," June said, looking away from them. "Who's doing the milking?"

"I reckon I am," the Kid said.

"God a'mighty, I'm tired of being a mother," June said, getting up and crashing through the brush in the darkness. Quietly, Pretty Shadow and the Kid followed him.

The sun stood hot and high in the afternoon. The wind tugged at the stiff, stained hatbrims, flapped the trouser legs and frayed shirtsleeves of the small group gathered around the blanket-wrapped body, and blew a fine layer of dust from the mound of quickly drying dirt piled beside the grave. The Preacher spoke quietly to the faces circled about the grave, and the wind sucked the words from his mouth and scattered them over the prairie.

"We don't none of us know anything about Gattis's previous life except what he told us, that he didn't do right by a girl back home. That was wrong, and Gattis confessed it. But we ain't here to bring up Gattis's past mistakes, and that wasn't the Gattis we knew. The Gattis we knew did right by us, and he done right by the cows. There are cows standing on this side of the river that wouldn't be here now if it hadn't been for Gattis and what he done. And for that we praise him. It wasn't because they was worth it, or because he owed it to them, that he died to save them. It was because that was the kind of feller Gattis McCullough was. He stayed with the herd. There was never a night so dark nor a river so deep but what Gattis stuck.

"But Gattis has another river to cross, and it's the deepest river and the blackest night he's ever faced. Deep as a bronc buster in his favorite saddle. Blacker than midnight in a dugout. Swifter than a hanging rope. And all a man's efforts as useless as sacking sand. But Gattis don't have to cross that river alone or afoot. There stands Somebody who walks the water like He's saddled a cloud, Somebody to set Gattis's foot in the stirrup and point the way to the end of the trail.

"Old Gattis don't live here any more. He ain't bound to no wagon. He ain't tied to no plow. He don't chase no cows. He don't smell no sheep. Old Gattis has saddled him a cloud. He's sitting safe beyond the rimrock. Safe for evermore. Amen."

Bowing his head, the Preacher began to sing, and one by one the others joined in.

> We who have lived our lives in the sun,
> Who have loved the day and the light,
> Must some day, we know, through the dark waters go,
> And cross through the river of night.
>
> O Jesus, we pray, from our side never stray
> As we ride through the river with Thee,
> Our sins we'll confess, Thy name we will bless
> When the end of the trail we see.

While the Preacher stood with bowed head and silently prayed, the men lowered the blanket-wrapped body into the grave with the rope and took turns shoveling the dirt over it.

Covina, her hair pushed back into the hat which was too big for her, stood at the foot of the grave holding the sleeping baby. The only sounds were the crunch of the shovel in the sand and the sigh of the dirt as it slid from the shovel and fell upon the blanket.

The baby began to fret, and without a word June handed the shovel to Lampassas and got the bucket out of the wagon. Pretty Shadow picked up his rope and fell into step with June and the Kid.

Lampassas and the Preacher took turns filling the grave, and then the Preacher replaced the shovel in the tool box. Taking the pen case from his bedroll, he recorded Gattis's death in the Bible. Lampassas started back to the herd, and the Preacher climbed up on the wagon seat. Covina pulled her carpetbag out of the wagon and took out the bonnet adorned with pink and purple flowers. She tore off the flowers and placed them on the grave. The wind lifted the brightly colored flowers and rolled them up at her feet. Stooping with the baby, she replaced the flowers, securing them with a rock. She tugged at a wide strip of rawhide which had been wrapped around her boot and sewed across the instep, settled the baby on her hip, and started after the herd.

Stopping once to push a wisp of hair into her hat and tug again at the ill-fitting boot, she looked back at the grave, where the freshly packed earth was beginning to blow and the bright flowers were beginning to tatter and soon would fade.

Chapter 6

A *FULL* yellow moon hung soft and heavy in the sky, reminding men of Comanches, tides, and love. The moonlight shone down on the bedground, softening the dusty hides and pointed horns of the bedded cattle, splashing the earth with pale gold. The Kid made his slow way around the cattle, dreamy and half asleep. On the other side of the herd, Pretty Shadow sang the sweet but melancholy tale of the cowboy

> *Who sold his saddle and went on a fling,*
> *Traded his horse for a wedding ring,*
> *His boots he swapped for a leather grip*
> *And packed his duds for a wedding trip.*
> *But when he got back he neglected to brag,*
> *For his horse was a ride, but his wife was a nag.*

The Kid listened to the song, feeling all soft and melancholy inside. Ever since he had crossed the river and had seen Gattis's lifeless body wrapped in a blanket and buried out nowhere, the Kid had been blue. He spent most of his time thinking of his mother and her grave behind the store, of Tertia and walking in the moonlight back home. Walking through the pale yellow and orange leaves and wading in the creek below the store. Watching Tertia wade through the water with her wet-tailed dress pulled halfway to her knees. He had tried to kiss her there beside the creek.

It was early fall, still warm, but not hot and brilliant like July, not hot and dead like August. He held Tertia's hand as they waded through the water. He caught her about the waist, pretending he was preventing her from falling. And after spending most of the afternoon missing opportunity after opportunity to take her in his arms and kiss her, he had at the worst possible moment tried to plant a kiss on her lips. Even then he might have succeeded except that, coward that he was, he had changed his mind and tried to divert his kiss to her cheek, and had been slapped for his trouble.

If he had asked her first, he believed she would have permitted him to kiss her. She liked him. He knew she liked him. But he had been so clumsy. And he had been so stunned by the slap that he had returned to the store without a word. Cursing himself for the fool that he was, Jamie had decided to go back and apologize to Tertia, taking a little present with him. He had been trying to pick out something when his father came in from his bedroom at the back of the store.

"Sit down, Jamie," Lampassas began.

With a show of annoyance, Jamie sat down in a cane-bottomed chair and waited, idly scanning the shelves for a suitable present while his father made appeals for his attention. Jamie hated these sessions with his father, and he sat embarrassed while his father tried to include him in his plans and plead for his enthusiasm. They always ended the same way. He did what his father wanted, but never freely, never gladly, always with a reluctance which drove his father into a rage.

"Jamie, I sold the store," Lampassas said.

Jamie did not look at his father, and he could not speak. He did not know what he felt. He did not like working in the store. He did not want to live there. He wanted to get away. But it was his mother's home. His father had sold his mother's grave.

Lampassas took out a thick wad of bills and laid them on

the counter. Then he picked up a dirty sack and emptied out some folded bills and an assortment of dusty coins. He raked them into a separate pile. "Your ma was saving this for your future," Lampassas said. "And I kept it for you, adding to it what I could. And now I reckon the time has come to spend it."

Jamie looked at the dirty, crumpled bills, wondering how much was there. Enough for a trip to New Orleans? There were trains and women there. But he didn't know how to get to New Orleans. He knew his father wouldn't go with him or even consent to his going at all, and the idea of going alone did not appeal to him. He thought of taking the money, laying it at Tertia's feet, and asking her to marry him. But then he decided he should first get a job on the railroad and then ask her to marry him. They could use the money to buy a house. Or perhaps one had to have money to get a job with the railroad. That seemed likely, else everyone would be a conductor or an engineer. As he thought about rolling down the tracks, up above the world looking down, the wind in his face, passing pretty girls who danced with excitement, swirling their dresses and clapping their hands, he even thought it might be best to work with the railroad for a while before asking Tertia to marry him.

"I think I know where I can get some cows," Lampassas said.

At first Jamie didn't understand. He had heard his father talk of driving cows to Trails End. He had lain in bed at night, trying to sleep, earnestly wishing the men would stop their eternal talk, talk, talk of horses, and cows, and trails. Sometimes his father would come and get him and make him sit on the porch, listening to their talk although he longed to be somewhere else. He pretended interest in their talk of rivers and stompedes, of throwing the houlihan and smoking up the town. The only time he really listened was when they talked about the women and the trains. Gilt-edged beds and gilt-lettered trains. Rose lamps and red lanterns. But it had been old men's talk, about old things that were dead and done with, things which had never been as the old men remembered and never would be.

"By rights, half of what I got for the store ought to be yours, too, but I thought you might like to throw in with me," Lampassas said.

The money was his. He could demand it. He could ask for what was coming to him and be perfectly within his rights. He could spend it anyway he wanted. He could—

"This here's a right smart of money. You got to put it in something worthwhile."

"Women and sin," Jamie thought. He would invest in that. The thought of being a by-word in the town, of being pointed out as a wild, reckless kid amused him.

"That's why I was thinking about the cows. A feller could buy cows pretty cheap here. He could drive them up the trail, not costing him anything except wages for the hands, and sell them for a big price at Trails End."

Trails End was where the women and the trains were. But was Trails End real? Was it still there? The women? The trains? Did they still buy cows in Trails End? Did men still drive cattle up the trail? Trails End was part of the old lies, the old glories, the untrue past. Jamie did not want to go back to an old way of life, even if it was an honest one. He did not want to discover an ancient city, even if it was a wicked one.

"You don't know nothing about cows, but I'll teach you that."

There was nothing at all that Jamie wanted to know about horses and cows and cowboys, not because he was perverse, but because he didn't see how such information would do him any good. He was going to work on the railroad, and he wasn't going to fill his head with things that didn't have anything to do with the railroad.

"It'll make a man of you, Jamie," Lampassas said. "Not that you ain't near a man now, but you've always been on the lean side and kinda sickly."

That had a certain appeal to him. Not that he'd ever considered himself unmanly. But he didn't know how to treat a lady like Tertia with confidence. The thought of coming back from Trails End too sure of himself to be denied, thrilled him. He wondered if he would be coming back. The railroad was in Trails End.

"I'm trying to think what's best for you."

Suddenly, Jamie was angry. His father had always wanted to go up the trail; he had planned it for years, and now he had the money and he was going to go. Why did he always have to pretend he was doing it for somebody else? Did he think his son wouldn't go unless he thought it was for himself? What else could he do? If a father wanted to make a fool of himself, then he guessed a son had to look pretty silly, too.

"And when we come back, we'll have enough money to buy us a little place and run us a few cows and be set for the rest of our lives."

"I'll go," Jamie thought. "I'll see that he gets there, but then I'm through. I won't come back."

"I kept us out a suit of clothes and two good saddles. Everthing else goes with the store. I reckon we'll strike out tomorrow to look for some cows," Lampassas said. "I thought you might want to say good-bye to somebody."

Jamie sat looking at nothing while his father stood waiting, reluctant to go. His father tried to tease him about Tertia, flattered him about his native abilities as a cowboy, and finally left the store, slamming the door behind him.

Jamie went to his room. There on the bed were the clothes he was to take, rough, sturdy clothes, along with a bedroll and a saddle. Everything else in the room now belonged to someone else. Jamie sat down on the clothes on the bed and looked about the room. Hanging in the chifforobe was the blue serge suit he had persuaded his father to let him have so that he would have something elegant in which to court Tertia. Hanging beside it was the cap the railroad men had given him. Jamie pulled out the drawers of the chifforobe, going through his personal possessions. There were the railroad book and two crumpled dollar bills. He unrolled the bedding, placed the cap, the suit, and the two dollars inside, and rolled it up again. "At least I won't have to ride into town looking like a cowboy," he thought. "I can go down to the train station in a suit."

About dusk, Jamie walked down to Tertia's house, taking the railroad book with him. He was going to humbly apologize, boldly ask for a good-bye kiss. He found her outside, airing herself.

"Tertia, Pa sold the store."

"To whom?"

"What?"

"To whom did he sell it?"

"I don't know. He's going to buy some cows and drive them up north."

"I don't think folks does that any more, Jamie."

"I know, Tertia, but Pa is, and I got to go with him. And it's—it's real dangerous work."

"Well, you take care, Jamie."

"I mean, it's bad. Real bad. Stompedes, and rivers, and cows and all. I may not ever be back."

"What do you aim to do up north?"

"I mean, I may get killed or something."

"Oh."

"And just in case I do, I want you to have this. My railroad book. To remember me by."

"I'll remember you, Jamie."

"Tertia, could I kiss you?"

"But you might get killed, and I'm not going to kiss anybody but the man I marry."

"It would be something to remember me by."

"You done give me the book."

Jamie made up his mind to grab her and kiss her whether she wanted to be kissed or not. "Tertia, do you want me to come back?"

"Is it as dangerous coming back as it is going?"

"I don't think so," Jamie said. "I'm going, Tertia," he said, warning her.

" 'Bye now," she said.

Cautiously, they eyed each other. The gallery groaned as her father came outside to hawk and spit over the lilac bush. "Do you need to go outdoors, Tertia?" he asked, referring to the privy, blithely ignoring the fact that she was already outdoors.

"Yes, Pa."

"Run along, then. I'll wait for you on the gallery."

"I bet you don't even read the book," Jamie said.

That night was a bad one for Jamie. He struggled with the covers all night, and with the first light of day, he went out back where his mother had been buried. He stood there trying to think of something to say. After a while, his father stood beside him. Once his father had started to speak, and then he had changed his mind and walked around to the front of the store, where he had two horses tethered. Jamie had walked beside him.

In front of him a cow shook its head, flapping its long ears and startling him out of his dreams. Jamie looked out over the herd; it was quiet, peaceful, nothing moved. He began walking again, thinking of Tertia, wondering if Tertia was awake now, perhaps lying in her bed looking at the moon and thinking of him. Perhaps beside the lilac bush. With someone else. Someone who had kissed her where he had failed.

He put the picture out of his mind and thought of her waiting for him at the end of the track. He would swing down out of the cab, pull off the cap and heavy gloves and hand them to the fireman. He would step up to her, and she would open her gown and wrap it around him to warm him. He would hold her gently and kiss her, but he wouldn't do anything bad to her. Not unless they were married. Not the way someone had done to Covina. And if someone else had kissed her, he would forgive it. The thought made him feel big and magnanimous. Even if someone had done her like Covina, he would stand by her, proud and protective, and he would take her for his wife. Jamie almost wished someone had done her wrong because it made him feel so generous and manly to forgive.

Pretty Shadow, who had completed his round in the opposite direction, stopped to wait for the Kid, needing to share the peace and beauty of the night. "Peaceful, ain't it?" he asked as the Kid came up. "Wish Gattis could see this." They pulled the makings from their pockets and leisurely rolled cigarettes to smoke in unhurried pleasure.

"Hell, I could stand watch forever on a night like this," Pretty Shadow said, licking his rolled cigarette and placing it between his lips. "You won't see nothing like this on no train, boy. Just smoke and noise."

"But I'll be getting somewheres."

"Yeah, you'll be getting somewheres," Pretty Shadow said. "You'll be traipsing all over the country and not even know what it is you're looking for."

"Do you know what it is?"

"What you got right here. Contentment," said Pretty Shadow, scratching his chest. "Pure contentment."

"Is that what you've been chasing all over looking for?"

"I reckon it is," Pretty Shadow said. "Except when you're young, you think it's the hell-raising at the end of the trail."

"Where is it, then?"

"I don't rightly know where it is," Pretty Shadow said. "Sometimes it's quiet like this, and other times there's real contentment in drinking, and brawling, and branding the girls. Sometimes it's doing a good day's work. And then there's the times when a man's alone, not a fence nor a campfire as far as the eye can see. You feel like the whole world was made just for you, the whole sky was watching over you. I reckon that's how old David must a felt."

"David who?"

"King David. The one that was a sheepherder."

"Why, Pretty Shadow, I didn't know you was religious."

"I ain't religious and anybody that says I am is a lying son of a bitch," Pretty Shadow said, belligerently. "But, hell, I got some feelings. I never muddied a water hole. I never sold my saddle or left the bunk house door open. I never killed anything that didn't need killing. I never hit a drunk for sport. I never took advantage of a man's wife if he was out on a legitimate cow hunt or off on a hoot. And when I die, I aim to have my debts paid."

"I'd say them was the qualities of a good man," said the Kid, trying to regain Pretty Shadow's favor.

"Hell, boy, it ain't that easy to tell a good man from a bad one," Pretty Shadow said, carefully pinching the fire from his cigarette and making sure it was out before dropping the shredded tobacco on the ground and wiping his fingers on his vest. "Why, I've knowed fellers that'd steal your last steer but wouldn't beat you out of a drink. There's men that wouldn't lie to a out-of-work sheepherder that would lie to a woman, and there's fellers that wouldn't cuss a horse that'd kill a man."

"Then how can you tell a good man from a bad one?"

"Like I say, it ain't that easy. But there's one thing you can tell for sure. A good man don't owe nobody nothing. No money, no cussing, no favors. He pays his debts and he keeps his word. And that's what I'm going to Trails End for, Kid. To settle up. Marry Diamond Annie."

"Pretty Shadow, is Annie—" Nervously, the Kid pulled off his hat and began rolling the brim in his hands. "Can you tell a good woman from a bad woman?"

"Why, hell, there's nothing easier. It's just like reading a brand. A woman is the opposite of a man, and the more opposite she is, the better a woman she is. A good woman don't act like a man, she don't laugh out loud in a man's presence, she don't enjoy a man's company unless she is married to him, she don't enjoy a man's pleasures even if she is married to him, and she don't try to draw a man's attentions to her opposites."

The Kid twisted his face and rolled the hatbrim even tighter between his hands. "Do you think Covina is a bad girl?"

"Boy, you talk like a feller that's been going around bareheaded in the sun."

"Are you sure, Pretty Shadow?"

"Sure as there's teats on a cow. A female traveling alone in the company of men? Wearing a man's clothing? Doing a man's work? Cussing like a cow hand? Those are indis-putable signs, boy. In-dis-putable. But the real earmark of a bad woman is traveling around the country with a fatherless child. That don't wash off."

The Kid rolled up his hat some more, clapped it on his head, and turning away from Pretty Shadow, started another turn around the herd. At first he walked slowly, saddened by thoughts of Covina and what was waiting for her at the end of the trail. He felt kindly toward her, even generous. It wasn't entirely her fault. Why should she be the one that had to pay? What was so bad about Covina anyway? In pants and a shirt she was kind of cute. And she was nice enough when they treated her right. She just didn't want any man pushing her around, that was all. Hell, she had to travel with somebody, he thought, gesturing to the herd. And putting on trousers to cross a river showed pioneer spirit and common sense besides. And what harm was there in doing a man's work if she could do it as well as anybody else? Hell, a woman shouldn't cuss. That wasn't right no matter how you looked at it, but she didn't mean anything by it. Like as not, if she liked a fellow and he didn't like to hear it, she'd cut it out. But having a brush baby. There wasn't but one way you could get those. And that wasn't right.

Still, that could happen to any girl. Especially if she was young and naturally friendly. And besides, the man had probably lied to her. Maybe he'd even given her whisky pretending it was tea. Well, hell, what could a girl do if they were alone and he decided to take advantage of her?

In his mind the Kid began to conjure up pictures of a brute taking advantage of Covina. Lying to her, forcing her, laughing at her tears. Jamie wanted to kill the man, so cruelly did he treat her. Jamie wanted to smash his sneering face. And then to tenderly pick up Covina and gently cover her naked body while he caressed her and smothered her tears against his shoulder. To hold her lightly as she sobbed, her body shaking against his, the clothes he had so gently wrapped around her falling away, revealing thigh, and belly, and her naked breasts throbbing against his chest—

The tranquillity of the night, the splendor of the moon seemed to touch the boy's heart. His body ached and sang of love. Of moonlight and roses. Cottages and children. Beds and bushes. She's already ruined, he thought. No question about that. One more time wouldn't make any difference. He wished he had some whisky, or knew some words. Soft words, sweet, seductive—

He hurried to his next meeting with Pretty Shadow. Again, looking over the sleeping herd, they rolled their cigarettes in silence, the Kid needing all his concentration to put the thing together.

"Pretty Shadow," he said, holding the cigarette together with both hands and puffing at it. "How does a feller—talk to a bad girl?"

"Well, boy, I don't know what'd work for you and what wouldn't, but I got a sure-fire spiel that ain't never missed yet. But maybe I oughtn't to tell you," Pretty Shadow said seriously. "Your pa might not like it, and then again, it might not be right to give you a unfair advantage over the girls."

"I wouldn't hurt nobody," the Kid said. "Honest. I probably wouldn't never even use it."

"Well, I sure used to strike terror in their little hearts with it," Pretty Shadow said. He studied his cigarette, overcoming his natural reluctance to speak of his romantic exploits. "I use to kinda sashay into the parlor, and at first I wouldn't say nothing. I'd just look around kinda bold-like until the girls began to blush and giggle. But I wouldn't let them rush me. I'd just take my time. Some girls appeal to your eyes, and some girls appeal to your ears, and some of them you just got to kiss or die. And then there's them that just strikes you hollow in the belly. I'd pick out one that struck me hollow in the belly, and I'd stroll over to her, and put my arm around her neck, and I'd say, 'Where you been keeping yourself, honey?'"

"And she don't slap your face or say nothing to you?" the Kid asked, his incredulous eyes big in the moonlight as he memorized the magic words.

"She don't say nothing. She just casts her eyes to the other side of the room and giggles a little. I say, 'Sugar, let me buy you a drink.' She gives me a look out of the corner of her eye, and she says, 'I don't drink,' kinda pious-like. So I squeeze her neck a little, and maybe feel of her shoulder, and I say, 'Sure you do, honey. You drink with me,' and she says, 'Well, just one.'

" 'One for the hire, two for the fire, three for the head, and four in bed,' I say, pulling her ear. She says, 'Don't talk naughty, you're in the presence of a lady.' I say, 'I knowed you was a lady the first time I laid eyes on you. Let's sit down.'

"So, we turn to go to a table, and I let my arm slide off her shoulder and down her back, to guide her. Not too far. Just far enough for her to grab my hand and squeeze it. We sit side by side at a table and I press my knee against her knee, and I slip my arm around her waist, and she says, 'What do you think you're doing?' And I say, 'I ain't doing, honey, I'm undoing,' and wink at her. She glances up at me like she's mad and puffs up a little and says, 'If you ain't nice, I'm going to leave.' I say, 'We'll both leave, honey. We'll go up to your room.' And she pouts a little but I don't let her rush me. I buy her another drink for the fire, and then I stretch a little so that my hand slips down on her flank, and she grabs it and jerks it up, and I act embarrassed and jerk it up too, so that between us, it sort of falls on her teat. And she jumps a little, and looks offended, and I apologize, and say how sorry I am, but that it's so crowded, and why don't we go up to her room where we can relax. She says, 'Okay, but don't try none of that funny stuff.' I promise her, and we go up to her room. But I don't let her rush me," said Pretty Shadow, yawning and stretching.

"What happens then?" the Kid asked breathlessly.

"Then I close the door."

"Aw, please, Pretty Shadow."

"Well, it gets kinda private."

"I won't never tell."

"Well," said Pretty Shadow, having to overcome his natural reluctance all over again. "In the room there is only one chair so she says, 'You sit there, and I'll sit here on the bed.' And I say, 'Let's be fair, honey. I ain't no better than you are.' So I sit down on the bed, close beside her so that the bed sags a little, throwing us together. I catch her around the waist so that she don't fall, and when she looks up at me to say something, I silence her lips with a kiss. And I keep kissing her until she loses her breath and falls on the bed."

"Then what?"

"Then I blow out the light."

The Kid thought Pretty Shadow was becoming reluctant again, but he was only rolling himself another cigarette. "By this time I'm a little breathless, too, so I fall down beside her, and for a while we just pant. Then I reach over to see if she's still there, and I pat her, and I say, 'Powder River, honey. Get ready to buck, I got my spurs on.' "

Impatiently, the Kid waited for Pretty Shadow to light his cigarette. "Then she says, 'You rough thing, I believe you tore my dress.' And I say, 'I'm sorry, honey. Here's ten dollars to fix it.' "

"Then—"

"From there on it's my own special, patented treatment, sacred between me and her, and not to be believed in any case."

"And that's all there is to it?" the Kid asked, not completely convinced.

"I ain't saying that it'll work for ever man that comes up the long trail, but it sure as hell always worked for me."

The Kid licked his lips, swallowed down the hollowness in his belly, and already feeling rushed, turned to start another round. The night lay before him, dew-sparkled, star-spangled, moon-bright, so that the Kid felt stunned by its brilliance and splendor and stumbled over the rough ground like a man drunk on dreams. Behind him he heard Pretty Shadow's loud whispering. "Kid. Hey, Kid. Our watch is over. Go in and get our relief."

In the days that followed his talk with Pretty Shadow, the Kid sought an opportunity to be alone with Covina. Coming in from the herd, he would quickly wash up and fill his plate in order to sit beside the girl before the other men could. Hurriedly, with aching jaws and knotting stomach, he would tear through his food, put aside his plate, and be on the very edge of speech when Lampassas would send him back to the herd, the Preacher would set him to washing dishes, or the baby would begin to cry.

"Covina," the Kid would whisper, so that the others, pretending nonchalance but stopping their chewing and pulling their ears, could not hear. "Where have you been hiding your—"

"I'm going to have some more of them frijoles," Covina would say, and rising cross-legged, she would return to the pot to fill her plate with the tender, bubbling beans. "Anybody else for the whistle-berries?"

On the trail, the Kid sang the saddest, sweetest songs he knew in his best nasal falsetto to catch Covina's ear, and sometimes he would drop back to work beside her in the drag, seeking a chance to speak to her.

"Let me buy you a drink, honey," he would say.

"What?" she would yell, her teeth set and her chapped lips tight against the cloud of dust that hung perpetually over the drag.

"Where have you been keeping—" the Kid would ask, attempting to throw his arms around her neck, just as she ran off to prod up some sore-footed cow.

"Damn cow," she would say, squinting into the dust. "What was it you wanted?"

The dust stirred up by the heavy-footed animals would envelop them, sifting through their clothing, down their necks, up their noses, and into their sweat-caked faces until their eyebrows turned bushy and gray with dust; and the Kid's mouth dried, his lips cracked open and bled, his desire shriveled, and his soft words were dissolved in a fit of coughing.

Lampassas didn't like for Covina to stand watch, feeling that an unmarried girl should be in bed early and that there was something especially immoral about a woman working beside men at night. However, the men grumbled because they were short-handed and overworked, and Lampassas compromised himself to the extent that Covina sometimes stood the first watch after getting the baby to sleep and leaving him in the care of the Preacher. Usually, Lampassas took the watch with her, but when he had to scout ahead of the herd looking for water holes near the trail, the watch was given to the other men. When June had the watch with Covina, he wouldn't trade, but by virtue of much pleading and after promising to stand two of Pretty Shadow's watches, the Kid managed to get a first watch alone with Covina.

It was a clear, dazzling night, and the impatient Kid made his way around the herd toward a rendezvous with Covina at a faster pace than usual, so that even his singing seemed rushed. June answered him from the wagon, giving the Kid an occasional rest. Covina was not allowed to sing because Lampassas believed a woman singing at night would stampede the herd. Besides which, the songs were not especially appropriate for the female voice.

When Covina and the Kid met, each of them having completed half a turn around the herd, Covina stopped, as was usual when the herd was quiet, to swap a few words.

"Hell of a pretty night, ain't it?" she asked, but the Kid's eagerness to meet with her had turned into anxiety to get away, and quickening his steps, he walked past her without speaking.

The next time they met, the swift-footed Kid had completed one turn and a quarter of another, while the girl, walking at a more leisurely pace, had not yet completed a round. Uncertainly, she slowed down, as did the Kid.

This time, upon meeting Covina, the Kid turned and looked over the herd, and she did likewise. Carefully, they studied the herd, unwilling to overlook the most minute sign of a stampede.

"Hell of a pretty night, ain't it?" she tried again.

"Damn yes," the Kid said, fidgeting.

"Roll me a cigarette, Kid," she said.

The Kid gaped at her in disbelief, but she was looking over the herd and seemed not to notice. Happy to have something to do, the Kid pulled out his sack of Bull Durham and with trembling fingers and a hollow belly tried to roll her a cigarette.

"What's your name, Kid?"

"Jamie."

"You mind if I call you Jamie?"

"No," said the Kid, who rather liked the way she said it.

"Then put her there, Jamie," the girl said, extending her hand.

The Kid took her soft, sweaty hand, gave it a perfunctory shake, and then dropped it, while the tobacco spilled out of the crushed cigarette he was holding between the fingertips of his left hand.

With nerves steeled by desperation, the Kid quickly rolled another cigarette, that even in the darkness looked more like a mesquite root than a grapevine. Raising the cigarette to his lips, he was overcome with embarrassment. Covertly, he watched her until she looked away, and then quickly he turned and touched the paper to the tip of his tongue to hold it securely. Handing her the cigarette, he rolled one for himself. Turning his back and ducking his head so that the flare would not startle the cattle, he struck the match inside his vest and lighted their cigarettes. For a time they smoked in silence.

"God, ain't it quiet," she said.

"Yeah."

"You can pretty near hear your heart beat."

"Sound sure travels," he agreed, as on the other side of the herd a cow noisily relieved itself.

"Back home on a night like this there'd be dancing, and partying, and carrying on, and by next fall, more marriages than you could shake a stick at."

"You wish you was back home?"

"No, I don't reckon I can ever go back home. Not that I'd want to," she said, pouting her mouth. "There's nothing there for me. Nothing but sand and sweat. I don't miss it."

With elaborate grace she brought the cigarette to her lips, inhaled, dropped it to the ground, and blew smoke at the moon. "You know what I do miss? That old well out in the yard. That old well that was about to fall in and that old gyp water. God, I can still taste it. When it was cold it was almost bearable. Of a

Saturday, I'd go out and draw water and draw water, till I got a tubful, and Pa would go out on the porch and smoke, and watch out for somebody coming down the road. Hell, you could see them coming a day's ride away. Pa was always scared someone would look in the window and see us taking a bath. God, you should a seen us. Legs hanging over the side of the tub," she said, laughing and stuffing her hands in the pockets of her oversize trousers, as the Kid busily tried to roll her another cigarette, scattering papers and tobacco down the wind.

"Then Pa would take a bath. He always waited till last because he was the dirtiest, and me and Ma refused to bathe after him. He'd send me and Ma out on the porch to watch for him, but Ma'd say, 'Pshaw, if anybody wants to look at him, let them. I wouldn't turn my head to see any man alive.' And she wouldn't, neither. Ma'd go gather the eggs or bring in the clothes with Pa sitting in the tub yelling that he heard somebody coming down the road. I'd hitch up the team, and as soon as Pa was dressed, we'd drive to town and watch the train come in. Then Pa'd go down to the wagon yard, and me and Ma'd go to the general store or the drug store and just admire all the pretty things, and listen to folks talk—"

"You like the trains?"

"Well, that's about the only thing that ever happened. The train'd come in. Sometimes it'd stop and somebody'd get off. Drummers mostly. My, they was fine-looking men. All pink and slicked down, and as clean as cat fur. I used to wonder how they kept so clean. They'd go down to the store and talk about where-all they'd been, and what-all they'd done, and try to sell stuff, and we'd just all stand around admiring to watch."

"That's what I'm going to do," Jamie said. "I'm going to travel all over the country, and when I get off the train and go down to the drug store, folks'll say, 'That there's the engineer. I wonder where-all he's been?' "

"I learned a lot at the drug store," Covina said, accepting the cigarette the Kid had twisted together. "Why, there was places and things I'd never even heard of before. And dance.

Everone of them knew some new kind of scandalous dance. There was the Dimmitt Wriggle, and the Quanah Stomp, and the—"

"I never danced much," the Kid said, lighting their cigarettes. "Pa don't believe in having fun. All he believes in is sitting around and talking. But I ain't going to be sitting around and talking when I get to Trails End. I'm going to dance and have fun."

"I wonder if I'll be doing a lot of dancing?" Covina asked.

"I'm going to paint the town red," the Kid said. "Then I'm going to put it back like it was and do it again."

"I guess I could dance if I worked in a saloon, but then maybe I'd get tired of it."

"I'm going to do everthing there is to do, and most of them I'm going to do twicet."

"Do you think it's better to work over a saloon, where you have to dance and drink with the customers, or on your own, where maybe you're alone a lot?" Covina asked.

The Kid, who had been only half listening, heard that plain enough. He puffed on the cigarette, sending up great clouds of smoke, pretending to mull over the problem. "If it was me," he said, trying to swallow the squeak in his voice, "I'd rather work in a saloon, where there was dancing and other people."

"That's kinda what I thought," Covina said, thoughtfully chewing a fingernail. "But then there's the baby. I don't want to raise him in a saloon."

"Maybe your own place would be better."

"Yeah. I could have friends come and see me. I mean, just to talk. You could come and see me," she said.

The Kid saw amber on the semaphore. He didn't want to be just friends. He knew that if he was ever going to declare himself, it had to be now. Feeling hot and rushed, he took a heady drag of the cigarette and dropped his arm around Covina's neck, squinting his eyes and looking at her boldly. "Where you been keeping yourself?" he asked.

Covina removed the cigarette from her mouth and applied it to the hand which was hanging about her neck. The Kid jerked his hand back and stood kissing it, mentally expressing his low opinion of Pretty Shadow's veracity and the girl's virtue. "How are you supposed to look bold in the dark?" he thought to himself. "And I never should a given her that cigarette. I bet the father of that child never gave her a cigarette." He thought of saying to hell with it and quitting the chase, the watch, and the girl, not necessarily in that order. But then he would have to admit failure to Pretty Shadow. He was trying to decide whether to risk Pretty Shadow's ridicule or Covina's cigarette when the girl spoke.

"Did I burn you bad? I didn't mean to hurt you," she said. "It's just that I don't like to be rushed."

The Kid wondered if she had been talking to Pretty Shadow, too. With some misgivings, he decided to give her one more chance. "Sugar, let me buy you a drink," he said, standing a respectful distance behind her.

"You mean you got some whisky with you?" Covina asked, dropping the cigarette.

Encouraged, the Kid carefully laid his hand on her shoulder and rubbed it a little. "Sure you do, honey, you drink with me."

"Well, break it out."

"One for the—uh—"

"One for the moonlight, one for the miss, one for the mister, and one for the kiss," Covina prompted.

"I knowed you was a lady the first time I laid eyes on you," he said.

"I'm sorry I burned you," she said, with her fingertips caressing his burned hand, which was resting on her shoulder.

The world seemed to be rushing by with dizzying velocity. The Kid laid his other hand on Covina's shoulder to steady himself, and she moved against him, laying her head on his shoulder. The Kid began to feel rushed. He closed his eyes and shook his head to clear it.

"What're you doing?" she asked.

The Kid held to her tightly. "I ain't doing, honey, I'm undoing," he said, and when he opened his eyes, she was looking up at him, her mouth open. He closed his eyes again and kissed her on the neck, the ear, and the hatbrim before finding her lips.

"It's working, it's working," the Kid thought, so elated he had to suppress a shout. "Let's sit down," he said, masterfully letting his hand fall off her shoulder and slide down her back until it shaped itself around her hip.

"None of that, now," she said, catching his hand and pulling it up to her waist. The Kid grabbed for her breast, catching his little finger in the pocket of her shirt and ripping it.

"Dammit, you tore my shirt," she said.

"Here's two dollars," the Kid said, feeling for the money with one hand and her buttock with the other.

Covina leaned her hip into his trembling fingers, and arching her neck, brought up her hand and laid it across his face with a force that brought the earth to a crashing halt inches in front of his nose, deposited his hat on the ground beside him, and split his lip in two places.

Placing his hand over his roaring ear, the Kid instinctively ducked when Covina reached for him, not realizing until she caught him by the arm and began dragging him along the ground that the roaring in his ears was the herd stampeding past as Covina tried to pull him clear. Jumping to his feet and grabbing her hand, they ran to safety and turned to watch as the cattle stampeded across the campground. In the bright moonlight they could see the men, carrying hats, boots, and the baby, scramble into the wagon for safety, as the sharp hooves scattered supplies, crushed cooking utensils, and trampled the bedrolls into the ground.

"God a'mighty, we was almost killed," said Pretty Shadow, warily looking over the side of the wagon for sight of a stray but malignant steer. Every cow had disappeared.

"Hell, I wasn't worried," June said. "If you stand your ground and look them—"

"Then why wasn't you standing there looking them in the eye?" asked the Preacher.

"Too dark," said June.

"Too dark, hell," said Lampassas.

"Look at that mess," the Preacher said. "The fire is out, the bedding is all cut up, the gear is scattered from yander to yon, and the coffee pot looks like a herd of cows run over it."

As the men, shaken and dazed, climbed out of the wagon, the girl trudged into camp, followed by the Kid, who was squinting out of one red, puffy eye and holding a soiled handkerchief to his mouth.

"What in the hell—" Pretty Shadow asked, climbing down from the wagon. Presumably he was going to inquire as to what had excited the herd, but a solid blow, accurately aimed at his right eye, disposed him peaceably under the wagon.

"I don't believe that about Old Snuff, neither," the Kid said.

Chapter 7

THE Preacher scraped the hot coals off the dutch oven, lifted the lid, and satisfied that the sourdoughs were browning properly, replaced the lid and the coals and took a last look around to see that everything was in order. The beans had cooked so long that not even Pretty Shadow could say they rattled in the plate, and the beef had been chopped with the butcher knife until it was malleable.

Deciding the coffee had boiled long enough, he moved the pot to the edge of the coals and threw in a dash of cold water to settle the grounds. Satisfied that everything was ready for the men's return from the herd, he picked up the baby from under the wagon where he had been playing with a spoon, ran his hands over the baby's legs to brush off any ants or spiders that might have gotten on him, and changed his diaper. He applied coal oil to the red welts caused by mosquitoes and chiggers and tickled the baby's stomach. "There'll be milk for you as soon as the men are fed," he said, shaking the baby's tiny fist. "And I aim to rush them." The baby, good-natured now that the sun had passed, taking the prickly heat and hot, heavy air with it, stared at the Preacher in near-sighted perplexity and smiled. Hearing the men returning to the wagon, he gave the baby an old, dried biscuit to suck on and set him on the ground under the wagon where he would not be stepped on.

The day had been sultry, and the exhausted, sweat-drenched, irritable men, who had been trailing the herd since daybreak without stopping for food or drink, returned to the wagon dreaming of cool clean water, light fluffy sourdoughs, and a night of uninterrupted sleep under the stars.

"Preacher, you got any fresh water?" Lampassas asked, splashing water from the washpan at his sweat-grimed face.

"After I made the coffee and beans, I only had a little dab left, so I put it in the sourdoughs. But there's water in the barrel."

"You call that water? Back home we'd use that to make 'dobes," Lampassas said, mopping his neck with his bandana and sitting down beside the wagon. "Jamie, would you take the bucket and go down to the spring and get us some fresh?"

"Sure, Pa."

"I can't wait," June said. "I'll just start off with some of this old muddy."

"Pour me out a little," Covina said. "After you've been in the drag all day, it all tastes like mud." Dropping her hat in the wagon, she bent over and dusted out her hair. Brushing it back with the grimy, gap-toothed comb, she put her hat back on, took the cup of water from June, rinsed her mouth, and stepped around to the other side of the wagon to spit. When she returned, June was already filling his plate. Taking a plate from the chuck-box lid, Covina fell in behind him.

"You-all go ahead," Lampassas said. "I can't eat a bite till I've wet my mouth with some of that fresh water." He rubbed his bare knee where it protruded through his trousers and pointed off to the northeast. "That valley I been telling you about is up ahead. I figure on driving the herd in there tomorrow and letting them graze three or four days to rest up and put on some weight. I figure after that last stompede we can use the rest, too. Maybe patch up our bedrolls and clothes some. Repair the wagon."

"I got to have another sole," June said. "I can't tell any more when I'm barefoot."

"We'll take care of that tomorrow," Lampassas said. "Covina, soon as you finish, you relieve Pretty Shadow so he can eat. June, as soon as he eats, I want you-all to—you-all can bring back some milk. Then you and Jamie take the next watch."

June groaned at the prospect of having to milk a cow and stand a watch before he could go to sleep. "You can rest tomorrow," Lampassas said.

The Kid returned with a bucket of fresh water and triumphantly set it before his father.

"Did you get it at the spring?" Lampassas asked.

"Yeah. I reached way out in the middle and I sunk the bucket down as far as I could reach where it was real cool."

"Thank you, boy, that's real water," Lampassas said, putting his hands around the bucket. He smiled at June and Covina. "Still cool."

"All things come to them that waits," said the Preacher.

"Impatience makes a long drive," said Lampassas.

The Kid got a cup from the wagon and handed it to his father. "Let's see what she tastes like," Lampassas said, as he dragged the cup across the dark surface of the water to brush back any dust or insects the Kid might have kicked up on his way back from the spring. He plunged the cup deep into the bucket and brought it up with water streaming down the sides. "As clean and fresh as the day the good Lord made it," he said, looking about to see that everyone was watching him with proper envy. Lampassas threw back his head and drank deeply as the water ran down his face and dripped from his beard in large drops, red in the firelight.

Grabbing more cups, the Kid was dipping out fresh water for everybody when Lampassas's eyes popped open and, spluttering and spitting, he threw down the cup and began coughing so violently that the Preacher and the Kid pounded him on the back, fearing he would choke to death.

"Sheep pills," Lampassas gasped, looking at the greenish-gray balls at his feet. "There's sheep pills in the water. Somebody fouled the spring."

The Preacher dipped a cup of water from the barrel on the wagon and handed it to Lampassas. "Here, take a drink of this. It's hot and it's muddy, but it's clean."

Gratefully, Lampassas took the cup, sipping the water through his teeth to strain out any foreign matter that might have gotten into the barrel. "I have drunk everthing from alkali to mud, but that was the goddamndest stuff I ever tasted," he said, making a face and spitting.

"I know it was bad, but that ain't no excuse for cussing in front of a lady," the Preacher said. "I don't think we should encourage her no more."

"You been using that spring water to cook with?" June asked, swallowing his last bite with an effort.

"Why, sure, I've been using the best water I could get," the Preacher said. "But it's been boiled in the coffee and the beans."

"I reckon I'm through," June said, setting aside his plate of beans and cup of coffee.

"I don't believe I want nothing neither," said the Kid, who was faint with hunger.

"Oh, hell," said Covina, biting into another biscuit. "Eat. It's just grass."

"June, you got a six-shooter," Lampassas said. "I want you to go out there and find the son of a bitch that fouled the water hole."

"There is a lady present," the Preacher reminded.

"And bring the brother to me," Lampassas said.

"Tonight? How will I find him?"

"If you can't find a herd of sheep without your eyes, you might as well go ahead and eat them beans; you won't know the difference."

"Don't you think I ought to take someone to help me?"

"What in the hell would you want help for?" asked Lampassas. "You are looking for a damn sheepherder, and there ain't a damn sheepherder in the whole damn country that ain't a damn coward."

"What if this one is a exception?"

"A man becomes like the thing he follows," the Preacher explained. "A feller that follows a plow walks in a straight line looking neither to the left nor the right. Them that follows the sea becomes restless and intemperate. Men that follow the long-horn cow are reckless, resourceful, and independent. And sheep-herders are always shiftless, sheepish, and—uh—shunned."

"How do you know he don't also follow bears?" asked June.

"You got a six-shooter," Lampassas said.

"Well, what if he's got one, too?"

"Then take it away from him," Lampassas explained. "Now get going, I can't spare you any help. Jamie and Pretty Shadow have got other things to do. Jamie, you go get Pretty Shadow and bring back something for the baby. Covina, you go take the watch."

Thoughtfully, the Preacher surveyed the uneaten food after the others had gone. "I purely hate to throw away all this good food," he said. "Maybe if I was to boil it some more and not tell the boys—"

"Throw it out," Lampassas said.

"Not enough time to cook some more beans," the Preacher said. "Maybe I could get one more meal off that beef in the wagon."

"Fine."

"That'll mean we don't have any more meat," the Preacher said, picking over the few supplies left in the chuck box. "We finished the last of the sow bosom two weeks ago, and this'll finish off the beef. You know, it don't seem to me like them cows are running like they use to. There was just one killed in that last run, and we've just about et it. If they don't stompede again soon, we're going to have to go out and kill one ourselves."

"Throw it out," Lampassas said, kicking over the reshaped coffee pot. "Throw out the whole damn mess. At night, how in the hell could you tell if it was beans you was chewing?"

The Preacher threw out the food, washed the pots in the

muddy water from the barrel, pulled the bones of a steer out of the wagon, and began chopping off bits of stringy flesh. Lampassas, too angry to lie down, and too tired to do anything else, sat down on the wagon tongue and amused himself by letting the baby play with the toe of his boot.

It was far into the second watch when the men returned. Covina was still trudging dutifully around the herd as no one had come to relieve her, and the Preacher was circling the wagon, trying to placate the hungry and fretting child. The Preacher stopped his pacing to stand beside Lampassas in front of the wagon as June, Pretty Shadow, and the Kid returned to the campfire.

"That him?" Lampassas asked, indicating the small, bearded man in the dirty clothes and worn sandals who stood before the fire trying to look humble with a rope about his neck, a pistol in his ear, and his hat in his hands.

June avowed that the man standing before them was the culprit who had fouled the water hole. "You know that little valley we was planning to rest the herd in? He has his sheep in there," June said.

Pretty Shadow was of the opinion that cattle would not graze after sheep.

Lampassas was positive that fouling a water hole and ruining a range were crimes against nature.

The Kid suggested they run the sheepherder out of the country.

June allowed they should burn his tent.

Pretty Shadow was of the persuasion that killing the sheep was the best means of restoring grass to the range and purity to the water.

The Preacher suggested that they give him the milk so that he could be feeding the baby while they weighed the requirements of justice.

"We don't have no milk," said Pretty Shadow.

The Preacher inquired into the disappearance of the milk.

June explained that he and the shepherd had come across

Pretty Shadow and the Kid milking the cow, and while he was helping them let the cow go, the shepherd had drunk the milk.

All signs of human compassion, generosity, and forgiveness disappeared from the men's faces as for the first time they looked upon total depravity.

The Preacher wondered where they were going to get some more milk for the baby.

Lampassas ruled that the shepherd had the prior claim to their attention.

Pretty Shadow suggested that the shepherd be tied to the wagon where he could listen to the baby crying for milk, but Lampassas held that legally and humanely, all they could do was hang him.

The Preacher affirmed that this was right since to coddle a coyote was to raise a snake.

June wondered how they were going to hang the shepherd as there was not a grown tree within a day's hard ride.

"We'll use the wagon tongue," Lampassas said.

Pretty Shadow slipped the rope off the shepherd's head, made a noose, tied it fast to the wagon tongue, and then ran the rope across the top of the wagon and around the rear axle. Pulling the rope taut, he raised the wagon tongue until it was almost vertical and then tied it off.

June inquired as to the fashion in which the shepherd would be hung.

Lampassas replied that they would stand the shepherd on the hub of the wheel, pull the noose tight about his neck, and then push him off.

Pretty Shadow observed that the shepherd appeared to be light of weight.

Lampassas proposed that June and the Kid attach themselves to the shepherd's legs when he began to swing in order to pull the rope tight.

Pretty Shadow bound the shepherd's hands with hobble strings, tying the ends to the rope which Inocente, the shepherd, had wrapped about his waist as a belt. After which, Inocente fell upon his knees, and the Preacher shifted the baby to his left arm and placed his right hand on the prisoner's head, praying that the Lord would receive one who had worn out his welcome on earth and asking for a strong rope and a quick passage.

"Thank you, friend," Inocente said. "That was a fine prayer."

"You're purely welcome," the Preacher replied, helping Lampassas and the Kid pass him up to the wagon hub, where he was fitted for the noose.

Whereupon the shepherd asked to hear the Bible read once more, as his mother had read it to him when he was a child. Pleased with the request, the Preacher promised the others it would not take long and suggested to Inocente that he read something about shepherds. Inocente was pleased with the suggestion.

The Preacher opened his worn Bible to Ezekiel, and standing close to the lantern, began to read in a loud, complaining voice: " 'Seemeth it a small thing unto you to have eaten up the good pasture, but ye must tread down with your feet the residue of your pasture? And to have drunk of the deep waters, but ye must foul the residue with your feet? And as for my flock, they eat that which ye have trodden with your feet; and they drink that which ye have fouled with your feet.' "

The Preacher closed the Bible and placed it in the wagon. Inocente spat on the ground. "Gringo book," he said.

Lampassas granted the accused a last request. Above all things on earth, Inocente desired a cigarette. Lampassas ordered someone to roll the prisoner a cigarette, but June was holding a pistol in one hand, Pretty Shadow was too proud, the Preacher was too pious, and the Kid was too clumsy. Lampassas loosened the knots tying the shepherd's hands to his waist and allowed him to roll his own.

Inocente inhaled deeply and pleaded for his life, arguing that he was a poor man, that his mother had died reading the Bible when he was born, that his father was killed by bandits while praying in church, that he had no brothers or sisters to speak of, no wife, no children he knew of, and therefore he should be pardoned.

Lampassas accepted testimony in behalf of the prisoner.

June testified that the prisoner did not put up a fight when arrested.

The Kid testified that the prisoner had helped them find their way back to the wagon when they got lost.

"He's got a smile like a coyote," said Lampassas.

"He smells like a sheep," said the Kid.

"He almost poisoned me," said Lampassas.

"He ruined the supper I fixed," said the Preacher.

"I had to walk all over the country to find him," said June.

"He drunk the baby's milk," said Pretty Shadow.

When all the evidence had been heard, the indignant jury turned on the accused. Guilty head hanging in shame, Inocente puffed glumly on the cigarette. Lampassas pardoned the accused for the crimes of being a Mexican, being a sheepherder, crossing his path, and being in the valley he planned to make use of. For the crimes of fouling a water hole and taking milk from a baby, he found no forgiveness and passed sentence.

Inocente rubbed out the cigarette on the rim of the wagon wheel and offered one thousand of the finest sheep in the country in exchange for his life, believing that a cow man wouldn't know the difference between a sheared sheep and a woolly jackrabbit.

Pretty Shadow signified their indifference to the sheep.

June inquired as to whether the shepherd had a horse.

Inocente explained that without a shepherd, sheep were helpless, and that they would be scattered and eaten by wolves.

June explained that they were not interested in sheep but only in justice.

Inocente studied the faces of the men, and selecting the Kid, gave the sheep to him, confessing that he was not unwilling to die if the sheep were safe and explaining that they would be no trouble as they would follow the wagon.

The Kid declined to accept.

The Preacher was unable to bear the humiliation of being followed by a flock of sheep.

Pretty Shadow was of the persuasion that sheep could not be driven with cattle.

Lampassas explained that it was not lawful to take the sheep and confessed no inclination to buy them.

The baby began fretting again, and the Preacher got a biscuit from the wagon with which to reconcile him. Lampassas looked suspiciously at the biscuit but said nothing.

The shepherd testified to his willingness to die but asked that they take his dog, a faithful creature which would not leave the flock until his master called but would stay with the sheep and die of hunger and thirst, a prey of coyotes and buzzards.

June recalled once having a dog of a similar nature.

Inocente gave the dog to June.

June declined to take the shepherd's last dog.

Pretty Shadow was of the persuasion that dogs and cattle did not travel together.

Inocente swore that with the dog June would never be alone.

June recalled that he was traveling in the company of eight hundred cows.

Inocente declared that the dog was the only true friend he had ever had and that he would gladly give his life for his dog; indeed, that he had once risked his life to save the dog from a panther and bore the scars on his neck to this day.

Pretty Shadow found there were scars on his neck.

The Preacher found that they closely resembled rope burns.

"There is no place on the trail for a dog," Lampassas said. "One bark and the whole herd would just stompede to hell. I'm right sorry for the dog, but that can't be helped, so let's get on with the business at hand."

Pretty Shadow retightened the noose, and the Kid tied the prisoner's hands to the rope about his waist.

Inocente began to weep for his poor nanny goat, that only

last week lost her kid to a coyote and would now have no one
to milk her.

"Did you say milk?" June asked.

"So much milk that I have to pour it upon the ground,"
Inocente said.

Lampassas motioned the men to one side, and pretending
disinterest, they strolled over and stood talking and gesturing,
turning now and then to study the prisoner. Inocente, finding
some slack in the rope, warily sat down on the wagon wheel,
taking care not to slip off and commit suicide.

Pretty Shadow was of the opinion they should take the goat.

Lampassas held that no self-respecting cow man would
accept a goat from a sheepherder.

The Kid felt that they should humble themselves for the
sake of the baby.

Pretty Shadow believed that he could not continue his
milking chores and maintain his self-respect.

Seeing that the men had turned around and were watching
him, Inocente called to them. "Señors, is that coffee I smell?"

"Jamie, get him a cup of coffee," Lampassas said.

"And another cigarette, if you please. It's a long time to
wait. A man gets impatient."

Gaining a cup of coffee, a cigarette, and some slack in the
rope that bound his hands to his waist, Inocente sat on the
wagon wheel, smoking in contentment while the cow men de-
liberated over his fate.

Lampassas decided they should trade the shepherd out of
the goat but found he had nothing to trade. The Kid suggested
trading the saddles. Lampassas reminded him that a cow man
did not sell his saddle. The Preacher volunteered to feed the
shepherd a good meal. Pretty Shadow offered the use of his fine
shirt he had hidden in his bedroll to get married in. The Kid
offered June's pistol.

"If we give him the six-shooter, what's to keep him from
hanging us?" Lampassas asked.

Aware that he had made a fool of himself, the Kid confessed the possession of two dollars.

"Now, keep quiet, and let me handle this," Lampassas said.

Casually, the men broke up the meeting and sauntered over to the wagon where Inocente was finishing his coffee.

"Sheepherder, what would you take for that goat?" Lampassas asked.

"The nanny goat?"

"Whatever damn goat gives milk."

"Señor, I give him to you," Inocente said magnanimously.

Lampassas leaned forward and caught the rope about the shepherd's neck. "We ain't accepting no damn gifts from no damn sheepherder. We aim to buy that damn goat. Now, Pretty Shadow here has a real pretty shirt he was planning on wearing to his wedding. We'll trade you that fine shirt for your goat. See all them buttons? And how long the sleeves is? Two pockets," said Lampassas. "What do you say?"

"Who wants to be hung in a fine shirt?" Inocente asked, shrugging his shoulders.

Lampassas took off his hat, brushed back his coarse gray hair with his fingers, and slowly replaced the hat on his head. "All right, we'll give you the shirt and throw in two dollars, pilon."

"Silver?"

"Greenback," said the Kid.

Inocente rolled his eyes to heaven and shrugged. Lampassas, less sure of himself now, turned around to demonstrate the perversity of the shepherd to his friends. They shrugged their shoulders and screwed up their mouths.

"In addition to which, the Preacher here will cook you a fine meal."

The shepherd confessed that he was not hungry.

Angrily, Lampassas turned away from the fire, catching the Preacher by the arm, and with the others following, they walked a short distance into the darkness where they reconvened with a great deal of cursing and demonstrative waving. After a few minutes the group became quiet, and together they strolled back to the wagon.

"The goat gives milk?"

"More than one man can drink."

"Can one man milk her?"

"The goat loves to be milked. She was given to me by my poor old grandmother, God rest her soul, who raised the goat as one would raise a child."

"You mean the goat can be milked by a woman?" June asked.

"The easiest thing in the world."

The men whooped and struck each other with their hats until Lampassas quieted them down.

"All right," Lampassas said. "We will trade you your life for the goat. But if we ever see that depraved face again, I'll put a noose around it. June, you go with him to see that he don't relieve himself in the water hole and bring back that goat. And if you don't want him swapping you out of your six-shooter, you'd better leave it here."

Pretty Shadow slipped the noose off the shepherd's neck and untied his hands.

"Señor," Inocente said, gently rubbing his wrists where the ropes had bound them and smoothing his neck where the noose had chafed it, "to show my gratitude, I will go with you to milk the goat."

"Oh no you don't," said the Preacher. "We don't want no flock of sheep following our goat."

"But, señor, for a man who has never milked a goat, it is very hard."

Lampassas placed his hands around the shepherd's neck, and June fingered his pistol. "You said the goat was easy to milk," Lampassas shouted.

"For a man who knows how to milk a goat it is very easy, but for a man who does not know how to milk a goat, it is very hard."

"Get the rope, Pretty Shadow," Lampassas said.

"No, wait," said the Preacher, catching Lampassas with his free hand while he juggled the baby in the other. "There's no need for that. This sheepherder can teach us how to milk a goat. Can't you?"

"Teaching a man to milk requires patience and takes much time."

"We'll give you the shirt, two greenbacks, and a meal for your time," the Preacher said. "And you can start teaching tonight."

"Jamie, you've eaten," Lampassas said. "You go and relieve Covina and tell her to get herself up here so she can learn. June, you go and get that damn goat while this sheepherder's eating. And if the goat won't come, shoot it."

"All right," said June, looking about uncertainly.

Inocente pointed off to the east. June started off in that direction and then stopped and looked back. "We promised him two dollars."

Lampassas pulled off his hat, threw it down, and called back the Kid, who grudgingly dug the two dollars out of his pocket and gave them to the shepherd.

The Preacher gave the fretting baby another cold biscuit to gum and laid him in the wagon while he finished the meal he had started earlier. Inocente sat by the fire, drinking coffee and smoking cigarettes. Lampassas, unwilling to sit at the same fire as a sheep man, stood at the front of the wagon, watching the sheep man's enjoyment with increasing violence to his inner peace.

By the time Covina returned to the wagon, the meal was ready, and Pretty Shadow, having retreated somewhat from the fire, was eating in silence, while Inocente held a bone in one hand and was trying to tear the meat off it.

"Well, it took you long enough to relieve me," Covina said, pouring herself some coffee. Pushing back her hat, she looked in the wagon and checked the baby's diaper. "Little Jake been fed yet?"

"No," said the Preacher. "But it shouldn't be long now."

Covina gave a sigh of disgust at such male incompetence and taking her cup of coffee, sat down on her torn and mended bedroll. "Is that the bastard that fouled the water hole?"

"That's him," said Pretty Shadow.

"Who invited him to the table?"

"I did," said the Preacher.

"Social, ain't you?"

"We got us a goat to milk," Pretty Shadow said. "June went to get him."

"A goat. Why, we can tie a goat to the wagon and have milk whenever we want it. And that's the best milk there is for a baby," Covina said. "I was raised on goat milk myself."

"You were raised on goat milk?" Lampassas asked.

"Yeah, we used to always keep a nanny around for milk. Hell, I bet I've spent half my life milking goats."

Because he was a little man, and nimble, the shepherd jumped to his feet and disappeared into the darkness before the men could grab him. Lampassas, brandishing a carving knife, pursued him into the night.

Lampassas returned to the wagon in time for breakfast, and after the hands had eaten, the wagon was repacked, the oxen yoked, and Lampassas, wearing a fine shirt which was minus one sleeve, led out past the little green valley and bore north. Behind Lampassas came the wagon, with the Preacher on the seat, the baby in the rear, and the nanny goat tied to the tailgate. Behind the goat came Old Blue, June, Pretty Shadow, and the rest of the herd. Behind the herd in the dust and heat of the drag walked Covina and the Kid. Behind them followed three hundred ragged sheep. Twice an hour Covina and the Kid stopped prodding the drag and turned around to drive off the sheep. The sheep stamped their feet and bleated in confusion.

That night half the hands stood watch over the cattle, and the other half stood watch over the sheep, to keep them away from the cattle. On the second day, Inocente appeared and offered to take the sheep for the price of one lame steer. Lampassas threatened him, Pretty Shadow cursed him, and Covina and the Kid drove him off with rocks and cow dung. June joined Covina and the Kid in the drag, and one of them prodded the cows while the other two held back the sheep. The nanny goat was paraded back and forth across the trail to confuse the sheep, and that night half the hands stood watch over the cattle, and the other half stood watch over the sheep to keep them away from the cattle.

On the third day, Lampassas gave the shepherd the shirt, the steer, and two greenback dollars, and left June behind to guard a line he had drawn across the trail. "Shoot anything that crosses that line," Lampassas said. "And I hope to hell it's a sheepherder."

"How am I supposed to find you?" June asked.

"Wilmer's Junction is supposed to be up ahead. "We're going to stop there and rest the herd three or four days. You can catch up to us there."

As soon as the wagon was out of sight in one direction and the sheepherder in the other. June, none too anxious to resume his duties, lay down beside the line to catch up on his sleep. He was awakened by an old ewe that stood astraddle the line.

"Back up, damn you, or I'll shoot," he said, pulling the six-shooter with one hand, and pushing the sheep out of his face with the other. "I've killed before and I'll do it again."

The old, watery-eyed sheep, which had become separated from the flock, only watched him stupidly. June yelled at the sheep and slapped at it with his hat, but the sheep only blinked its eyes and turned its head. He tried to run the sheep off, but it would turn and follow him every time he stopped chasing it.

"I got to shoot it," he said reluctantly. "That's what Lampasses give me the six-shooter for. If I go back to the wagon with this sheep following me, he'll take the six-shooter away from me.

"I ain't going to give up my six-shooter," he said to the sheep, cocking and pointing the gun to scare it. The sheep watched him out of its stupid, watery eyes.

June knew the value of a gun. No one had ever noticed him until he had one. Back home he had been an orphan stable boy, cleaning out the horse stalls in Mr. Kitchell's stables. When folks saw him, they would say, "Looka there. June's been working in his gold mine again." Or, "Girls, girls, hold your nose. Here comes June in his dirty clothes." He had no friends, and when he walked down the street, girls turned their heads as though he were indecent to look upon.

June worked steadily in the dusty, ammoniac barn. He led the horses out of the stables and turned them loose in the lot behind the barn. He got the rake, shovel, and pitchfork from the harness shed and placed them in the two-wheel cart, which he pushed along the row of stalls that lined the barn on both sides. Taking the long-handled rake, he raked out the fresh droppings in the stall, shoveling them into the cart. Then he raked over the straw bedding, piling it lightly in front of the stall to allow the urine-dampened dirt floor to dry. When the cart was full, he pushed it out of the barn and across the lot where he dumped it onto the growing and aging dung heap. Twice a month he loaded the manure into the wagon and scattered it through the piny hillsides of east Texas.

At the end of the day, after filling the holes pawed in the floor, spreading out the straw bedding, feeding and watering the horses, and returning them to the stalls, June walked to Tom Kitchell's house, set back from the road on the other side of town, to eat supper, wash the dishes, and sweep the kitchen. Afterward, he would sometimes sit on the porch listening to the girls' laughter, catching the girls' smells, like wisps of honeysuckle. Sometimes he would lie down on his bed, usually with his clothes on, since they were at least as clean as the bed, and stare into the darkness out the window. The night wind carried the odors of pine, and dogwood, and honeysuckle, which got mixed up with the stable smells of the room, so that at night, to June, the whole world seemed to smell of horses and despair.

No one had ever noticed June until an old recluse from the hollow had ridden into town, killed Bert Carmichael, and ridden out again. Mr. Kitchell was too busy helping the gay, heavily armed men saddle and mount their horses to notice that June had taken the old single-barrel, muzzle-loading shotgun from the harness shed and a horse from the lot and joined the posse.

In profane brotherhood the posse had ridden out of town, making enough noise and raising enough dust to scare every recluse in east Texas. They had spent the afternoon and most of the night blasting away with alacrity at the house, splintering the wooden shutters, riddling the already blasted door, cutting away the porch posts, and chewing up the corners of the house, content with smoke and noise and flying splinters, full of the fellowship of battle.

When refreshments arrived from town, just before sunup, they fell back to regroup, to count casualties, and to refresh themselves with whisky. Old comrades were reunited, new friendships were formed with every drink. June found himself surrounded by friends, and no one mentioned his occupation or noticed the caked manure on his boots. Roll call revealed only one casualty, Roscoe Pennyworth, who had shot himself in the foot while scratching his piles with the front sight of his pistol.

At dawn, after two false starts, the men charged recklessly into the hollow, to collide breathless against the walls of the house until their accumulation burst open the door of the cabin. Broken dishes and ripped pans lay about the floor among the fallen shingles and splintered wood. The old man lay in a corner as though he had been tossed there, his beard tangled, his coat askew, his shirt-tail hanging out, his trousers twisted. A trail of ants led across the floor and up a bare and bloody foot.

Quietly, but with haste, the men backed out of the house and headed for their horses. Silently, but close together, they rode back to town to a glorious reception. Bloody deeds had been done, and the town fully intended to have its holiday. The tired, sullen men, who wanted only the forgetfulness of a drink, had to listen to a speech by the mayor acclaiming their bravery and dedication to the town's welfare. Then somebody struck up a tune on a fiddle, and they were argued over, claimed, and pushed about the floor by thrill-seeking women. Girls who had tilted their noses at June now lifted their skirts to dance with him.

One by one the men hitched up their trousers and strode across the street to the saloon where they tried to revive their spirit of camaraderie. Instead they got mean drunk and abused each other. Sadly, June left their company to sleep in the stable on a pile of hay.

"Boy," the sheriff called, without recognizing or even looking at his old comrade at arms. "Brush up my horse. I want him to look good for the funeral."

"Who are you to go to a funeral?" asked Mr. Kitchell, when June indicated a desire to attend.

"I was with the posse, Mr. Kitchell. I was in the fight. I was a part of it."

"You ain't going to no funeral. You get a rake and a shovel and get them droppings up before I get back."

June watched the funeral procession until it passed from sight behind the trees, and then he got Mr. Kitchell's shotgun and Mr. Kitchell's horse and headed for open country, just west. He rode the rest of the day and all night before stopping at a farmhouse to ask for food and a place to sleep. He swapped Mr. Kitchell's sore-footed horse for a paddle-footed pinto and rode on in the pursuit of his future.

June could find work easily, horse work, but it wasn't what he wanted. He wanted to carry a gun, so that people would notice him. He wanted to ride with brave companions, and he wanted, some day, tough of mouth, hard of eye, to go back home and strike terror in the hearts of bad men and young girls.

June sought jobs with various peace-keeping organizations, and despite rejections that would have driven lesser men to despair, June never doubted. He decided the only way to be recognized was to demonstrate his ability to dispense justice and right wrongs.

Carrying across the saddle the heavy shotgun, for which he had been unable to find ammunition, June rode in search of injustice. He was delighted to see a near-sighted Mexican beating a horse with a buggy whip. June grabbed the man by the suspender straps of his overalls the way he would grab a horse by the halter, and giving him a firm shake, said, "Quit that, now." The man reversed the whip, and reaching back over his shoulder, laid June out in the ditch with the handle. When June came to he discovered that the shotgun and the pinto were gone, and that the lick had also laid open his cheek. He was embarrassed at having a purple welt under his eye, but when it healed into a scar, he was rather proud of it as it gave him a mean look.

Without a horse and a gun, June ended up as he had begun, raking manure. When Lampassas offered him work as a cowboy, June accepted, although he didn't care much for spending all his time with cows. But when Lampassas mentioned they were going to Trails End, June knew this was what he had been waiting for. Trails End was Mecca for gunmen. All the great law men had made their reputations there shooting one another. And all the great bad men had made their reputation by going up the trail and becoming law men. To go up the trail, to stand at the bar in the Red Dog Saloon, elbow to elbow with man-killers, to see the elephant and hear the owl hoot in Trails End, that would make him somebody back home. Men would whisper his name as he passed, and young girls would shiver and clutch their throbbing breasts.

"We could use an experienced wrangler," Lampassas said.

"No sir, not as a wrangler. But I'll go to look after the herd."

"All right, I reckon we can use you."

"What about a six-shooter? I'm going to need a six-shooter if I'm going to look after the herd. I know how to use one."

"What would you use it for?"

"What if the herd stompedes?"

"What would you aim to do with it? Scare them?"

"We might run across a rattlesnake or a lobo."

"I reckon we could use one all right," Lampassas admitted. "Just in case a horse or a cow was to break a leg. But you'll have to be the one that's responsible for it. The one that does the killing."

"I've killed before," June said, picking out a heavy pearl-handled, nickel-plated, fourteen-dollar, single-action .45. "I'll need a holster."

"Don't you think we'd better leave that thing in the wagon? It's against the law to carry a six-shooter."

"But I'm carrying it to protect the herd. It'll be like I was deputized."

June walked out of the store, the heavy six-shooter dragging at his hip, and stopped on the porch to survey the town. Unfortunately, all was quiet. Not a person moved in the street. There was no sound of gunfire from any of the five buildings in town. Wet clothes flapped softly from a washline. June walked down the steps and mounted his horse, riding for the herd without a single glance over his shoulder. He hoped rustlers would try to take the herd from him.

"I reckon he ought to have a nickname," Lampassas said, as the crew looked over the new member who stood before them, his right hand resting on the pearl-handled butt of an enormous six-shooter. "It don't seem right for a cow hand to be called June."

"Hell, ain't June a nickname already?" Pretty Shadow asked.

"Don't nobody know what my name is," June said. "I was called after the month I was born."

"Lucky for you it wasn't May," Pretty Shadow said.

June turned to face Pretty Shadow squarely, his gun hand at his side. He studied Pretty Shadow's face to see if his name had been made light of. There was no trace of challenge in Pretty Shadow's eyes. June decided that Pretty Shadow was merely being friendly. He smiled and Pretty Shadow smiled in return. June let him live.

June stopped and looked over his shoulder. Sure enough, he was being followed by a sheep. "I'm going to kill you," he said, turning around and glaring at the wet-eyed sheep. The sheep bleated.

"If I'd a knowed I'd have to shoot all them crippled cows, I might not a asked for the six-shooter," June lied to the sheep. "But I got it now, and I aim to keep it. I'm going to shoot, damn you. I can't wait no longer. I got to get to Wilmer's Junction and catch up to the wagon."

Annoyed by the sheep's stupidity, June fired the pistol into the ground in front of its nose, but the old ewe only blinked its eyes and turned its head.

"I told you, damn you," June said. Cocking the six-shooter again, he shot the sheep between the eyes. The old ewe jerked, fell forward with its neck twisted, and lay quivering on the ground.

With the smoking pistol still in his hand, June looked about him guiltily. "There wasn't nothing else to do," he said. Suddenly afraid, he turned and hurried toward Wilmer's Junction, carrying the six-shooter in his hand.

Chapter 8

IN Wilmer's Junction, Maury Clegg slid his feet off the bed and paused to see if the movement had disturbed Sad Sal's sleep. It had not. Sad Sal, her mouth hanging open in a sneer, continued the low, moaning snore followed by the pitiful sigh that had inspired her name. With his feet on the floor, Maury slowly rolled off the bed and hurriedly began to dress.

Maury was a man of regular habits. Not knowing at what hour of the day or night he would be obliged to leave a place, he always laid out his clothing in the same place every night, careful as a fireman, so that he could dress in the dark quickly and quietly, without unnecessary fumbling and moving about, and without disturbing anyone who might happen to be in the bed, or listening outside the door. He put on his clothes, loosely knotted his four-in-hand, attached his genuine gold nugget cufflinks, his authentic solid-carat diamond stickpin, his money-back-guarantee gold watch with the Albert chain, and sitting down in the chair beside the bed, began putting on his shoes. They were shiny black patent-leather shoes, half a size too small and tapered to a point to catch the girls' eyes.

Maury knew from experience that four days was the maximum time he could safely spend in one town. After that there was too great a risk that the owner of the original and authentic waybill of the Lost Dutchman mine might meet the owner of an identical original and authentic waybill, and that the two of them in turn might find a third, a fourth, and a mob. All the men had sworn on their honor never to mention the waybill nor the name of the person from whom they had purchased it, but Maury had already discovered to his great sorrow what such honor was worth.

Maury had been in Wilmer's Junction six days, foolishly taking a chance because he had not been able to see Katrinka alone. Katrinka, the full-bodied, blond-haired farmer's daughter who waited on tables at the one room and cook shack Virginia Plantation Inn, had been fascinated by his gold cufflinks, his pointed shoes, and his hand-painted, orange-sunset tie. Maury had waited around Wilmer's Junction for two extra days to take her to a dance.

They had been a sensation, Maury in his yellow-checked coat and flowered vest and Katrinka in a dress cut way down to her collarbone and exposing a mole at the nape of her neck. Maury and Katrinka had demonstrated the Ringgold Wriggle and the Stamford Stomp, to the delight of the gents and the scandal of the ladies. Sweating and panting, he had swung her around, conscious of the attention the men were giving him. At first he thought it was due to his skillful dancing and the beauty of his partner. But when the men began gathering in groups of twos and threes in conspicuous places like the doors and windows, Maury began to believe that someone had broken their sacred oath and had talked about the waybill. He began looking for a way out.

Discovering how hot it was, Maury wondered if Katrinka would care to take a stroll outside. Katrinka agreed, and they walked about the grounds, accompanied by three armed men. Maury wondered if she had ever seen the inside of the livery barn at night. She had not. Maury promised her that if she would go into the barn with him and remain perfectly still, she could hear the toadstools growing. Maury escorted her inside the barn, closed the door, and leaving her listening for the toadstools, he ran through the barn and out the back door. Slipping past the

three men who stood with their ears to the barn wall, listening
for the rustle of hay, Maury sprinted down an alley, climbed the
back stairs of the hotel, and slipped into his room unseen. Grabbing his carpetbag, which was always kept packed and ready, he
was about to decamp when Sad Sal came in, flushed from over-
work.

For a moment, hope deserted him, but when he realized
that Sal did not as yet suspect anything, Maury knew he had one
last chance. Quickly, he undressed and got in bed, hoping to get
Sal asleep and to slip out of the room before the citizens came
pounding up the stairs and broke in the door demanding his
hide. Sal had other ideas. First she was hungry and had to have
something to eat. She gnawed on a turkey drumstick until the
bone looked polished, and then she had to have something to
drink. Maury encouraged her to drink, hoping she would pass out.
Instead, she felt inspired to dance. While Maury alternated between urging her to come to bed and pretending to be asleep, Sal
paraded around in her flannel nightgown, grinding away his
chances to escape.

Sad Sal, who was the official chambermaid, was unofficially
the hotel's well-used welcoming service and at the moment had
the additional duty of house detective. Sal had been assigned the
task of keeping an eye on Maury so that he did not leave without satisfying his debt to the management and, incidentally, to
Sal.

A brilliant strategist, Sal had devised a scheme for keeping
track of Maury. It seemed to her that he could scarcely walk out
of the hotel in broad daylight without paying his bills, so the
time to watch him was at night. Consequently, Sal spent each
night with Maury, going to his room as soon as her other chores
were completed.

At first, Maury had found the arrangement to his liking, but
after four days it had become restrictive. Sal was never ready for
bed when she came to his room. After work, she was restless and
hungry. After eating, she was thirsty. After two drinks, she
wanted to dance for him.

Sleepily, he would watch her puff, red-faced, about the room, her scrawny flanks flapping uncontrollably, her misshapen thighs, the color and texture of turkey skin, slapping together. Maury would doze off and wake up to find the lamp burning and Sal sitting beside him on the bed talking of her disastrous love affairs, of which there seemed to be an unending variety. While he dozed, Sal droned on, seeming neither to notice his inattention nor to care. When at last the lamp was blown out, Maury would sigh gratefully, but before he could roll over and sink back once more into sleep, Sal would begin her whining, sighing snore. Maury built nightmares around those snores, full of trains, and mourning, and weeping women. He would awaken in a cold sweat to find Sal's hand reaching for him in the darkness. Sad Sal had a habit of reaching across the bed in her sleep to feel if he was still there; a habit, he supposed, of her trade. It always gave him a start to find her checking on him in her sleep, and he would lie awake scarcely daring to move.

Maury sweated profusely while putting on his shoes, knowing that the long flabby arm would fall across the place where he was supposed to be; and not finding him there, Sal would wake up and see him sitting fully dressed in the chair, struggling with that damn shoelace.

Fully dressed, Maury picked up the carpetbag, and opening the door, peered down the hall. The corridor was empty and no lights shone under the doors. Noiselessly, he slipped out into the hall, pulled the door closed behind him, made his way to the end of the corridor, and stepped through the window to the outside staircase, where day was breaking in the street. Now all he had to do was get out of town, walk down the road a piece, and wait under a shade tree for the mail hack to take him to Mobeetie. With a carefree air, after poking a cigar between his lips so he'd remember not to whistle, Maury started down the stairs.

He had almost reached the bottom of the steps when he heard someone coming down the street. He pressed himself into the long early morning shadows and watched a delegation of men,

carrying stones, clubs, a rail, a tub of something black, and two
bulging sacks of feathers, stop in front of the hotel.

"Maury, Maury," he heard Sad Sal calling. "Help, help, he's
gone!" Whereupon the delegation seemed to be sucked into the
hotel with a banging of doors and breaking of glass. Maury rushed
down the remaining steps and peeked around the corner to as-
sure himself that all the men had entered the hotel. Not daring
to cross in front of the hotel, he turned and hurried down the
street, swinging the carpetbag. Which brought him to the attention of several playful dogs. The dogs barked merrily as they followed Maury. The delegation erupted from the hotel in something resembling an explosion and ran after Maury, splashing tar
and scattering feathers down the street. Maury spit out the cigar,
pulled his hat down tight on his forehead, and ran in earnest.

Old Man Seibert, who lived in a one-room shack at the end
of town, was awakened by the noise and excitement, and, near-
sighted and drunk, believed the town was being attacked by
Indians. Grabbing his shotgun, he ran out of the house in his
red woolies and discharged both barrels of the shotgun down the
middle of the street, ruining three hats and a set of false teeth,
and raising a cloud composed of equal parts of dust, smoke, and
feathers. The old man was reloading when he was knocked down
and tripped over by a half dozen people carrying a tub of tar and
two bags of feathers. The men emerged from the dust and smoke
at the end of town, brushed the feathers from their faces, and
discovered that Maury was no longer with them.

In the confusion, they took the man covered with tar and
feathers to be Maury, and pounded Old Man Seibert with sticks
and stones. When the mistake was finally cleared up, the old
man was roughly treated for getting in the way, and the posse
was split into searching parties.

The dogs got wind of Maury behind a privy and began barking, bringing the posse in a run. Maury jumped up and started
back through town after first colliding with Old Man Seibert, who
was standing in the middle of the street trying to reload his tar-

smeared shotgun while waving one fist in the air and yelling, "Come back, you red bastards, I'm not through yet."

Maury hit the old man about chest high and they went down together in a heap with the dogs. Maury extricated himself from the sticky old man, beat back the dogs with his hat, and ran for his life.

The old man got unsteadily to his feet and waved an angry fist in the air. "By God, I been shot at with everthing you got, boiled in oil, and run over by a pack of horses, but I ain't through yet."

He was loading his shotgun when he was knocked down and tripped over by a half dozen people who were carrying a fresh tub of tar and three sacks of feathers. "Forget about me," the old man groaned, as they tried to pull him from the pool of tar. "Save the women and children."

In the interest of speed, Maury dropped the carpetbag, spilling the contents: original and authentic waybills to the Lost Dutchman mine, a roll of cowhide, a vial of chicken blood, two worn brushes, some rather effete underwear, a roll of greenbacks, a bottle of whisky, and a bottle of Honeysuckle Hair Tonic and Dandruff Remover. The men stopped to divide the money, sample the whisky, and admire the underwear. When they remembered Maury, they discovered that he was well out of town and still running. With their firearms, they sped him on his way.

While the herd rested and grazed contentedly in the little valley below, the herders sat around the wagon repairing boots, sewing up torn clothing, washing personal items, feeding the goat, and cussing sheepherders. The Preacher was trimming Pretty Shadow's hair with a straight razor, and Covina was lying in the shade of the wagon teasing the baby's stomach. No one turned to watch as a man, his face swollen and angry from exertion in the sun, his clothing dirty and torn, limped up the little rise to where the wagon stood.

Leaning against the wagon for support, Maury mopped his face with his handkerchief, pulled off his hat, brushed it on his sleeve, and fanned himself with it. "Howdy, gents," he said. Without stopping their work or looking at him, they nodded.

"Hot day for a walk, ain't it?" he said, sizing them up. They allowed that it was without finding it necessary to speak.

Eyeing them shrewdly, Maury pulled a cigar out of his vest pocket and chewed on it. "Nice goat you got there," he said, removing the cigar from his teeth and spitting in the general direction of the goat to indicate that that goat, which was the only goat within sight of eye or knowledge of man, was the goat to which he was referring. The hands turned to look at the ragged, gotch-eyed goat. "Never hurts to have a goat when you're camping out," Maury assured them.

With a disconsolate eye, Maury looked about to see what they had that he could possibly want. The dirty, ragged men obviously had nothing of their own. The wagon belonged in a museum or a junk yard; and while he was no expert on cattle, the herd scattered in the valley looked like the greatest collection of soup bones ever assembled. Maury wondered if they would be of any value to a circus or maybe a zoo. Although he could not discover them, cows and cowboys meant horses, and even a shirttail outfit like this one should have one horse that was fit to ride. Maury needed a horse.

"I wonder if you could spare a cup of coffee?" Maury asked.

"Help yourself," said the Preacher.

Taking a cup, Maury poured himself some coffee from the pot kept hanging at the edge of the fire.

"Man at the pot," yelled June, who had quietly rejoined the group during the night.

"What say?"

"That means while you're at the pot, you got to give everone a refill that wants it," explained the Preacher.

"Surely," Maury said, good-naturedly picking up the heavy, battered coffee pot and making the rounds pouring coffee, nodding his head, smiling, and patting the boys on the shoulder. One of them, a young boy, was lying in the shade of the wagon with his hand on a bundle of rags. Maury looked at him curiously, but the boy ignored him.

Taking up his cup, Maury found it harder to sit down than he had anticipated. He was too fat to squat, and he didn't know how to sit cross-legged the way the others were sitting. Bending over, he set his cup on the ground, then sat down sideways beside it.

"Ain't there a town over thataways?" the Preacher asked.

"That's right, that's right," Maury said. "I come from there this morning."

"Any excitement over that way?"

"Oh, that. Could you hear that from here? That was a big celebration."

"Sounded like a fare-thee-well," June said.

"That's right, that's right," Maury said, wide-eyed and chuckling. "They was giving me a big send-off."

"Seemed to me I heard shooting," Lampassas said.

"Must a been the drum you heard, brother."

June stared at something white fluttering from the shoulder of Maury's coat. "Seems to be something stuck to your coat," he said.

Maury reached over his shoulder to remove the last memento of his encounter with Old Man Seibert. Together they looked at the black, gummy smear with three puffy, soiled feathers adhering to it, and then Maury solemnly wiped the feathers off on a rock. "Would you believe I was run out of town?" he asked.

They would.

Maury leaned forward to speak in confidence; and after looking around to be sure no strangers were eavesdropping, he tapped the breast pocket of his coat with the hand holding the cigar. "But they didn't get what they was after," he said, sitting up and watching them.

No questions were forthcoming, so Maury cleared his throat, studied their faces, and leaned forward again. "I have found the only true and authentic waybill to the Lost Dutchman mine."

While Maury nodded his head in satisfaction, the herders said nothing, watching him.

"Gold mine," he said carefully, wondering at their ignorance. "Written by an Apache chief on a piece of buckskin in his own blood." Again the herders said nothing, watching him warily. "You're asking yourself how I come to have this treasure," Maury said, interpreting their looks. "How this map has eluded the wealthy and wise to be possessed by me." He took a long swill of coffee which puckered his lips and brought tears to his eyes, and for a moment chewed on the cigar, reading their thoughts. "Would you believe me if I told you I won this waybill in a poker game with a drunk army scout?"

The hands shook their heads as a token of their unbelief.

"If I told you I found the waybill in an old trunk in a house burned down by Indians, would you believe it?"

Again the men demonstrated their little faith.

"Then, gentlemen, this story will test your credulity," Maury said, clamping the cigar between his teeth and nodding his head. And while the herders darned socks, mended shirts, and rinsed underwear, Maury told them the tale of the true waybill.

In his extensive travels about the country, Maury had once come upon an old Indian who had been wounded in the side and thrown in a ravine to die. The poor Indian, sick with his wounds, was unable to crawl to the water hole a few feet away and was thus dying of thirst and treachery. Maury took pity on the Indian, bound up his wound, gave him water, and tried to make him ready for the great trek to the happy hunting grounds. The Indian took Maury's hand, drew him close, and pulled the knife from Maury's belt. Maury shrank back in horror, thinking his own end near; but the Indian made a sign of brotherhood and motioning Maury closer, confessed that he was not a poor Indian but a great chief, and because Maury had shown himself a brother, he was going to make Maury a rich man. With the knife, the chief cut a corner from his breechclout. Then, pulling the hair from his head, he twisted it into a crude brush, dipped it into his bloody wound, and on the buckskin breechclout he drew up the waybill to the Lost Dutchman mine.

"Gold mine," Maury said.

"If you bound up his wound, how did he dip the brush in it?" asked June.

"It was a deep wound," Maury said. "Come out the other side."

The men began stretching and moving about, and Maury knew he was about to lose his audience. "Maybe you'd like to see it," he suggested.

"Sure, bring it out," Pretty Shadow said.

"Let me speak frankly," Maury said, patting the breast of his torn coat. "Getting this map cost me a lot of money."

"How did giving a dying Indian a drink of water cost you money?" Pretty Shadow asked.

Maury looked at him and blinked once. "Finding him cost me a lot of money. It was finding him that cost the money. And to be frank with you gentlemen, I am a little short of capital and a little down on my luck. That's why I'm going to offer you a look at this waybill, a quaint and authentic museum piece, for the price of one horse."

The herders looked at each other and laughed.

"I'll tell you what I'll do," Maury said, prepared to bargain. "I'll give you-all a look at this waybill drawn in human blood and tell you how it come to be in my possession, all for the price of one horse."

"We done heard it," June said.

"But did I tell you about the beautiful Indian maiden, the old chief's daughter that I found hiding half naked in the rocks and later became the toast of New Orleans?"

"I don't believe we want to hear that story," the Preacher said.

"We don't have a horse," Lampassas said. "But if we did, we wouldn't trade it for ten gold mines."

"And we ain't trading for the goat, neither," June said.

Maury sat on the ground in defeat. Never before had he left

a place without making something off of it. Once more he looked about him, looking for something, looking for anything to salve his pride. After some cogitation and chewing of the cigar, Maury decided that the young gent lying in the shade of the wagon was in reality a young girl in a young gent's clothing. Having decided that, he next decided that the bundle lying beside her was a baby. But Maury could not decide what the girl was doing there nor what was the significance of the baby.

"That's a nice-looking baby you got there," he said, carefully watching the men to see which one displayed signs of ownership. "Boy or girl?"

"Boy," said Covina.

Again Maury studied the rather unlikely-looking candidates, none of whom seemed to have the application necessary to engender a child. "Who's the proud father?"

"Sure as hell ain't you," Covina said without looking at him.

"That's right, that's right," Maury said, removing the cigar so he could chuckle at the joke and then replacing it so he could study the girl. "There ain't nothing better than a cup of coffee on a fine morning with a pretty girl and a pretty baby," he said, flashing his eyes and smiling at Covina.

"Bullshit," said Covina.

Maury chewed on his cigar and thought some more. It wasn't much but it seemed to be all they had to offer. "Where you boys headed?"

"Trails End," Lampassas said.

"Just where I was headed," Maury said. "Mind if I tag along with you?"

"There's nothing to stop a feller from walking behind the cows if he's a mind to," Lampassas said. "But if he's going to sit by my fire, he's going to have to drive them during the day and stand a watch at night."

Maury didn't know what the work entailed; but he was of a mind to string along, at least until such time as he could make something off the girl. Which, in his estimation, wouldn't take long.

However, he had not foreseen the closeness of the group nor the fondness the men felt for Covina. Throughout the day, she was never alone. When she took the watch, Lampassas walked it with her. When she sat down to eat, she was surrounded by the men. At night, when she threw down her bedroll, other bedrolls were thrown nearby in a rough square, while Maury had to share the soogans of whoever was on watch. And strange to say, no matter whose soogans they were, Maury always found them on the other side of the wagon by themselves.

Lampassas held the herd in the valley two extra days hoping Maury would leave; and then, unable to wait longer, he had pointed the herd north once again, reluctantly putting Maury in the drag with Covina and the Kid. Steadfastly, the Kid imposed his virtue between Maury and the girl.

Covina, bored with the monotony of the drive, was pleased to see a new face. She was even more pleased to find that the new face was interested in her. As a woman. Since the Kid's awkward and abortive attempt, no one had looked at her like a woman, not even the shepherd. She was flattered by Maury's interest, amused by the attempt of the hands to protect her from him. Covina was determined to see Maury and to see him alone, not only for her own amusement but also to show the drovers. They had thought evil of her, and now she was going to give them something to think about. She smiled as she thought of herself as a Scarlet Woman. Bold, shocking, yet secretly admired for her beauty and daring.

Covina had always wanted to be bold, courageous, daring. She had wanted to be the Joan of Arc of the Indians, or temperance, or suffrage, or free love. But living on a farm offered few chances for daring causes; and boldness, courage, and daring, while considered virtues in a man, were considered vices in a woman. Her father called her tomboy, let her do a man's work, and was ashamed of her for doing it. Her mother chided her, thought her silly; and when she looked at Covina's rough, sunburned face and callused hands, she shook her head and bit back her tears, afraid Covina would be an old maid.

Her mother had reason to be afraid. The boys she knew seldom thought of her at all and never as a girl. Boys helped other girls into the wagon, but Covina tucked up her skirts and climbed over the wheel. They held the door for other girls while Covina slapped it back against the wall. They danced with other girls while Covina sat alone or played mumblety-peg with the rough boys in a corner. And after a dance, the boys found a special girl to sit beside on the ride home while Covina sat alone, chewing straw or making a whistle out of a leaf. At such times she did not feel bold and daring but lonely and afraid; so she did foolish things, like slipping away from a dance with some boys to steal watermelons, smoking cigars on a dare, and getting drunk with Wilfred Gidney behind the mule barn.

And then John Scott Renovard came selling lightning rods with engraved, beribboned, lifetime guarantees. When John Scott came to their house, Covina and her mother stared open-mouthed at the elegant man and the elegant certificates, but her father picked up the shotgun and ordered the drummer off the place.

The next Saturday, Covina saw John Scott again, this time in town. John Scott was fingering an indecent watch-fob charm and talking to a group of sunburned farm boys in overalls and brogans, who admired his finery and eloquence and giggled at his jokes, snickering and jabbing one another with elbows. Covina, embarrassed because of the snickering boys, and because of the inhospitable way her father had treated John Scott, walked by pretending not to see him. But John Scott dismissed the boys, caught up with her, and walked beside her down the street.

Covina was flattered by his attention but afraid to be seen talking to him on the street. When John Scott asked if he could call on her, Covina said no because her father would not allow it. When he asked if she would meet him on the road by her house, she said yes because it was daring, because no man had ever noticed her before, and because she wanted him to go before her father caught her talking to a drummer in public and shot them both.

Covina's courage almost failed her; but because it was daring and bold, she slipped out of the house as soon as her parents were asleep and ran far enough down the road so that they would not hear the buggy stop. John Scott came along, helped her into the buggy, and drove past the house to the top of a little rise. There was nothing to see. The moon filtered down through light clouds and shone over flat, treeless fields and waste places. The wind blew over the plains, tangling her hair.

"God, do people really live here?" John Scott asked, depressed by the desolate view.

Covina had never heard anyone disparage the country before. Whenever she mentioned wanting to get away, the boys, who were fiercely proud of the flat dry land which was either intemperately hot or intemperately cold but always windy and always sandy, had become fiercely angry. But now she saw it as he saw it, a dead, dry, hopeless country; and she wanted to get away. John Scott told her about a valley, the San Joaquin valley, where there wasn't any sand, and there wasn't any wind except a cool breeze from the ocean at night, and the sun was gentle and didn't burn your face or freckle your skin.

Silently, John Scott took her hand and stroked it. "I'm afraid they're kinda rough," Covina said. "That's from working in the field. Mama says it'll ruin my face and bleach my hair."

John Scott touched her face with his fingertips and ran his hand over her hair.

"Mama's afraid I'll get freckles and wrinkles and my hair will get stiff and stringy. Mama wants me to be soft and fluffy."

"A girl should be soft and fluffy," John Scott said, feeling her softness.

"Don't," Covina said.

John Scott felt sorry for her. She was just a kid, alone with a man for the first time, and there was no one who could hear her, and no one likely to happen down the road. John Scott thought of giving her a stern lecture about meeting strange men at night and then taking her home. Then he remembered how her father had chased him off and he decided to show the old bastard. "Now, there ain't no need of that," he said. "You come of your own free will."

Afterward, as always, he felt some remorse. "I'll come by tomorrow night and take you to California," he said, almost believing it himself. He waited for her to answer, but she did not. "Maybe I'd better not stop," he said, watching the house. "It might wake up your father." And when he reached over to squeeze her hand as a token of gratitude and sincerity, he found that she had already jumped out of the buggy.

"He's not coming back," she said, yet the next night she slipped out of the house again to wait beside the road with her bag. For a long time she stood listening, knowing that he was not coming. She sat down on the bag and after a time dozed off, waking with a start. At the first warning of dawn, she picked up the bag, dried her eyes, and walked back to the house.

Three months later she stopped working in the field and told her mother why. Her mother told her father. Her father came into the bedroom where she was waiting for sleep, slapped her, called her names, and hoped she would die. At the breakfast table he would hardly look at her; but at night he would come to the supper table filled with a whole day's anger and frustration; he would abuse her until she ran from the house in tears. She tried going without supper, but he would come into her room, call her evil names, and drag her into the kitchen to wait on him. "You'd better get used to it," he said. "This is all that's left for you."

She thought of killing herself. She thought of killing the baby. She thought of running away. She thought she could not endure her father's hatred any longer. She thought she could not stand her mother's eyes, accusing her for causing her father's misery. She lay awake at night, sometimes crying out of pity for herself, sometimes wishing she would die out of hatred for herself. And then she had her fill of it. Not only of her father's abuse but also her own self-pity. "It's all a lot of crap," she said, resolving to do whatever she had to do to raise the child.

When her father next began his tirade, heaping his scorn and shame on her, she watched him without tears. "You've ruined ever chance you ever had. You've ruined ever plan I had for you. Ever thing I ever did, I did for you, and you ruined it."

"Bullshit," Covina said.

Her father stopped, his mouth open. Her mother began to cry softly. "I'm not taking any more of that crap," Covina said. "You're thinking of yourself and I'm thinking of myself. And as soon as the baby is big enough to travel, I'm leaving. So until then, let's just forget about it, because if you don't leave me alone, I'll stay right here and have another one just for you."

"How are you going to take care of a baby by yourself?" he asked.

"I'm a woman," she said. "I got ways."

The way her father looked at her, she thought he was going to hit her, but instead, he put down the knife and fork he was holding and left the table. He never spoke of the baby again. When the baby came, he stayed in the field although the doctor's buggy was clearly visible from where he was working and although it remained at the house for fifteen hours. He never held the baby and looked at him only when necessary. Covina's mother played with the baby and carried him about but only when her husband was in the field and not likely to know.

Neighbors still occasionally dropped by the house. At first Covina stayed in her room; but after the baby came, she would sit with her parents on the porch, talking to the company, all of them pretending there wasn't a bastard in the house. When the baby cried, Covina would go inside, feed or change the child, and then return as if nothing had happened.

Once the Bishops, a poor family nesting in a dugout down the road, stopped by to visit; and Mrs. Bishop hinted that her half-wit son was thinking of getting married and might be willing to take Covina to the dance. Covina's parents thought it would be nice for her to get out for a change.

"Bullshit," Covina said, getting up and going into the house, leaving her parents to pretend nothing had happened, and the startled Bishops to find the way to their wagon alone. When her mother came in to reprimand her, she found Covina packing her bag; and although she sat down on the bed and cried, she did not ask her to stay.

Covina started out bravely enough, riding in the back of Mr. Bishop's wagon as far as Slicknasty Creek and then cutting across country, stopping at farmhouses for milk and something to eat. But when, wet and hungry, she stood with the baby beside the river with no way to cross, she knew how hopeless getting to Trails End was. When the Kid found her, she was sitting in the rain, unable to go forward, ready to die before going back.

When Maury Clegg joined the drive, Covina watched him shrewdly, recognizing him as the kind of man with whom she would have to deal. And when Maury let some cows stray so that the Kid would have to chase them, leaving them alone, Covina listened to what Maury had to say.

"With the proper handling you could go far," Maury said, and although it didn't look very promising, he figured he could turn a buck or two. "I could help you."

"What do I need you for?" she asked.

"What are you going to do, sit back and wait for them to find you? Too slow. Go out and find them? Too much competition. What you need is someone to handle you, drop your name in the right places. A little advertising. You can't hang out a shingle, you know."

"I hadn't thought about that."

"You want to talk?"

"When?"

"I'll let you know," Maury said, having to break off the conversation as the Kid returned with the strays. But he felt better now. At least he had something to work on.

The Kid lost no time in reporting the fact that Maury had been alone with Covina.

"We've got to do something," said the Preacher, who was washing Little Jake in the dutch oven. "We got ample evidence that she can't handle men on her own."

The men agreed to double their surveillance, that Covina and Maury were never to be left alone, that if there were strays, either Covina or Maury would chase them, but never both of them at the same time, and that Maury would not be encouraged to travel with them. They left the meeting, each man resolved in his heart to protect the helpless girl from the snares of the deceiver.

"Up ahead there is Sandy Creek, and beyond that is Buttermilk Flats," Lampassas said to Maury, who was tired and disinterested. "We could cross Sandy Creek and make good time across the flats, but what I keep thinking is, suppose there's not any water in the creek. And this time of the year, there might not be a blade of grass on the flats. So I was thinking of maybe swinging down Sandy Creek and crossing it at Three Mile Fork."

Maury said nothing, and in fact appeared not to be listening, looking about him without curiosity.

"That seems like it'd be a good idea, but there's one hitch. That would throw us close to the settlements. Why, we'd be near able to see Tascosa, we'd be so close. What I'm afraid of is that one of the hands might take it in his head to walk over to Tascosa to get a drink or see the girls, and not even come back. What do you think?"

"Suits me," said Maury.

"No sir, I couldn't sell this six-shooter even if I wanted to. Not even for a gold mine," June said, pulling out the pistol and aiming it across the bedded herd, squinting one eye so that the scar on his cheek looked raw and mean. "This six-shooter was give to me for a special purpose," he said, hoping Maury would ask what the purpose was, but he didn't.

"This six-shooter was give to me for the protection of this herd and them are with it. And that's what I aim to use it for.

If I have to. Anybody that comes to hurt the herd or any of the hands is going to come to hurt, hisself," June said, wiping the pistol under his armpit to clean it and shoving it back into the holster.

"Worth about four dollars," Maury figured, fingering the map inside his coat pocket.

"There ain't nothing lower than a man that don't carry his share of the load," the Kid said.

Maury, who had his head down against the afternoon sun, his eyes squinted, and his mouth closed against the dust, seemed not to hear. The herd moved slowly, heavily before them. Covina was chasing strays on the right flank. The Kid sized up Maury. The way he figured it, Maury had weight and experience; and he had youth, reflexes, and right on his side.

"Except maybe for a drummer," the Kid said, walking close beside Maury. Too close, so that they frequently bumped together. "I said a drummer. There ain't nothing lower than a drummer, is there?" he asked, poking Maury with an elbow. Maury vaguely nodded.

The Kid paused to spit the dust out of his mouth, and then caught up with Maury. "I never seen a drummer yet that I couldn't lick. One hand tied behind me. I never seen one yet that wasn't a thief. And a liar. A son of a bitch," he shouted. "I think you're yellow. You want to fight? I'm not afraid to fight you."

The Kid danced alongside Maury, occasionally stopping to spit the dust from his mouth, while Maury plodded along, no longer even trying to save his fancy, sharp-pointed shoes from the piles of cow droppings.

"There ain't nothing lower than a man that'd trifle with a girl," the Kid said. "You leave her alone or you'll have me to deal with. You bother her and I'll let you have it. I'll give you a thrashing you won't soon forget. Do you understand? Do you hear me?" he asked, giving Maury another shove. "Keep away from her."

"When I'm on guard and the others are asleep," Maury thought. "That would be the best time."

"Goodness is like a river," the Preacher said. "It runs deeper in some folks than it does in others. Sometimes there don't appear to be nothing there atall. But that's a delusion. It's just underground where a man has to probe a little to find it. He has to clear a way for it. But I believe it's there in all men," the Preacher said, watching Maury, who was looking over the wagon to see what was worth stealing.

"I believe that in ever man there is a spark of goodness, and when that spark is found and fanned to life, a man starts thinking of others instead of just hisself. I don't believe any man, if he'd stop and think about it, would want to hurt a young girl and a little baby. Do you?"

There was nothing in the wagon except the steer carcass, the useless saddles, and the bedrolls. Maury decided to go through the bedrolls the first chance he got in case the men had anything valuable rolled up in them. There was nothing in the chuck box but cheap staples and medicine and the Preacher's Bible. Maury wondered if the Bible was worth anything. You could sell the Bible to almost anybody. But this one was so old and worn he had his doubts. Nobody wanted a used Bible. He picked up the Bible and leafed through it. He might be able to use the family tree and the records. Make him look respectable. Or maybe he could sell the Bible to an orphan who needed family background.

The Preacher, seeing that his words had set Maury to reflecting and reading the Bible, decided to drive the message home. "The feller that puts others first don't come in last," he said.

"I'm minded of the feller that was out on the prairie alone and got his horse stole," Pretty Shadow said. Maury was already in his soogans, but Pretty Shadow was still sitting, smoking, and passing the time of day.

"Of course, there wasn't nothing for him to do but pick up his saddle and strike out for the closest civilization. Which he done. He walked along bad-naming the thief and whoever made such a heavy saddle, when it come to him that there was something following him. He looked around and there was three familiar steers, lean and snaky, their noses stuck out and their eyes sunk back into their heads. He yelled and waved at them, thinking to run them off, but they just looked at him, so he turned around and started walking again, the steers right behind him. They followed him the rest of the day, but he didn't mind; he was kinda glad of the company. He walked as far as he could and lay down to go to sleep. But them steers wouldn't let him sleep. They started bawling, and nosing him, and keeping him awake. He sat up and they just stood there waiting for him to lead them some more. He tried running them off, but before he'd be good asleep, they'd be back nosing him and bawling some more. Finally, he just got up and struck out again, them steers right in behind him.

"It got to worrying him having them steers tagging along behind him, so he tried to run them off. He throwed rocks at them, but they'd just trot back a ways and wait for him to start moving again. He tried throwing his saddle on one of them to ride, but they'd just back off, and he got to where he couldn't lift the saddle any more, but had to leave it. He tried running away from them but they'd run along behind him. He tried hiding but they'd find him ever time. And ever time he'd lay down to rest, they'd start bawling and nosing him, trying to get him started again.

"We spotted him one day while we were out trying to cut the trail of some lost horses. The poor feller was trying to lay down and die, but them steers wouldn't let him. When we picked him up he was so thin we had to wrap a blanket around him to keep him together, but them steers followed us right on back to the wagon. They was so dried up and poor, we had to throw water on them to stretch their hides before they could eat."

Maury had been pretending to be asleep and must have succeeded because Pretty Shadow stopped. After a moment of silence, Maury rolled over and looked at Pretty Shadow. "That all of it?"

"Well, sir, for the first week, it was real close. The feller near died of superstition. But when he got well enough to put his pants on, he had the boys throw them steers and tie their tails together, and then he took off running for a mesquite thicket with them three steers right behind him."

Maury, who knew a come-on as well as anybody in the business, knew he was trapped. "What happened?" he asked, against his better judgment.

"Well, sir, them three steers caught their tails on a big mesquite, and run right out of their skins."

With a sigh, Maury rolled over and closed his eyes.

Pretty Shadow took a long drag off the cigarette and tossed it into the fire. "Out here a feller oughtn't to get too familiar if he wants to keep his hide," Pretty Shadow said before turning in.

"Covina," Maury whispered. "Meet me in the draw."

Covina waited until she couldn't hear Maury moving about any more, then rolled over and sat up. Everyone seemed to be asleep. Slipping out of her soogans, she picked up her hat and boots and listened a moment for the baby. Little Jake's breathing was regular, so she stepped over the Preacher's body and stopped by the wagon to put on her hat and boots, then followed Maury to the draw. "You're supposed to be on watch," she said, catching up with him.

"June's looking after things."

"What do you want?"

"I want to help you."

"Bullshit."

"You're going to have to stop saying that," Maury said. "A whore's got to look respectable. That means she has to know how to dress, act, and talk like a lady."

"I already know how to act like a lady."

"And how to take orders. From now on I'll tell you who to see, what to do, and how to do it."

"Hell, I might as well be married."

"Turn around and let's see what you've got that we can use," Maury said, examining her. "We can't say much about your figure. No bust and no hips."

"Hey, cut that out."

"Nothing special about your face."

"Stop pawing me."

"Maybe there's something I'm missing," Maury said doubtfully. "Can you sing?"

"Hell no. Lampassas won't even let me sing to the cows."

Maury walked around her again, and even in the darkness, even dressed in pants and a shirt, he knew for certain. Covina would not do. Not worth two dollars if you threw in a silk dress and a feather bed. "You'll do fine," Maury said. "But first there's a few things you'll need to know. I'll teach them to you."

Maury was scarcely into the first lesson when Covina struck him in the stomach with her elbow, and when he reached out a hand to steady himself, she grabbed it and threw him to the ground. When he looked up, she was pulling back the hair from her face and tugging at her sleeves, apparently ready for another lesson. Maury decided she had learned enough for one night and sent her back to the wagon, staying on the ground until he was sure she was gone.

For a moment he just thought of giving up and admitting defeat. The girl wasn't worth talking about and the men had nothing of value, so there was nothing he could make off them. Maury very nearly resigned himself to failure, but his years of practice, the habits of a lifetime stood him in good stead. If they didn't have anything that was of value to him, then he would take what was valuable to them. Getting to his feet, he sneaked back to the wagon to look for their treasures.

"He disappeared sometime during the night," June said. "The first time around, I figured maybe he had gone to the bushes, but when I didn't see him the second time around, I thought I'd better check."

"He's gone," Lampassas said quietly, and the men looked at Covina, peacefully asleep in her soogans.

"Maybe we ought to leave before he comes back," the Kid said.

"He won't come back," the Preacher said. "We won't see no more of him."

"We run him off," Lampassas said. "We saved the girl."

Solemnly, the men nodded their heads, their hearts swelling with the satisfaction of a job well done. Clapping one another on the back in wordless fraternity, they went quietly to bed to lie sleepless with virtue.

"The Last Survivor of Little Big Horn," Maury thought. Not believable. "The Last of the Texas Steers." Not important enough. "The Last of the Five Thousand." Not familiar enough. "A Bull and Bear Contest."

Maury looked back at the cow plodding along behind him at the end of a rope. It had horns. Now if he could just find somebody who owned a bear. The thin, tangle-horned cow stopped to graze, jerking the rope. Maury turned around and struck the cow over the head with the heavy Bible. The cow raised its head, and chewing a mouthful of grass, patiently followed.

"This Bible Was Taken in the Battle of the Little Big Horn by an Indian Chief Who—" "This Bible Saved the Life of Billy Dixon at the Battle of Adobe Walls—" Maury looked at the Bible. What it needed was a bullet hole and maybe some blood stains. If he had taken the pistol. "I Found the Lord at Little Big Horn—Out of the Clutches of Sitting Bull He Lifted Me— I Was a Tinhorn Gambler Until Jesus Cut the Deck."

Maury's thoughts went back to the pistol. If he'd had time, he'd have gotten the pistol and the girl. Not that the girl was worth much, he thought, touching his stomach, which was still unsettled. But the pistol was worth at least four dollars. Cash. That would have given him some working capital. The cow and the Bible were long-term investments requiring patient preparation, careful marketing, and ready cash.

Maury stopped and looked at the goat tied to the cow, worth three or four dollars as it stood. Maybe he could even teach it some tricks. "This goat once belonged to General George Custer," he would say. "What kind of an Indian was Sitting Bull?" "Baaaad," the goat would say.

Chapter **9**

MARTIN FOSTER became aware of a trickle of dirt falling in his ear. Then he felt something drop lightly onto the bed and scamper away. Some small, harmless, burrowing creature, he decided. Martin pulled the counterpin of stitched flour sacks over his head to ward off any falling centipedes and rolled over against a wet and messy child. Grunting, he turned again, rolling this time against the knotted back of his wife. Sliding his hand along her angular body, he felt his way to her dry, stringy breast, pinching the hard button of her nipple between his fingers. His wife responded by jabbing him in the eye with her sharp elbow. Martin, annoyed at such a reception, gave her a sharper pinch, and when she tried to back away from his hand, brought up his knee, thumping her in the rump.

"Come on, Opal. Time to get up," he said.

Opal Lee groaned through gritted teeth, grotesquely stretching her long, thin arms, and licked her lips before sitting up on the grass-filled mat. Martin watched as she stood up, hunched tall and round-shouldered in the dark dugout that, in the four years she had inhabited it, had never allowed her to stand straight. With both hands she scratched through the long, shapeless gown before going outside to search for sticks and roots for fuel.

Martin thumped the mat to frighten off any spiders or scorpions that might have come to rest there and rolled over in her place. The wet baby and the tangle of other children followed him as if he were a magnet.

Martin Foster next awakened to the smell of breakfast and to the smoke of dried grass and green leaves that burned the eyes and nostrils. Martin sat up, kicked his feet into his shoes, placed his hat on his head, and in his dingy long underwear, stumbled out of the dugout to the barren spot of sour-smelling ground where he had relieved himself with such regularity that not even the weeds would grow through the salty crust. He walked down to Three Mile Fork where he washed his hands and face in Sandy Creek. Taking a bandana from his hat, he dried his hands, wiped his bald head, and stood for a moment enjoying the sunrise over the creek. Martin Foster was something of a poet, being able to see the sunrise on the creek without seeing the weeds in the cotton patch nor the fence which was falling into the corn.

Martin enjoyed the sunrise until his wife called, destroying his mood. He blew his nose into the bandana, placed the bandana in his hat, put his hat on his head, and made his way through the tangle of kids who, standing and squatting, were performing their morning chores about the entrance to the dugout. He ducked his head when he entered the dugout just as his wife had done, although on Martin's part it was an affectation. Martin was a careful man, and to avoid unnecessary work had, in digging the dugout, measured off just the height he would need to safely stand erect with his shoes on. The fact that his wife was taller than he had escaped his notice.

Martin sat down at the rickety table made of boards which had been nailed to a keg. Placing his hands beside his plate, he looked down at the cup of hot water tinted by thrice-boiled coffee grounds, a small bowl of clotted gravy, a pan of runny cornbread, and six hungry, sleepy-eyed children who had somehow gotten to the table as quickly as he had. Martin looked up reproachfully at his gaunt wife, who stood hunched under the low roof, her hands rolled up in a dirty apron that had once been pink.

"I can't help it," Opal Lee said, waving a limp hand over the table to annoy the flies that rose to bump against her and then settled back on the table. "I been out of coffee for three days, we ain't had bacon in four weeks, and we got just enough corn-meal left for dinner. Last week you ate the hen, so there won't be no more eggs."

Martin lifted his long-suffering eyes to the earthen roof of the dugout. There between the warped and crooked sticks that held back the world, a root protruded, hanging into space. The root, as always when he had something important to think about, caught Martin's eye. Martin wondered what was at the other end of it, and whether it was growing up or down. Martin did not like problems. He especially did not like problems in the morning, and he particularly did not like problems on an empty stomach.

The winter had been a long one, draining them of their carefully hoarded provisions. Spring had come; and Opal Lee had planted a garden; but it had blown away. The wheat had been hailed out; the corn had burned up; and the little patch of stunted cotton wouldn't be ready until late fall. He would have no money until he sold the cotton.

"You better walk into town and get something," Martin said.

"I went to town week before last and they wouldn't give me nothing till we paid some on what we owe."

Sadly, Martin shook his head at the cupidity of the merchants. "They would sit and watch us starve," Martin said.

"They said a man that could afford a ten-dollar pair of yellow shoes could afford flour for his kids."

With a sigh, Martin looked down at his shoes. They were the only real good shoes he had ever owned, and folks reproached him for it. "A man that works on his feet all day to feed his wife and kids ought to be allowed a good pair of shoes to stand in," he said, saddened by the injustice of it all. "Whyn't you stop by the church?"

"That's where I got the cornmeal."

Martin closed his eyes on a church so chary as to give corn-meal to the wretched mother of six starvelings. "Well, go back and get some more."

"They said next time I'd have to come on Sunday and bring the children."

"Well, you got to do something. A man can't live on that," he said, pointing at the thin, lumpy gravy.

"If you'd ever go and ask yourself—" Opal Lee began, and then stopped, seeing the hurt in Martin's face. Martin Foster was independent, and he was proud. He had never asked for any-thing; he had merely taken. Whatever land was vacant, what-ever house, or tent, or dugout was empty, whatever woman was available, whatever food one of his women or wives had managed to beg for a hungry child. Whenever his independence had been threatened, Martin had moved on. He had left a string of aban-doned children, pregnant women, and unpaid bills across six states and territories; but his pride and his independence were still intact. He had seen his children go naked and his wives starve, but he had never lowered himself to ask for help.

"I'll go out today and see if I can find some poke salad," Opal Lee said contritely. "Maybe there's still some berries the birds ain't got."

"Take the gun in case you scare up a rabbit," he said.

"You going to work the cotton today, or fix the fence?"

"I ain't got no time for that today. Thought I might go down to the crick and see if I could catch a fish, or some frogs. Or even a turtle'd taste good, wouldn't it?"

Opal Lee smiled wanly. For four years Martin had fished in the creek and never caught anything, not even a snake.

Si Foster, the dirtiest and hungriest of the children, had withstood the torture as long as he could bear. Pretending to wipe back the fat, green flies, he dipped his finger into the gravy, dis-lodged one of the lumps, and stuck it into his mouth. He was reaching for more when his father pinned his hand to the table.

"None of that," Martin said, slapping the boy on top of his

scaly head. "We may be poor, and we may be hungry, but we ain't so hungry or so ungrateful as to fail to thank the Lord for what little He has sent us."

Like most men, Martin's gratitude was conditional upon the provisions before him. When the table sagged under the weight of sausage, green onions, black-eyed peas, berries in cream, and potatoes fried in hog fat, Martin's prayers were concise, to the point, and concluded with a great deal of reaching and grabbing. But when the table was bare, Martin's prayers were long, filled with gratitude, and concluded with great sighs of thanksgiving. Martin, in other words, was a Christian.

"O Lord, we are poor and hungry, nigh naked of clothing, and destitute of the worldly goods the wicked enjoy. But we ain't asking for nothing, Lord, but accepting anything You send us, and grateful for ever blessing that comes our way. Cornbread and water gravy is mighty poor food for one of Thy children, O Lord. But he complaineth not. Neither doth he ask for flour, salt, corn, potatoes, sugar, and tobacco, food worthy of Thy faithful servant. But O Lord, a piece of meat would season what little we got."

"And a packet of needles, and a card of large white buttons," Opal Lee added.

"In Thy generous and giving name, Amen."

Rubbing his hands together, Martin reached for the bowl of gravy just as a shower of dirt fell from the roof, burying the cornbread and gravy and spilling onto the table. Opal Lee gasped. The children began to cry. Martin, feeling that his independence had been threatened, lifted up his eyes to curse God and die when he beheld the leg of a steer protruding through the roof.

"God be praised!" Martin shouted. "He has sent us a beef."

The wagon led the way to Sandy Creek. While the Kid unhitched the oxen, hobbled them, and turned them out to graze, the Preacher studied the chuck box for something to cook. Since losing the goat, the men had been dispirited and cross. Even the Preacher's morale had been shattered by the total depravity

Maury had demonstrated in stealing the Bible. The Preacher thought a little something special would cheer them all up and searched the chuck box for ideas. The flour and salt were low, the coffee, tobacco, and molasses were running out, and the bacon and beans were gone. The only thing there was plenty of was beef. Fighting down his repugnance, the Preacher caught hold of a slab of the beef and began chopping it up for supper.

The Kid had built a fire with the wood he had stored in the cooney slung under the wagon, and was now scouting around looking for some more with which to replenish it. He stopped and watched the Preacher hacking at the side of meat. "Beef again?"

"That's all we got left, so I reckon you'd better get used to it," the Preacher said.

"I'm used to it," the Kid said. "I just hope to grow up to where I can chew it."

The hands brought the herd to water, swinging them upstream so that the latecomers got clean water that hadn't been muddied by the leaders. After the watering, they let the cattle scatter out to graze and came in for a hurried meal.

The Kid, who had wandered off down the creek looking for fuel, came running back to the wagon. "There's a man down to the creek and he appears to be dying. Looked like a nester."

"What's the matter with him?"

"I don't rightly know," the Kid said. "He was swole in a strut, and rolling on the ground."

"Sounds kinda like the ruby-oller," Lampassas said.

"Well, I don't know," the Preacher said. "Was he fevered?"

"Well, he was red in the face and his eyes looked like they was about to pop out of his head," the Kid said. "He kept mumbling, 'Not another bite, not another bite.' And he'd groan and thrash around, foaming at the mouth. Then he'd start yelling, 'I'm swelling, I'm swelling.' "

"My God," Lampassas said. "The infectious quinsy."

"I ain't real sure of that," the Preacher said. "With them symptoms it could be Jacob's malady or the bride's lament."

"What do you think we ought to do?" Lampassas asked.

"Well, the feller needs our help. We can't just pass by on the other side of the trail," the Preacher said. His face wrinkled in thought. "I think we ought to wait and see what happens. If he don't die, that shows the disease ain't fatal, in which instance we ought to treat him."

Lampassas saw June and Pretty Shadow coming in from the herd, leaving Covina to hold the cattle while they ate. Pretty Shadow had his coiled lariat slung over his shoulder. The loose end, which he had knotted to discourage the steers from getting too close, he snapped at the weeds as he walked along, improving his aim. "Pretty Shadow, there's a sick man down the creek there. I want you and June to go down and bring him in."

Sulkily, Pretty Shadow stared at him, and then, snapping the knotted rope at the toe of his boot, he turned and walked off with June.

"Don't bring him too close to the wagon," the Preacher said, examining the medicine in the chuck box. "If it's on the outside we'll treat it with coal oil, and if it's on the inside, with castor oil."

Lampassas and the Kid hurriedly ate their beef, and the Kid went back to the herd to relieve Covina. Pretty Shadow and June hauled in the patient by a length of rope which was attached to the patient's heel. Standing in a loose circle about the groaning man, they studied his symptoms.

"What's the matter with you?" the Preacher asked, jabbing a stiff finger into the man's stomach. "Does that hurt?" The man screamed and thrashed about on the ground. "Something the matter with his stomach," the Preacher said. "Hard as a rock. I believe it's the appendicitis."

"It must be highly contagious, then," said Pretty Shadow. "Because there's a dugout down there with a woman and six kids in it and they everone looked just like this one."

"My wife, my children," Martin groaned.

"We done found them," Pretty Shadow shouted, as though

the man were also deaf. "Whatever you got, you give it to the whole damn bunch."

"Let's treat this one, and if he don't die, we'll know what to do with the rest of them," the Preacher said.

"Okay, boys," Lampassas said. "You can put him on the wagon sheet for treatment."

"God, God," Martin groaned as they rolled him over on the wagon sheet.

"Ain't no need to cuss," the Preacher said.

"The Lord sent it. He sent it."

"The Lord tries us all, but he don't send no more than we can bear."

"Too much. It was too much."

"Then pray for greater endurance."

"God, God."

"He's cussing again," Pretty Shadow said, but the Preacher silenced him with a look.

"Pray," the Preacher said.

All his life Martin had believed in an all-powerful God who could give or withhold as the mood struck Him. And most of his life Martin had practiced prayer, although the Lord had never seen fit to answer him. But now that Martin had experienced the magnanimity of the Lord, he was awe-struck. "I'm afraid," he said.

"God answers prayer."

"That's why I'm afraid."

"Then I'll pray for you," the Preacher said. "I'll pray that the Lord delivers you from this suffering."

"Alive," Martin gasped.

"What?"

"Delivers me alive," Martin said, knowing first-hand the Lord's bent for overdoing things.

Covina marched up to the group assembled before the sick man and threw a wet cowhide on the ground. "Is that our trail brand or ain't it?" she asked. The men admitted that it was. "Somebody killed one of our steers, skinned it, and threw the hide in the creek thinking nobody'd ever find it," Covina said, picking up the hide and shaking it at them.

"Get it away," Martin said. "Get it away."

They looked at him curiously as his body was wracked by convulsions. "I have heard that a Indian will always confess his crime if the evidence is held before him," Pretty Shadow said.

"Look at this," Covina said, shaking the wet hide before Martin. "You seen this before, ain't you?"

Martin groaned, rolling over on his side away from the sight of the hide. Pretty Shadow stuck a boot heel in his shoulder and rolled him on his back.

"Where's the rest of it?" Covina demanded, shaking the hide in Martin's face where he could get a good smell of it. Martin held his nose with one hand and his mouth with the other. "You ate it, didn't you?"

"I couldn't stop," Martin moaned. "The more I chewed, the bigger it got."

"What was you doing down at the crick?" Pretty Shadow asked. "Getting rid of the hide?"

"Thirsty," Martin gasped. "The more I drank, the more it swelled."

Wearily, Lampassas sat down on the wagon tongue to consider the evidence. He took off his hat, placed it on his knees, and ran his fingers through his tough gray hair.

"Three things are inviolable in this country," said the Preacher. "A man's word, a woman's name, and a critter's brand."

Martin gave his word he had never taken a woman's name in vain.

"We have what you might call a moral obligation to punish him," said Pretty Shadow. "Else he might be persuaded into thinking he could steal somebody else's cows."

"I done been punished," Martin groaned. "I done paid."

"I reckon if a feller was to come to me and tell me his bosom companion and the fruits of his marriage was starving, I'd not be the last man to cut out a old, sore-footed cow and give it to him," Lampassas said. "And if a man was to take advantage of one of my steers and eat him, and tell me about it, I reckon I'd forgive him after roughing him up a little. But the man that'd kill a cow and throw the hide in the river—he ain't fit for nothing but a neck rope."

"We couldn't stand the sight—the smell—"

"You should a hung the hide, brand side up, over the fence," Pretty Shadow said. "That's the accepted way."

"It weren't much of a cow anyhow," groaned Martin, who had never eaten meat so tough and indigestible.

"It ain't that he was worth a whole lot," Lampassas said. "It's the fact that man and boy, horseback and afoot, we have drove that steer nigh onto a thousand miles, and we didn't do it to have some nester eat him for breakfast."

"If I had any way to do it, I'd pay you for the cow."

"Nope. Wouldn't take it," Lampassas said. "You have to pay for a steer before you eat him. Otherwise, it's stealing."

"I don't reckon you got a milk cow?" June asked. "Or a goat?"

"She took sick and we et her."

"Then I reckon you et your last chance," June said.

Now that the issue was settled, Lampassas felt a tremor of self-doubt. "We ain't had much luck with hanging lately," he said, thinking of the shepherd.

"That's because you take all the fun out of it," Covina said. "For a real good lynching, you got to get all worked up. Dancing, and singing, and speech-making. If we're not going to enjoy it, there don't seem to be a whole lot of point in doing it."

"By God, the thing to do is do," Lampassas said. "Thinking never stopped a thief or stretched a hanging rope."

"Wait a minute," said the Preacher, as Pretty Shadow began fashioning a noose. "We can't hang him yet. This here's a sick man. We can't hang him without first treating him for his ailment."

"Why not?"

"Because it ain't civilized, and it ain't Christian. If you're going to hang a feller, the least you can do is make sure he's in good health before he dies."

"Give him some medicine and let's get on with it," Lampassas said.

The Preacher got out the castor oil, and after studying Martin's condition, poured some into a cup. "Give him more than that," Pretty Shadow said. "We ain't got a whole lot of time to wait for him to get well."

The Preacher poured the cup full and gave it to Martin. "Drink it down. It'll fix you up, and after we've disposed of you, I'll go by and give some to your wife and kids. And now, was I you, I'd say my prayers."

Martin confessed that he didn't feel much like praying at the moment and requested instead that they read him a few words from the Good Book.

"The Preacher's done loaned out his Bible," Pretty Shadow said. "I reckon you'll just have to pray." Lifting Martin from the ground, he placed him on his knees. The position was an uncomfortable one for Martin, but with Christian forbearance, he adapted himself to it with groans and complaints.

"Well, ain't you even going to shut your eyes?" he asked.

"I'll put my hand on his shoulder, and if he makes a move to run, I'll yell," the Preacher said.

The men closed their eyes and bowed their heads, and Martin began to pray. "O Lord, I ain't asking for nothing, just thanking You for ever blessing that has come my way. Bless this food—"

Martin glanced up to see if anyone had noticed his mistake. Thankful that he had not been caught, yet saddened to discover that they were not listening, Martin began praying again, thanking the Lord for his wife he didn't deserve and the children he didn't ask for. Still no one seemed to be listening. Raising his voice, Martin loudly began to prophesy the doom of his wife and the destruction of his children. The terrors of the plains would beat at their door. Without his restraining hand, the boys would run away to California and go hungry, the girls would run away to Kansas City and go bad. His wife would dry up like a horse apple.

Surprised at the rush of compassion he felt for his wife and children, Martin looked up, sure they must have felt it too. Every face was set against him. Martin began praying again.

"I don't hold You to blame, O Lord, for permitting that steer to come my way, knocking down my fence, trespassing upon my corn, and breaking down my roof, but O Lord, when he ruined the last breakfast I had, I was sorely tried, and I come near to cussing You, Lord. But I have ever been one to wait until Thy hast made Thy purposes clear. And when I seen that steer had broke his own leg, I done what I thought You wanted, Lord. I ended his suffering. I hit him in the head with a axe, and I cut his throat to be certain. And when the sun commenced getting hot I cleaned the carcass so it wouldn't spoil. It is a sin to waste food, Lord. And when my wife and the children Thy hast sent me commenced begging for food, I weakened, Lord. I cut off a steak because I could not bear to see their suffering. But such is the nature of sin, that when I had once yielded myself to it, I could not stop. I cut them another, and another. I weakened some more and cut me off a steak. And a roast. Some liver. Short ribs. O Lord, for my sin I have suffered."

Overcome by his own earnestness, Martin was unable to continue. Sniffing and wiping his nose with his sleeve, he stood up.

"Just a minute," Lampassas said, and drew the hands aside where they could talk without being overheard. "Do you reckon that steer broke his leg?"

June didn't believe an innocent man would have waited so long to mention a steer's leg.

Covina didn't believe an innocent man would have tried to dispose of the hide.

Pretty Shadow didn't believe the dugout was substantial enough to bend a snake.

The Preacher didn't believe a nester could be expected to tell the truth.

Confirming their private opinions, they walked back, picked up Martin, placed his feet on the wagon hub and the noose about his neck. "Is there any last word you'd like to say?" Lampassas asked.

"I got to be excused."

"What?"

"I got to be excused," Martin said, jumping up and down on his toes at the risk of falling off the wheel and hanging himself.

"You picked a fine time," Lampassas said angrily.

"I can't help it," Martin said, doubling over as far as the rope would allow.

"Well, don't go far," Lampassas said, taking the noose from around his neck. "We ain't got all day."

Martin hurried off and the hands settled down beside the wagon to wait. Lampassas linked his hands behind his head and lay down on the ground, looking up at the cloudless blue sky. The wind rustled the wagon sheet they had placed on the ground for the sick man, and in the distance the cattle bawled.

"I don't think he's coming back," June said, breaking the silence.

Lampassas gave the nester a few minutes of grace and then sat up. "You don't reckon he run off, do you?"

"Damn nesters," Pretty Shadow said. "You can't trust them for nothing."

"Well, we ain't got no time to go looking for him," the Preacher said.

"Our job is to get the herd to Trails End," Lampassas said.

"If we had horses we could find him quick enough," June said. "But we ain't."

"He's probably in the next county by now," Pretty Shadow said.

"He probably ain't stopped running long enough to let down his trousers," Covina said.

"There he is," June said.

"Is he getting away?"

"No, he's just laying on the ground."

"That's him, all right," Lampassas said. "Well, come on, let's go get him."

Martin was carried back to the wagon and placed on the wagon hub, June and Pretty Shadow standing on either side to hold him in place, as he sagged badly. Lampassas tried to fit the noose, but Martin toppled over on him. Lampassas helped to restore Martin to his proper place and to hold him there while the Preacher took the noose and tried to place it over Martin's head, which was rolling about Martin's shoulders. Martin's knees also buckled, so that the Preacher not only had to determine the pitch and roll of his head but also the elevation.

"He's as hard to get a rope on as a muley cow," the Preacher said.

"Well, hurry up," said June, who found that Martin was no longer standing on the wagon but astride his head.

"Put him down, put him down," Lampassas said. "We got to figure this out."

After much planning and debate, the Preacher took the noose in both hands, Lampassas held Martin's limber head with both hands, June and Pretty Shadow lifted the pliant Martin up to the noose, and Covina kept him from pitching forward. Making a wide noose, the Preacher slipped it over Martin's head and Lampassas's arms; and while Lampassas worked his arms out, the Preacher jerked the rope tight. The knot caught Martin under the chin, and limply, he doubled over backward and fell under the wagon, carrying June, Pretty Shadow, Covina, and the Preacher with him, and leaving Lampassas swinging by one arm.

"I got to be excused," Martin said weakly from the bottom of the pile, and they all began scrambling to extricate themselves from Martin, who slowly crawled away from the wagon.

June and Pretty Shadow helped Lampassas down, and they all sat down again in the shade of the wagon to wait.

Lampassas was of the opinion that hanging a fellow was not much fun.

June had never realized how much work went into a hanging. "That's something folks don't never tell you," he said.

Covina was disgusted. She felt that the men knew very little about hanging and nothing at all about having fun. "This is the dullest drive I ever seen," she said. "There's nothing to do."

The Preacher was of the opinion that it wasn't a question of whether or not it was fun, but whether or not it was right. And since they had decided that it was right to hang Martin, not to do so would constitute a wrong.

Lampassas recalled that the steer had broken its leg, therefore justifying its death, and that the nester was praying when he told about it. "That ought to count for something."

The Preacher demonstrated his lack of faith in the nester.

Pretty Shadow inquired as to whether the Preacher would accept the nester's Christian testimony. "Taking into consideration that he is the husband of one wife and the father of six children."

"And that he's a mean son of a bitch to hang," June added.

The Preacher believed he would be bound to accept a Christian's testimony.

"Let's hope to hell he ain't out of his head when he gets back," June said. "He might forget the way it happened."

Martin crawled back under the wagon and lay down. Lampassas bent under the wagon and looked into his glazed eyes. "What's your name, feller?"

"Martin Foster."

"Martin Foster, are you a Christian?"

"God, God," Martin groaned.

"He believes in God," Lampassas said. "Now, Martin, we been doing some thinking while you was gone. We hate like hell to make a mistake in hanging a feller, so I want you to tell me the truth on your Christian word. Did that steer have a broke leg?"

"God, God," Martin groaned.

"He swears to God," Lampassas said. "And we believe him,

don't we, fellers?" With the exception of the Preacher, the men enthusiastically agreed. "We believe your story about that steer breaking his damn leg, so we're going to let you go." Lampassas had to shake Martin to get his attention. "We're going to let you go."

"I'm obliged," Martin groaned.

"Well, go on, you're free," Lampassas said, motioning Martin out from under the wagon. "Crawl on out of there."

Martin looked at them through glassy eyes. "I don't believe I can make it by myself," he said.

Reaching under the wagon, Lampassas caught Martin by the collar, dragged him out, and set him up against a wheel. "We got to get him out of camp and get moving again," Lampassas said. "Preacher, give him some of your coffee. That'll cut through anything."

The Preacher poured Martin a cup of coffee, and Martin lay back against the wheel, drinking it slowly, letting the strong black liquid revive him. Gradually, he regained his strength and was able to sit up and talk coherently. "I don't envy you fellers none having to drive them cows all the way to Trails End. Not since Crazy Woman Creek dried up."

"Dried up?"

"Yeah, the farmers have dried up all the water around here, cultivating, and irrigating, and damming. And what they ain't dried up, they turned to mud. There ain't nothing running between here and Ruby Draw."

"Son of a bitch," Lampassas said. "What next?"

"Yes sir, that's a fur piece to drive cows without water," Martin said cheerfully.

"The herd can't make it," June said. "Not in the condition they're in."

"Hell, we can't make it neither," Covina said.

For a moment they sat in thoughtful silence. "We ain't got no place to go back to, and we ain't got no place to stop, so I reckon we'll go on," Lampassas said.

"If we was to rest the herd up for a few days, water them

good, and drive them like hell, we might make it," Pretty Shadow said.

"I bet we could," June said.

"Hell yes, we can do it," said Covina.

"That's what I figure," said the Preacher.

"First thing to do is cross the creek at Three Mile Fork," Lampassas said.

The herd forded Sandy Creek without difficulty, while Martin's fence collapsed, his corn fell down, and his dugout caved in on his sick wife and children. Martin, feeling his independence had been threatened, moved on.

For two weeks the herd rested and watered while the hands built a fence, dug a dugout, gathered corn, nursed Martin's family back to health, and searched for Martin.

"Son of a bitch has a new wife and is on his way to Arkansas," June reported.

For two more days the herd rested and watered while the hands encouraged Opal Lee to take the children and go back home. When she began making eyes at Pretty Shadow and talking of cotton-picking time, they departed suddenly in the middle of the night, leaving a few head of cattle behind in their haste.

Chapter 10

THE first day was like any other day on the trail, hot, dusty, and long. The cattle, their sore feet rested, their bellies full of water and grass, trailed at an easy but distance-covering gait. The long column moved smoothly, evenly, without stragglers. Only the men suffered the first day. Only they were aware of the miles, counting the hours to water, watching the progress of the sun.

To cover as much distance as possible while the cattle were still fresh, they did not stop at mid-day. Since the only water was in the wagon, which the herd had already overtaken and passed, the men suffered terribly from the heat and dust through the long afternoon. Dusk came on, but the herd kept moving, pressed on by Lampassas, who was determined to drive them as far as possible the first day. Night came on, and stars twinkled through the cloud of dust that hung over the herd, but still they plodded on. With hoarse, painful voices, the men cursed the sultry night and the pale moon that rose to light their way. The cattle began to balk and had to be prodded by the weary, stumbling men the last hour before Lampassas threw the herd off the trail to rest. It was near midnight when the last dry-throated man reached the bedground, followed by the Preacher with the wagon and a barrel of water. The herd, overtired and restless after a long day's drive without water, refused to bed down, so that half the hands stood watch, walking around the milling cattle and singing, while the others ate.

"Don't waste no water washing," Lampassas said. "Let's save it for the oxen and the coffee."

The men wiped their hands and faces on their grimy bandanas and sweaty shirts, dusted off their clothes, spat the dust out of their mouths, and drank enormous quantities of water while the Preacher fried beef.

"We better all figure on standing the watch tonight," Lampassas said. "We can't take a chance on losing the herd out here without water."

The hands sat sprawled on the ground, sipping their coffee, too tired to complain. Their jaws worked slowly as they tried to chew the tough meat. Their lips were cracked open and bleeding, their tongues and throats were swollen and raw from lack of water and shouting at the cattle in the dust.

"I'll keep the coffee boiling all night so's you can get some when you make a round," the Preacher said.

"We'll have to take it a little easier tomorrow on account of the cows," Lampassas said. "We'll start as soon as it's light and let them rest some in the heat of the day. That way they won't suffer as much and it'll give us a chance to get a drink. We'll be going slower tomorrow and the Preacher ought to be able to keep up. Maybe even have supper ready for us when we get there."

Pretty Shadow pushed his food away uneaten and reached for his sack of tobacco before he remembered that it was all gone. He pinched his mouth, wondering if a man could smoke twice-boiled coffee grounds. Behind him, the baby began to whimper.

"You boys hurry now so you can go milk," the Preacher said.

After the hands had eaten, the Preacher watered the steers that were pulling the wagon, banked the fire, and scoured the dishes with sand. Pouring a little water in a pan, he washed the cross, sour-smelling baby. The dust had worked into the

folds of the baby's skin, turning his flesh raw and inflaming his
eyes. Taking no heed of his screams, the Preacher bathed him
and redressed him in his dirty clothes after first shaking them
out. Then he fed the baby the milk which the Kid brought and
put him to bed in the wagon. Little Jake had grown accustomed
to his irregular life, eating in the middle of the night, sleeping
through the day in the moving wagon, days of leisure during
which he was petted and played with, and periods of activity
during which he was largely ignored. Clean and fed, he went
quickly to sleep.

Finishing a turn about the herd, Covina walked to the
wagon to get a cup of coffee and to check the baby. Little Jake
was lying on his stomach, his head on one folded arm, breathing quietly through his mouth. Covina bent down and brushed
her chapped lips across his cheek. Little Jake squirmed and
sighed heavily, but he did not awaken. Covina smiled and
smoothed down his hair, surprised that it was not stiff with sweat
and dust like her own. Getting a cup of coffee, she sat down on the
ground and rested her head on her arm, which lay along the
wagon tongue.

The Preacher had already bedded down, but he woke every
time someone came to the wagon for coffee. Knowing that he
would have just a couple of hours to sleep before it was time to
begin breakfast, he only allowed himself to doze, afraid of over-
sleeping. "Herd quiet?" he asked.

"That's the noisiest herd I ever seen not to be running."

"Well, if we can hold them another hour, it'll be light
enough to trail."

"If I'm going to be walking, I'd just as soon be going somewheres as to be walking around in circles," Covina said. With
her little finger, she felt of her puffed, cracked lips. "Little Jake
all right?"

"Best eater I got," the Preacher said, and they both smiled.
"Only one that'll eat them sourdoughs without complaining."

"Must be good for him," she said. "He don't cry as much as
he used to."

"About the only time he cries any more is when I stop the wagon."

"That boy's got moving in his bones," Covina said. "I wonder if he'll ever be content to stay put when we get there?"

"By the time he gets to Trails End, he'll probably be ready to settle down to a normal life," the Preacher said, and then remembered. He wondered if he should make a point of explaining to Covina that he did not consider her life either normal or settled.

"At first I hoped we wouldn't never get there, but now I just want to get it over with," Covina said, feeling the ends of her hair where the dust and sweat had caked.

The Preacher tried to think of something to say, a warning or a rebuke. "It ain't far now," he mumbled, and throwing back his soogans and putting on his hat, he got up to fry some beef for breakfast.

Before daylight, the hands had, two at a time, eaten the tough, stringy meat, washed it down with coffee, and started the herd moving toward water. The sun rose hot and high over a pale, cloudless sky, a day devoid of wind. The dust kicked up by the sharp hooves billowed up to hang motionless over the herd, blinding and choking the men. The hands turned up their collars, turned down the brims of their hats, tied their bandanas over their mouths and noses. Still they were racked by dry coughs and sneezing. Their irritated eyes turned red and swelled. Tears stained their faces. The cattle, tired and thirsty, hung back uncertainly, stopped to mill and bawl. The wagon was able to keep the pace and took the point, while the number of hands in the drag had to be increased to keep the herd moving.

The hands lost all track of time as, with the vision of water before them, they pushed and prodded the cattle through dawn and breathless morning, the stale air and blinding heat of the long afternoon, into the promise of dusk, on into the night as long as they could hold the herd together, as far as they could push them toward water. And when the herd stopped, the men kept going, around and around the edgy cows, that would not lie down but stood sulkily about, motion implied, ready to run at the slightest provocation, so that the night was full of the threat of stampede.

The men ate whenever they could, usually two or three at a time in the darkness before the drive began or after it was over for the day. They ate hurriedly, whatever the Preacher found time to cook, not tasting, nor caring, mechanically chewing and swallowing, their tongues and throats painfully swollen. They drank the coffee whenever they could get it, aware of the diminishing supply of water in the barrel. They slept not at all, or at least not lying down. Sometimes they slept on their feet, stumbling over rocks or walking blindly into the cattle that also walked blindly, with eyes swollen shut, tongues hanging out, gaunt sides heaving for the stale, dead air. Overhead, the sun bleached everything, turning the cloudless sky, the thin, dry vegetation to the color of dust. And through this vale of dust walked the panting, bawling herd, that was also turning the color of dust, pushed on by the stalking brown figures who no longer fought the dust, no longer brushed it from their clothing, dug it from their ears, or spat it from their lips, but stumbled and staggered through it into the darkness at the end of the day. And even in the darkness, the smell of dust was in their nostrils. Even when at the end of the day they slowly drank the precious water, the dust gritted between their teeth.

Covina walked through the dust, scarcely knowing where she was, not driving the cattle but following them, believing blindly, steadfastly, that somewhere, at the front of the herd, someone was pointing the way to water. Beyond anger or care, she no longer cursed and shouted at the cows, chased the strays, prodded the stragglers. When a cow stopped, she leaned against it until it began moving again, sometimes draping one arm over its neck to steady herself while she dozed on her feet. Not all of the cows would move at her urging. Some of them would drop down on their knees, slowly collapsing on trembling limbs. At first she had tried to prod them back on their feet, but now she knew it was hopeless. There was nothing she could do but leave them behind to die. A dun-colored, lineback cow, one of those the men had been milking, stopped and stood head down before her in the trail. Covina felt a kinship with the cow, a sense of gratitude. Besides, the cow was valuable to her, and she was determined to save it for the baby's sake. If she could keep the cow going until they reached the bedground tonight, perhaps tomorrow they could find water. Leaning against the cow, Covina pushed against its bony, manure-caked hide and prodded it in the flank. The exhausted cow spun around to face Covina with a quickness the startled girl would not have believed. Shaking its head, the cow backed slowly away, dragging its hooves, its eyes rolling wildly, its dark and swollen tongue hanging from its mouth. Covina realized that the cow had been driven mad by heat and thirst. The cow swung its head slowly from side to side as though it were having difficulty seeing, trembling with fatigue and excitement, its thin flanks heaving.

Covina looked about her, but she was alone. The herd and the drovers had disappeared into the dust. She was alone, without any cover in sight. She stood motionless, watching the cow, trying to think what to do. Her head ached from the bright sun, and she was too tired to think clearly. If she stood perfectly still, perhaps the cow would lose interest or go away, or perhaps, in its exhaustion, lie down. But she was afraid of being left behind like one of the straggling cows, forgotten, left to die of thirst.

Slowly, Covina began backing away from the cow, moving after the herd, believing that if she increased the distance between them, the cow would lose interest. The cow jerked its head up one time and then lunged at her. Covina tried to run but stumbled and fell on the ground as the cow charged over her and then whirled around looking for her. The cow was nearly blind from the sun. Swinging its head from side to side, raising its nose to sniff, legs trembling, flanks heaving, the cow searched for her. Covina lay on the ground, not daring to move, watching the cloud of dust moving slowly away. The cow trotted toward her, nose in the air, walking as though on tiptoes. It had found her. Covina jumped up and ran again until she could hear the cow close behind her, and then she threw herself to one side as the cow charged past and turned about looking for her.

Covina lost all sense of time as she lay on the ground panting, her head splitting from the sun and the effort of running, praying that the cow would not find her. Then jumping up and running again until she could run no farther and falling on the ground while the heat-crazed cow looked for her. Sometimes she ran in circles. Sometimes she ran south instead of north, but always she kept the dust cloud of the herd in sight. That was where she must go if she could. That was the direction from which help would come, if any did.

Raising her head, Covina saw that the cow was looking at her. Scarcely caring any more what happened, she lay waiting for the cow to charge, but the cow did not move. Its eyes were hollow, its long tongue had turned black. From where she lay, Covina could smell the hot stench of its breath. Gathering itself, the cow staggered forward a few steps, tottered, and with a groan, fell to its knees. Its head rolled back, and Covina could hear its strangled gasps as she got to her feet and, her knees shaking so she could hardly stand, trudged after the herd. Long after the cow was out of sight, Covina continued to look back over her shoulder.

Because of the straggling condition of the herd, it was difficult to know when she had caught up with it. Covina passed cows that were down, others that were standing but unable to move, still others that were slowly plodding in the chewed-up path of the cows that had passed before. Covina made no effort to prod up the cows, to drive them on, but walked beside them, united with them in the effort to reach water in time.

Covina had kept her hatbrim turned down and her bandana covering her nose, mouth, and throat, to protect her face from the blistering sun. Even so, her cheeks had chapped. Her sleeve had been ripped from shoulder to wrist, and the sun had burned the exposed flesh, raising water blisters. Waves of heat rose from the ground and beat against her legs. The sunlight glinted off the ground broken up by the cows' hooves. Her eyes ached at the slightest movement, and she looked neither to left nor right. When she could bear it no longer, she dropped her arm over a steer's back and stumbled along beside it, her eyes closed, into the sunset, into the cooling darkness that bathed her eyes. Still walking, Covina dozed off; and when she was awakened by the bawling of the cattle, she realized that the herd had stopped and that she was standing in the midst of it, her head resting on the steer's back, having no idea which way it was to the wagon and water. Blindly, she worked her way through the standing, bawling cattle, trying to find the outside of the herd where the hands stood watch, and beyond that the wagon with water and coffee. But in the confusion of the milling, bawling herd, and in her own sleepy dull-wittedness, she could not find the limits of the herd, and coming to a solitary rock which was as big as a washtub and almost as round, she sat down, too tired to find the wagon, not caring that the herd might stampede with her in the middle of it. Placing her elbows on her knees and her head in her hands, she went to sleep.

Pretty Shadow had been on the point all day, and in a way he was glad to be free of the heavy dust and driving of the drag. But the last two days, the point had been different from anything he had ever experienced. Regularly, the job of the point was to pinch back the leaders when they began moving too fast and allow the drags to catch up. Before, it had been unnecessary to drive the leaders. He and Lampassas had only to point the cattle in the right direction between them. But the last two days it had sometimes been necessary to prod the leaders, and today he had worked desperately trying to keep the leaders from turning back, as some of them wanted to do. And even though he was far ahead of those working in the drag, they had some comfort in thinking perhaps those ahead had already reached water. There was a special despair in being on the point, able to see across the dust-free miles ahead and see no sign of water.

Because he was on the point, Pretty Shadow was one of the first to eat when they threw the herd off the trail. And even though his tongue was swollen, it was small comfort to be the first to the food and water, because there was nothing more to anticipate, and it only reminded him of how long it would be before he ate again.

Pretty Shadow began his watch by promising himself that he would only make one or two circles about the herd, and then he would slip off somewhere and lie down to sleep. He lost track of the rounds he had made, and still he promised himself sleep after one more round. His feet were so sore he could not walk without limping; and even if this had not been so, he would still have had to limp because of the broken-down condition of his boots. The sweat ran down his calves, burning the sores on his ankles. Something—Pretty Shadow supposed it was chiggers or spiders—had bitten him about the ankles. The places had itched, and by flexing his boots, he had scratched them into open sores. The Preacher had treated them with coal oil, and that had helped, but now the salty sweat was irritating them, setting them to itching and burning again. Bending over, Pretty Shadow thrust his hand into his sockless boots and clawed at the sores until they bled.

Bending over made him dizzy, and he thought perhaps he had better sit down until he felt better. Then he thought of the other men, who were also walking around the herd, and was ashamed of his weakness. He knew if he ever sat down, he would not get up. He straightened up with the half-wish that he might pass out, and began walking again. To encourage himself, for inspiration, he tried to think of Diamond Annie. He had to go on, to keep the herd moving; he had to get to Trails End for Diamond Annie. Clad only in her embroidered flannel drawers, with a lacy silver garter on her leg, she was reclining against the red satin bolster of the brass bed, waiting for him. Her rosy lips curled back in a smile as she ran a brush through her black and sparkling hair.

Jervis Applewhite met Diamond Annie on his first trip up the trail when he was barely eighteen years old. After the cattle had been sold, Jervis had hurried to town to wash away the cow smell and trail dust and to drink away the monotony of a hundred days in the saddle. He wanted to drown the memory of riding fourteen hours a day in the choking dust behind the herd. He wanted to forget falling off his horse in the dark at the end of the day, so exhausted he could scarcely stand or eat, and then jumping up before he was asleep good to chase the herd all night. He wanted to forget the monotony of eating the same food, hearing the same lowing and bawling, seeing the same men, riding the same horses after the same cows, over a never-ending and never-changing prairie, under a sun that seemed to hang motionless in the high, pale sky. He wanted to forget a monotony so heavy that he had found relief in the danger of a river crossing, the discomfort of a hail storm, or the sickening lurch of a stumbling horse in a stampede.

After getting all duded up in new boots, hat, and corduroy suit, Jervis joined the boys in the Red Dog Saloon. He didn't stop to admire the scenery on the way in, being anxious to see the boys he had been so tired of seeing on the trail. But they looked different now, their hair cut and oiled, their mustaches trimmed and waxed, their faces pink from close shaving and talcum powder, their clothes creased and stiffly new. They were his bosom companions, the friends of his youth, partners of the dust. They had shared thousands of experiences, hundreds of scares, scores of disasters, a half dozen delights. Together they had heard the owl hoot. Together they would see the elephant.

After admiring one another's attire, they drank to the health of each member, present and unaccounted for, singly and collectively, dead and alive, and had started on the horses in the remuda before Jervis had an opportunity to admire his surroundings. Leaning an elbow on the bar, Jervis surveyed the room. The bar was of heavy wood, darkly stained by glass and foam. The mirror and the two paintings, which were hung one on either side to balance it (one of them depicting the Indians' last stand before the sword and pistol of General Custer, and the other portraying a lady of proportion and propensity the like of which Jervis had never seen), were framed in gold gilt which was none the less genuine because of the smoke and soot from the kerosene lamps; which smoke and soot accented the purity of the gold, changed the race of Custer's victims—indeed, the race of General Custer himself—and provided the only veil over the lady's enormous expanse of pink flesh.

"That's real painting," said one of Jervis's friends, who, with one eye closed and the other squinted, was expertly appraising the picture. "It takes a real artist to paint that much of a woman without showing anything important."

Above the mirror hung a set of dusty cow horns mounted on moth-eaten red velvet. A few feet past the end of the bar were stairs which led to the rooms above where a commodity older than whisky was sold. The rails of the stairs had been polished shiny by sweaty hands; and the carpet, red like the dusty curtains that shut out any sunlight from the room's two windows, was stained and worn. The room itself would have been middling large had twenty less people occupied it, or had they been twenty times quieter. Tables were pushed into the corners, and a few men sat drinking with female companions. Other men tried to dance their ladies in the small space left them, to the tune which was being banged on the piano through the smoke and noise. The ladies drifted up and down the stairs, adjusting their costumes, smiling, and eying the men lined up at the bar. Generally, Jervis noticed, the ladies changed partners and directions at the same time, coming down the stairs with one man, turning around and going back up with another. This marching up and down the stairs seemed to have an ill effect upon the ladies, as most of them were sallow skinned and hollow cheeked.

"When does the excitement start?" one of Jervis's companions shouted at the bartender.

"Soon's it's dark."

The most beautiful girl Jervis had ever seen danced past him in the arms of a bearded buffalo skinner. The dark-eyed, dark-haired, fair-skinned girl was wearing a green velvet dress cut low enough to reveal the smoothness of her neck and shoulders and the soft white flesh of her bosom. Her red-kid-and-cloth shoes kicked high, exposing her lacy, ruffled petticoat. Three bright feathers waved from her hair as she spun around, her ruby lips open, her teeth flashing as she laughed. Pushing back his hat, Jervis turned to admire the flounce of her bustle.

When the music stopped, the girl pushed the skinner away and walked along the bar eying the men. She stopped in front of Jervis and invited him to dance. The skinner, stunned by whisky and noise, stalked after her, shoved Jervis against the bar, and grabbed the girl around the waist. Jervis separated them with an empty whisky bottle, and his friends directed the man outside.

"I ain't known for dancing," Jervis said.

"Just hang on," the girl said, taking him in her arms. Jervis was unable to match the steps she was doing, but neither was he willing to let her go. Holding tightly, he stayed with her, not even releasing her when the dance was over.

When the music stopped, the men escorted their ladies up the stairs or to the bar. The huffing, perspiring ladies at the bar sipped their drinks, looking over the crowd for more adventuresome prospects, all except Jervis's girl, who stood beside him at the end of the bar, seemingly content with his company.

"What do they call you?" he asked.

"My name's Annie, but most of the men call me Diamond Annie. They say my hair sparkles and I got diamonds in my eyes," she said, matter-of-factly, tossing her hair.

"They're sure right about that."

"What do they call you?"

"Jervis."

"Jervis? Don't they ever call you anything but Jervis?"

"After my horse threw me one time, they got to calling me Duster."

"Jervis is a name for a tailor or a bank clerk. I'm going to call you Pretty Shadow."

The Professor downed his drink and began playing the piano again. Jervis took Annie's hand and led her to the dance floor.

"We're only allowed two dances with the same man," she said.

"Why's that?"

"Just the rules."

"You're in my corral now," Jervis said, swinging Annie about the room, oblivious to the crowd, the noise, and the music, aware only that he had her in his arms and that he wanted to dance and shout and hold her forever.

As they passed near the piano, the Professor leaned back and looked at them over his glasses. "Look, kid, you better roll your tail for home," he said. As he spoke, ashes fell from the cigarette drooping in the corner of his mouth and trickled down the front of his flowered vest.

Jervis pushed Annie aside and looked at the man. He was a little hunchback with a thin yellow face and leering eyes. The man was too monstrous to curse, too small to shoot, and too crippled to fight, those being the only defenses Jervis knew.

"You keep out of this," Annie said to the Professor.

"That's three dances with the same fellow," the Professor said, without looking at the piano or slacking in his playing. "Bill ain't going to like it."

"Come on," Annie said, leading Jervis back into the dance.

"Who's Bill?"

"He's just a man that thinks he owns everbody," Annie said.

"Well, he don't own me," Jervis said, and to prove it, he drew her close and swung her about the floor.

When the music stopped again, Annie caught his arm as he headed for the bar. "I think we'd better go upstairs," she said. Jervis took off his hat, offered her his arm, and escorted her up the stairs the way his mother had taught him. At the top of the stairs, Annie stopped long enough to look back in the direction of the piano.

"Damn piano player. He's always spying on us," she said, as she led Jervis down the dark, narrow hall.

"Nice room you got here," Jervis said, casting about the room for a place where his eyes could light.

The room was small, and even so it seemed almost barren of furniture. There was a worn red carpet on the floor, a small round table holding an ornately painted lamp, which was not lighted as it was still day, and another small table covered with a lace doily, holding a bowl and a pitcher. A lovesick Indian maid lying languidly beside a pool was painted on the bowl; and the pitcher was decorated with an Indian buck who was staring resolutely toward the horizon, doomed never to see the maiden until someone picked up the pitcher and poured water into the bowl. A painted screen stood in one corner of the room with a clothes tree beside it. The rest of the room was dominated by a large brass bed decorated with brass flowers, and a red satin counterpane.

Jervis was disconcerted by the fact that there was no chair in the room. He couldn't stand up forever. He chose the snow-capped mountains painted on the screen to rest his eyes upon. "Ain't that pretty?" he said.

"You can sit here," she said.

Jervis sat down on the bed beside her, holding his hat between his knees and humming quietly to himself. "You can hear the piano plumb up here."

"Yes. We're only allowed to stay up here for two dances."

"Oh," said Jervis, somewhat discouraged. He couldn't imagine what they could talk about for more than one dance or what they could do in less than three.

Jervis looked at her out of the side of his eye. With a tongue-moistened little finger, she was rubbing at a spot on her green dress. He wanted desperately to kiss her. Hooking his hat over his knee, he slipped one arm around her while looking steadfastly the other way to disclaim any intention in the action. She leaned her head against his shoulder.

Jervis tightened his arm about her waist and was trying to figure a way to get his head far enough over to kiss her and still make it look like an accident when he heard the sound of blows being struck in the next room, deliberate blows followed by moans and sobs. Jervis jumped up, reaching for his pistol, but Annie threw her arms around him. "No, no," she whispered in his ear.

A door opened and closed, and the sound of footsteps faded down the hall. "Wait here," Annie said, looking back to see that he obeyed, and then she left the room.

Jervis sat back on the bed to await her return. He hummed along with the piano. He tossed his hat in the air and caught it with his toe. He felt the smoothness of the satin counterpane and tested the mattress springs. He looked nonchalantly about, then strode across the room and took a peek behind the screen. He saw another washstand with a bowl and pitcher. He sat down on the bed, looked up, studied the ceiling, and then dropped to one knee and looked under the bed. There was nothing but a chamber pot decorated with Niagara Falls. Jervis was checking the level of water in the basin on the table when Annie returned.

"He'll never beat me like that," she said grimly, leaning against the door and closing her eyes on what she had just seen.

"Who?"

"The girl next door."

"Who beat her?"

"The man that put her here."

"What did he beat her for?" Jervis asked, incredulous that anyone would beat anything as soft and lovely as a woman.

"He caught her with another man."

"Didn't he put her here to be with other men?"

"She was sweet on this one. Now she's afraid they'll kill each other."

"Seems more likely they'll kill her," said Jervis, who was not wise in the ways of the world.

"She'll have to leave now," Annie said with a shudder.

"You mean he'll put her out?"

"He ruined her face," Annie said. "Now she'll have to go down to the railroad tracks. Look." She opened the small velvet bag which was attached to her belt. Inside, under a lacy white handkerchief, was a small nickel-plated revolver. "Just in case."

"You won't need that while I'm around," Jervis said. "I won't let nobody bother you."

Annie looked up at him and smiled. Gently, she took his face in her hands and kissed him. The steady drum of the piano stopped and she dropped her hands and stepped back. "Oh, God, how many times is that?" she asked, tugging at the top of her dress and straightening her belt. Pretty Shadow didn't know but he thought there had been three or four songs. "We've got to go," she said.

"I'm dancing ever dance with you."

"No, you can't. You've got to go. When we get downstairs you can pinch me, and then leave, and don't look back."

"When can I see you again?"

"Don't come back for several hours. Wait at the bar until I come down, and then you can dance with me. Come on, let's go," she said, taking his arm and fluffing her hair at the back of her head. "Wait," she said, looking at him in dismay. "Put your hat on your head."

"It ain't polite."

Taking his hat, she placed it on the back of his head at a go-to-hell angle, and while he fidgeted, loosed his tie, unbuttoned his vest, and pulled his shirttail out. Then she stepped back and inspected him. "Can't you even smile?" she asked. "Not like that. Pleased with yourself. We're going downstairs."

Downstairs, Annie invited him to dance again, but Jervis did as he had been told, pinched her arm, and in the company of two friends, he left the Red Dog for a change of scenery in an identical saloon down the street.

Jervis's head was already sitting uncertainly on his shoulders. He was not well acquainted with liquor or women, and it was difficult to say which had confused him more. He didn't want to drink any more, wishing to save all his money for Diamond Annie; but his friends insisted that he have a drink with them before they went looking for a faro game to make enough money to start all over. Just as they were leaving, they were joined by more of their friends and had to have a drink with them. They met a waddie from Copperas Cove and had to drink to Copperas Cove, which led to drinks in honor of Jacksboro, Cotulla, Frio Town, Cuero, Uvalde, and Red River. The mention of the river opened up an entirely new subject for drinks which exhausted their capacity to drink and to remember at about the same time, and left them hung up on the Platte, the Stinkingwater, and the Susquehanna. The last-named of which almost set off a gun fight, as one of those present chose not to believe in the existence of any such-named river. The argument was settled without bloodshed to the satisfaction of all by deciding that there was a Susquehanna River, but that it was in Mexico. This compromise necessitated a last drink to prove that no hard feelings or sensitivity of any kind still persisted. Then Jervis and his two friends set out as a scouting party to search for the door.

Jervis and his two companions did considerable wandering about in search of a faro game; and when they at last found one, Jervis discovered that his friends were nowhere about, that he was in a place he had no recollection of entering and no idea of how he got there, and that he was betting the last dollar he had. The dealer turned up a ten and raked in Jervis's money.

Jervis didn't know how long he had been in the game nor what had happened to his money, but he felt cheated. Leaning back in his chair, he jerked out his six-shooter and emptied it at the hooded kerosene lamp above the table. The room disappeared in blackness. Everyone that had a pistol and the urge pulled it and blazed away in the darkness. Screaming and shouting, the occupants of the building tried to vacate it. Jervis dived through a window, landing on a pile of folks who had previously used that exit. Rolling away from the others who jumped through the window behind him, he scrambled to his feet and fled down the dark street.

Jervis stopped behind the blacksmith shop to catch his breath and to clear his head. As his senses returned, the enormity of what he had done came to him. With all the shooting, it would be a miracle if no one had been shot; and since it would be impossible to say who had fired what shot, he would be blamed for the whole thing. The sheriff would be looking for him now. Maybe for murder. Jervis was frightened. He had to get out of town, but he was broke. He had to find his friends and borrow enough money to catch a train to Kansas City or maybe a Dakota stage.

Keeping to the shadows, Jervis made the rounds looking for someone from his brand; but they had either found a poker game in a back room, were sleeping off their drinks under a porch, or had retired for the night in one of the shacks along the railroad. Jervis thought of going down to the shacks, knocking on the doors, and asking who was within; but he gave it up as too chancy. The doors did not look substantial enough to stop a bullet.

There was nothing to do but stay out of sight and hope to find someone from his outfit before daylight. He didn't have a watch, but Jervis knew that it was very late and that he had promised Annie he would come back and see her. It was a risk, but he decided to take it. Since he had no money to stand at the bar, he waited outside until the music stopped. When he stepped inside, Annie was coming down the stairs with a railroader. She invited the man to dance again; but he shook his head ruefully, patted her on the backside, and left. Jervis caught her in his arms, danced her around the room, and when the piano stopped again, led her up the stairs.

"I told you I'd come back," he said.

"Yes," she said, unhooking her dress, stepping out of it, and hanging it on the clothes tree. Then she pulled off her bustle and slipped out of her ruffled petticoat. Sitting down on the bed in her flannel drawers, she leaned back against the bolster.

Jervis was astonished. He was astonished to see such garments as he had never before imagined. He was doubly astonished that they could be removed so quickly, and triply astonished that they had been removed for him. At what they had been concealing, he was astounded.

"Come here," she said, patting the bed beside her.

Jervis walked across the room and fell down on the bed beside her. Annie reached up and removed his hat, dropping it beside the bed. "Don't you think you should take off your boots?"

Pretty Shadow sat up on the side of the bed to remove his boots, but the stiff new boots were something to be bargained with. Grunting, Jervis pulled off one boot and was working on the other when there was a knock on the door.

"Annie, this is Billy Meadows. Who's in there with you?"

"That's the sheriff," Jervis whispered to Annie, signaling her not to give him away. Jumping from the bed, he tried to stamp his foot back into the boot he had just removed.

"Just a minute," Annie called at the door, picking up Jervis's hat and placing it on his head. "Hurry. Out the window," she said, pushing him along while he hopped on one foot, pulling on his boot. "Get out of town."

Jervis tugged into his boot, straightened his hat, and braced himself to avoid being pushed backward out the window. "I don't have any money," he said.

"Annie, open this door or I'm going to break it down."

"Oh, God," she said, running to the clothes tree and opening a hidden pocket in her petticoat. "Here's ten dollars. Now go."

"I'll pay you back," he said, as a body crashed against the door with a thud.

"Just get out."

Jervis was touched by her concern for him, the risk she was taking to help him escape, her generosity in giving him the money to get out of town. "I'll come back, Annie." The whole room seemed to shake and rattle as the heavy body again thudded against the door. "I'll come back and marry you, Annie."

"Just go."

"Will you wait for me, Annie?"

"I'll wait, I'll wait," she said, as the body again slammed against the door and the wood cracked and splintered.

Jervis gave her a quick kiss, pulled back the curtain, and jumped out the window. The last thing he heard before he jumped to the street below was Annie crying his name, "Pretty Shadow."

With the ten dollars, Jervis caught the stage to Milestone to hide out until he received word from Trails End that the sheriff had been shot, fired, or bought off. Impatiently, he waited, fired by the remembrance of his whispered name. But the good news did not come. Because he had no money, he worked at the wagon yard for three meals and a bed in the straw until such time as he could return to Trails End for Annie. When the chance came to work at the blacksmith shop for three meals and a bed in the back of the shop, he took it; and later, he took a job in the Platte Saloon for three meals, a bed in the hotel, and ten dollars a month spending money.

The spending money gave Jervis new hope. Some of it he saved for Annie and some of it he spent on drink, and when he had had enough to drink, on women. Jervis saw more rooms like Annie's room, and he met more girls like Annie. Jervis did not forget Annie. He remembered the way she looked in the green dress, the way she looked on the red counterpane. He saw other women in identical dresses and identical poses, but no one else ever called him Pretty Shadow the way Annie had. In time, Jervis came to understand the indestructability of the girls; and although he did not consider for one moment backing out of his promise to marry Annie, he did become more patient.

The cattle season drew to a close and Billy Meadows was re-hired for another season. Not wishing to hang around and wait him out, Jervis drifted, riding the chuck line, working in saloons, skinning mules. He holed up on the Powder River. He worked along the Yellowstone and the Musselshell. He revealed no inclination to settle down, working a roundup here, a drive there, a full season somewhere else. The trail he left was a crooked one which crossed and crisscrossed the western states over the years, revealing only one overall pattern. He was drifting, but the general direction of that drift was back to Texas. Jervis was going home.

One morning Jervis awoke in a one-room adobe in a small New Mexico town. By the light of day, the room looked only a little better than it had in the darkness. The ceiling was thatched and oppressively low, the floor earthen, the walls unpainted adobe, the bed a straw pad over strips of rawhide. Jervis picked up his hat from the floor and set it on his head. He picked up the empty whisky bottle in which he had deposited his cigar the night be-

fore, shook out the butt, and stuck it in his mouth. There was a
shelf built into the thick adobe wall; and in a jar on the shelf,
Jervis found three matches. He selected one, lighted the cigar,
burning his nose, and leaning back against the wall, wondered
how long it would be before someone would come along, and how
he could talk them into bringing him some clothes.

Jervis picked a flea from his stomach, crushed it between the
nails of his thumb and first finger, and dropped it on the floor.
While waiting for some trousers to come along, Jervis pondered
the vagaries of fate. Being naked gave him a philosophical inclination.

The day before Jervis had learned that Billy Meadows was
dead, his throat cut by a careless barber who had an equally careless and public wife. Now he could go back to Trails End and
marry Annie. Jervis had drawn his pay, bought a wedding suit, a
pair of boots, and a ticket to Trails End. Then he had set out to
take one last glimpse of the joys of being a free man. He had
stopped by the cantina, had a few drinks, met a girl who had not
seemed too bright, but willing, and had followed her home. After
that, things were hazy, but the meaning was clear.

Jervis was almost fifteen years older than when he first made
his way up the long trail. All he had to show for those years were
the lines about his eyes, a bum knee from the time his horse fell
on him, a bad stomach from a steady diet of beef, beans, and gyp
water, a shoulder which had never been right since he had tangled
with a cow after digging her out of a bog, and the dent in his nose
which had been put there by a bull that was reluctant to become
a steer. There were the horse, stripped of saddle and bridle and
left only because the authorities might laugh at the theft of a
man's money and trousers but had no sense of humor about
horses, the hat which was not worth stealing, and a red welt on
his stomach left by the flea. He hoped the girl had not left him
with a more lasting souvenir.

Diamond Annie would have to wait a little longer. The
money, the train ticket, the saddle and bridle, his boots and clothes

were gone. He had nothing left but his self-respect. That was still intact. He still kept his word. He still paid his debts.

Jervis went back to drifting, back to work, saving up money to marry Diamond Annie. When a man came to the ranch where he was working to get together a herd to take to Trails End, it seemed to Jervis like the hand of fate, too strong to ignore. It might not be his kind of drive, but it was going where he wanted to go.

"What do they call you?" the old man asked.

"Call me Pretty Shadow," he said.

Pretty Shadow recalled a song he had made up once about Annie. He had been working a roundup in Wyoming, long days, short nights, little sleep. He had made up the song accidentally, the words coming to him as he rode along. But the song had amused the crew and they had all begun singing it. Pretty Shadow wondered if any of them still remembered it, still sang it. He wondered if Annie had ever heard it. He'd never been one for writing letters, but if she had heard the song, she would have known it was Pretty Shadow who wrote it.

For a moment Pretty Shadow tried to recall the words, and then, even though it was not a night-herding song, he began to sing it, soft and slow.

> I got a gal whose name is Annie,
> She's got freckles on her fanny,
> Dark-brown eyes as big as any,
> And diamonds in her hair.

> When she smiles it's like a penny,
> When she loves she's got aplenty,
> She ain't fat but she ain't skinny,
> And diamonds in her hair.

Pretty Shadow was so tired and so caught up in the song and the memories it brought to mind, that he ventured too near the edgy cattle, bumping into one of them. The cow turned and hooked at him; and Pretty Shadow jumped back, collided with something else, and fell down, instinctively throwing his hands up to protect his face before he realized that it was Covina he had bumped into. "What are you doing here?" he asked, pretending anger to hide his fear.

"Watching the herd," she said curtly, afraid she had been caught sleeping on guard. "What are you doing?"

"I was just—Old Blue was after me."

"I didn't see Old Blue."

"Well, it was one of them cows. It don't make no difference which one it was. They're all mean enough to eat snakes."

"Yeah, one of them got after me today," Covina said.

Neither of them bothered to get up. Pretty Shadow lay on the ground where he had fallen, and Covina sat on the rock where she had been sitting when Pretty Shadow bumped into her. Both of them tried to think of something to say, each knowing that if one made an effort to get up, the other would have to do the same.

"June says if you look them in the eye, they won't bother you," Covina said.

"June can say that because if they did, you wouldn't be able to tell nobody about it," Pretty Shadow said.

"How much farther do you think it is?"

"I don't know, but if we don't get there tomorrow, we won't never get there. There won't be no holding the herd. They remember where they watered last, and when they get thirsty like this, they don't have no sense. They keep trying to go back."

"I don't know if I can last another day."

"Don't you worry. If we get to water tomorrow, you won't have much to do. The moment them cows smell water they'll start running, and you can just let the drags go. It's the point that'll have trouble. We'll have to hold them back and spread them out, or they'll just pile up on top of each other."

Covina looked up at the brilliant stars, cold and crisp as ice and a thousand miles away. "How do we know Ruby Draw ain't dry, too?"

"It ain't. The Preacher's leaving as soon as it's light, and he ain't stopping the wagon till he hits water."

"What if he gets lost? What if he misses it?"

"He won't."

"But what if he does?"

"Then we will get lost, lose the herd, and keep right on walking till we all fall down dead."

"That's what I wanted to know," Covina said, encouraged. "I got to go check the baby and see if there's any water left. Which way's the wagon?"

"Oh, hell, it's over that way somewhere," Pretty Shadow said.

"The only thing is," Covina said, "if we make it, I'm willing to forget that that sheepherder fouled our water. But if we don't get there, I hate like hell to think that Martin Foster is still tormenting women and that Maury has our goat."

"I'd like to settle with them horse rustlers, too."

"Pretty Shadow, do you think that nester's prayers helped him any? I thought he was as good as hung, but he's still alive," Covina said, deciding that Martin's prayers had aided and abetted him.

Pretty Shadow was distressed at the uncertain nature of prayer. "You can't never tell."

Covina declared with certainty that her prayers had never been answered, recalling that she had once asked for a doll for Christmas.

"Did you get one?"

"Yeah, but not the kind I wanted. I got a homemade one."

"You have to be specific," Pretty Shadow said, ruling the prayer answered.

Covina recalled praying for a pinto pony and never getting it.

"Do you still pray for it?"

"Hell no, I quit praying for horses when I was a kid."

"You got to be persistent," Pretty Shadow said, ruling the example invalid.

Covina recalled praying that her cat would have kittens.

"Did she?"

"Hell no, it was a tom."

"You got to be sincere," Pretty Shadow said, ruling the example inapplicable.

Covina wondered if Pretty Shadow's knowledge came from experience, or if he was stating theory.

Pretty Shadow confessed that he had experimented with prayer during lightning storms and while crossing rivers. "I never said much. Mainly, I just wanted the Lord to know which one I was in case He had a choice."

Covina inquired as to whether Pretty Shadow was going to address his talent at prayer to their present circumstances.

Pretty Shadow reminded her of the sweet-tasting water they had found at Beaver Creek and suggested they apply for some just in case the Preacher was to miss Ruby Draw.

Covina admitted it was about the best water she had ever tasted. "Hell, I'm so dry I could drink some of that gyp water out of the well back home without curling a lip."

Pretty Shadow suggested they put their faith to the test, recalling how good beer tasted when one's throat was tight and one was dry plumb through to the marrow.

Covina recalled drinking beer with a fellow behind a fence. As she remembered it, it wasn't much better than gyp water.

Pretty Shadow assured her that beer or whisky either would slide easily down his throat; but to demonstrate himself free of prejudice, he would accept gin, rum, or rye.

"You know what really satisfies a thirst?" Covina asked, and her tongue got thick at the thought of it. "Cold buttermilk." She said the words slowly, thinking how the cold, heavy liquid would feel on her swollen lips and parched throat.

Pretty Shadow made a face, spat, and suggested they approach the throne of grace.

"You don't think it'd be bad luck or anything?"

"I ain't superstitious," Pretty Shadow said. "But I ain't going to go it alone."

Covina, never one to desert a fellow when the going got rough, stiffly dropped to her knees beside the rock.

"You say the words," Pretty Shadow said, working himself

into a position that looked religious but felt comfortable. "I'll keep my fingers crossed."

"O Lord, we ain't asking You for nothing, just thanking—" Covina began, glancing at Pretty Shadow, who was vigorously shaking his head. "Except for something to drink. O Lord, we are dry clear through. We have been without water all day, and it looks like we might not get none tomorrow neither. And we'd appreciate it if You'd send us something to drink. Amen."

Pretty Shadow suggested they be more specific.

Covina prayed for buckets of water.

"From Beaver Creek," Pretty Shadow interjected, unwilling to leave anything to chance.

Covina nodded and got to her feet.

Pretty Shadow demonstrated his exasperation with people who tried to rush him and suggested they had not yet put their faith to the test. "Water gets mighty ordinary when you have it."

"You want me to pray for beer?" Covina asked, shocked at the impudence of it.

"As long as you're at it," Pretty Shadow said, assuring her that it was all right and explaining that the prayer would go on his record, not hers.

Dubiously, Covina prayed again. "Lord, send us buckets of beer." She paused, waiting; nothing happened. She looked up.

Pretty Shadow expressed his approval. "Amen," he said.

Covina felt uplifted. "Prayer is heady stuff," she said, and encouraged by the absence of calamity, decided to try again. "O Lord, send us buckets of whisky," she said, and Pretty Shadow winked his eye and happily nodded his head. "O Lord, send us buckets of gin," she prayed, and Pretty Shadow demonstrated his approval. "Send us buckets of rum. Buckets of rye. Buckets of buttermilk."

"That's way to hell too much buttermilk," Pretty Shadow said.

The sun rose slowly, remorselessly in the pale sky above the bedground, deserted now except for a few cows that had been unable to leave with the herd and lay helpless in the sunlight, grateful for the brief, flitting shadows cast by the soaring, circling buzzards.

The torn and broken ground, the trampled vegetation, the dust that still hung above the ground clearly marked the trail that the herd had taken. Along that trail, like beads from a broken string, were other cows that had left the bedground in the predawn darkness but had been unable to stay with the leaders and were down, never to rise, or, scarcely able to stand, awaited death with lowered heads. Farther up the trail, a few lowing cows straggled back toward the water they remembered, a life's journey away. Dominated by a blind instinct to return to the last place they had watered, they tossed their heads at anything in their way, turned from their path by nothing.

The trail ended in a thick cloud of fine dust where the hands fought the stubborn cattle. The leaders, blinded by the brilliant sun that burned in the sky and glinted off the ground before them, turned back. The drag overtook the point. All semblance of herd order disappeared. The hands, knowing that the back trail was too long for the cattle to return to Sandy Creek alive, pushed them on to the only possible water, in Ruby Draw, somewhere ahead. Throughout the heat of the day, the men and the cattle exhausted one another. Waving shirts and hats, yelling and cursing, beating the cattle with sticks and fists, the men pushed the herd closer to Ruby Draw. The cattle milled and bawled, rattled horns, and died of exhaustion in the suffocating dust and heat at the center of the herd. A few of the cows, senseless with thirst, walked stupidly, stolidly through the curses and blows the overwrought hands threw at them. Nothing could stop them. The hands let them go.

The cattle had sulled, stood facing the hands with their heads down and would not budge. As Covina tried to turn them north, a cow darted past her and started down the back trail. With a yell, Covina turned and tried to head the cow off. As she did, four or five more cows broke away from the herd. She chased after them; but she could not get around them; and to run behind them was to drive them down the trail. Picking up rocks, she threw them at the cows and stood panting. She looked back at the herd, hoping miraculously the men had been able to turn the cattle toward water. The cows stood watching her, their eyes wide with fright. She knew they were close to panic, on the edge of stampeding; but she did not care. Covina fell to her knees, throwing her arms over her hat to protect her head from the splitting rays of the sun. She did not care if they lost the herd. She did not care if someone else did her share of the work. She did not care who saw her sitting down.

The Kid, weeping in frustration, tried to turn a mean-faced brindle steer that started down the back trail. He beat on the steer until his fists throbbed with pain, but the steer did not seem to feel the blows and would not turn. Driven by an irrational impulse to make the steer obey his will, the Kid stationed himself in the steer's path; and when the animal tried to walk over him, he caught it by the horns, trying to twist its head around. He was unable to turn the animal, but he held on while the steer pushed him along. The Kid wrestled with it until the brindle shook him off. For a moment he lay on the ground, picking the stickers out of his arm. He watched the animal march solemnly down the trail and wished for a gun or knife so he could kill it. Getting to his feet, he wiped his cheeks with his sleeves and started after a lineback cow.

Pretty Shadow snapped his knotted rope at the cattle and yelled until his throat was so dry and inflamed that he could scarcely swallow. June stationed himself before the straggling cattle and, risking a stampede, fired the pistol into the ground at their feet. Even that did not turn them. They did not seem to hear the shot but plodded on in their slow, inexorable way. He beat them and prodded them with the barrel of the six-shooter, managing to turn some of them.

Knowing that this day would be crucial, Lampassas had prepared himself for it. He had set himself to reach water before stopping, and he had driven himself and the herd relentlessly in the seesaw battle toward Ruby Draw. Grimly, he battled the cows, unmindful of the buzzing in his head and the pains in his lungs when he gasped for breath. His legs quivered so that he could not stand still but kept moving, stumbling after first this remnant of the herd, then that one. He was chasing three wild-eyed, raw-boned cows when his legs suddenly refused to function and he fell face down on the ground. The abrupt cessation of movement was unbearable. His head pounded, the blood rushed to his head until he felt it would explode from the pressure. His vision blurred. He gasped and retched, unable to catch his breath. Lampassas tried to get up, but his muscles, old and overstrained, would not obey. He could not get up. He tried to call for help but no words came. He could not swallow. For a moment he thought he was going to die and in panic lay jerking on the ground, trying to get to his feet. Then he lapsed into semiconsciousness.

For a time Lampassas was conscious only of the sounds of his breathing and the ache in his throat. His mouth was dry; and he thought his throat would swell closed, choking him to death. He closed his eyes, aware that time was passing. When he opened them again, he could see clearly. He realized his hand was stinging; and when he looked at it, he saw that it was covered with little black ants. He brushed them off and raised his head to look for the herd. The men had lost more ground. The herd was getting farther and farther away from the water, and he knew the end had come. He had faced disaster before. He had lost the horses. He had lost some of the hands. From time to time he had momentarily lost his picture of the way. But he had always held on to the herd. And now there was no herd; and because there was no herd, there was no way he could hold on to it. All he and his men could do was battle the individual cows, and they were losing that battle.

Lampassas tried to resurrect the old dream of success, pitting his courage, enterprise, and daring against the odds and winning. But the dream was gone. Dead. He could not bring it to life again. In its place he saw himself as a fool wagering the spent strength and mad dreams of his old age against change and all the machinery of fate: the railroad, the stockyard, the plow. The thought enraged him, and the rage lent him strength. Rising to his feet, he tottered after the herd, an old and beaten man.

"To hell with them," he yelled. "Let the sons of bitches go. I don't give a damn." But his voice was hoarse and weak, and the drovers could not hear him above the bawling of the cattle. Squinting his eyes and sealing his lips against the dust, Lampassas stumbled through the cattle trying to help his men until he could find them and tell them to quit.

A late afternoon breeze blew up, giving them some relief from the dust and heat. Encouraged by it, Covina got to her feet but could do little to restrain the cattle. The men stopped for a moment to feel the breeze cool their blistered, sweaty faces and to breathe the freshened air. Old Blue stopped, raising his head, and stood sniffing the air. Trotting forward a few yards, the steer sniffed again, and then, lowing, headed north at a trot.

Lampassas saw the peculiar action of the big steer, but, his mind dulled by heat and exhaustion, he could not interpret it. Then, seeing other cattle sniffing the air and following Old Blue, he realized they had smelled water.

"Old Blue's smelled water," he called. "Hold up the leaders." One by one, and then in larger and larger groups, the cattle turned about and headed toward the draw in a deliberate walk that quickened into a swinging, ground-eating gait, and finally broke into a desperate, head-down, lowing trot. Knowing that he had to gain control of the herd, Lampassas doggedly set out after them.

Short of breath, doubled over with stomach cramps, Lampassas chased the cattle. He was only vaguely aware of the other hands, who were running along somewhere behind him, and sometimes completely forgot the herd in front of him and ran head-down, thinking only of the water in the draw. He stumbled and fell. For a moment he lay on the ground resting, unable to get up, and then the thought of water drove him on.

After running awhile, the cattle slowed to a walk, and then stopped altogether to stand, sides heaving, sniffing the air for smell of water. Seeing them stop, Lampassas ran harder to catch them. He passed the stragglers that could not keep up and was heading the herd when the leaders began running again. Sobbing and cursing, he slowed to a walk, hunched over against the pain in his side.

His hatred of the cattle knew no bounds. He believed the cows acted as they did only to torment him; and although his purpose was to save the cattle by preventing mills and pile-ups in the draw, he would gladly have killed them instead.

When Pretty Shadow caught up with him, Lampassas began trotting again, partly because he had caught his breath but also because he did not want the hands to slacken their efforts. They saw the Preacher coming out to meet the herd; and they knew the draw was near; but they also knew that something was wrong because the Preacher was waving to them and trying to turn the cattle. Lampassas and Pretty Shadow stopped to get their breath and looked at each other, for a moment unable to face whatever the Preacher was trying to tell them. Then they began again, running to his assistance.

"Bank's too steep," the Preacher yelled, when they got near enough to hear. "Got to turn them. Spread them out." But already the leaders had gotten past the Preacher and the thirsty cattle were plunging off the bank and into the shallow water, crowding, crushing, and piling up. Swinging sticks and lariats, the men tried to drive them apart, to spread them out.

The cattle, mad with thirst, knew no fear. In a solid mass they surged toward the water, hooking and trampling, oblivious to the men's attempts to direct them, turning on the men only when the men got between them and the water. The hands kicked and prodded at the cows, their only protection the confusion and mass of the herd.

A runty white steer, one horn pointing forward and one horn pointing back over its head, tried to get past Pretty Shadow. Pretty Shadow kicked him in the neck, but instead of ignoring the blow and crowding into the mass of cattle along the bank as the others had done, this steer jumped back and dropped its head, very much on the prod. Had it been full size, Pretty Shadow would have ducked behind some other cows, but he was too tired to run from a stunted, half-size steer. He snapped the knotted rope at the steer's nose; and it backed up, tossed its head, and lunged forward before Pretty Shadow could recoil the rope.

Pretty Shadow tried to jump out of the way, throwing out his hands to push the steer's single forward horn out of the way; but the short, curved horn struck him in the left side, just above the groin. Grunting, Pretty Shadow threw himself forward, over the steer's neck, trying to hold its head down until he could roll off the horn. The animal not powerful enough to throw Pretty Shadow, kept tossing its head, driving its horns upward in a series of sharp thrusts. Unable to scream, Pretty Shadow grunted, the sound jerked from his throat by the driving horn. Catching the horn with both hands, he pushed himself free and fell to the ground.

Pretty Shadow lay doubled up on the ground, feeling nothing except the sticky wetness that lay against his arms and a sickness in his throat. He was scarcely aware of the cattle running about him. Sometimes a hoof kicked him, or a cockleburr-loaded tail lashed his face. Once a cow, seeing something in its path, hooked blindly at him, tearing his shirt and back. He knew that June was standing over him, beating at the cows with the six-shooter. Later, the Preacher stood beside June. Pretty Shadow felt himself being lifted. He screamed and fought at the hands that held him while the horn once more tore at his belly. Then he felt nothing except that he was going up, up into the air, and the grasping fingers could not hold him down.

Covina lay across a dead cow, her head in the water. Feeling someone touch her back she raised her head and, wiping back her hair, saw that it was Lampassas.

"Upstream," Lampassas gasped. "Water's not so muddy."

Pushing herself out of the water, she got to her feet and pulled back her tangled and muddy hair; and putting her hat on her head, she followed Lampassas upstream where the water was untrampled by the cattle. After washing her face in the clear water, she began drinking from her hands. The Kid joined them, and they lay on the bank drinking water until they were sick.

It was dark and they could hear the cattle moving about, some of them still in the water, others scattering out to graze.

Many of them had bedded down wherever they happened to be. Downstream, a cow slipped off the bank and fell into the water with a splash. "To hell with them," Lampassas said. "Let's go look for the wagon."

Getting stiffly to their feet, they started upstream in search of the campfire, so logy from the water and sore from cooling off that they had difficulty walking over the rough ground in the darkness.

June was holding the lantern in one hand; and when they saw his face, they stopped. The Preacher looked up at them and then looked away. Quietly, they walked up and knelt on the wagon sheet beside Pretty Shadow. His face was pale and drawn. His eyes were closed.

"What happened?" Lampassas asked, laying a thick, stiff hand on the blanket over Pretty Shadow's shoulder.

Pretty Shadow's eyes opened. "I reckon I got too close to the herd," he said, trying to laugh but unable to.

Lampassas patted the blanket with his worn, swollen hand. He looked at his hand as though he were ashamed of the thick yellow nails and gnarled fingers. "I'm real sorry," he said. "Is there anything we can get you?"

"Since I come all this way," Pretty Shadow said, running his tongue over his cracked lips, "I'd like to have some of that water."

"It won't do you no good to be drinking water," the Preacher said.

"It won't do no harm, will it?" he asked.

"I'll get some," Covina said, taking the bucket from the wagon.

"How many did we lose?" Pretty Shadow asked hoarsely.

"I reckon there's about a hundred cows down between here and last night's bedground," Lampassas said. "About the same number still on their feet that ain't made it to water yet. Some of them will come in before morning. I don't know how many was killed or crippled in the pile-up."

"We tried to hold them," Pretty Shadow said.

"We done the best we could," Lampassas said. "There wasn't nothing else we could do."

"If we'd a had horses we could a handled them," June said.

Covina came back with a bucket of water and worked her way between Lampassas and the Preacher. "Pretty Shadow," she said. "Pretty Shadow, do you want some water? Fresh from Beaver Creek. That other you asked for, I couldn't get."

The water choked Pretty Shadow, and he coughed, groaning with pain. The men looked away. Lampassas picked up the bucket, and tipping back his head, drank from it, then passed it around. Unable to look at Pretty Shadow, the men followed the progress of the bucket until it was set aside. Then they looked at Covina.

"You're the one that said a cow wouldn't bother you if you looked him in the eye," Covina said, turning on June.

"I was talking about a stompede," June said. "I didn't mean a man could stand between a thirsty cow and water and not get run into."

"That wasn't a stompede?"

"No, I wouldn't call that a stompede."

"No, you wouldn't," she said. "You wouldn't call yourself a horse's ass neither, would you?"

June said nothing, believing his face to be impassive but looking exactly like a man who has just had his foot stepped on while helping his wife out of the wagon. Hurt, yet more than hurt; angry at himself for putting his foot where it could be hurt.

"June," Pretty Shadow said. "I looked away."

"Then that's what did it. Sure, they'll charge you if you look away. I told you you had to look him right in the eye." June dropped his head, and at first they thought he was crying; but when he looked up, his eyes were dry. "Tell me which one it was, Pretty Shadow. I'll kill him."

"Don't do that," Pretty Shadow said. "You're going to make it now." Pretty Shadow looked at the Preacher, and the Preacher leaned close to hear. "I always been one to keep my word and pay my debts. I ain't never backed down on my word."

"We know that."

"I give my word to this gal, Diamond Annie, that I'd come back and marry her. I meant to do that, Preacher."

"You done your best."

"Tell her not to wait no more. I couldn't ask that of her."

"I'll tell her."

"I'm obliged. Tell her I meant to come," Pretty Shadow said. "Preacher, I got in a scrape once. Had to get out of town. She loaned me ten dollars."

"Is this the same girl?"

"Diamond Annie. Give her whatever wages is coming to me. Tell her not to wait no more. I couldn't ask that of her."

"How will I find her?"

"Ask for Diamond Annie. Red Dog Saloon. No mistaking her. Long black hair. Eyes sparkle. Why they call her Diamond Annie. Soft, gently face. Rosy lips. Wearing a lo-and-behold shiny green dress. Red slippers. Feathers in her hair. When I seen her coming down the stairs that way, I thought she was the prettiest gal I ever saw."

"I'll find her for you," the Preacher said. "You just rest easy."

Pretty Shadow began to shiver and Covina got his bedroll from the wagon and spread it over him to keep him warm. Sitting down beside him, she tenderly stroked his head.

"Preacher, I ain't going to see Trails End again," he said.

The Preacher bowed his head. He had faced death with others many times, and each time he had felt this. What was there to say? What had he learned from those times that would give ease and comfort to this man? His hands flexed unconsciously, yearning for the familiar heft and feel of the thick, heavy Bible, filled with words of warning and comfort. He knew the words, as old and familiar as death itself, as thick and heavy as the Bible. He had pronounced them how many times? Letting them roll off his tongue to sting or comfort as the Lord willed. He had never studied what to say; he had only prayed; and when he had opened his mouth, the words were there, without having to be called, without having to be thought. But now the words were gone. He had set out on a mission for the Lord; and in getting there, he had forgotten not only the words but the mission and the Lord, too.

"It's a better city than Trails End you're going to," the Preacher said. "No plows, no fences, no rivers to cross. Just sit easy in the saddle."

"Preacher, I don't reckon anybody has been throwed as often as I have. And this last horse is the worst in the string."

The Preacher explained that every man had his own horses to ride, that Pretty Shadow had had a mean string, and that what counted wasn't the kind of horses a man rode, or how many times he was thrown, but how many times he got back in the saddle. "There never was a man that couldn't be throwed," the Preacher said. "And there never was a horse that couldn't be rode, if a man had Jesus to top for him. That's what He come to earth for. Why He was born in a manger and grew up like a man. He had a pretty mean string of horses to ride, too, but He rode them. All the way to breakfast. And He showed everybody else the way they ought to ride but don't, and how they could ride if they'd ride with him. And He topped Old Death, the meanest horse in a man's string. You can ride it, Pretty Shadow. Just set your heels in the stirrups and lean back."

"Jervis Applewhite," Pretty Shadow said, and everyone started and looked about, half expecting an apparition. "That's who I am. Nobody ever called me Pretty Shadow except Annie. And then you boys. All them women I told you about. They didn't call me Pretty Shadow. They didn't know who I was."

The men sat in silence over Pretty Shadow, each deep in his own thoughts. Covina got the baby out of the wagon to have something to hold. The night was still, and they could hear the cattle going back to the water to drink and the frogs singing for rain. June slapped a mosquito on his face. The Preacher tapped the nodding Kid on the shoulder; and when the Kid looked, he knew Pretty Shadow was dead.

Lampassas got up and walked to the wagon. Leaning against the wagon, his foot on the tongue, Lampassas looked out over the dark land. Overhead the stars glittered brilliantly just above his fingertips, like reflections from his campfire. The water was like a pale ribbon in the night, and scattered along it were the dark and peaceful shapes of the bedded cattle. It was a comforting scene, like an illustration from an old family Bible.

Lampassas rested in the quietness of the moment. He was tired, very old, and he had very nearly lost. The horses were gone and over half the cattle he had started with. Gattis and Pretty Shadow were dead. But he was going to make it now. He had won. He tried to feel what it was like to have won. He waited for relief, for triumph, for joy. Below him a broken-backed cow thrashed in the draw, grotesquely tried to rise on its forelegs, and then fell back in the water. "June," he called, his forlorn voice echoing along the draw. "Go down there and shoot that damn cow."

Earlier in the day June would gladly have killed the whole herd. When he had seen Pretty Shadow on the ground, he had looked for a bloody horn, wanting to kill that cow. Tomorrow he would walk back down the trail, killing the cattle that could not make it. But today he had had enough of killing. He wanted no more.

Taking cartridges from the wagon, he loaded the six-shooter and walked along the bank above the cow. "One shot," he thought, swallowing down the sickness in his throat. "Just one shot." He tried to pick out the animal's head in the darkness and, slipping, fell into the water beside the thrashing horror.

Rolling over in the water, he fired at the cow, that crawled after him on broken stumps of legs. Again and again he shot at the groaning and trembling cow and in the flash of powder saw blood running from the empty eye that loomed above him. He fired until the gun was empty and then he beat at the cow with the barrel until it was still.

Only after he got to his feet did June discover that the cow lay on its side, its twisted head upstream, and that it had been trying to get away from him, to escape his bullets. In darkness and fear, he had shot the cow six times in the rump. Leaning against the bank, June threw up the bitter water of Ruby Draw.

At dawn June got the shovel and began digging the grave, and the Kid fashioned a cross out of two sticks of wood. Because there was no Bible in which to record his death, the Preacher asked that they mark his grave with his name so there would be some record of his dying. Finding nothing on which to write his name, Lampassas took the axe and chopped a piece out of one of the side rails on the wagon.

The Kid got out his pocket knife, rounded off the edges of the board, and prepared to cut the name into it. "What did he say his name was?"

"Pretty Shadow," the Preacher said.

The Kid carved the name into the piece of wood and blackened it by burning the letters with a heated pothook. With a length cut from Pretty Shadow's rope, he hung it over the cross.

Chapter 11

FROM where they held the herd, the town stood above them on the brow of a low hill. A fretwork of corrals and loading pens decorated the base of the hill. Red pendant stock cars were strung along the tracks between the red depot and the towering red water tank that seemed to rise up into the town, where building fronts reached upward two and three stories toward the sky and tumbled away in all directions until they covered the hill. The rooftops of the town were bright in the early morning sunlight, the chimneys stood etched against the soft pink morning clouds, and the windowpanes glinted the gold of the sun. From the very center of town, above the water tower and the dome of the courthouse, rose the church steeple. At the top of the steeple, a crucified weather vane indicated the direction of the wind.

"There she is," Lampassas said. "That's Trails End."

"God a'mighty," June said reverently, removing his hat. "God a'mighty."

"That's what we come to see," said the Preacher, seeing the promised city through misted eyes.

Covina was terrified, for the first time realizing the size of the city. "God, ain't it big?" Protectively, she held the baby close to her.

"I don't reckon they've seen us yet," the Kid said. "Don't seem to be nobody coming out to meet us."

Lampassas had expected a tumultuous welcome. He expected crowds of people to come out and look at the herd with curiosity and at the drovers with admiration. He expected young girls to dance and clap their hands with joy, young boys to run along beside the cattle, old men to throw their hats in the air and shout. He expected cattle buyers to meet him with bags of money to bid for the herd. "I reckon they sleep late in the city," he said.

"God a'mighty," June said softly. "God a'mighty."

"I reckon I'd better go wake them up," Lampassas said, and they chuckled nervously. Lampassas looked up at the bright but forbidding city on the hill. "Well, you-all can bring the herd up slow and easy. We want them to look tame. Leave the wagon by the depot," he said, squaring his hat and jaw at the same time. "I'm going up there to do some powerful trading, and when I get done, I reckon we'll all be rich men."

Unable to contain their excitement, the men slapped each other on the back, including Covina in their camaraderie; and then Lampassas turned, and hitching up his torn and dirty trousers, which were now several sizes too big for him, he began the last solitary mile to the far end of the trail to claim the prize.

Wordlessly, the hands turned to watch Lampassas as he made his way across the open prairie and up the rise that led into the town. And now that the ordeal was over, and over so quickly, they felt a sadness.

"I can't believe it's over," Covina said, wetting her hand with her tongue and smoothing down the baby's tousled hair.

"You know, it wasn't so bad," the Kid said. "Not like I thought it would be."

Lampassas walked toward the city slowly to give himself time to think. He was frightened by the suddenness with which the end had come. He had reached the end of the trail. His ambition, the dream of his life was over. He needed time to prepare himself. In a few more minutes he would be free of the herd, the men, the girl. He could go to sleep at night without listening to the cattle. He could wake up in the morning without worrying over what he would have to require of the men. If he forgot the way, he would also forget its hardships; and if his mind chose to remember it, it would be something to talk about to folks who stopped by his place to sit on the porch and rock.

Lampassas looked at the ground before him, because the sight of the big and wonderful city frightened him. But tonight, bathed and shaved, with money in the pockets of their new clothes, they would own the town.

When Lampassas looked up, he was surprised to see that weeds were growing in the cattle pens, and the fences were old and rotten and in some places had fallen down. The streets were empty. "Must be earlier than I thought," he said, mounting the steps of the depot.

The station agent, a thin, pale, bespectacled man with a thin, pale mustache, had a bit of dust trapped in a corner of the room when he heard the door open. "Do fer you?" he asked, bending over with his duster to whisk the dust into the pan.

"You the cattle buyer for the railroad?" Lampassas asked.

"Huh? What? Who, me?" the agent asked, looking back over his shoulder at the door. What he saw was a shriveled, dirty, long-haired, bearded man in a large frayed hat, torn and patched clothes, and unrecognizable footwear. The agent whirled around and jumped erect, dropping the dustpan, pushing back his eyeshade, and jerking a crick in his back. "You, you," he said, pointing at Lampassas. "Get out of here. Go on," he said shooing Lampassas with his hand. "Go on down to—Jake's Place. They'll feed you," he said, groping in the pocket of his vest. "Here. Here's two bits. Get yourself some breakfast."

"Where's the cattle buyer?" Lampassas asked.

"Cattle buyer? There ain't no cattle buyer here. This here is the railroad depot."

"I reckon there are some buyers in town," Lampassas said.

"Could be. There ain't nothing else."

"I reckon it's all right if I put my herd in your holding pens."

"You got a cow?" the agent asked, warily eyeing Lampassas.

"Six hundred head."

"Where'd you get six hundred cows?"

"Texas."

"That so?" the agent said, trying to humor him. "Huh, huh, huh," he laughed. In the corner the telegraph clattered.

"They're right out there," Lampassas said, pointing out the window.

"Let me look at them cattle." Keeping the desk between himself and Lampassas, the agent edged along the wall. Still facing Lampasses, he turned his head and looked out the window, and then turned and looked again. "My God," he said, slapping off his eyeshade. "Them ain't cows. Them's horny toads."

"I drove them all the way from Texas," Lampassas said proudly.

"I can see that," the agent said. "There ain't nothing left but legs and horns. My God, look at that one. There ain't enough hide on him to make a shoelace."

"They're all for sale," Lampassas said. "Ever last one."

The agent looked at Lampassas and backed away from him, bumping into the wall. "You brought them here from Texas to sell?"

Puzzled, Lampassas stared at him. "Ain't this Trails End?"

"No, it ain't. This here is Grandview."

"Grandview?" Lampassas felt dizzy. Reality seemed to be falling away from him. "I followed the trail just the way they told me. They couldn't a been hurrahing me. I—I never heard of no Grandview before. You sure this ain't Trails End?"

"I think it used to be Trails End," the agent said. "But folks didn't like that name. Said it wasn't progressive enough. So they changed it to Grandview."

"Don't they ever have any cows in them pens out there?"

"Not since I been here."

"Don't the trains come through here any more?"

"Ever Thursday evening. Drummer special."

Lampassas sank down on a bench along the wall. The agent, keeping his eyes on Lampassas, slid along the wall to the door of the baggage room, reaching down and pushing it open. "Ab," he called without looking inside the room.

Beyond the door, five men sat huddled around a small table. No one spoke. There was a sigh, a sweeping of the hands; one man pronounced an oath, another slid his cards across the table, shifted the fat cigar in his mouth, and stood up. "Yeah?"

Ab walked into the office, closing the door behind him. He was a large man, wearing black shiny boots, a big white Stetson, fawn-colored coat and trousers, and the thinnest of string ties and the widest of leather belts, each held by a silver buckle. "What do you want?"

"Feller there says he wants to sell some cows," the agent said, gesturing to Lampassas.

Ab looked at the old tramp sitting against the wall and then back at the agent. "This your idea of a joke?"

"He's got a herd right out here."

Ab walked over to the window and looked out. Deliberately, he reached up and removed the cigar from his mouth. "God almighty, I ain't seen anything like that in ten years."

"You ain't a cattle buyer," Lampassas said.

Ab looked at Lampassas, squinting through the smoke and rolling the cigar in his mouth. "I used to be one," he said. "I used to be the best there was. Right now I'm selling windmills. Everlasting windmills. It's profitable, interesting, and I'm doing a real service for the people of our great West. What the hell are you?"

"Cow man," Lampassas said. "Ever last one of them cows is for sale."

"I used to buy cows like that," Ab said, staring at his cigar as he rolled it between his thumb and middle finger. "I've seen them cows come in here till it looked like the world was made of horns. Hell, I'll never forget them days. When the cattle come, the women and flies come with them. It's hard to say which was the thicker, but the flies you could brush off. Good-lookers too, them women was, with silk parasols, and high-heel shoes. Hell, with all them cows in the street, the women had to wear high heels. But them days are gone," Ab said with a sigh, spitting a bit of the chewed cigar out the window. "Ten years. And out here that's a long time. There ain't a cow in this country less it's a moo cow, and you couldn't find a decent-looking woman in the whole town. And if you did, she'd be respectable. Hell, you have to close the door to play poker any more."

Lampassas sat on the bench, his drooping eyes fixed on the floor. Ab leaned his elbows on the window and looked out at the small herd grazing toward him. "I've been rich and busted more times than most folks has been drunk, and all on cattle. I was a millionaire twice, and I can't even count the times I had to cadge a drink. Yeah, I used to buy them. But I'm respectable now. The Everlasting Windmill Company of Emporia, Kansas. That's me. Lord, I didn't know there was another one of them critters left in the world."

"There's six hundred of them," Lampassas said without looking up. "All for sale."

"Yeah, but who would you sell them to? You might be able to sell a few of them to a circus. Their hides might be worth something if they weren't all scarred up. You might could sell some of the horns. Look nice over a bar or a big fireplace. Not even an Indian would eat one of them now. Too civilized. I might could offer you something for your horses."

"We done lost all the horses. We walked them cows. All the way from Texas."

"Too bad, but you'd a done better to just let the cows go. They ain't worth nothing here."

"But maybe they are someplace else."

"I don't know where, unless it's where they came from. I used to could sell them cows. Hell, I used to could sell cows to a sheepherder. I don't know any more, though. Who would I sell them to?"

Lampassas did not know. His concern had been to round them up, brand them, and drive them to Trails End as quickly as possible with a minimum of suffering and weight loss on the part of the cattle. He thought if he could get them there somebody would buy them.

Lampassas looked up at Ab. The fight had gone out of him. He did not have the heart to bargain, scheme, and bluff. It was not his game. "I ain't trying to make money any more," he said. "But I got to have enough to pay the boys and what I owe to Mr. Fulton back home."

"How many boys you got?"

"Seven," Lampassas said, including Covina, Pretty Shadow, Gattis, and himself.

"A man'd be a fool to buy them wore-out old cows," Ab said. "But I reckon I made my share off of them. I reckon I owe it to them old cows to make a offer. I'll swap you a railroad ticket to Denison per man for the herd."

"We don't want no railroad ticket," Lampassas said, getting to his feet. "We aim to go back the way we intended to come. Horseback."

"Well, at least my conscience is clear," Ab said. "I made an offer. Now I better get back to the game. I was right smack in the middle of a string of luck."

Lampassas sank down on the bench. Ab walked over to him, placing his fat hand on Lampassas's shoulder. "Look, old-timer, I ain't going to let a cattleman down," he said, squeezing Lampassas's shoulder. "I owe them too much, I reckon. I'll give you a dollar a head for the hides."

"I owe more than that to the boys," Lampassas said. "After what they went through to get the herd here I got to give them something. And I got to take that five hundred dollars back to Mr. Fulton. I give my word."

"Sure, I'd like to help you, but that's the best I can do," Ab said. "Why, their hides is so scarred up with brands, you'd be lucky to get a watch fob out of them. Look, pardner, let me give you a piece of advice. You take the money. You earned it.

You buy the boys a drink and then light out for California. You don't have to go back to Texas. Why, as old as you are, that money will take care of you the rest of your life."

"I can't do that," Lampassas said. "I ain't hoping to get rich any more. I ain't even hoping to break even. But I aim to take care of the boys and go back to Texas with five hundred dollars if I have to drive them cows to Chicago."

"Excuse me a moment," Ab said, stepping into the back room. Patiently, he waited until the boys finished their hand and gave him their attention. "Who wants part of some Texas cows? If we take the whole six hundred we can get them for four dollars a head."

"What do they look like?"

. "Worst-looking bunch of cows I ever saw."

"I'll take a hundred head for the Wild West show," said one player, pushing a stack of chips to Ab's side of the table.

"I'll take the best eighty pairs of horns," said another.

"Hell, give me a hundred," said the third. "Have them butchered and I'll send them to that orphanage in Illinois. I promised the senator I'd do something for them."

They turned and looked at the fourth player. "I don't deal in cows," he said. They waited. "Oh, hell, give me twenty-five I'll have their horns knocked off and peddle them for milk cows. Only hurry up. I'm losing money ever hand you ain't here."

"I'll expect you boys to cut me in on something some time," Ab said, and then he stepped back into the office and closed the door behind him.

"I talked to my friends in there," he said to Lampassas, "and they offered to back me up to two dollars a head. That'd be twelve hundred dollars. That's the best I can do, and it's costing me money to talk to you."

"Hides is four dollars in Texas," Lampassas said.

"Then you should a sold them in Texas. Or maybe you want to turn them around and drive them all the way back. Twelve hundred, that's my final offer."

Squinting, Lampassas tried to figure it out. It came to five hundred dollars for Mr. Fulton and a hundred dollars apiece for him and the boys.

"Here, I'll write a draft for it, and I'll take your head count," Ab said magnanimously. Taking up a pen, he wrote out the draft, signing it with a flourish and sticking the paper in Lampassas's hand. He walked to the outside door, threw it open, and whistled. "Newt, go tell John I got a job for him and two or three of the boys. Tell them to bring some axes. I got a herd of cattle out there, and I want him to knock them in the head and jerk the hides off of them. All except a hundred and twenty-five that Murl is going to cut out." He caught Newt by the arm as the man hurried off. "Tell him not to damage the horns if he can help it."

Ab picked up a sheet of paper from the agent's desk and rapidly scribbled on it, then handed it to Lampassas with the pen. "Here, you sign this bill of sale."

"We drove them from Texas," Lampassas said. "The last of their kind. And they walked the whole way. They swum the rivers. They went without water—"

"I can't give you no more money," Ab said. "I done told you that."

"It ain't the money any more," Lampassas said. "Hell, them cows are— Maybe they are kinda skinny and bony. Maybe they're not much good for eating. Don't belong in fancy restaurants. But they belong. By God, they're cows. And by God, I never brought them all that way to sell for hides."

"Then why didn't you leave them alone? Why didn't you leave them back there in the brush to die out? They're freaks, don't you know that? They're so damned tough they've outlived their times. There ain't no use for them any more. If they ain't any good for eating, what are they good for? Why, killing is the only thing you can do with them. Get rid of them. There ain't no place for them. Hell, I used to admire them too, but they're just freaks now. Two dollars a head, that's what they're worth to me. If they're worth more than that to you, why, by God, you keep them; put them in a museum."

"I got to have that five hundred dollars," Lampassas said. "I got to pay the boys."

Ab shrugged. Lampassas picked up the pen, dipped it in the inkwell, and deliberately wrote his name. The agent snatched the draft out of his hand. "I'll translate this into cash," he said. He opened the safe, took out a box, lifted out a handful of bills, and deftly sorted out the money. "There you are," he said, shoving the pile of bills at Lampassas. "One thousand dollars." Then he counted out two hundred dollars for himself. "Commission and stock-pen charges," he said. Busily, he stuck the money in his pocket, and closed and locked the safe.

Ab picked up the stack of bills, placed them in Lampassas's hand, and catching him by the elbow, helped him to his feet and guided him to the door. "It has been a pleasure dealing with you, my friend," Ab said, patting Lampassas on the back and gently shoving him out of the office.

Lampassas stumbled out of the door and sat down on the steps. Spreading out before him was the herd, which the hands were slowly, hopefully grazing behind the wagon toward the stock pens.

Lampassas waved them in. Seeing his signal, the hands looked at one another, not wishing to be the first to quit the herd and go rushing to town. Together, they sauntered through the grazing herd and up to the depot.

"Nobody's watching the herd," the Kid warned as they crowded around Lampassas.

"Let them go to hell for all I care," Lampassas said. "Don't none of them belong to us any more."

"Whoopee," they shouted, throwing their hats into the air, dancing around and startling the cattle. June pulled out the six-shooter and tried to fire it into the air, but the hammer fell on a spent cartridge. Before he could pull the trigger again, the Preacher twisted the gun out of his hand and silenced the cheering with a gesture.

"You'll stompede the herd," he said angrily.

"They don't belong to us no more," June said.

"It don't make no difference. They belong to somebody."

Lampassas looked up at them standing above him. "Boys, they wouldn't give me nothing for the cows."

"How come?" June asked.

"Because they ain't worth nothing," Lampassas said. "Nobody wants them any more."

They stared at him in disbelief. In the past months, the cattle had assumed a worth greater than anything they knew, more valuable than their own lives. They could not comprehend the kind of world in which the cattle were of no importance.

"You mean them cows?" Covina asked, hitching the baby up on her shoulder and pointing at the ragged, thin-flanked, hump-shouldered, sway-backed cattle. "Them cows ain't worth nothing?"

"That's the finest herd of cows I ever seen," June said. "They can outwalk, outrun, outfight, and outswim any damn herd in the country."

"He give me a thousand dollars for the hides," Lampassas said.

"The hides!" Covina said, stricken at the thought that they had driven the cattle a thousand miles to sell for leather.

"You mean he's going to kill them cows?" June asked.

"That's all they're good for," Lampassas said bitterly. "They're freaks. That's what they are. Freaks."

"Who said that?" asked June.

"The buyer."

"By God, he'll take that back," June said, vaulting up the steps past Lampassas and throwing open the office door.

By the time the others had reached the top of the steps, June had the thin, pale station agent bent backward over the desk and was holding the pistol at his throat.

"Apologize."

"I'm sorry, I'm sorry," the agent screamed.

"That ain't the one," Lampassas said. "It was the big feller."

"In there," the agent said in a strangled voice, pointing to the side door.

June was across the room in two steps and kicked the door open. There was a flurry of action, and when it was over, the men sat leaning back in their chairs, puffing on their cigars, not a card, chip, or coin in sight.

"The feller that bad-named them cows out there is going to apologize or be full of more holes than he can likely use," June said.

The poker players cheerfully agreed that the herd represented the finest bunch of cows they had ever seen and were a credit to the drovers, the Creator, and the state of Texas. Accepting the apology, June nodded and began backing out of the room, the other hands retreating behind him.

"You oughtn't to a done that," Covina said, when they had stopped outside the depot.

"They apologized, didn't they?"

"Yeah, but you ought to a let them finish their hand."

"I got a thousand dollars for the hides," Lampassas said. "Five hundred of that I promised to Mr. Fulton, and I reckon I'll keep my word. I can't get back what I paid for the herd noways, so I'm dividing the other five hundred dollars among us equally. I figure we ought to give Gattis a full share and send it to his folks. We wouldn't a got across the river without him. The Preacher's taking Pretty Shadow's share to his sweetheart. I'm giving Covina a share so she can—fix herself up. She worked like the rest of us."

"That's less than a hundred dollars a man," the Kid said.

"It ain't much for the hardest work a man was ever called to do, but it's all there is. If this other five hundred was mine, I'd share it with you, but it ain't. It belongs to Mr. Fulton."

"Well, I reckon it's enough for a drink, a horse, and a suit of clothes," June said. "And if a feller got a cheap horse, a cheap drink, and a cheap suit of clothes, he might have enough left over for a cheap sack of tobacco."

Grimly, Lampassas counted out the money, paying off the

hands. "I thought after we got all cleaned up, we might get together at the Red Dog Saloon and pay our respects to Gattis and Pretty Shadow," he said.

"Wait a minute. Hold up there," shouted a grim, official-looking man who was waving a tally book in one hand. "Is them your cows?"

"Nope," Lampassas said. "Done sold them."

"Did you bring them here?"

"All the way from Texas."

"They look ticky to me," the man said.

"Don't cast no aspirations on them cows," June said, his hand resting on the butt of his six-shooter.

"There ain't enough to them to keep a tick alive," said Covina.

June turned on her, then decided to limit his objections to outsiders.

"Well, just the same," the man said in a politer tone of voice. "There's a fee for inspecting cattle in this town. Two bits a head."

"Then you go talk to the man that owns them," Lampassas said.

"Don't make no difference. The fee has to be paid before the cattle are sold. How many head you got?" the inspector asked, thumbing through his tally book.

"Four hundred head," the Preacher said, feeling a conservative estimate to be in order.

"I thought it was six hundred."

The Preacher bristled at the insult to his integrity. June's hand tightened around the butt of the six-shooter. "All right. Four hundred head. That's an even hundred dollars."

"You thieving carpetbaggers have got the last cent you'll get out of me," Lampassas said. "I ain't paying."

"It ain't me," the inspector said. "It's the law. I'll go back and tell them you wouldn't pay the fine, and then the constable will have to come and put you in jail. I don't want no trouble."

"I don't have a hundred dollars," Lampassas said.

"It's the law."

"I don't reckon any of us would want to see Lampassas go to jail," the Preacher said, taking off his hat. "I think Pretty Shadow would have wanted to chip in fifteen dollars at least, and I don't see how I could do any less."

Placing the money in the hat, the Preacher solemnly passed it around. After everyone had contributed, Lampassas counted up the money, made up the difference out of his pocket, and the Preacher handed it to the inspector, who made a note in his tally book.

"When do you aim to inspect the herd?" Lampassas asked.

"Oh, they been inspected. I'm just collecting my fee now," he said, counting the money as he walked away.

"Wait a minute," June said, grabbing the man by the collar and spinning him around. "You forgot to pay us for cutting out the cows so you could inspect them."

The inspector glowered at June and started to say something; then his eyes dropped to June's hand, resting on the pistol. "Don't you know it's against the law to carry a gun?"

"You trying to rile me?" June asked.

The inspector peeled off a five-dollar bill and handed it to June, but June did not move. He added another five to it and June accepted it.

"You'll hear about this," the inspector said, angrily backing away. "I'll go to the law."

June pulled the six-shooter out of the holster, and the man backed over the railroad tracks and fell down. Getting to his feet, he backed on down the street, waving his fist at June. "You'll hear about this."

"This'll pay for our drinks at the Red Dog," June said, waving the ten dollars.

"Was I you, I'd put that six-shooter in the wagon before I got in trouble," the Preacher said, but June declined.

In neat trail order, Lampassas on the point, June and the Preacher in the swing, Covina and the Kid in the drag, they walked across the railroad tracks, between cars broken and devoid of running gear, and started along the street into town. The big doors of the fire house were hanging uselessly, emptily from the hinges. The roof of the opera house had caved in. The courthouse was boarded up, and sunlight glittered from the broken and curtainless windows of the St. George Hotel.

Lampassas stopped. "We're here," he said. "I reckon we might as well split up."

After readily agreeing, they all stood waiting for someone to make the first move, a little frightened at the thought of being alone.

"I reckon this is my street," the Preacher said, picking a street and then waiting to see if anyone was going with him.

"I'm going that way," Lampassas said, pointing in the opposite direction.

Self-consciously, each of them picked a different street, and after promising to meet later at the Red Dog Saloon, they started on their way, scarcely looking back.

As soon as he was out of sight of the others, the Kid stepped through the open door of an empty shell of a building, walked across the rotten floor, jumped out a back window, ran down a weed-filled alley, and came out directly behind Covina.

She turned and looked at him, and he looked away, unable to think of anything to say. He heard the wooden sidewalk creak and saw that she had turned and was walking toward town. He walked a few yards behind her, glad that the street was deserted, not only because he wanted to be alone with her, but also because he did not wish to be seen in his filthy, ragged clothes and recognized as a shiftless cowboy instead of a serious-minded railroad hand.

"Where are you going? What're you going to do?" he asked, walking along behind her, but she did not answer.

"Maybe you don't have to—do that. Maybe you could do something else."

They passed a broken-backed building, from the doorway of which three ragged children stared curiously. A drab-haired woman in apron and bare feet jerked the children back and closed the door. A sign, threatening to fall from its single remaining chain, hung over the sidewalk. DUGGAN'S was still discernible in the cracked and peeling paint. Unconsciously lifting a protective shoulder over the baby, Covina walked around it.

"Maybe you could cook. You could sew. Or—or—"

There was a dull crack as Covina stepped through the rotten plank sidewalk. The Kid ran up to help her, but she pulled her foot out and stepped into the street where the footing was surer.

"Maybe you could get married," he said, struck with admiration for his own idea. "There must be men who aren't married. I mean, just because— Why, I bet a lot of men would marry a girl that—"

"Bullshit," she said.

For almost eight years Trails End was the brightest town on the frontier. By the end of the first season there were thirty cattle pens, a railroad depot, five saloons, a dance hall, fifteen brothels, and two homes. Subsequent years showed comparable growth. The future was in longhorn cows and attendant businesses, which business was to give money to the cowboys for bringing the cows to the city and then to take the money back through various entertainments such as murder, robbery, adultery, and the subtle poisons the saloons offered. This was called a system of free enterprise, and the freer the enterprise, the better.

Occasionally, there was trouble when a man who had worked a hundred days for about the same number of dollars lost it all in a throw of the dice, the dark of an alley, or the privacy of a girl's room. Such disappointments often led a man to relieve his feelings by emptying his pistol in available targets such as mirrors, signs, and people. These excitements stimulated population growth in the person of a preacher, a doctor, three undertakers, and six law men.

The town, determined to protect lawful business interests from their victims, hired Billy Meadows, a gunman wanted for murder in four states, to police the town. He in turn hired five more murderers to help him keep the law and built a reputation for himself as a peace officer by killing three men and a girl. He killed a farmer for seeing his current girl after her quitting time, a deputy for wanting to be sheriff, and another deputy for looking like a cowboy the sheriff was looking for. The girl he killed for getting up after he had knocked her down the third time. Billy Meadows had pride in his punch.

In addition to his reputation for keeping the peace, Billy had a reputation with the girls and kept the dance halls supplied with his castoffs. As they had no place to go when he got through with them, he generously placed them in the dance hall, accepting a cut from the proprietor for their performances.

The whole town was too busy trading thirty minutes' worth of affection for two days' worth of work, selling five cents' worth of whisky for two bits, and peddling violence for law, to notice that the railroad was moving west and so was the trail, and with them, the easy money. The town awoke from its orgy of blood and money to find that the stock pens were empty; the cowboys, gamblers, and prostitutes were gone.

The panic-stricken town passed an ordinance making drinking, gambling, prostitution, and murder illegal. Then they hired a newspaperman to report the booming future of the town. An expert came from Chicago to survey the town's needs and found that the town's name was all wrong.

"Too dreary," he said. "Not enough romance. When people think of the West, they think of romance."

The town council voted to change the name of the town to Grandview.

"Got a nice ring to it," said the man from Chicago, stuffing his pockets.

People moved away from Grandview just as they had left Trails End, leaving empty hotels, empty saloons, empty shacks. The sand piled up against the sides of the buildings, weeds grew through the floors, and the wind worried doors on rusting hinges.

Billy Meadows prowled the dying town, his black-holstered six-shooters ineffectual against decay and vandalism, and with his boots on, died on the dusty floor of the barber shop. The town did not want another killer-type sheriff. Instead they selected as part-time constable a dark, thickset blacksmith who sharpened plow points and dreamed of glory. When not occupied shoeing mules and repairing wagons, the constable patrolled the town, checking doors and windows of the stores, and cursing mischievous boys who hid in deserted buildings and scared him as he passed.

The constable maintained an enviable record, never making an arrest or shooting anybody. Occasionally he would rough up a drunk drummer who tried to get familiar, before carrying him to his room above Jake's saloon. Once he had simultaneously beaten the sense into and out of a farmer who wanted to shoot the town fellow that ruined his daughter. And once he had cuffed Red-haired Retta because she was illegal anyway and not very good. For these services the town gave him a badge, a second-hand shot-gun, fifteen dollars a month, and a license to kill, thereby not only gaining a law man but keeping the town's only blacksmith.

Some people stayed on in Grandview because they had no place else to go, and the railroad stopped every Thursday to rescue the drummers who plunged recklessly into the heart of the country to ferret out a last treasured dollar hidden in a fruit jar in the cellar or in a can beneath the hearth in exchange for the dream of getting on, of having one more futility than their neighbor could afford.

If the trip was a successful one, the drummers returned to Grandview just in time to catch the train. But if things had gone badly, they came to town early to console themselves with drink, cards, and lies at Jake's Place, and with Red-haired Retta on Texas Street.

Even in daylight, Texas Street was the darkest street in Grandview. Lying below the hill, the street began near the old loading pens and ran a few hundred yards parallel to the railroad tracks, ending at the new hog pens. Texas Street was not really a street at all but a weed-guarded trail between the tracks and the row of gray, rotting shacks. Most of the shacks were vacant, but it was hard to tell which ones because they all had broken shingles, broken windows, and unpainted walls. But those who knew Texas

Street knew that Red-haired Retta had the widest path beaten through the weeds to her door.

The sun, rising above the hill and the town, shone through the broken window and fell on Retta's loose, puffy face. Blinking her thick yellow eyelids against the sunlight, she turned over to see who was in bed with her, her memory not being what it used to be. "Harry again. Oh, God," she thought. "And here it is Wednesday and the drummers will be coming in."

"Get up," she said, digging her elbow into the ribs of the large, dark, hairy man beside her. "Get up, this is Wednesday."

Retta stretched and yawned, throwing the back of her hand over her mouth, and then fingering the triangular scar on her lip. "Damn Billy Meadows," she said without passion, remembering how beautiful she had been before Billy had hit her in the mouth with his pistol barrel, knocking out a large chunk of her lip and three front teeth. The blow had spoiled her looks, and she had had to move out of the dance hall with its fancy love rooms and high-paying clientele and take up a shack on Texas Street. "What the hell," she thought. "The farmers don't pay much, but they're nice. And the drummers—the drummers only come on Wednesday."

"Get up," she said, punching the dark-armed man again. "Get up. I got things to do."

The farmer groaned, pulled the pillow over his head and commenced snoring.

"I better do something with my hair," she thought, running her broken nails through her tangled, lifeless hair.

In the good old days when she had worked in the dance hall, she didn't have to do much with her hair. Just give it a good brushing, and it would sparkle. But on Texas Street the men never noticed her hair; and she didn't have much time to brush it, and soon it lost its sparkle. She began dyeing it red, and calling herself Red-haired Retta. It gave her a new outlook, the farmers liked it, and it added color to their lives.

"Get up," she said, shaking the farmer. The two-room house

was a shambles. Harry had come in drinking; and as always when he had been drinking, he wanted to fight first. They had yelled and wrestled around, knocking over chairs, breaking the jar that held her dried cattails, and stepping on her polished seashell, the one from California that the drummer had given her in lieu of two dollars and in which she could hear the ocean waves. Remembering, she viciously hit the man with her elbow. He snorted, turned over, and threw his powerful arms around her, pulling her close.

"That's the trouble with farmers," she thought. "The cowboys hung their six-shooters on the bedposts, the railroad hands hung their lanterns on the door, but the farmers just hung on."

She reached behind him, grabbed a handful of his long dirty hair, and pulled his head away from her. The farmer woke up. His dark eyes blinked open and then shut again as with one hand he pulled her to him, running the other down her back.

"Oh, God," she thought, feeling his rough hand tugging at her flaccid hip. "Oh, well."

A sudden rapping on the door arrested the farmer in his exertions. "Beat it," he yelled.

"It's a drummer," Retta said. "It's Wednesday."

"Let him wait," the farmer said, pushing her back on the bed and forcing the interruption from his mind.

"Just a minute," Retta called, not wishing to lose a customer.

The farmer was on the verge of recapturing his former ardor when the rapping was sharply repeated. Snarling, he looked up, his fists clenched. "Wait your turn," he yelled. Belligerently, he watched the door until Retta pulled his head down. Returning his attention to her, he took her savagely in his arms, just as the rapping began again.

With a shout, he was halfway off the bed when Retta, with a strength and agility surprising in such a limp and shapeless body, pushed him back and ran to the door. She jerked the door open just enough to pop out her head at a freshly bathed and shaved gentleman, dressed in store-new black, high-heeled boots and a black broadcloth suit, and holding a white Stetson in his hand.

"Didn't I tell you to wait?"

"Yes ma'am, you see, I'm—"

"Then dammit, wait," Retta said, slamming the door and trotting back to the bed where the farmer was sitting up. "Hurry up," she said. "This one looks rich."

"I couldn't wait," he said.

Retta looked at him. "Damn you, you're just trying to get out of paying."

"With all that banging going on, how's a man suppose to keep his mind on his business?"

Angrily, Retta picked up his clothes and tossed them to him. "You do that again and you'll have to pay anyhow. I'm not responsible for what you do on your own. Now, you get behind that curtain and get dressed. I've got a gentleman waiting."

"I got to go. I got work to do," the farmer protested. There was no back door.

"You'll just have to wait. This is a paying customer," she said with savage sarcasm.

While the farmer picked up his shoes and disappeared behind the curtain, Retta slipped into the egg-yellow negligee that went so well with her red hair, dusted her wrinkled, yellow bosom with powder, threw the spread up over the mussed bed, and replaced the stained bolster.

"Come in," she called sweetly, reclining on the bolster.

For a moment she thought the man had gone, but then there was a gentle knocking at the door.

"Come in," she said, a little more firmly, but still keeping a sweet edge to her voice.

The gentleman rapped sharply on the door.

Cursing to herself but still keeping the smile on her face, Retta opened the door and leaned seductively in the doorway. "Did you hear me say come in?"

"Yes ma'am. You see, I'm—"

"Then dammit, come in," she said, taking his hand and pulling him inside so quickly that he dropped his hat. While he stopped to pick it up, she closed the door and leaned against it. She had handled these rich, shy ones before.

"Hope I didn't get you out of bed," said the Preacher, who was a little startled at her manner of dress.

"The son of a bitch was just piddling anyway," she said.

"Maybe I'd better come back later," the Preacher said, holding the hat under his chin and backing into the room.

"I won't have no time for you later," she said.

The Preacher decided to put his hand to the plow and not look back. "What I come to see you about was a business matter," he said as solemnly as possible.

"Yeah, and I know the business," she said, giving him a push.

"No, you see, I'm—I'm looking for Diamond Annie."

"What do you want her for?" Retta asked cautiously.

"I come to give her some money," the Preacher explained.

"Then you found her, Pretty Shadow," she said, and pursing her thick red lips, she walked toward him with outstretched arms.

"I reckon I'll have to require some proof," he said.

"All you can stand, Pretty Shadow," she said, throwing her heavy arms around his neck.

"No, you don't understand. I ain't Pretty Shadow. I'm what you might call a—a emissary," the Preacher said, backing into and abruptly sitting down on the bed.

"I'll vouch for that," Retta said, gracefully sinking down on the bed beside him and seductively throwing back her head and shoulders.

"You don't need to wait for Pretty Shadow no longer," he said, placing his soft new hat on his lap and crossing his arms over it, so that it crumpled.

"I'm mighty glad to hear that," Retta said, blowing in his ear and nibbling his neck. "But I hope in the future you'll be a bit more patient after knocking on the door, as there is certain things a lady's got to do before she answers."

Only by throwing his elbows behind him did the Preacher escape a reclining position. With one hand he felt along the bed for the hat, which had been knocked out of his lap, accidentally brushing Retta's knee. "I regret to tell you that Pretty Shadow won't be able to marry you," he said.

"I'm right sorry to hear that," Retta said, blowing down his collar. "But even knowing don't change my feelings."

"Pretty Shadow is dead," the Preacher said sadly, averting his face to escape her wet, lippy kisses.

"Not yet he ain't," Retta said, passionately embracing him.

"Yes he is."

"No he ain't," Retta said, embracing him some more.

"I—I got something for you," the Preacher said, trying to slip out from under her suffocating weight.

"I thought you might," Retta said. "Gray hairs don't mean nothing."

"You give Pretty Shadow something once," the Preacher said.

"I never give nobody nothing," Retta said. "If you got it, you got it from somebody else."

"Is ten dollars correct?" the Preacher asked.

"Ten dollars!" Retta said, scarcely able to conceal her surprise. "Why, yes, that's right. Ten dollars."

"I ain't going to give you ten dollars," the Preacher said.

"Say you ain't?"

"I'm going to make restitution."

"Not with me you ain't."

"Yes sir," the Preacher said. Sitting up and putting his hat on his head, he pulled out a roll of bills. "I'm going to give you a drover's remuneration."

Retta, who had a low opinion of most men, wasn't partial to this kind at all. In terms which were certain and picturesque, she expressed her sorry opinion of his habits, character, and dress. "I don't cotton to your kind," she said. "So you can take your money and your fancy suit and your remuneration where it's appreciated. I'm respectable."

"Whoring may have become respectable," said the Preacher, offended by the woman's profession, personal opinion, and manner of speaking. "But it sure ain't Christian."

"Pretty Shadow," Retta called.

"Yeah."

"Pretty Shadow, this man insulted me."

"I was only trying to give you what was coming to you," said the Preacher, sliding away from her across the bed.

"Don't you touch me," she said, striking at him.

The Preacher decided to throw the money on the floor and run, without explanation, and was backing off the bed when he bumped against a huge, half-dressed man who towered over the bed, his enormous arms crossed over his chest.

"What's the matter, Retta?" the farmer asked.

"Pretty Shadow, this man insulted me," she simpered, huddled in a large heap in one corner of the bed.

"I was only trying—" the Preacher began, but before he could finish, he was lifted bodily from the bed and slammed against the wall with a force that rattled the dishes in the cupboard as well as the teeth in his head.

"Be careful, Pretty Shadow," Retta screamed. "He's an emissary."

The Preacher came to himself in a pigpen. A large, fat sow nuzzled at his ear. A small, white, pink-eared pig stood grunting on his back. Shooing them away, the Preacher raised his head. He had been stripped and robbed and left for dead. All he had left were his new woolies, which were soiled with mire, and several ribs which were sensitive to the labors of breathing.

For a moment, with the fat sow grunting inquisitively in his ear and the stench of the pigpen in his nostrils, the Preacher was provoked to wrath. With murder in his heart, he looked about for a pole large enough to break the farmer's head and to bring the whore to remembrance. Then he thought better of it and peace returned to his heart.

"I may be in a pigpen, but I ain't a pig," he said, generously leaving the obverse unstated. "It's better to be robbed than be a robber." Kneeling in the mire, he offered up a prayer of thanksgiving that he had lost nothing worse than his money and his clothes.

Shining with a bath, a shave, and a haircut, decked out in new clothes, ready for the whisky and girls of the Red Dog Saloon with money in his pockets and spurs on his boots, June strode down the street, his boot heels bouncing unfamiliarly on the plank sidewalk. He felt so good he pushed back his hat with his thumb, jammed his hands in his pockets, and whistled. The only problem he had left in the world was finding the Red Dog Saloon. But that was a problem, because the tailor had acted very strangely and June couldn't find anybody else to ask. Every time he saw somebody they ducked out of sight.

About a block up the street, June saw a man step out of a store and start across the street. June threw up a hand. "Hey, you son of a bitch," he yelled in a friendly fashion, and the man stood petrified for a moment and then dived under a building. "Shyest damn people I've ever seen," June muttered.

June walked down to the store the man had dived under and looked inside. The place was deserted. June stepped inside and looked around. No one. "Son of a bitch is still under the floor," June muttered. He thought of shooting through the floor to bring him out but then decided it might scare him. Instead, he stomped on the floor with his boot heel. "Come out from under there," he yelled, and a man arose from behind the counter with his hands over his head. June was so startled he forgot what he had come in for. "Give me some cigars," he said. The man slowly lowered one hand, picked up a handful of cigars, jammed them in June's pocket, and then elevated his hand again. June flipped him a coin and the man caught it one-handed in midair and then returned his hand to its previous position.

June strolled outside, took one of the cigars, bit the end off it, and spat the end into the street. Poking the cigar in the corner of his mouth, he searched his pockets. "Got a match?" he called over his shoulder. The man lowered one hand, struck a match, and with the other hand still high in the air, walked outside and lighted June's cigar.

"Thanks," June said, throwing back his head and blowing blue smoke into the air. When he looked around, the man had disappeared.

Roger McSwain, Ladies' French Lingerie, addressed the bar, head up, shoulders back, and thumbs hooked into the pockets of his flowered vest. Finishing his story about the drummer who sold hair remover to an Indian squaw, he lifted his glass and sipped like a humming bird.

His companion, Joe McMasters, who sold prairie-dog poison and magic corn-remover out of the same bottle, allowed himself one loud snort to show his appreciation of the tale and then began his favorite lie about the girl fresh from milking the cows whom he had met on the train outside Quincy.

"Gangway, step back, gents, and let a thirsty man to the trough," shouted June as he batted the doors back against the wall and swaggered to the bar, half expecting to see the occupants disappear. "Whisky," he shouted, slapping the bar with his hand.

The bartender, a short, buck-toothed man with black hair combed straight down the sides, poured a neat drink, shrugging at the drummers, who stared at June with obvious distaste.

"I've drunk whisky near and whisky far, but this here is just like tar," June said, throwing the drink past his lips, teeth, and tongue, so that it splashed against the dry back of his throat.

"Another one," June said. "And then you can direct me to the Red Dog."

"This is it," the barkeep said. "Or used to be. Jake's Place now. Changed the name when the girls moved out. Changed hands three times since then."

"I've tasted good and I've tasted fair, but this here will curl your hair," June said. He emptied the glass and looked about. The room was dark, the only light spilling in through the two dirty and curtainless windows. The floor was bare, the boards worn and cracked open and soft underfoot. Two tables, each with a circle of chairs, stood in orderly arrangement, gathering dust and cob-webs. Behind the bar were a dark, cracked mirror past reflecting, a fare rate for the railroad, and a stuffed two-headed dog, with one head sniffing the ground and the other baying at the moon.

"The drummers like it," the barkeep said, seeing June's frown of disgust.

"I sure hope my friends can find this place," June said, doubtfully.

"They can if they're looking for a drink. Only saloon in town still open. Every night from seven to ten, all day Wednesday and Thursday. Got some beds upstairs if you need a place to sleep."

"Another whisky for me, and one for my friends here," June said, waving the two drummers into his circle of acquaintance.

"No thanks," said Roger McSwain addressing the bar.

June turned from the bar and looked down at the man. "You refusing to drink with me, Shorty?"

Roger McSwain's fat pink face turned schoolgirl white.

"Not at all," said the friendly Joe McMasters. "We would just prefer a cordial."

"That's right," said Roger McSwain, giggling nervously.

"Okay," said June, somewhat mollified. "If you won't have a drink with me, I'll have a drink with you. Three of whatever they're having."

McMasters leaned farther back across the bar and, turning his head away from June, winked at the bartender, who nodded in reply. The bartender quickly prepared two of the drinks, and then, with special care and ingenuity, he prepared the third, setting it before June.

"I won't ask, and I won't beg, but I'll accept a drink for my holler leg," June said, tipping back his head and pouring down the drink.

While the two drummers sipped their drinks with studied nonchalance and the bartender busily polished a bottle of four-bit whisky, June took a firm grip on the bar, blinked to focus his eyes, and took a tentative and shaky breath.

"Fix," he said, having to stop and swallow. "Fix another." The bartender looked uncertainly at Joe McMasters, who shrugged his shoulders and then nodded his head. Roger McSwain giggled. Turning his back, the bartender prepared a lethal drink, setting it before June with a trembling hand.

"All right," June said, brushing back his coat. On the second try, he caught the butt of his six-shooter and aimed the wavering barrel in the general direction of the bartender's head. "You drink it," he gasped, "and we'll die together."

At the sight of the pistol, the bartender took a step backward, Joe McMasters came to attention beside the bar, and Roger McSwain threw his arms into the air. The bartender took a sip of the drink, his short nose quivering. "All of it," June said, leaning across the bar on his elbows to steady his aim. The bartender, spilling half the drink over his shaking hand, managed by closing his eyes to get the drink down, then dropped the glass and placed both palms on the bar. June, by using both hands, returned the six-shooter to his holster and then secured himself to the bar with his elbows.

Taking advantage of the pall which had come over the saloon, Joe McMasters picked up the fallen Roger McSwain, who had fainted dead away with his hands still outstretched, and began dragging him outside.

"Where do you think you're going?" June called over his shoulder, not daring to let go of the bar.

"Just taking my friend out to get some fresh air," McMasters said. "I guess he had too much to drink."

"I knowed them cordials was too much for a little feller like that," June said.

When Lampassas found them, June and the bartender were propped up over the bar, singing a loud, incoherent, and blasphemous lullaby. "Give me a whisky and one for my friend here," Lampassas interrupted, patting June on the back.

"Make it a short one," June said, trying with both hands to indicate the size, in a gesture that would have included everything from a half teaspoon of castor oil to a tall lemonade. Turning his head, June tried to focus his eyes upon the face of his benefactor.

"Hidy, Lampassas," he said. "I want you to have a cordial."

The bartender succeeded in finding a bottle of whisky and after sloshing some of it into their glasses, placed the bottle between them.

"Here's to the trail back home," Lampassas said, hoisting his glass.

"That don't rhyme," the bartender said.

"Anything I can't stand, it's a drunk barkeep," June said, putting his hand in the man's face and pushing him away. The man folded up against the back wall like a pleated buggy top.

Hearing the doors open, they turned to see the Preacher, bareheaded, barefooted, and wearing a long saddle blanket wrapped around him Indian fashion. "God a'mighty," June said. "The Preacher's been in a poker game."

"Daniel in the lion's den was not tried as I have been tried," the Preacher said, tenderly feeling his nose.

"What happened to them clothes you bought?"

"Joseph lost his garment before Potiphar's wife, and I done the same," the Preacher said, scratching beneath the sweat-stiffened saddle blanket. "Wouldn't you think the mange would a had time to get out of these blankets?"

"You found Pretty Shadow's sweetheart?"

"I found her, all right."

"Did you tell her about Pretty Shadow?"

"I told her," said the Preacher, who knew now that Diamond Annie had called every man Pretty Shadow and that Red-haired Retta had no recollection of Jervis Applewhite. But he could not bring himself to tell Lampassas and June these things. "I ain't sure she understood."

"Did you give her the money?"

"I never had a chance. There was a man with her, and before I could give it, they took it. They took everthing I had."

"Why didn't you call for help?" June asked. "I'd a helped you."

"If I'd a opened my mouth, they'd a taken the gold out of my teeth."

"Did you tell the law?" Lampassas asked.

"I thought about it," the Preacher said. "I thought it over for a long time. But would you like to go to the law and tell them that you're a parson and that a whore robbed you?"

June shook his head in sympathy and understanding. "Not unless I had my pants on," he said.

The Preacher narrowed his eyes at June and would have said something fittingly sharp and to the point had not Covina come in, followed by the Kid, who was carrying the baby. Little Jake, dressed in a fresh blue gown and a new blue cap, and scrubbed pink, recognized the men and smiled happily, jabbering and trying to stand in the Kid's arms.

The men, already made shy by the strangeness of shaven faces, cut hair, and new clothes, were awestruck at the sight of Covina in a bright yellow dress with padded shoulders, puffed sleeves, and hourglass waist.

"It ain't right you should be in a place like this," Lampassas said.

"You asked me to come."

"But that was when—when you looked like a man," Lampassas said. "A lady wouldn't never come in a place like this."

"I'm trying to act like a lady," Covina said. "But, hell, this is my first day."

Critically, Lampassas studied the Kid, who was wearing a fancy vest, a bowler, and congress gaiters instead of boots. The Kid, fidgeting under his father's steady gaze, set the baby on the bar. "Pa, I come with you because you wanted me to, and I tried to do what you wanted. But I'm nineteen now, and Covina here is seventeen. Eighteen," he said, after looking at her. "And there's the baby to be looked after and all and, well, we thought we'd kinda throw in together."

Covina stood bravely beside the Kid, trying very hard to be a lady but ready to fight if necessary. No one looked at anyone as Lampassas felt around for words.

"Well, Jamie, I knowed this would happen some day. There comes a time to ever man when he wants to cut his own herd and brand his own name. I was kinda hoping—" Lampassas stopped, remembering Marfa. Not very suitable for a wife, folks had said. Not pretty enough. Not gentle enough. Not the kind of girl a man would choose to marry. But he had chosen Marfa. And she had suited him. The memory softened, mellowed him. Some things a man had to do on his own, and Jamie was a man now. He had crossed the river. "Covina is right smart of a woman to start out with," he began again. "But I reckon you're right smart of a man, too."

Lampassas laid his hand on Jamie's shoulder and gripped it. After a moment's hesitation over whether he should kiss Covina or shake her hand, he took her hand, and she kissed his cheek.

"He just wouldn't take no," Covina said, trying to smile.

"Let's drink to that," June said, trying unsuccessfully to resurrect the bartender and then pouring his own drink.

"If you folks want to get married," the Preacher said, pulling the blanket about him, "I'll marry you as soon as I can borrow a Bible."

"I'll give the bride away," Lampassas said, still blushing from Covina's kiss. "And June can be best man. We'll have a real Texas wedding."

"That's mighty kind of you," Covina said. "But we done married."

"That's where we been," the Kid said, blushing and grinning.

The Preacher could not hide his disappointment. Lampassas was chagrined at having been left out on such an important occasion, but decided there were other compensations—having his son near him, watching the baby grow, seeing other babies come. He did not intend to let his hurt mar his son's wedding day. June, however, faced life's disappointments from a more philosophical foundation. "Let's drink to that," he said.

"I was kinda looking forward—" the Preacher said. "I mean, you was one of my flock."

"Well, we thought it seemed more regular this way," Covina said. "I mean, he was a real preacher. He had a collar, and a church. And he didn't know us or anything."

"It seemed more regular," the Kid said.

"Well, it don't matter who does it," the Preacher said, looking self-consciously at his bare feet. "What matters is getting it done." He looked at Lampassas and smiled, and with a corner of the blanket, he loudly blew his nose.

"Things might look kinda tough right now," Lampassas said, taking Covina by the arm. "But me and Jamie has always managed to pull through. So don't you fret none. We'll take care of you and the baby. If I have to, I can work in a store. For a while. And it'll be kinda nice having a little feller around the house again," he said, patting the baby on the head. The baby laughed, jumping up and down so that Covina had to restrain him lest he topple off the bar.

"Pa, I ain't going back," the Kid said.

"You ain't going back home?"

"Jamie's got a job," Covina said.

"But I always thought—I planned for us to go back together and—"

"You planned, Pa. I never planned."

"Jamie's got a job here," Covina said.

"Me and Covina thought we'd stay here and make it on our own."

"I was figuring on letting you be the head of the house now that you're married and a father. I'd get a job. I wouldn't be in the way. Be a burden or nothing."

"We don't want to go back there," Covina said.

"There's nothing for us back there, Pa."

"I know there ain't nothing now. But we could build something. Together we could. The three of us."

"Pa, I got a job on the railroad."

"The railroad!" Lampassas said. Bitter disappointment welled up in him. He could not hold it back. "I reckon if there was any sheep here you'd be a sheepherder."

The Kid was stung by his father's remark but fought back his resentment at being misunderstood and tried once again to explain. "The railroad's the future, Pa. It's something we can put our lives into."

But Lampassas did not understand. His son was repudiating everything he had been taught, denying every value his father lived for. Lampassas could understand no explanation for it except spite and vengeance.

The Preacher understood the Kid no better than his father did, but seeing Lampassas's suffering, he tried to console him. "Why, Jamie'll be trailing all over the country on a pair of rails," he said. "Ain't that right, Jamie? He'll be riding that big engine and doing more and seeing more than you and me ever dreamed of."

For a moment, Lampassas caught a glimpse of the vision, seeing his son churning across the earth on an iron horse. "You'll be driving one of them big trains," he said.

"Pa, that's a big job," the Kid said. "They don't give it to beginners. A man has to be trained. Go to school. But maybe someday I can work my way up to it."

"You going to be the conductor?"

"Pa, the conductor runs the train. It'll be years before I can get a job like that. I'm a section hand, Pa."

"He'll work in a crew, just like cowboys," Covina said. "They'll all work together and be friends and everthing."

"Road gang," the Kid said. "We'll take care of a section of the track. Dress the right of way."

"It's an important job," Covina said. "Responsibility."

"We'll have to keep the track safe for the trains. Replace stringers, align the tracks, oil the side plates, cut weeds along the right of way—"

"Cut weeds? Like a nester? A damn farmer?" Lampassas asked. "That's what you want to do? That's your idea of a man's life?"

"It's just the beginning," the Kid said. "Pa, I have to start at the bottom."

"You've lost it," Lampassas said. "The dream I tried to give you. Of being your own man. Riding free. Finding your own way."

"Pa, I never had it," the Kid said. "I don't want to be alone. I don't want to be left out. I want to belong. I want to be part of something big. Don't you see, Pa? I'm going to be part of the railroad. That's something important."

But Lampassas did not see. Lampassas saw his son as one of the grubbers of the earth, one of the vast horde of bent and faceless men who tore and dug at the earth instead of riding free above it, who stooped before the great machines of the age and carried them on their backs. The vision brought him to despair. He was an old man. Unable to talk to his son. Incapable of dealing with the world. Useless. He had been left behind. Slowly, he turned away from them and poured himself a drink.

The Kid stared at his father's shoulders, which were beginning to sag with age, at the deeply lined patch of white skin left by the barber's razor just above the collar. He felt pity, complicated by feelings of guilt, for the old man who had outlived his day and now had nothing to do but wait for death to come along and get him out of the way. He wanted to explain that he could not wait because life called to him, that he could not follow his father's path because time had passed it by. But he did not know the words. He felt Covina squeeze his arm, but he did not look at her.

"Jamie's lucky to get any kind of job at all," Covina said. "There's not much to do in this town."

"What are you going to do?" the Preacher asked.

"I guess I'll have to learn to cook. And mend clothes," Covina said. "I'll be a good wife, Preacher. Honest I will. And a good mother, too."

"After these first seventeen years being a wife and mother is going to seem kinda dull."

The thought seemed to bother her. "We'll get on," she said. "Jamie'll do good, and we can get a house. It'll keep me busy keeping up with the baby. And we'll have more kids, and—I can buy things."

The Kid straightened his father's collar, cleared his throat, and pulled an enormous, second-hand railroad watch from his vest pocket. Holding it shoulder high, he studied its face. "We got to be going," he said. "I got to work tomorrow."

"First a drink to Gattis and Pretty Shadow," June said.

They all took a glass, except the Preacher, who proposed the toast. "To those who died to get us here: Gattis and Pretty Shadow."

Lampassas proposed a toast to Covina, Jamie, and Little Jake.

"It ain't Little Jake any more. We decided to call him Jamie after his father. Don't you think that's better?" Covina asked the Preacher.

"It's—more regular," he admitted.

They drank a toast to little Jamie, patting him on the head to see him laugh, then shook hands all around with Covina and the Kid, who were making eyes at each other, anxious to get away.

"Wait," June said. "I want to make a toast to Old Blue and the finest herd of cows that ever stompeded up the trail."

"We won't see no more like them," Lampassas said. "There may be other cows, but these was prodigies."

"They probably done started killing them," June said.

"How art the mighty fallen," said the Preacher. "Littleness has inherited the earth."

"Amen," said Lampassas.

"Commonness has become a virtue," said the Preacher. "And all cows are tame."

The station agent said it was Billy the Kid.

The constable said Billy the Kid had been in a New Mexico grave for at least ten years.

The station agent agreed that was what folks said, but allowed that if he was the Kid, he'd like to pass himself off for dead also.

Ab wasn't certain who it was, but he was certain that it was a Texas gunman. "Have you seen the way he handles a gun?"

The station agent declared that not only had he seen him handle a gun but only his quick, cool thinking had prevented his seeing it mishandled on himself.

The poker players and the inspector also admitted to having seen the gun at close range.

A man declared that he had been standing in the street when the gunman had jumped him, cursed him, picked a fight, gone for his gun, and would have shot him had he not had the foresight to jump under a building.

The inspector told how the gunman had held him up and robbed him of a large sum of money.

The storekeeper told how he had been minding the store when the killer came in, took a handful of cigars, forced him to light one, and threatened to shoot him if the match went out.

Roger McSwain told how the gunman had threatened him and his companion, Joe McMasters, and how at gunpoint he had forced the bartender to drink a concoction that was possibly poisonous and definitely harmful to the health.

The constable was not convinced. He admitted that, strictly speaking, it was against the law to carry a gun in town, and, in principle, it was wrong to go around threatening and robbing people with it and making them do things they didn't want to do. Still and all, he had heard no shots and seen no dead men.

The man on the street described how the killer walked through the street looking for trouble, his hat pushed back on his head, his hand hovering near the gun, his mean eyes looking like they had seen hell. "There ain't been nobody to walk through this town like that since Billy Meadows," he said.

The constable wiped his face with his bandana, spat into the glowing forge, and suggested that they not provoke the man and then maybe he would leave them alone.

Ab declared the man had come to town to add a notch to his gun and wouldn't leave until he had one.

The station agent declared the man had come to town to rob the depot safe and wouldn't leave until he had done so.

Roger McSwain had heard him asking for a woman. "As soon as he gets all the liquor he wants, he'll go looking for a woman, and who's to stop him."

The constable suggested sending for Red-haired Retta.

The inspector said a man that had come all that way would expect something better.

The constable suggested sending for the U.S. marshal.

Ab said there wasn't time, as the train wouldn't come in for another day and the man might already have killed the bartender and started raping the women.

"I ain't heard no shots nor screams," the constable said. "I know the women of this town, and I know they wouldn't give up nothing without a holler."

The men declared that the gunman could not be left alone all night as there was no telling what he might do after dark.

The constable suggested they go to the saloon with him, ask the man what he wanted, and if it wasn't much, give it to him.

The men believed that if they once gave in to him, he would keep asking for more and more until he owned the town. The only course was to shoot him or put him in jail.

The constable suggested they get their guns and go down to the saloon with him and arrest or shoot the man.

The station agent didn't have a gun.

Ab had never fired a gun in his life.

The storekeeper didn't believe in violence.

Roger McSwain said he was just passing through.

The man on the street said he didn't have a wife.

"If I'd a wanted to get shot, I could a done it this morning sitting down," said one of the poker players.

The constable thought it unfair that he should have to go down to the saloon alone and face five armed men.

The storekeeper said it was the constable's sworn duty to protect the women and children and the business interests of the community.

Joe McMasters said the constable would be a hero.

"We've been giving you five dollars a month extra just for the freedom to play poker at the depot without interference, and that freedom no longer exists," said one of the poker players.

His moral obligations having been explained, the constable wiped his nose and reached for the shotgun. The others warily stepped back to give him room, with his responsibility. It was a twelve-gauge, double-barreled breech loader. He broke it open and looked down the barrels, spying a dirt-dauber nest. Digging it out with a grimy finger, he blew down the barrels, making a funny, squeaking sound. Loading the gun with half-paper ready loads, he closed it with a snap and turned around. The men jumped away from the muzzle of the gun.

"Don't let none of them get behind you," they said, as he took down his shirt from the nail where it hung when he worked.

"Watch his hands. If they move, let him have it."

"Watch his eyes. A man will always blink before he goes for his gun."

"Watch out for tricks. He'll try to get you to look away."

"Belle Starr used to carry a derringer wrapped up with her baby in a blanket."

"Billy the Kid use to have one of his men carry a pistol strapped to his back, and when the Kid seen a law man, all he had to do was pat his friend on the back, and Powder River."

"Clay Allison shot up a Texas town wearing nothing but a Mexican blanket over his shoulders and two six-shooters strapped around his waist."

"Wes Hardin used to pretend to hand over his pistol butt-first and then flip it over and shoot you when you reached for it. Don't let him hand you the gun."

With such encouragements, the men entertained the constable as he stepped out into the sunlight. The saloon was up the street and around the corner.

Self-consciously, the constable walked in the dust of the street, avoiding the noisy sidewalks, aware of the spectators watching him. Storekeepers and drummers followed him, ducking from one doorway to another and dodging behind empty rain barrels. Young boys stood in groups along the street, laughing at him.

"What you carrying that shotgun for? Going to shoot somebody?"

"Naw, he's going crow-hunting."

"Look out, Mr. Badman, here comes the constable."

"Look out, somebody's behind you."

Despite himself, the constable had to turn around and look; and, sure enough, a boy was sneaking up behind him to yell boo. Angrily, the constable motioned for them to be silent and waved them out of the way, but his actions only increased their amusement. They played tag, running across the street and catching at his overalls or grabbing at the barrel of the shotgun. The constable was trying to decide whether or not the law gave him the right to shoot them for interfering with the performance of his duties when, mercifully, a woman ran out into the street and shooed them away.

The constable stepped up on the sidewalk that creaked and popped under his weight, and with one eye looked around the building. The street was deserted. He could hear laughter in the saloon. "Drunk," he thought. Then the laughter stopped and their voices dropped to a murmur. "But dangerous," he added. He heard some shouts and then the voices dropped to a murmur again. "Planning what they're going to do with the town," he thought. "Once they get rid of me."

He wiped his sweating hand on the bib of his overalls. He saw now that for him there was no way out, whether he provoked them or not. They had plans; and to carry them out, they had to get him out of the way. He wondered why he had ever taken the job for fifteen dollars a month and blamed his wife for it. With satisfaction he imagined the look of guilt and sorrow on her face when she saw him lying dead, riddled with bullets, and realized that it was all her fault. Angrily, he turned and waved at the men to take cover, and the boards clattered and rattled as they jumped into doorways or ducked behind buildings.

He had to have a plan. He thought of sneaking up to the door, stepping quickly inside and letting go with both barrels. But the bartender might be in the way. And one of them was a girl. Besides, he only had two shots and it wouldn't kill all of them no matter how close together they were standing. One of them would be left to shoot him before he could reload. He would sneak up to the door, trying not to make a sound, step quickly inside, catch them by surprise, yell "Hands up," and shoot the first one that moved.

Cocking both hammers of the noisy shotgun, he slipped around the corner of the building and began sliding along the sidewalk, that popped and snapped at each step. He moved slowly, with sweat beading on his forehead and running into his eyes, blinding him. He wiped the sweat away with the back of his hand, enraged that Providence should be on the side of the sweatless man.

The constable looked down. He had forgotten his badge. Cursing himself, he ran his hands over his pockets. The badge was in his pocket. He fixed the star to his bib, took a deep breath and looked back. The men were peeping around the side of the building. He waved them back, took another deep breath, and crashed through the door yelling, "Don't move, none of you. Get your hands up."

It took a moment for his mind to register what his eyes saw. Standing at the bar was the hardest set of killers he had ever seen. One man stood practically naked, holding a six-shooter beneath the blanket that was thrown over his shoulders. Beside him stood a mean-eyed girl, hiding a derringer beneath the baby's blue gown. A young man and an old one stood side by side, each holding a gun behind the other's back. In the center of the group, his hat pushed back from his cold, murderous eyes, the right side of his coat bulging from the immense six-shooter he made no attempt to conceal, stood the killer, holding a glass in one hand and a bottle in the other.

"Watch that bottle," the constable told himself. "He'll throw the bottle and go for the gun." He watched them, wondering what to do next. He had them, but what was he going to do with them? Seconds ticked away. The gang watched him with cold, grim eyes, looking for a chance to kill him. Behind him, he could hear the drummers whispering and the creak of the sidewalk under their footsteps.

"Where's the bartender?" he asked, trying to sound gruff.

"Behind the bar," said the one in the blanket.

From the side of his eye, the constable could see a foot protruding from behind the bar. "They done killed him," he thought. He was shaken by their calm deadliness. "I've got to get their guns," he thought. "Start with the easiest one, work up to the killer."

"Set that baby on the floor and then step back real slow," he said, waving the shotgun at the girl. She did not move. "Drop that blanket," he shouted, turning the shotgun on the half-naked man.

"Not for you nor no man."

"God, what a cold-blooded bunch," the constable thought, wishing he had enough barrels to shoot them all. That was the easy way. Sweat ran along his hand, making the grip slick. He wished he had waited until now to cock the big, noisy hammers. That would impress them. "This gun is loaded," he said.

He turned the shotgun on the two men who stood side by side, holding guns behind each other's back. "Drop them guns behind you and no quick movements," he said, steeling himself not to jump at the thud of the heavy pistols. The men only stared back at him.

There was nothing to do but to face the killer, the ringleader. If he could force him to give up his gun, the others would do the same. If he failed to get that gun, he was a dead man. Slowly, he focused the gun on the killer. "I'm taking your gun," he said with as much assurance as he could muster.

"I didn't mean nothing," the killer said. "I was just having fun."

"Either you give up the gun or I'm going to kill you," the constable said.

"Okay, you can have it," the gunman said, holding out his hands, which still held the bottle and the glass.

This was too easy. The constable knew it was a trick. "You touch that gun and I'll kill you," he said.

"Wait," said the man in the blanket. "He'll give it to me."

"Don't move," the constable said, swinging the gun on him.

June, stupefied by the alcohol, was puzzled by the belligerent attitude of the constable. He did not know why the man was so angry, why he had broken up their party, or why he was bullying them. He had heard that there were such bullies at the end of the trail, masquerading as law men and hiding behind their badges. He had met such men before, men who bullied him because he was an orphan and because he swept up after horses. The old hurt came back, the old insult that he thought he had erased forever. But it was different, too, because he was not being insulted for himself, but because he was a cow hand, and Lampassas, the Preacher, Covina, and the Kid were being insulted, too; men who had ridden the long trail, who had crossed the river, who deserved better. June thought of defying the man, of standing up to him. He did not want to give up the six-shooter. He did not want to see the others humiliated, and he was the man who carried the gun. But the constable had a shotgun and acted like he wanted to use it. June was afraid the man wouldn't take much defiance. And June was almighty tired of the town and its petty crooks and un-friendly people. All he wanted was to buy a horse with the money he had left and to hit the trail for Texas. He had been to Trails End, and now he no longer cared whether he went home as a hero or as a coward, only that he go.

"You take it, Preacher," he said, turning to the Preacher and brushing back his coat to enable the Preacher to take the six-shooter. He had forgotten that his right hand held the whisky bottle. As he grasped his coat, the bottle fell to the floor.

When the constable saw the killer turn away so that the gun and the right hand were hidden from him, he knew it was a trick. "He's going for the gun," the constable said to himself. "Shoot quick, it's a trick." But he could not move. He saw a ripple across the back of the coat; and he knew the gunman had brushed his coat back to free his pistol; but he could not move. Then the bottle crashed to the floor.

The two shots were almost simultaneous, the blast slam-ming June back against the bar, the roar of the shotgun deafen-ing in the quiet town. For an instant, June stood looking at the blood that sprang to the surface of his blue coat, and then he fell face down on the floor.

The constable stood holding the shotgun on the gang, but

they had forgotten his presence, and he likewise was watching not them but the killer, who rolled on the floor, gasping for breath. Behind him the drummers and shopkeepers crowded into the room to look. The constable looked down at the shotgun and saw that both hammers were down. For the first time he realized that both shots had been his.

Unable to get his breath, June flopped on the floor, thrashing and kicking his legs, propelling himself erratically along the splintered and glass-strewn floor. Lampassas and the Preacher vainly tried to hold him down.

In his struggles, June's six-shooter was dislodged from the holster. Seeing it, several men in the crowd ran forward to pick it up. The constable, suddenly vicious, shoved them back with the barrel of the shotgun. Keeping his distance from June, who was throwing blood with every kick, the constable bent down and picked up the blood-smeared pistol by the barrel, looked at it, and slipped it into the back pocket of his overalls.

"How many notches?" someone yelled over the commotion of the crowd. "How many men did the son of a bitch kill?"

The constable turned and, pushing his way through the crowd, tried to get outside.

June's struggles subsided, and the room became quiet as the spectators stopped snickering and calling to one another to listen to June's hoarse and infrequent breaths. In the quietness of the room, they became aware of another sound, already growing faint. At first the spectators did not know what it was, but to the hands it was old and familiar, strangely exciting, and full of hope. From habit they raised their heads and stiffened.

"Stompede," June groaned, reaching for his hat. "Stompede."

"I hope they run clear back to Texas," the Preacher said. "I hope they cave in ever dugout, roll up ever fence, and knock down ever town they come to. O Lord, give them wings of destruction that they might tromple underfoot the signs, and machines, and works of man. Let them scatter the nesters and carpetbaggers the way Thou didst scatter Pharaoh's army. Let them wipe the slate clean, O God, that we might start all over and do it right."

Lampassas and the Preacher sat at a table while the organizers put things in order. The floor was mopped, the chairs and tables arranged, and June's body was measured, examined, and dispossessed of earthly valuables.

"What do you aim to do with them things?" Lampassas asked.

"Hold them for the next of kin."

"I was hoping to use that money to see that he was decently buried," Lampassas said.

"That's okay by me, but you have to get the permission of the next of kin. That's the law."

"He don't have no kin."

"Then I guess his things belong to the city," the man said, neatly sacking and tagging the meager possessions before putting them in his pocket.

"Well, what do you think we ought to do with him?" the Preacher asked.

"I thought it might be nice if we laid him to rest out on the prairie," Lampassas said. "You could say a few words over him, and we could put up his saddle for a headstone."

"Maybe we ought to bury him in a regular cemetery with a regular headstone and a regular preacher and everything," the Preacher said.

"You do it," Lampassas said. "Maybe his things belong to the city, but I reckon he belongs to us."

The undertaker had finished the examining and measuring and now stood to one side jotting notes in a little book he carried. Fortune had smiled on him and he knew it. This man, a stranger in the town, was like a gift from heaven, enriching his present livelihood without diminishing his future prospects. "Terrible thing," he said to Lampassas and the Preacher. "Terrible thing. But it won't be no bother to you. I'll take care of everthing."

Lampassas explained that they would not require his services.

The undertaker reviewed the Ethical Code of Undertaking Practices, which required the body to be prepared in the approved manner, placed in an approved coffin, and buried in an approved cemetery. All for a hundred and fifty dollars.

"We thought the Preacher here might handle the services," Lampassas said.

"It isn't regular."

"And we got our own wagon for transportation," the Preacher said.

"Me and the Preacher can dig the grave."

"What we want," the Preacher said, "is a approved preparation, a approved lot, and a approved coffin."

"A hundred dollars."

"We ain't got it," Lampassas said.

"Seventy-five dollars. That's my cheapest offer."

"We ain't got that neither."

The undertaker closed his book with a snap. "Look me up when you decide what you want to do with your friend." He started out and then stopped to look back at the Preacher, sitting barefooted and bareheaded with the saddle blanket over his long woolen drawers. "Did I understand you to say you're a preacher?"

"I ain't regular, I don't reckon, but I'm called of God," the Preacher said.

"I bet folks around here would be mighty interested to hear what you have to say," the undertaker said, studying the Preacher some more. "You must have many unusual stories to tell."

"I've had some experiences with the Lord," the Preacher said modestly, pleased at the way the Lord had prepared the people for his coming.

The undertaker did some quick thinking. In a few days people all over the country would know that the last of the Texas gunmen had been killed in Grandview, and that he had done the burying. That would stir up business, especially among the farmers, who did most of their burying over at Lewiston because they had a Swedish funeral parlor and some trees in the cemetery. But not any more. Folks would start coming to Grandview to be put away by the man who had buried the last of the Texas gunmen. Why, Grandview would have the biggest cemetery in the country. Especially if he could get that fellow in the Indian blanket to throw in with him and do an Indian lament or a rain dance of some kind. They'd have funeral services that no one west of Chicago could touch.

"I got a tent I use some for graveside services when the occasion calls for it," the undertaker said. "And I wouldn't mind if you was to set it up down by the river."

"I come here to preach, and I mean to do it out of doors," the Preacher said, astonished once more by the way things worked together for the good of those who served the Lord. And although he had never lost faith, he was relieved that God had thus given him a sign of His blessing.

"Of course we need to spread the word around so folks would come, but I figure if you was to let folks know you aimed to tell the true story of your dead friend, word would get around."

"I could tell how he walked on the bottom of the river," the Preacher said. "And how he always looked the cows in the eye, but took his eye off the law. Maybe I could find a lesson in that."

"Yes sir, word would get around," the undertaker said. "We might have a parade with you in your Indian blanket and a headdress, and maybe a choir of young girls in white robes behind you. And I'd welcome folks and tell them about our friendly, special services to the bereaved and pass out free fans with the Lord's Prayer printed on one—"

"Chauncey T. Gray," the Preacher said with such vehemence that the undertaker paused. "I will preach to anybody, but I will be a spectacle to none."

"I'd be willing to take you in as—"

"I come to this town to preach the word of God," the Preacher said, standing up so fast that his chair fell over backward. "To do the will of the Lord. And not for no man's money, and not for no man's praise, and not to be seen by nobody. I come to preach the word as a man knows it, out under the sky where a man lives."

"If that's all you're going to do, you could have saved yourself the trouble," the undertaker said. "We got a regular church here and a regular parson with a wife and a education. What do we need with somebody like you? This is a respectable community."

"It may be respectable," the Preacher said, "but it sure ain't Christian."

They sat in silence after the undertaker had gone, the Preacher brooding over a call that had sent him wandering through the wilderness, only to be rejected when he had reached the end of the trail. There was no place in his theology for such an error. Lampassas said nothing, respecting his mood.

"He wouldn't a talked to me so loose if I'd a had on my new clothes," the Preacher said.

"I wouldn't pay him no mind," Lampassas said.

"No, he's right. Here I ain't nothing but a curiosity."

"The Lord told you to come here."

"Well, I come, didn't I? I crossed the Red, the Washita, the Cimarron, like He said. Maybe Trails End is where you got to go before you can get to Nineveh."

"Well, if you think Nineveh is south, I'd be obliged to have you along," Lampassas said.

"I got to have some clothes first," the Preacher said.

"I got just enough money to buy a horse to ride home. The rest is Mr. Fulton's money and I don't know no way to ask him for a loan."

"I ain't wearing this blanket home," the Preacher said.

"What you done with your money is your business," Lampassas said.

"I never done nothing with my money and you know it."

"What you never done with your money is your business, too."

"You got me here and it's your responsibility to get me home," the Preacher said. "Ever real cow man knows that."

"I don't see how I could do no more than buy you a cheap pair of boots and a second-hand suit of clothes."

"That's all I'm asking," the Preacher said. "And I'd kinda like to have a Bible. Not too big. And not too new, neither."

"We'll be afoot."

"I reckon we can walk it one way as well as the other."

"We got to take care of June first," Lampassas said. "I'll sell the wagon, but that won't bury nobody."

"Since we're walking, we don't have no way to carry the saddles," the Preacher said thoughtfully.

"It ain't right," Lampassas said.

"I know it ain't respectable," the Preacher said. "But it's Christian."

June was placed in a pine box and hauled to the cemetery in the wagon, which had been sold, by mules which had been borrowed. The Preacher drove the wagon slowly through the street, and Lampassas and Covina followed behind. The Kid was cutting weeds on the railroad right of way, and the baby was being kept by a neighbor. The meager procession was met at the cemetery by a crowd of drummers, farmers, and storekeepers, dressed in Sunday clothes and come to see the last of the Texas gunmen laid to rest.

June was buried between two storekeepers, in a grave Lampassas and the Preacher had dug early that morning, and paid for with eight absurdly large western saddles. The Preacher read the eighth chapter of Romans from a small second-hand Bible, and Covina cried. It was in the fall of the year, and the first norther carried sand on its icy breath.

Chapter 12

"HELLO the house," the Preacher called. He and Lampassas stood at the edge of a brown, dead corn field, the collars of their dirty coats turned up against the wind at their backs, their hatbrims rippling. Before them, exposed to the elements on the bare prairie, stood a sod house. A coyote hide covered the single window, a washtub lay overturned at the corner. A bristling yellow dog stood before the house barking, his black lips curled back from his teeth. "Hello the house."

"What do you want?" a woman called back, suddenly appearing in the doorway. The wind flattened the faded gray dress and dingy apron against her body and blew her hair in tangles about her head. Assorted children's heads appeared behind her. With the back of her wrist she swept the hair from her face. "Shut up, Tige."

Courteously, Lampassas and the Preacher removed their hats, and the wind ruffled their long gray hair. "Would you like us to chop some wood?" the Preacher called, shouting over the distance, the wind, and the barking of the dog.

"You looking for a handout?" she called back. "Shut up, Tige."

"We're looking for work."

The woman reached back inside the house and produced a corn-shuck broom with which she swatted the backside of the barking dog. Disconcerted, the dog yelped and ran around the corner of the house, its tail between its legs, leaving a trail of water on the bare ground.

"I don't need no wood chopped," she said, talking now that the dog was quiet and the men had come closer. The dog watched them from the corner of the house, growling and baring his teeth. "What else can you do?"

The two men looked at each other, hunching against the wind, trying to think of some profitable skill they possessed. "We can mend harness," the Preacher said.

"Don't need mending."

"Or repair a wagon."

"Don't need repairing."

"I'm a fair cook," the Preacher said.

"I do the cooking."

"Gather corn?" Lampassas asked shamefully.

"My husband'll get up with that soon as he gets back. Our mule run off last night," she said. "First time that ever happened. Something must a got after him in the pasture."

"We're making our way back home, ma'am," Lampassas said. "Back to Texas. And we'd do most anything for a little food and a place to spend the night."

"How far you come?"

"From Grandview," Lampassas said. The woman gave no indication of ever having heard of such an unlikely place. "A far piece."

"We ain't eaten since yesterday," the Preacher said.

The woman studied them, her face stern, suspicious. Having acquired over some forty years a husband, four children, and a roof of her own, she did not easily forgive need in others. "Can you milk a cow?"

The men shifted uncomfortably, looking over the empty miles to the next house, the next possible meal, trying to measure the other's hunger against their own. The Preacher, who knew more of humility, more of man's frailty, was the first to speak. "What was you planning on fixing, ma'am?"

"Well, I thought I might kill a rooster. I got some turnips and some hominy. I could fry some potatoes and onions in bacon fat. Make a raisin cobbler. I guess you could sleep behind the house out of the wind."

Lampassas, who had eaten nothing but beef for several months and nothing at all for several hours, was tantalized by the thought of chicken, fried potatoes, and boggy top. Seeing the Preacher looking at him, he closed his mouth. "We're cow men, not milkers," he said.

"Suit yourself," the woman said. "I don't reward laziness."

The Preacher waited, politely holding his hat in his hands, but the woman showed no signs of relenting. "We're cow men, ma'am, but we're also Christians," the Preacher said. "And I reckon we'd do a lady a favor."

"The last I seen them cows, they was way back down over yonder," the woman said, pointing back over her shoulder. "You go down there and bring them up to the house. You reckon you can drive them?"

"I reckon so," the Preacher said.

"Well, I don't want you running the milk out of them. If you get to it, you can be done by dark. My husband will be back by then, and I'll have supper ready. So get at it."

Setting their hats firmly against the wind, they walked around the house, ignoring the yellow dog that followed barking and snapping at their heels and then lay down in ambush to await their return. Slowly, they plodded across the rough ground, their run-over boot heels slipping and turning painfully. A hint of snow was in the air.

"Milking cows," Lampassas said.

"It's a case of the ox in the ditch," the Preacher said. "We got to get back to Texas before the snow starts flying."

"Milking cows," said Lampassas, who could not believe it even after he had said it. "We have fallen on evil days."

"I don't reckon it's a disgrace as long as we're ashamed of it," the Preacher said.

"Damn sheepherder," Lampassas said as they walked along.

"Damn drummer. Damn Martin Foster. Damn them fellers that stole our horses. They got the best of us, didn't they?"

"Well, we got to Trails End," the Preacher said. "And they never."

"It wasn't worth it, was it?" Lampassas asked. "Coming all that way. Losing Gattis and Pretty Shadow to get us there. And then when we got there they didn't have no use for us. They didn't have no use for my cows. They didn't have no use for your preaching. They killed June and put Jamie to cutting weeds like a damn farmer."

"Well, maybe we ain't where we aimed to be, but we ain't where we was, neither," the Preacher said.

"I paid good money for them worthless cows. It costs me good horses and better men to get them there. And then they rob me. They take my cows, they take my money, they take my son, they rob me of my self-respect. I ain't got nothing left but what I got on and that five hundred dollars I owe Mr. Fulton. I've been a fool," Lampassas said.

"I notice how it's the first feller that does something that is the hero and the last feller that does it that is the fool," the Preacher said.

"That's right," Lampassas said. "Even though it may be harder the last time."

"The first feller that come to this country was a pilgrim and the last one to come was a foreigner."

"I reckon it don't matter what a feller does or how well he does it so long as he does it before everbody else gives it up," Lampassas said.

"Well, I have give up trailing cattle," the Preacher said.

"You ain't give up preaching?"

"The Lord ain't put me out to pasture yet," the Preacher said. "Maybe the church I was supposed to build was the church we had going up the trail. You and Gattis, Pretty Shadow, June, the Kid, Covina, was the congregation, and I was the Preacher. We had the grass for a floor, the sky for a ceiling. We was out in the open where we could worship God as we pleased. Maybe

the Lord sent me to take care of you, bury Gattis and Pretty
Shadow and June, and look after Covina and the baby."

"Well, if He did, you done lost your congregation," Lampassas said.

The Preacher nodded. It was true. The Lord did seem to be
done with him. Well, he wouldn't question the Lord's will. He
was old, useless. This last adventure had been foolishness. He
wondered how he could have so misinterpreted the Lord's purpose. Could it have been the voice of the devil he heard? But
if that were true, how many times in the past had it been the
voice of the devil he had followed and not the Lord? Had his
whole life been spent going up one trail after another only to
find at the end of it, not the Promised Land, not the City of
God, but the whited sepulcher of his own folly?

The question made him tired, and he put it out of his mind.
He no longer cared. His body ached with fatigue and hunger; the
muscles of his legs trembled so that he walked clumsily, awk-
wardly over the rough ground. The only thing that mattered
now was food and rest. Tomorrow maybe he could go on.

The Preacher's boot heel slipped off a rock and his ankle
turned under him as he fell heavily to the ground. Sharp pains
shot up his leg as he groaned and rolled over.

"What's the matter?" Lampassas asked.

"It's my ankle. I think I sprained it," the Preacher said,
lying back and gritting his teeth against the pain.

"Can you stand on it?"

"I don't think so."

"Let's try," Lampassas said, helping him up.

The Preacher tested his foot and sank back down, shaking
his head. "I almost wish I'd a bought walking shoes," he said.

"You rest here and I'll go get them cows," Lampassas said.
"You can help me milk, can't you?"

"I'll try," the Preacher said.

Lampassas walked away a few steps and stopped to look
back. It was clear to him that the Preacher could go no farther.
They could probably stay at the farmhouse milking cows until
the Preacher's foot was better, but what was the use? Winter

was at their backs. Ahead of them was nothing. They were through.

In his pocket was Mr. Fulton's five hundred dollars. That would get them home. He had given his word, but the word of a man who milked cows couldn't be much. "It ain't no use fooling ourselves," he said, sitting down beside the Preacher. "It was slim enough that we could walk it when you had two good feet. Now your ankle's sprained and it's fixing up to snow. I still got that five hundred dollars. If we can just make it to the train, I'll buy us tickets home."

"I hate to ask it of you," the Preacher said. "I know how much it meant to you to be able to take that money back, but I can't go no farther."

"I'll just explain to Mr. Fulton how we had to have that money and offer to work to pay it back."

They stretched out on the ground, leaning back on their elbows, their shoulders hunched against the wind, looking up at the gray and forbidding sky. The ground was cold and their muscles were stiffening, but they did not care. Soon they would have a hot meal, a warm place to sleep, and a railroad ticket home. Just as soon as the cows were milked. Counting the steps to supper, the Preacher looked down to where the fat brown cows stood chewing their cuds. They looked easy to drive, easy to milk, and he was thankful for it. Something nearer at hand caught his eye and he raised up to get a better view. "Ain't that one of them longhorn cows?"

"Where?"

"Right there," the Preacher said, pointing at the well-hidden cow. "And there's another one right over there."

"Damned if it ain't," Lampassas said, sitting up to look at the long thin face and the sharp-pointed horns. "That's that old mealy-mouthed steer that carried Pretty Shadow across the river."

"Yeah, and that one over there looks like that lame cow we give that sheepherder."

Lampassas began to feel the warmth of happiness, of purpose returning to him. "Them cows is taking the same trail home as we are," he said, hitting the Preacher on the back. "By God, we can just round them up and trail them back as we go."

"That's still a long way to go," the Preacher said, doubtfully.

"Hell, it ain't far now," Lampassas said. "And when we get back we'll have something. Do you think you could make it if I give you a hand?"

The Preacher sighed and felt of his ankle through his boot. "Like a steer, all I can do is try," he said, as Lampassas helped him to his feet.

Resting his weight on Lampassas, the Preacher hobbled along toward the two cows. Seeing them approach, the two cows broke from cover, trotted a few yards and then stopped to watch the two men struggling after them.

"Maybe you can ride one of them," Lampassas said.

"I think I'll wait till they get to know us a little better," the Preacher said. "If we can get enough of these cows together we can give them to Mr. Fulton for that five hundred dollars."

"I was thinking if we could catch up with Old Blue, we could start us a herd of our own," Lampassas said. "'Swap the first crop of calves for horses, the second crop for a piece of land, build us a house—"

"Bullshit," said the Preacher, slapping his hat against his leg to start the cows again. "Old Blue's a steer."

The yellow dog leapt from ambush, snapped at one of the steers, and was sent sailing through the air. Howling, he limped for the house with his tail between his legs. The steers jumped a fence and ran through the corn field.

"Stompede," the Preacher yelled, and forgetting his sprained foot, he released Lampassas and chased after one cow while Lampassas tried to head the other. The cow tried to double back; and the Preacher jerked off his hat and sailed it through the air, hitting the cow on the ear and turning it. Lampassas scared up a third cow hiding in the corn patch, and bunching the cows together, they were chasing them south when the first snow-flakes fell.

Trails

MUCH OF MAN'S STORY is told in terms of trails: trails he has blazed through forests, over oceans, across the skies; trails he has followed; trails he has dreamed of; trails he has camped beside.

There are forbidden trails, forgotten trails, trails not taken. There are the old trails that run deep in our psyche, deeper than our bones. We enclose them with fences. We build our homes and churches, schools and pesthouses, jails and seats of government over them. And we try to forget them while pursuing comfort and commerce.

But there is a lure to old trails, a magic to them. Sometimes that call to the wild is so strong in us that some, against the advice of others, against their own better judgment, despite the folly and pain of it, just for the sheer hell of it, go storming up the trail again, with ruin in their wake and disappointment in their future, but satisfied for a while just to be on the trail.

Lampassas was such a man. Lampassas dreamed of the other trail, the one not taken, the trail of his youth that would have given him adventure instead of safety, meaning instead of means. Despite the fact that it wasn't good business, it wasn't politically smart, it wasn't neighborly, maybe not even Christian, he went up the trail. Whether it was worth it or not is something only he can know.

Robert Flynn